THE BIG BOOK OF NECON

THE BIG BOOK OF
NECON

EDITED BY **BOB BOOTH**

Cemetery Dance Publications

BALTIMORE 2009

Cemetery Dance Publications 2009
ISBN 978-1-58767-202-6
ISBN 1-58767-202-2

Dust Jacket Art © 2009 pottsdesign, www.pottsdesign.com
Dust Jacket and Book Design: pottsdesign
Printed in the United States of America

Cemetery Dance Publications
132B Industry Lane
Unit 7
Forest Hill, Maryland 21050
http://www.cemeterydance.com

10 9 8 7 6 5 4 3 2 1

First Edition

For Mary

The love of my life,

the co-founder of Necon,

the actual mother of Dan and Sara,

the symbolic Mother of all the Necon Campers

contents

Part II Necon: The First Twenty Years

contents

Part III Necon: New Blood

Part IV Necon: Visitors From Across The Pond

"On the Last Night of the Festival of the Dead" copyright © 1994 by Darrell Schweitzer. Originally published in *Interzone (December)*. Reprinted with permission of the author.

"Exercise of Faith" copyright © 1987 by Lucius Shepard. Originally published in *Rod Serling's Twilight Zone Magazine (June)*. Reprinted with permission of the author.

"Erotorium" copyright © 1998 by Stephen Spruill. Originally published in *Imagination Fully Dilated*. Reprinted with permission of the author.

"Response from a Surprised But Pleased Recipient" copyright © 2000 by Peter Straub. Originally published in *Necon XX*. Reprinted with permission of the author.

"Nocturne" copyright © 2000 by Thomas Tessier. Originally published in *Necon XX*. Reprinted with permission of the author.

"Night Deposits" copyright © 1987 by Chet Williamson. Originally published in *University Man*. Reprinted with permission of the author.

"Demonsong" copyright © 1979 by F. Paul Wilson. Originally published in *Heroic Fantasy*. Reprinted with permission of the author.

"Necon Proceedings" (illustration) copyright © 1998 by Cortney Skinner. Originally published in *Necon 18*. Reprinted with permission of the artist.

"Red Paint" (illustration and text) copyright © 2005 by Jill Bauman. Originally published in *Necon 25 Flash Fiction*. Reprinted with permission of the author.

"A Death In the Day Of" copyright © 1987 by Gary A. Braunbeck. Originally published in *Horror Show (Winter)*. Reprinted with permission of the author.

"And We'll Be Jolly Friends For Evermore" copyright © 2002 by P. D. Cacek. Originally published in *Necon 22*. Reprinted with permission of the author.

"Becoming Men" copyright © 1999 by Douglas Clegg. Originally published in *Subterranean Gallery*. Reprinted with permission of the author.

"Tryptich" copyright © 2005 by David Cram. Originally published in *Necon 25 Flash Fiction*. Reprinted with permission of the author.

"Somebody Put Me Together" copyright © 2002 by Sephera Giron. Originally published in *Random Acts of Weirdness*. Reprinted with permission of the author.

"The Girl With No Name" copyright © 2003 by Elizabeth Hand. Originally published in *Necon 23*. Reprinted with permission of the author.

"Little Brother" copyright © 1991 by Rick Hautala. Originally published in *Night Visions #9*. Reprinted with permission of the author.

"I Am an Exit" copyright © 2004 by Brian Keene. Originally published in *Fear of Gravity*. Reprinted with permission of the author.

"Virtually Perfect" copyright © 2003 by James A. Moore. Originally published in *Necon 23*. Reprinted with permission of the author.

"Necon Bat Camper" (illustration) copyright © 2005 by Gahan Wilson. Originally published in *Necon 25 Flash Fiction*. Reprinted with permission of the artist.

"Burning" copyright © 2000 by Ramsey Campbell. Originally published in *Necon XX*. Reprinted with permission of the author.

"Clearly Dead" copyright © 2004 by Simon Clark. Originally published in *Necon 24*. Reprinted with permission of the author.

"Days of the Wheel" copyright © 2000 by Peter Crowther. Originally published in *Strange Attraction*. Reprinted with permission of the author.

"Fifteen Painted Cards from a Vampire Tarot" copyright © 1998 by Neil Gaiman. Originally published in *Necon 18*. Reprinted with permission of the author.

"Partial Eclipse" copyright © 2000 by Graham Joyce. Originally published on *SCIFI.COM*. Reprinted with permission of the author.

"Recipe for Disaster" copyright © 2000 by Tim Lebbon. Originally published in *As the Sun Goes Down*. Reprinted with permission of the author.

"Memories Of Lydia, Leaving" copyright © 1993 by Phil Nutman. Originally published in *After the Darkness*. Reprinted with permission of the author.

"Camp Necon Skeleton" (illustration) copyright © 2006 by Gahan Wilson. Originally published in *Necon 26*. Reprinted with permission of the artist.

BOB GOES TO NECON

Charles Lang

Preface

BY BOB BOOTH

WELCOME TO MY BOOK.

WELCOME TO MY WORLD.

IT'S TRUE. MY FAMILY AND I THINK ABOUT NECON ALL YEAR LONG.

My wife Mary and I began it on a lark in the warm afterglow of the Fifth World Fantasy Convention in 1979. I had chaired that historic convention in Providence with Stephen King as Guest of Honor along with Frank Belknap Long and Michael Whelan. Charles L. Grant was the toastmaster.

Roger Williams College was trying to find a way to generate revenue during the idle summer months. The person given this task read about the convention in the *Providence Journal* and called me. I explained that World Fantasy always happened in October and could draw up to a thousand guests.

She said she was sorry to have bothered me and out of politeness I asked her what the price would be. She said $15 per day per person which would include a room, three meals, and of course all function space would be free.

How could I turn that down? If there was no convention for the horror/fantasy crowd in the summer then by God we'd make one. How could we not?

And so it began. Necon's well-known loose structure and casual sense of community came about because we were all in a college dorm in a beautifully isolated spot on the ocean, beneath the Mount Hope Bridge to Newport. Very few attendees had cars so in a very real sense we were stuck with each other for three days. Also, because the committee was tired from World Fantasy we put a very loose event structure in place and let folks do pretty much what they wanted to do. This turned out to be drinking, talking endlessly, and playing competitive games.

Most of the attendees at Necon were, sadly, the last kids chosen for their neighborhood teams. After all we were readers, not jocks. As a result when we play the competition is intense and cutthroat. For Necon 20 we certified a few of these events with Necon Olympic Medals designed by the guest artist each year and cast by Richard Sardinha. They are prized possessions. Over the years the events have included such diverse games as hi-lo-jack, croquet, softball, darts, horseshoes, bocce ball, basketball, miniature golf, and bowling.

The game show, the talent show, the farewell picnic, the guitar gathering, the midnight salsa dance, the Beatles sing-a-long, and the Koi pond swim were all ideas of attendees, not the committee.

In the 1980's I sold a little fiction and a little non-fiction to professional markets. Some of it wasn't all that bad. One even made Honorable Mention in the first Datlow/Windling anthology. But I soon realized that there were an awful lot of people doing it better and more frequently than I was.

I came to realize that my art form was the convention. I had been part of six World Fantasy Conventions (and was on the board), a World Horror Convention, and several academic/fantasy events at Rhode Island College and Providence College. And, now there was Necon.

Almost thirty years have gone by and the family still runs Necon with the help of loyal friends. Mary and I are still heavily involved though our son Dan has been chairman for the last eleven years. His sister Sara is waiting in the wings for him to get tired. This year our granddaughter Jillian (age 9) sold soda to campers at registration (to raise money to buy Webkinz). It was a job her mother and her uncle did over twenty years ago.

Roger Williams College is now Roger Williams University. Necon now sells out every year and there is always a waiting list. People regularly come from all over the country, Canada, and Britain on their own dimes. For a few years we had a regular attendee from Israel. Over the years I've had many books dedicated to me or to Mary and I. The last few have been simply to "The Booths," to include the family. I can't tell you how gratifying that is. On good days I like to think it's akin to "The Kennedys." Realistically, it's probably closer to "The Osbournes."

The Big Book of Necon is my book and it celebrates Necon, which is my art. I hope you like it.

There are many kudos and thanks to be handed out for a project like this and I know I'll miss some, but here goes: to Brian Freeman and Richard Chizmar, who prodded me into giving them an idea, which they then accepted;

to all the writers and artists who have contributed to this book and the program books it was selected from;

to Doug Winter who contributed the only original piece to the book. It serves as a much better introduction to Necon than anything I could have written. I pestered him for it unfairly but he did it and it is brilliant;

to the string of coordinators at Roger Williams who have made us feel at home and pretty much let us do what we wanted (almost within reason), the most recent of whom have been Kaye Nevis and Jonathan Smith;

to the campers who come every year and have a good time, thus making it worth the effort;

to Donald M. Grant who gave me my entré into the world of horror and dark fantasy in the first place;

to Stephen King who has been more than generous to me and to Necon with his art, his time, and his good will;

to the ever loyal Necon committee, who are also my closest friends: Bob Plante, Patty Riendeau, Bob Lavoie, Steve Gervais, Dick Brisson, Stan Wiater, Jim Anderson, Les Daniels, Craig and Barbara Gardner, John and Dot Godin, Chris Golden, Jose Nieto, Matt Bechtel, Andy Dangelas, John McIlveen, Kelly Laymon, Mickey Sardinha, Richard Sardinha, the late Jinx Cates, the late Joe Crawford, and especially my book-hunting buddy Paul Dobish;

to my former co-worker (in the Providence College publications center) the gifted Emily Potts, who put up with my babbling about Necon for five years and still consented to design the book you are holding;

and most of all to the family;

Dan, who has run Necon better and longer than anyone;

Sara, who labors hard and quietly while waiting for her brother to step down;

Jillian, the presumptive chairman of Necon 40;

and of course Mary who personifies her screen name (Neconmom). She has been the warm smile and the kind words that have been Necon's secret weapons for nearly thirty years. She is tireless. She is saintly (she'd have to be, wouldn't she). And I love her very much. This book is dedicated to her.

LIVE TO WRITE / WRITE TO LIVE
Glenn Chadbourne

FBI Report No. QY-202

Behavioral Sciences Unit
QUANTICO, VIRGINIA

FILE: **Project Megiddo**

SUBJECT: Necon (aka "North Eastern Regional Fantasy Conference")

DESCRIPTION: Writer's Conference

DURATION: July 1980 - present

LOCATION: Roger Williams University, Bristol, Rhode Island (1980-1990, 1995-2003, 2005-present); Bryant University, Smithfield, Rhode Island (1991-1994); Salve Regina University, Newport, Rhode Island (2004)

KEY WORDS: Cults, mass delusion, extremism, readers

EXECUTIVE SUMMARY

Acting on information received from REDACTED, Special Agents Raymond Frisk and Dante Spinnelli, Providence Field Office, issued National Security Letter NSL-00789810 to Robert ("Bob") Booth and Mary Booth, occupants of 67 Birchland Avenue, Pawtucket, Rhode Island.

Said agents then seized paper and electronic files containing recipes (bean dip, beef agnolotti, beef cannelloni, beef linguine, beef manicotti, beef moscatelli, beef ravioli, beef tordelli, beef tortellini, beef Beefaroni surprise); lascivious photographs of actress/comedienne Fran Drescher; and a series of texts and illustrations labeled *The Big Book of Necon*. Examination of the latter materials confirmed their connection to a cult of annual visitors to semi-rural Rhode Island college campuses who celebrate the enigmatic event known as "Necon."

Given the apparent homeland security implications, FBI Deputy Director Garrison Goss asked Behavioral Sciences to review and assess this collection of texts and illustrations preliminary to its publication. Review was conducted by Special Agent Arnold M. Polen and consultant Brian W. Middlestone, M.D., Department of Forensic Psychiatry, Georgetown University School of Medicine. After Dr. Middlestone's breakdown and subsequent commitment, review was continued by consultant K. Michael Howell, Ph. D., Chair, Department of Psychology, Catholic University. After Dr. Howell's breakdown and subsequent commitment, Agent Polen completed the review.

After Agent Polen's breakdown and subsequent commitment, a series of note cards was found among his effects. Each contained handwritten ruminations tied to personal names and other words and phrases that will assist reader comprehension of Necon and the diverse, often baffling narratives that have been compiled here in its name. Behavioral Sciences thus assembled those notes into the following alphabetical lexicon of words and phrases indigenous to the Necon cultists known as "Campers."

A NECON LEXICON

Agar, John. Departed ex-husband of Shirley Temple, star of *The Brain from the Planet Arous* and *Mr. No Legs*, proprietor of *Agar's World of Kong*, and Patron Saint of Necon.

Artists' Reception. Saturday afternoon festivity populated by artists and an effete few in search of wine and cheese, which typically proved to be Mogen David and Velveeta.

Authors. Designation used to distinguish certain Campers based on level of guileless self-promotion.

Baruru. Punch-line of epic humorous anecdote known as "Death or Baruru," famously misdelivered by attending author. See Monteleone, Thomas F.

Bats. Enduring symbol of Necon, adopted after gerbils refused to sign the licensing agreement.

Baumann, Jill. Artist-in-residence with uncanny ability to duplicate book covers as large, canvas-sized paintings.

Books. Obsolete paper products whose prominence at Necon may one day explain the peculiar dementia afflicting Campers.

Booth Family. Descendants of presidential assassin, acolytes of the Reverend Jim Jones, founders and purveyors of Necon.

Booth, Bob. Ernest Hemingway reborn as Ralph Kramden. One-half of "The Two Bobs" (the one on the left).

Booth, Dan. The sins of the father descended.

Booth, Mary. Unwitting accomplice. Or was she?

Booth, Sara. Soft-spoken. Sweet. Innocent. In other words, guilty.

Breakfast. Least-attended Necon repast, typically consisting of coffee, dry toast, and Excedrin.

Buchanan, Ginjer. Publishing industry representative whose attendance can be likened to a driver slowing down at the scene of an accident. See Editors.

The Cafeteria (aka "The Caf"). Feeding ground for Campers, overseen by charm school dropouts and sanitation worker trainees. Source of severe linoleum exposure and repetitive tray return syndrome.

Campers. Desperate souls willing to spend money to cloister for 72 hours in abandoned dormitory rooms in failed search for illumination (or, at the least, one decent meal). Demographics skewed toward (in descending order of magnitude) authors, artists, editors, event coordinators, fans, and the sane.

Clegg, Douglas. Attending author and world-class tchotchke designer, best known for a "Signature Edition" that included the Doug Clegg Hypodermic Pen, Doug Clegg Beach Ball, and Doug Clegg Colostomy Bag.

Dancing on the Quad. Necon equivalent of the dance band on the Titanic, without the dance band or the Titanic.

Daniels, Les. One of only three authors to attend every Necon, as evidenced by inexplicable banjo-picking and tendency to drool uncontrollably at the sound of the word "home."

Dealer's Room. The place where obsolete paper products known as "books" go to die.

Editors. Mythical creatures once said to have determined whether novels and short stories would be published or remain mercifully hidden from the sight of all but their creators.

Food-like Substances. The repast of Campers, served in the Cafeteria and consisting primarily of starch, sawdust, and leftovers from the previous week's Hockey Camp.

Free SpongeBob. Long-planned liberation of square pants-wearing icon from the bondage of Ritual Satanic Animated Character Abuse.

The Game Show. An annual ritual of humiliation and thinning of the Camper herd, overseen by the two most noble and erudite males in attendance.

> RELATED TOPICS:
>
> **EuroContestant.** A game show contestant of un-American origin and fey demeanor, often heard to use words like "hooligan" and "ruffian."
>
> **Necon Champion.** Contestant of such great acumen and good fortune that he or

she found glory and Valuable Prizes as winner of the Game Show (unless, of course, the fix was in).

The Rules. Concise, unchanging, and easy-to-follow instructions intoned at the commencement of each Game Show.

The Other Rules. Concise, unchanging, and easy-to-follow instructions intoned at the commencement of the commencement of each Game Show, to wit: The First Rule of the Necon Game Show is: *You don't talk about the Necon Game Show.* The Second Rule of the Necon Game Show is: *You don't talk about the Necon Game Show.* The Third Rule of the Necon Game Show is: *If this is your first Necon Game Show, you fight.*

Valuable Prizes. The magnificent array of artistic masterpieces, technological marvels, and high-end collectibles at stake in the Game Show.

Vanna. Lovely assistant known for revealing clues as well as revealing attire. Depending on mood and availability, appeared as alternative incarnations Vanna White, Vanna Black, and NirVanna.

Gardner, Craig Shaw (aka "Craig Show Gardner"). The silence behind the violence, and one of three authors to survive each and every Necon. Often works with life-sized ventriloquist dummy. See Skinner, Cortney.

Gay Mafia. Clique of Campers identifiable by their clean clothes and their control of Hollywood.

Golden, Christopher. Billy Mays lookalike and intimate friend of *Battlestar Galactica's* Captain Apollo, Richard Hatch.

Goodie Bags. Paper containers distributed charitably to Campers and filled with books destined for the dealer's room and other castoff publishing merchandise that feature Campers shilling for other Campers, usually by repeated and senseless comparisons to Stephen King.

Grant, Charles. The Godfather. Within one degree of separation of every attending author.

Guest of Honor. Author or artist who serves as unwitting tool for attracting fresh Campers. "Honor" consists of complimentary accommodations (if shared with others) and generous supply of petroleum jelly.

Hautala, Rick. Attending author known for loving any cover a publisher might give him and for authoring a novel whose holographic cover ignited brief-lived trend of books as bicycle reflectors.

Hawaiian Shirt Contest. Friday evening event held to confirm the Campers' impeccable and ever-evolving sense of contemporary fashion.

The Heathers. Female vocal ensemble whose dulcet rendition of "Mr. Sandman" assured that Neil Gaiman did not attend another Necon. See Buchanan, Ginjer; Monteleone, Elizabeth; Winter, Lynne.

Hi-Lo Jack. Saturday evening competition in which certain Campers sat at square tables, dealt hands of playing cards, and pretended they were awake.

Ketchum, Jack. Reclusive novelist who never actually attended Necon. See Mayr, Dallas.

King, Stephen. Legendary author and one-time Necon attendee who, in response to the experience, devoted his life to writing obsessively about horror and death. Rumors of his messianic return to Necon were used on numerous occasions to lure more Campers into the cult.

Legend. The attending author or artist who is the most likely to die within the succeeding 12 months.

Liver Chicken. The most popular game at Necon: Playing chicken with your liver.

Maker's Mark. Brand name of a distilled bourbon whiskey believed by some Campers to increase their bonhomie, wit, and attractiveness to opposite and/or non-opposite sex.

Massie, Elizabeth. Virginia author and former Elliot Spitzer campaign adviser. Does best work in garish eye shadow and torn fishnets.

Mayr, Dallas. Regular Camper and identity thief. Persuaded most everyone he met, particularly females, that he was reclusive novelist Jack Ketchum.

Mini-Golf. Friday morning event for adrenaline-stoked thrill-junkies.

Monteleone, Elizabeth. Necon's Miss Congeniality and persistent foe of the concept of silence.

Monteleone, Thomas F. Attending author, publisher, joke-flubber, Sicilian-rights activist, and future Depends spokes model.

Moonlight Basketball. Late night tourney popular in the fledgling years of Necon, usually pairing shorts versus skins.

Mosquitoes. Non-paying attendees whose interaction with authors and artists resembles that of major publishers, television networks, and film studios.

Necon Hall of Fame. Valhalla for those authors, artists, and editors who returned to Necon so many times that they were rewarded with a shirt.

Necon Olympics. In the words of all known witnesses: Special.

Necon Update. Warm-up to the Saturday evening Game Show or Talent Show. Cautionary reminder to wannabe comedians that they're not laughing with you, but at you.

Necon Whores. Also known as Necon Harlots, Necon Hookers, Necon Hussies, Necon Slatterns, Necon Sluts, Necon Strumpets, Necon Tarts, and Necon Tramps, these women provide the event's feminist conscience.

Newley, Anthony. Late thespian, crooner, composer of "Goldfinger" and "Pure Imagination," and answer to numerous Game Show questions. Channeled on demand by Dallas Mayr and/or Chet Williamson.

Nutman, Philip. British expatriate author who never met a microphone he didn't like. Voted by schoolmates most likely to grow up to be Pete Best.

Panel. A communal hour-long event in which select authors, artists, and/or editors sought forgiveness for past indiscretions while promoting future ones.

> **RELATED TOPICS:**
> **The Future of Horror.** The theme of each year's central panel, intended to deflect any thoughtful examination of the present state of horror.
>
> **Goon Panel.** Saturday at 9:00 a.m.
>
> **New Writers Panel.** Unique seminar in which speakers outnumber their audience.

Picnic (aka "Farewell Picnic"). Concluding event held Sunday at noon, attended only by those not in need of immediate medical attention or admission to rehab.

Plante, Bob. Co-founder of Necon and former member of "The Two Bobs" (the one on the right). Disappeared under mysterious circumstances circa 1983. Reappeared. Disappeared. Reappeared. Disappeared. Last seen on milk carton.

The Quad. Necon's Grassy Knoll. Site of conspiratorial conversations, riveting dance moves, the Saugie Roast, the Sing-Along, Sidewalk Diving, and the 5.8 Richter-scale temblor felt annually by those who have had enough to drink.

Quahog. Son of Cthulhu. Waits dreaming in Seekonk.

Readers. Aficionados of obsolete paper products known as "books." This unpatriotic distraction from *American Idol*, *Fox News*, and *YouTube* demands further investigation.

Registration Ladies (aka "Mary, Patty, Dot, Barbara"). Local coven devoted to arming Campers with "badges" and "card keys" that permit access to all Necon events save those really worth attending.

The Roast. Saturday night ritual in which attending authors, artists, and editors provide an honest, thoughtful, and restrained appraisal of a worthy peer.

Roll Call. An interruption of Friday evening activities for the Toastmaster to read aloud (and, if possible, mispronounce) the names of most anyone and everyone in attendance save maintenance and security staff.

Saugie. A tube-like comestible consisting of "meat" of unknown origin. Served on Thursday night and in communion-like sacrament on Saturday near midnight, after the ingestion of mass quantities of alcohol and occasional mind-altering chemicals.

Saugie Nazi. Purveyor of the tube-like comestible, to be played by Tom Cruise in forthcoming feature film *The Good Saugie Nazi*.

Schweitzer, Darrell. Former top dashiki model turned author, editor, and bookseller. Attended every Necon while blissfully unaware that every Camper has sworn an oath never to buy a book from him.

Secret Masters. Neither secret nor masters.

The 1776 (aka "The '76"). Vendor of alcohol in mass quantities. First stop for arriving Campers. Last stop for certain departing ones.

Sidewalk Diving (aka "Face Surfing"). A sport pursued by attending medical professionals (among others) after suitable self-medication.

The Signing. Probable title of a horror novel circa 2005. Also refers to Friday evening ceremony in which Campers vie with each other to locate an attending author whose signature might return more than $1.98 on eBay.

The Sing-Along. The sad cacophonous howl of intoxicated, Saugie-swollen Campers failing to vocalize once-popular songs in unison and/or harmony. Notable selections include "Country Roads," "Sweet Caroline," and "Hey Jude" (in which the chorus is sustained for fifteen or more minutes).

Skinner, Cortney. Attending artist best known for long-time stage magic partnership with Penn Jillette.

Softball. Saturday afternoon event in which a team of attending authors takes to the field of dreams, where they challenge younger, faster, and more skillful attendees and lose.

Spruill, Steven. Author, psychologist, and body double for Dick Cheney. Voted the last person Campers ever want to see in a dress again.

Straub, Peter. Best-selling novelist and frequent Camper until receipt of doctor's orders.

The Talent Show. Occasional ritual of humiliation and thinning of the Camper herd, held less often than the Game Show due to the limited availability of talent.

Team Koi. Clique of Campers identifiable by an enduring love of pond water (and, in time, the Innsmouth look.)

Technicolor Yawn. Final evening (or early morning) act of certain Campers before losing consciousness.

Toastmaster. Lesser "Guest of Honor" tasked with unenviable duties that do not include making toasts. See Roll Call.

Town Hall Meeting. Sunday morning self-appraisal and planning session devoted mainly to asking whether Stephen King will attend next year.

Vodka. Beverage of choice for edified Campers. See Straub, Peter.

Williamson, Chet. Author, musician, and real-life inspiration for *Waiting for Guffman's* Corky St. Clair.

Wilson, F. Paul. Regularly attending author and physician best known for his kooky, offbeat novelization of the beloved Michael Mann film *The Keep*.

Wilson, Gahan. Artist, author, friend to those who have no friends, enemy to those who would make him an enemy. The reason most attending Campers purchased *Playboy*.

Winter, Douglas E. Otherwise undistinguished attendee who once swore to set his ass on fire if he had to hear five more minutes of Campers singing "Hey Jude."

Winter, Lynne. Original Vanna. Original Heather. Original Sin.

CONCLUSION

In the interests of economy and taste, many attendees have gone unnamed and undescribed in a happenstance that some of them may perceive as a sign of neglect rather than one of mercy. The seemingly uncontrollable desire for public humiliation remains a salient psychological trait of certain authors and artists that deserves further study, but not in these pages. Instead, readers should now turn to the entries in this collection, considering each on its own merits and, if possible, divorced from its relationship to the troubled and troubling cult behavior that is the subject of this report.

With that in mind, we will not comment further on the texts and illustrations that follow, other than to note that their relentless themes of despair, madness, mayhem, and death do not disturb Behavioral Sciences as much as their stirring invitation to read. We find here only additional evidence that ongoing programs to marginalize and, in time, eliminate print media should be accelerated at any and all costs.

PART I
NECON:
WHAT IT IS

Necon: What It Is

BY CHARLES L. GRANT

YOU WOULD THINK IT WOULD BE EASY, WOULDN'T YOU? IN A FEW PARAGRAPHS, explain to those who bother to read this stuff what Necon means to me, and to all the others who have organized their summers around this single event.

The problem is, the words are there, but they don't mean very much, because they're never quite right; the emotions are there, but they can't be put into words without sounding artificial; and the memories are there, but they're my memories, they're important memories, but they would bore anyone else if I dragged them into the open.

What's truly required for a piece like this is eloquence, and I don't have it; what's necessary to adequately and fairly commemorate fifteen years of a gathering of friends is a book, not a few rambling paragraphs; and what's unique about Necon isn't anything you can read about anyway.

You must experience it.

Panels that regularly fill the lecture hall; night basketball on a court the size of Ross Perot; an art show that is both small and exquisite; Sunday lunch on the grass, butter dripping off the corn, catsup sliding off the hamburgers, and nobody wanting to be the first to have to leave; movies in the rathskeller; a pool tournament, a hearts tournament, a poker game, and a watermelon that has been fermenting in gin all day: humidity that would frizz steel; Newport; a dealers' room that doubles as a sauna; walking by the men's/women's shower room and cramping your neck trying not to look; the dorm common room well past midnight, talking about stuff that doesn't mean a damn thing; Bristol; Camp Necon T-shirts: the weekend-long desperation of someone who is positive he's going to be roasted on Sunday: sunburn, poison ivy, and cafeteria food; sitting on the wall at twilight; sitting in the student center; sitting on the steps; sitting. Just . . . sitting. Necon isn't a convention. It's Necon. Trust me, there's a difference.

The Dark Campers

BY LINDA ADDISON

We dissect dreams,
    breathing and smiling on the edge of a thought,
tasting the flames of yesterdays in our open mouths,
    our blood carry unborn constructs rejected by reason
we open our eyes to visions running sharp in the shadows
    our lives, unlikely canvas for things: love, desire, pain, tears
opening, always opening veins to show the wonder, sweet and bitter
    the gentleness of determination
to tell a story.

A View From The Botton, Or Necon 18 from the Virgin Standpoint
BY MATT BECHTEL

I'VE DONE A LOT OF REFLECTING UPON THAT THIRD WEEKEND OF JULY, 1998. Let's face facts, a person simply cannot go through a life changing experience such as his first Necon and not think about it from time to time. But as I sit down to forever immortalize the scenes which replay constantly through my head, I'm struck with the problem of where to begin. After all, an event like Necon 18 can't just happen spontaneously. Years of chance encounters, decades of personality-forming events, centuries of genetic breeding, and yes, even millennia of evolution are required to produce all the necessary components, each inexplicably drawn to the one place and time at which their collective destiny will be met. Just my luck, it was Bristol, Rhode Island. Rhode Island? Can't destiny ever send me someplace cool?

I can't speak for all those campers who converged upon Necon 18's now historical backdrop, but I still remember what was responsible for bringing me to the convention that year. It was a bus. I'd gotten leave from my position as a petroleum engineer at a fueling combine (i.e. pumping gas at a Mobil) for the weekend, and hopped a bus into Providence. From there, the patriarch of Necon himself, Bob Booth, delivered me the rest of the way to the Promised Land.

Which brings me back to where I started, or, where exactly I should start. Does anyone really care who the hell I am? Probably not. That's my name at the top of the page, what more do you need to know about me? However, there is the matter of how I ever fell in league with Mr. Booth and the First Family of Necon in the first place. And that, quite honestly, is a story in and of itself, and too long of one to include at this point. Besides, negotiations are still being held for the movie rights to that tale, and I'd hate to ruin the feel good movie of next summer by spoiling the plot here now. All I can say is if the rumors I'm hearing about RuPaul playing Mary Booth are true, I don't think it's premature to start planning the Oscar speeches.

Anyhow, Bob picked me up Friday afternoon at the Providence bus station, and he'd brought Les Daniels along with him. Needless to say, I was immediately impressed. Not by Mr. Daniels himself, mind you; quite frankly, I'd never heard of him, didn't know he was a writer, and I couldn't name you one of his books if my life depended on it (still can't, for that matter). But that mustache! Dear God, I'd never seen such a fabulous display of facial hair! Every time I attempt to grow a mustache, the feeble result looks like I've just eaten a Hostess cinnamon donut. Les should seriously think about writing a horror novel in which a giant, mutant mustache kills people while its hapless owner can do nothing to stop the carnage. Then again, maybe such a plot would hit a little too close to home for Les. I mean, there have been a number of Necon campers alone who've met Mr. Daniels and have never been heard from again. Maybe I'm on to something here ...

But I digress. After arriving at the campus of Roger Williams University, Bob hurried me through the check-in process so we could catch the three o'clock panel that afternoon, something about comic books. Anyway, as Bob led me back to his room (being a poor student at the time, the Booths had magnanimously offered to let me crash on their couch that weekend for free), we came face to face with an enormous, hairy man surrounded by what appeared to be a flock of groupies.

"Here's someone you should meet," Bob opened. "Chris Golden, I'd like you to meet Matt Bechtel."

"You don't need to introduce us, we've already met!" Golden interrupted as he shook my hand. "We shared an ...intimate ...evening in New York together, remember?" ...

Now, I don't know much in this world. But if there's one thing I learned from my stretch in San Quentin, it's that if a 6'6" guy declares you his bitch, you just don't disagree. "I thought we agreed to keep that between us ..." I hedged.

Later on, I learned that Mr. Golden's confusion regarding my identity was linked to misunderstanding my Necon bio. Bob had made some lame-ass joke that was supposed to paint me as Daredevil, about whom Golden had just finished a novel. Instead, the entirety of Necon 18 thought I'd picked him up in a bar one night. Thanks again for that, Bob.

Anyway, after stashing my bags in the Booth's living room, I got my first true taste of Necon. No, I'm not talking about that before-mentioned panel. I'm talking about the Gordon's Gin and tonic Bob mixed me to take with us.

"It's Necon," he explained. "You can't go anywhere sober."

That was when I knew, I'd truly found a home. Thanks again for that, Bob ... and this time, I really mean it.

As any experienced Neconer knows, Bob Booth mixes one hell of a gin and tonic. Needless to say, I don't remember squat from that panel, nor do I remember too much from the rest of that afternoon. Well, I remember the food at dinner sucked, but again, that's pretty common Necon knowledge. So I'll fast forward to my next moment of lucidity amongst the alcoholic haze, Friday night's Author's Party.

Friday night's party started on a slightly embarrassing note for yours truly. Being a Necon virgin, meeting all these important literary figures for the first time, I definitely wanted to blend in to the crowd, to be "one of the gang." And I could have sworn I heard someone say it was a toga party. Oh well; at least I got a five dollar bill and a room key tucked into the waist of my bed sheet. Unfortunately, both came from Chris Golden.

Fortunately for me, the Author's Party featured two of my absolute favorite pastimes—beer and pool. Within half an hour, I was partnered off with Dallas Mayr for a game of eight ball against Bob and Dan Booth. The game was mostly uneventful, with no one shooting all that well (of course, the steady stream of alcohol didn't help matters). Halfway through the rack, Bob pulled me aside.

"Do you know who your partner is?" he asked.

"I'm guessing his name is Dallas ..." I joked back.

"Yeah, his real name is. He's better known as Jack Ketchum! You are shooting pool with Jack Ketchum!"

Needless to say, I was floored. I mean, for such a huge name, he was so unassuming, so down to earth, so cool. The next opening I had, I decided to let him know what a fan I was.

"Bob just told me something," I opened. "You're Jack Ketchum?"

He smiled. "Yeah. In fact, I am."

I shook his hand again.

"I'm a big fan of your work," I gushed. "And, if you'll let me say, you look really good for your age!"

Dallas looked at me with a raised eyebrow. "Gee, thanks ..." he muttered.

"I mean, I loved you in *The Odd Couple!*"

After a long, long silence, Dallas explained, "That was Jack Klugman."

"Jack Klugman?" I asked, to which he nodded. "Oh. Who are you again?"

"Jack Ketchum."

"How would I know you?"

"*Off Season, Stranglehold, Girl Next Door,*" he rattled off.

"Oh," I responded. "Was Tony Randall in any of those?"

Dallas excused himself to take his next shot, and unfortunately, cost us the game by sinking the eight ball prematurely. Funny, since the eight ball was all the way at the other end of the table from the two balls we had left.

As I wandered out of the game room, F. Paul Wilson staggered by. Seizing the opportunity, I pushed Chris Golden's room key card into his hand. "Here," I told him, "Chris wants to see you in his room later." Wilson mumbled something incoherent in reply, but since I was no longer in possession of the key, I figured I'd dodged a bullet.

Even though I don't smoke (it's the only bad habit I've managed to avoid over the years), I always hang out with those who do at parties. Maybe I'm addicted to second hand smoke. Anyway, I spent the rest of the Authors' Party on the patio, drinking the illegal "bootleg" liquor and floating amongst conversations. That was when my ears overheard a topic about which I knew I could hold my own—sports. I mean, you don't win four straight amateur gold gloves and set your state's high school record in competitive bass fishing without picking up a thing or two about athletics. So I casually glided my way into the discussion ... only to realize it was about soccer. I'm sorry, but soccer is not a real sport. All real sports are shown with commercials, because all real sports are watched by real sports fans who are drinking real beer, and need an occasional break to hit the bathroom. However, towards the end of the World Cup chatter, Charlie Grant delighted the rest of us with his "Seven Words You Can't Say On TV" routine, which was a real treat.

Around this time, the official Authors' Party broke off into the unofficial, outdoor, everybody-offer-up-all-the-booze-ya-got party. And I found myself talking with a really great-tempered guy named Larry. Larry was a Necon first-timer, which gave us common ground right off the bat. Also, we fluked into discovering we were both huge fans of the underground punk bank from the 80's named *The Replacements*. Most importantly, Larry had a thirty pack of Red Dog, and he was more than happy to share.

"So," Larry asked me, "do you write?"

I nodded as I slurped my beer.

"What do you write?"

Now, if there's one thing I learned from my stint as a C.I.A. operative, it's never, ever admit to having no real experience in the field in which you're currently dealing. So I covered, "I'm one of the foremost authors of Internet Erotica. You've probably read some of my work."

Larry's jaw dropped, which was exactly the reaction I'd hoped to get. When he immediately asked, "Are you Dr. Spankenstein? Or Baron Von Climitia?" my jaw dropped. Needless to say, two years later, I have diplomatically avoided ever talking to Larry again.

At this point in the festivities, Bob emerged from his room beaming from ear to ear and holding something waddled in a blanket. Proudly, he announced he'd passed his Annual Necon Kidney Stone! And there was much rejoicing. When Bob polled the peanut gallery for possible names for the stone, his daughter Sara offered up, "Well, is it a girl kidney stone? Cuz I kinda like the name Jillian ..."

I'm not exactly proud of what happened next that evening, but in the interest of honesty, I'll tell it. Oh, who the hell am I kidding? I'm damn proud of what happened next. Necon has a tradition of barring costume-wearing freaks from junking up our fun. Unfortunately, someone at Necon 18 found a loophole. You see, 1998's Guest of Honor was Neil Gaiman, creator of *The Sandman* comic book series. One look at Neil, and then one look at his work, and you immediately realize that he based the appearance of his dream-lord hero on his own personal fashion taste (black pants, black leather jacket, nothing too outrageous). However, one look at one particular camper—a camper whom no one had ever seen before, and who hovered around Gaiman like a moth to a light—and it was crystal clear that this guy had come dressed as The Sandman. The clothes were just normal enough to give the dude plausible deniability, but anyone with four functioning brain cells could see right through the facade. I mean, who wears a heavy jacket like that in July?

So, in my ever-increasingly drunken zeal, I decided to make this guy's wish come true. If he wanted to be The Sandman, I was more than happy to oblige. "Hey!" I shouted at him from across the lawn, "What the hell's the deal with the dream you keep sending me about my mom and lime jello? What about the one with Adolf Hitler in the all girl cabaret???

Hey, I'm talking to you, Dream-Boy!!!"

Later, I learned that I'd scared the poor dude so much that he spent the rest of Necon hiding under his bed, sucking his thumb. Needless to say, he has never returned to the convention. Mission accomplished.

Much of the rest of my first night at Necon is, understandably, a blur. I do recall that when I saw Dallas swinging from tree vine to tree vine in nothing but a loincloth, I decided that it was time for bed.

Necon Saturday was filled with the standard fare of riveting panels, brilliant art displays, a treasure-trove of a dealer's room, bad food, and one very, very special occasion which remains near and dear to my heart. Sometimes wonderful things do just fall into your lap, and all of us there that summer got to bear witness to such an event. Necon 18 marked the convention's first ever marriage ceremony … and an alternative lifestyle ceremony at that, as Chris Golden and F. Paul Wilson were joined as life partners. The blissful couple was so grateful to me for slipping Paul the room key that they asked me to serve as their flower girl. Naturally, I was touched, and honored to play a role in their special day. The twosome exchanged wedding vows barefoot on the beach, and Paul looked stunning in his tasteful, white satin gown. It was a moment I'm sure none will forget.

Naturally, all of Saturday's activities led up to the infamous Necon Game Show that night. In what was surely the high point of his weekend (hell, maybe the high point of his life), Steve Bissette conquered Les Daniels in the finals. All in all, I could have correctly answered two questions if I'd been in the hot seat. The shared worthless knowledge around this convention really does border on a cult sometimes.

However, the Game Show did feature a side attraction, so to speak.

As Guest of Honor Neil Gaiman was introduced as a participant, he was serenaded with a Necon-style version of "Mr. Sandman" by the all-girl singing group, The Heathers. The Heathers are comprised of the trio of Ginjer Buchanan, Lynn Winter and Elizabeth Monteleone, whose combined ability to carry a tune rivals that of a strangled Canadian goose. Watching The Heathers perform was like witnessing a cross between The Spice Girls and The Golden Girls; in fact, Elizabeth Monteleone even offered to cook everyone at the convention veal parmesan later that night.

The Game Show was followed by more random acts of alcoholism, otherwise known as another night of Necon partying. As all were gathered around The Meeting Place, someone had the bright idea of holding a contest—who could come up with the best reason that Stephen King failed to grace us with his presence that year? I had high hopes for my entry, but apparently no one appreciates a good joke about Abe Vigoda's toenail fungus anymore.

Slightly depressed by this setback, I decided to jump into one of the many card games that was taking place. After all, after spending four summers as a blackjack dealer on a Mississippi Riverboat Casino, I figured I knew pretty much all there was to know about cards. That was when I met Paul Dobish. To call Paul slightly anal regarding cards is an insult to the alimentary tract. For Paul, there are certain rules to follow when playing High-Low-Jack, rules that simply can not be deviated from. Unbeknownst to me, rule number one is that Paul himself must always win. When I broke this rule by over-trumping his partner and stealing the Jack, Paul responded by pulling a dirty sweat sock puppet out of his pants, putting it on his hand, and jamming his fingers into my gullet. By the time I came to, the card game was pretty much over.

What happened next to me at Necon 18 is the stuff that legends are made out of. I guess I was still slightly dazed from Mr. Dobish's attack, because I thought nothing of it when two robust, muscular sisters asked me if I knew what time it was. A quick glance at my watch told that it was midnight, and I informed them that it was time to wander back to the dorms for another outdoor party. With a combined five teeth amidst their two grinning faces, they thanked me.

As I staggered my way towards the party, I was tackled from behind by what felt like two water buffalo. Looking back, I wish it were two water buffalo. "We's just so grateful of ya'll telling us'n what time it is," one explained to me, as the other hoisted me over her shoulder like a sack of potatoes. "Tellin' time's jus too dang complitimacated for country gals like us'n. Now, we's gats to thanks ya the best way we knows how ta ..."

At this point, I still had no idea who the two behemoths that assailed me even were. Later, Bob would fill me in on the messy details. Debbie Sue and Patti LuLu Dombroski mistakenly followed Charlie Grant to Necon from rural Pennsylvania; apparently, they came under the misconception that Necon featured a tractor pulling contest. I still think the two of them planned on pulling a tractor with their bare hands.

Anyway, the smaller of the duo stood 6'2", and had to top 325 lbs. of pure muscle. The larger of the two would have made a bull moose look like a hamster. And, after two straight days of moonshine and pizza goldfish crackers, the Dombroski Sisters decided that they wanted to get themselves some loving. Lucky me, I was the one who (quite literally) gave them the time of day.

The next thing I knew, I was thrown behind the Tidewater Dorm dumpster, pinned up against the wall by a combined 600 lbs. of the best muscle that shucking Pennsylvania corn can build. There was simply no denying their animal lust. And, by the time, they had ripped off my shirt and started to pour Cheez-Whiz all over my chest ...

I'm ... I'm sorry. I ... I just can't go on any further. I really, really thought I was ready to talk about what happened to me that night. My therapist thought it was a good idea for me to discuss the incident, too. A chance to begin the healing process, to put that hellish night behind me and actually move on. But I just can't. Maybe it's for the best that I never fully remember the time I spent in their clutches. For the sake of the story, you'll all just have to use your imagination as to what transpired behind that dumpster. I'm sure reality is far worse than anything any of you can dream up.

Anyhow, I woke up the next morning outside of the Booth's door.

I guess when they'd had their fill of me, Debbie Sue and Patti LuLu deposited me there. They'd stuffed a note into my mouth. It read, "Matt—We's jus' too much philly for any one bull. It's best that we's goes now, and not ta break'n yours heart anymores than we's already did it. Thanks for the fun, the Dombroski Sisters."

Necon Sunday got off on a bittersweet note. Chris Golden and F. Paul Wilson went to get their marriage license, and it was discovered that Paul was already legally married to Steve Spruill. Therefore, their union was illegal and not binding. The couple parted friends, deciding it was best for all involved to allow the magic they'd shared that weekend to remain just that.

Sunday's roast victim, in what was surely the low point of his entire life, was Steve Bissette. Watching Steve get skewered, I made a mental note to never become enough of a Necon regular to ever even be considered for roasting. Of course, a couple more weekends like this one, and I wouldn't have anything to worry about—I'd be dead long before my roasting time ever arrived.

The rest of the convention was, gratefully, uneventful. Following the farewell barbecue, Bob kindly dropped me off at the Providence bus station, and I promptly went into a coma for the duration of my trip. As I crawled my way through my front door, my mom's reaction of pure horror would have been the envy of any of the writers I'd just met.

"Jesus!" she blurted. "What happened to you?"

I was too exhausted to even reply, so I just aimed my body towards the couch and fell backwards. Luckily, I hit my target.

"You look like you've been through hell!"

I opened one eye just enough to look at her, and my withered mouth cracked a smile in spite of itself. "Nah," I grunted, "Hell is for wimps. Necon is for writers."

AUTHOR'S NOTE: You must remember this; certain names have been changed or omitted to protect the integrity of the innocent (you know exactly who you are). Other actual names have been added for my own amusement. Besides, we all know the subjects are guilty anyway, so why not have some fun with them? Like my grandfather always said, never let the truth get in the way of a good story.

Four Views of Necon

BY GINJER BUCHANAN

THURSDAY: THE COOKOUT

Those with no jobs come
Early, seeking free food. They
Eat many Saugies.

FRIDAY: THE AUTOGRAPHING

We bring books, stand in
Lines, search for the great. We ask
"Who is the Bob Booth?"

SATURDAY: IN THE EVENING

The game show goes on
And on and on and on and
On. And then Les wins.

SUNDAY: THE ROAST

Feet to the flames, this
Year's victim writhes. We laugh and
Pray we won't be next.

Conning at Roger Williams on a Summer's Weekend

BY ELIZABETH MASSIE

Whose Con this is I think I know,
It's hiding in Rhode Island, though.
They keep the membership quite small
But the big names, Ah! Do they show!

My little van must think it queer
To Con without a Big Town near
Amid the dorms and dining hall (and Baptists and football players),
The best damn gathering of the year.

It gives its old engine a shake
To ask if there is some mistake.
But in we drive; see there, you car?
Enough to make you yelp and quake.

There's Charlie Grant and Stephen Spruill,
There's Doug, there's Vanna—such a jewel!
There's spooky Neil and lovely Von,
All whom the horror world do rule.

Les Daniels spouting movie names,
Alan Ryan checking out the dames,
Jack Ketchum's singing Newley tunes,
And Craig creating killer games.

Rick Hautala and Rick Berr-y,
Down orange juice and eggs with glee,
Whilst Chet and Ginjer both talk shop,
And Monteleone gives advice for free.

Humidity, the river fair,
Late-night parties—beer to spare,
Climbing underneath the bridge,
The dealers' room with books so rare.

Panels, slide shows, softball, fun,
Staying up until the sun,
Crashing on a new friend's floor,
Char-black hotdog on a bun.

This con is lovely, dark; and yet
I should go home to feed my pet.
And water plants and write some books
And pay some bills, those lousy crooks.

But if I could I'd stay right here,
And talk and play and eat and cheer,
'Til Bob outs me on my rear.
'Til Bob outs me on my rear.

My Favorite Necon Moment

BY THOMAS F. MONTELEONE

ACTUALLY, THAT'S NOT TRUE. I DON'T HAVE A FAVORITE NECON MOMENT, I HAVE LOTS OF THEM.

And at the risk of sounding mawkish, I am duty bound on the request of Dan Booth to list only a handful of them herewith.

1. The first time I was a contestant on the game show, and failed to provide even one correct answer.

2. Learning, after several years of watching Les Daniels and Steve Bissette trade Game Show Championships, that neither of them had anything even closely resembling A Life, and still wishing that maybe someday, I too, could be a Game Show Grand Master.

3. Defeating Les Daniels in the Game Show, thereby achieving my lifelong dream of becoming a Grand Master. (Years later, I went on to record an astounding 2nd Championship to the strains of The Theme from *Rocky*).

4. Being able to roast Rick McCammon, giving me an excuse to do a performance-piece rendition of my "Ba-Roo-Roo" joke.

5. Getting down on my knees in thanks for being roasted several years before Elizabeth came to her first Necon. Somehow, I don't think she would have appreciated the "humor."

6. Bringing Elizabeth to her first Necon, and finding out that Paul Wilson and I were, in her words, "a couple of geeks."

7. In one of the manifold softball games in which my team lost, making a diving stop to my right of a vicious short-hop, then getting up in time to throw out the fleet Hank Wagner.

8. Getting the shock of my life when I discovered you guys decided to roast my wife, Elizabeth, then absorbing enough collateral damage to take out a convoy.

9. Being invited to contribute to this book, which will be read by the biggest, best family of friends in the literary universe. Thanks, guys and dolls.

Necon X: a fond memory from the other side of sanity

BY YVONNE NAVARRO

Dateline: 7.19.90 Thursday

3:10 P.M. EASTERN STANDARD TIME—YVONNE NAVARRO AND JEFF OSIER ARRIVE at Green Airport in Providence [actually Warwick], Rhode Island and rendezvous with Beth Massie, Lisa Lepovetsky and Mark Rainey. A subcompact car is rented, and after some discussion and man-handling of luggage, it is agreed that it is not necessary to tie Mark to the roof of the car to save space. Concern was expressed that insects might stick to his eyeglasses during the ride.

A stop is made at a warehouse food outlet for NECondiments, those wonderful, sauces and flavors that are oh-so-necessary to bring out the best of the NECON cuisine. The final arrival phase finds Our Group swarming through 1776 Liquors for the ice and liquid sustenance that is required for sane survival. It is once again recommended that Mark be tied to the roof in order to make room in the vehicle for three coolers; Yvonne takes pity upon his poor, wasted form and miraculously packs everything in the trunk, thus saving him, once again, from a windy demise.

5:00 p.m.—After arriving at Roger Williams College and registering to become official NECONites (a complicated process requiring incredible motor dexterity in that one must have the ability to take and hold a key and an envelope containing panel information, *NECON Stories* and the special edition of *Footsteps*) Our Group members locate their rooms. Given the luxury and decadence of the dorms, the buttery soft beds and inviting lighting, it is a wonder each even desires to leave those fine comforts.

5:30 p.m.—Our Group consumes its first NECON dinner. Fragments of shells and tomato sauce, chicken wings and green beans splatter in all directions; fortunately, all survive.

6:30 p.m.—Selected souls depart for Providence to view Lovecraft's residence and drink bubbly over his moldering remains. Alas, the resulting tour takes the would-be adventurers only to the dead Edgar Allen Poe's dead girlfriend's house and imbibes only wine in a cemetery that probably looks a lot like the one in which Lovecraft is really buried.

7:00 p.m.—The members of Our Group begin to disperse, each seeking final frontiers and brave new worl—uh, new acquaintances, old friends, and, most probably, mass quantities of additional liquid sustenance. In the Student Union, dealers' tables are arranged, movies are watched, and chips, beer and soda are taken in by the crowd at a rate comparable only to the relish with which *The Blob* viewed its latest town. By 8:00 the Pub is open and operating.

10:00 p.m.—Slack-jawed convention-goers stare with unabashed awe as they are treated to such stunning pearls of the cinema world as *Horror Workout* and other flicks which have become so passionately desired in the genre that they can no longer be named lest demand surpass supply.

11:30 p.m.—NECONites grope their way to the Dorm Party Room in an attempt to prepare themselves for the weekend to come.

Yes folks, the excitement builds.

Dateline: 7.20.90 Friday

9:03 a.m. Eastern Standard Time—Late and fearful of missing the exquisite taste sensations of a NECON breakfast, Jeff Osier slinks into a cafeteria serving line momentarily empty of watchful employees, leaps the metal barrier and plunges his hands into mounds of hot, delicious meat. Moments later he flees, upheld fists clutching sausage patties the size of beer bottle bottoms.

10:00 a.m. - 12:00 p.m.—NECONites are treated to Continuing Better Education as they listen with rapturous attention to Those Who Supposedly Have Tremendous Knowledge About This Stuff recite a multitude of stories, advice, opinions and other unidentifiable and unclassifiable postulations on the scintillating subjects of poetry, violence, men, and women. Had someone thoughtfully combined these two panels, it may well have become a shining example of an outline for the average hysterical romance novel.

12:00 p.m.—Ah, the first NECON lunch! Tension escalates as debate flares over which of the three luncheon salads actually is the shrimp. Those not courageous enough to surrender their bodies to salads opt for the delectable looking grilled ham and Swiss on rye slabs. No mercy is shown to those writhing on the floor after the meal; it is assumed these are people hired to keep the cafeteria floor clean.

1:00 - 5:00 p.m.—A veritable avalanche of learning ensues as conventioneers are bludgeoned with tips by the pros and not-so-pros about Big Time Saviors, Breaking In Small Swamps, Starting Your Own Males, You And Women, and Publishing Deadly Companies. This afternoon's debate highlight is generously supplied by Darrell Schweitzer and Kathleen Jurgens.

Elsewhere in the lecture building, the bookroom opens and wealthy and poor alike flock to gaze with envious eyes upon a multitude of items, not the least of which include such things as uncorrected page proofs of *Twilight Eyes* by Dean Koontz, plastic-covered editions of *The Monster Men* by Edgar Rice Burroughs, and yes, even musty smelling collections of Hans Christian Anderson. Trembling fingers rummage in pockets for currency that they too might possess the wild thing of their own fantasies while next door the art show begins its slow transformation from bland classroom to horrific showcase.

5:00 p.m.—Friday dinner, a feast for only the starved among us. Fried fish, fried fries, fried potato skins and a wonderful casserole-type dish of white and red lumps resembling beef (?!) and macaroni which cafeteria servers insist on calling "chop suey." If only the Chinese knew the truth.

7:00 p.m. - ?—In the Student Union the autograph party begins. Rick McCammon sits hunched over a table writing unknown things with cramped, clawed fingers; F. Paul Wilson models patiently for the camera as he scrawls a prescription-like signature. A card game ensues. The stakes remain unknown, although a noted presence was John Betancourt, then co-editor of *Weird Tales*. Rumor has it that Lovecraft's true resting place is in a locked and nearly forgotten bottom desk drawer at the *Weird Tales* offices and that John bet the key. He won that hand, so the world will never know. Camera flashes fizzle and pop like dud firecrackers as images from *Reanimator* and *From Beyond* flicker crazily on the faces of Pub patrons.

Gradually the Student Union and Pub begin to disgorge their pulsing pieces of humanity and the Dorm Party Room accepts this offering with green carpeting and a ceiling that occasionally reminds a too-tall visitor that someone should have held back on the growth hormones. A guitar is produced and David Wilson and Mark Rainey stupefy the partiers with their strategic strumming and melodic singing. Beer abounds, accompanied occasionally by such wondrous seasonings as root beer schnapps and honey-flavored lacquer thinner—or wait, maybe that was honey-flavored schnapps? Most importantly, it is learned by all at the party that ELVIS LIVES (last seen out by the woodshed)!

Dateline: 7.21.90 Saturday
8:50 a.m. Eastern Standard Time—A breakfast obviously meant to soothe those fledgling NECONites feeling the questionable after-effects of the mass quantities of alcohol and other unidentifiable substances ingested the previous night: pancakes resembling wet paper circles served with brown maple water and slices of dead pig flesh. Yum.

9:00 a.m. - 12:00—The Real World continues to force-feed The Facts to NECON attendees. Slides are viewed, reviewers reviewed, and The State Of The World As We Know It stated in abundant and confusing detail. This morning's debate is generously supplied by Ginger Buchanan and the audience.

12:00 p.m.—Ole! Please write me if you attended this *mucho gusto* luncheon and think you can identify the meat in those tacos. 25 cents prize for the best answer.

1:00 p.m. - 4:00 p.m.—Saturday Afternoon Panels: Home towns are discussed, prose barriers and how to erect them, Real Writers share the secrets of their work habits with The Wannabes. To the ordinary eye, many NECONites appear to be dozing in the comfortable 85 degree lecture hall. The more experienced writer/poet/illustrator is sympathetically aware, however, that these naive conference attendees have, in fact, become so overwhelmed by the sheer immensity of the knowledge that has been imparted that they have, sadly, collapsed under its volume.

4:00 p.m.—The more hardy patrons of the lecture hall feel the tug of maternal instinct as they use humane (well, almost) methods to return the collapsed NECONites to consciousness so that all might drag themselves to the foyer and partake of the wines (two varieties, in attractive plastic cups) and flavorful cheeses which have been set out in honor of this year's attending arteests.

5:30 p.m.—How sad—the final NECON dinner. Succulent pork chops and gravy (oh God, I hope that was gravy!), and chicken pot pies. Say what? Your pot pie didn't have any chicken? It's amazing how many people don't recognize chicken toenails when they eat them.

7:00 p.m.—The moment everyone has been waiting for: The Celebrity Roastee is revealed. Rick McCammon is trussed to a verbal spit and spun repeatedly, but someone forgot to light the fire and the Honorary Nice Guy not only easily survives the babaruba without feeling the least bit puely, but counter-attacks with laser-like words that meld his attackers right into their plastic seats.

8:00 p.m.—*The Horror Game Show*, once again high-lighted by the lovely Vanna Lynn Winter. Fun contestants, obscure questions, silly prizes, what more should be said?

10:00 p.m. - ?—More films in the Pub, more booze in the bellies, books and magazines clutched in sweaty hands. A stew of bodies, some clad in neon-swirled tee shirts while others prefer leather wristbands and black sandals. The crowd surges to the Dorm Party Room for fabled Domino's Pizza and the final social frenzy. A few poor folk are forced to accept the brutal reality that there is simply no place open in Bristol for booze after ten on Saturday night. Beth Massie brings 60s nostalgia to those among the crowd with a mini boom box and a succession of taped hits which include such gems as "Stop in the Name of Love" and "Hair," while Joan Vanderputten paralyzes party goers with her dance skills. Amy Wimberger joins Beth and Joan in song as Yvonne Navarro conducts; the crowd is… speechless.

Dateline: 7.22.90 Sunday

10:00 a.m. Eastern Standard Time—Alas, due to strenuous Saturday night responsibilities and the horrible chore of re-packing a mountain of possessions into suitcases roughly the size of sandwich bags, most of Our Group has missed the final NECON breakfast and is forced to acquire sustenance at The Donut Barn. A sad thing. Really.

At this very point in time, panelists and dead puppies are writhing with NECON's final spasms in the lecture hall.

11:00 a.m.—At last! The NECON Tenth Anniversary Celebration! A mass of fetid breath explodes into the lecture hall as all those people who've been holding their breath let go. Jokes, awards, tears, and seizures; we have it all. Picture, if you *dare*, an hour of: Tammi (Bambi's sister), the 1990 Misnomer Award, Mon-ta-lee-ohn-ne, rhymes with ba-lohn-nee, stallions, lost and found videotapes, and NECON skull awards with blinking red and green eyes and clacking lower jaws. How can you stand it?

12:00 p.m.—Oh, tears! The heavens spit upon the NECON conventioneers and they are forced to celebrate the grand finale of the NECON social calendar, the cookout, within the cheery confines of the cafeteria. But the burgers and dawgs are just as good as in previous years— I mean that—as final conversations are held and warm wishes bestowed. NECondiments are, as has become tradition, passed on to Joe Cherkes for his family's feasting enjoyment.

1:30 p.m.—Packed and ready, the members of Our Group depart Roger Williams College, leaving as the only evidence of their passage a stinking, decomposing red starfish, plucked from its rocky resting place at the shore of Narragansett Bay and draped over the rock by the door of their dorm building. Farewell!

2:30 p.m.—Anguished goodbyes at the airport as Beth Massie doles out a purse full of nearly forgotten plastic flies.

In closing, no one says it better than Stanley Wiater:

"Other people have lives; we have NECON."

Whores Just Wanna Have Fun!

BY HOLLY NEWSTEIN

FOR THE INQUIRING CAMPER, BETH MASSIE AND I WOULD LIKE TO SHARE THIS EMAIL EXCHANGE REGARDING THE ORIGINS OF A FINE, UPSTANDING NECON TRADITION:

To: Beth Massie
From: Holly Newstein
Subject: Necon Whores

I love the Necon Whores. What a satirical indictment of the things writers are forced to do for money—a savage commentary on how we have to compromise our principles and artistic integrity—and maybe a bit of career counseling on how to supplement our ridiculous writing incomes.

To: Holly Newstein
From: Beth Massie
Re: **Necon Whores**

The origin of the Necon whores is actually kinda mundane. Barb and I will jump on any chance to perform (sorry, we have no impulse control…). We discussed what would be appropriately rude for Necon, and light bulbs popped over our heads. "Why, whores" we said. So, we came up with the Necon whore song, made up business cards, found fuzzy pens and matching datebooks, and performed it in over-the-top tacky clothes.

Moral of the story: Campers just wanna have fun, so check your brain at the door.

NECON 25
Camper Activity Page
BY CAMPER CORTNEY SKINNER

HI CAMPERS! "HORRY" HERE, THE NEW NECON HORROR MASCOT! GET READY FOR SOME SWELL FUN!

THE NECON 25 CAMPER SONG!

SUNG TO THE TUNE OF YANKEE DOODLE

OH NECON IS A HAPPY PLACE
WE ARE SO HAPPY OF THERE
THE SAUGIES FLOW
JUST LIKE CHEAP WINE
AND THAT IS THE FIRST VERSE
(CHORUS)
NECON-HAPPY, HAPPY TIME!
HAPPY LIKE A MONKEY
HORROR'S FUN JUST LIKE A BUN
YOU-ENKAY WHY SPELLS UNKY

OH NECON MAKES US HAPPY NOW
WHEN IT'S GONE WE ARE SADDY
OUR BUTT-OX CLENCH
WHEN WE DEPART
RICE IS GROWN ON A PADDY
(CHORUS)
NECON-HAPPY, HAPPY TIME!
HAPPY LIKE A CHIMPY
HORROR'S KEEN JUST LIKE A SPLEEN
THERE'S NO SUCH WORD AS MIMPY

OUR CHEEKS ARE SPREAD WIDE IN A SMILE
YOU THOUGHT I'D SAY SOME-THING ELSE
OH NECON JOY OH NECON JOY
WHAT'S WITH THIS OBSESSION WITH BUTT-OX?
(CHORUS)
NECON-HAPPY, HAPPY TIME!
HAPPY LIKE AN O-RANG
THOUGH ORANGUTANS LOOK GLUM ON THE OUTSIDE
THEY'RE PROBABLY BASICALLY AT PEACE WITH THE WORLD.
HEY!

OPTICAL ILLUSION

STARE AT THE DOT IN THE MIDDLE OF THIS SHAPE WHILE SHAKING THE PAGE FROM TOP TO BOTTOM. THE SHAPE WILL APPEAR TO MOVE UP & DOWN.

Magic Necon Money Puzzle

COMPLETE THIS PUZZLE & TAPE TOGETHER THE PIECES. GIVE THIS MAGIC MONEY PUZZLE TO YOUR FAVORITE BANK EMPLOYEE & THEY WILL GIVE YOU MONEY LIKE MAGIC!

GIVE ME ALL YOUR MONEY

FREE NECON SILVER DOLLAR!

IF YOUR FREE NECON SILVER DOLLAR IS NOT GLUED HERE ASK JACK KETCHAM FOR YOURS NOW!!

necon quiz!

1. NECON?
2. N-E-C-O-N SPELLS ...?
3. YOU ARE _ _ _ _
4. THE ANSWER TO QUESTION #5 IS
5. WHAT IS THE ANSWER TO #4?

ANSWERS:
1. ! 2. NONCE 3. HERE 4. SEE ABOVE 5. SEE ANSWER #5

NECON REBUS TIME!

ANSWER: T PLUS B PLUS BANANA MINUS DOG

CAMPER ACTIVITY PAGE

Cortney Skinner

VALUABLE PRIZES

Gahan Wilson

Necon

BY HANK WAGNER

The first rule about Necon is you don't talk about Necon.

The second rule about Necon is you don't talk about Necon.

You don't say anything because Necon exists only in the hours between when Necon starts and when Necon ends.

Only 200 hundred per year. Only one panel at a time. Panels go on as long as they have to. Those are the other rules of Necon.

Who people are at Necon is not who they are in the real world.

Who I am at Necon is not someone my boss knows.

After a weekend at Necon, everything in the real world gets the volume turned down.

The first Necon was just some of the Booths pounding on each other.

Hinchberger and I still go to Necon, together. Necon is in the basement of a student center, now, after the center closes, and every year there's more guys there.

What you see at Necon is a generation of guys raised on Creature Features and scary stories told around a campfire.

The other rules: one picnic on Sunday, no costumes.

Still another: if this is your first year at Necon, you have to attend the Sunday morning panels.

Necon gets to be the reason for reading a lot of books, going to movies you wouldn't otherwise see, talking to folks you might never otherwise get to know.

What happens at Necon doesn't happen in words.

You aren't alive anywhere like you're alive at Necon. When it's you and 199 other guys in a hot conference room. Necon isn't about winning and losing. Necon isn't about words. You see a guy come to Necon for the first time, and his ass is a loaf of white bread. You see this same guy there next year, and his ass is still a loaf of white bread. But, the guy trusts himself to handle anything. There's grunting and noise at Necon, but Necon isn't about looking good, it's about wearing ugly Hawaiian shirts. There's hysterical shouting in tongues like at church, and when you wake up Sunday afternoon you feel saved.

The last rule about Necon, is, of course, you don't talk about Necon.

A Report on Necon '82

BY STANLEY WIATER

Author's Note: WHEN GIVEN THIS CHANCE TO WRITE ABOUT NECON, SEVERAL IDEAS shot through my mind about how I could best serve its history. Naturally, I first went through the file I had kept over the years since first attending Necon in 1981. There I discovered the only article ever assigned to me by *Fangoria* magazine in 1982 which, for reasons unknown, never saw publication. Since Necon in many ways provided me with the means to pursue a career as a journalist specializing in horror (I've always conducted three or four major interviews here; the majority first saw print in *Fangoria* or *Rod Serling's Twilight Zone Magazine*), it seemed only fitting to have that "Report on Necon '82" finally make its appearance. And since it appears just as it was originally written, I trust the reader will bear in mind that my own skills as a writer have improved just a bit since then.

As witnessed by the 40th World Science Fiction Convention held recently in Chicago, the science fiction community has for some time been celebrating its own existence. Readers of *Fangoria* have certainly heard of similar conventions (such as "Star Trek" Cons, Comic Cons), even if they've not yet had a chance to experience one. But for those whose tastes run more to Stephen King than Arthur C. Clarke, or Robert Bloch rather than Isaac Asimov, there was simply no convention designed expressly for *us*. Now there is one— (actually there's two; the other is the World Fantasy Convention, which will be reported on in a future issue) and it's called Necon.

Necon (which is a quicker way of saying the North Eastern Horror and Fantasy Convention) had its third annual incarnation this past July 16-18 on the Roger Williams College campus, which is located in Bristol, Rhode Island. However, considering the reputation (usually negative) some conventions have acquired over the years, Necon is better described as more of a conference than a convention. This is partially because the organizers allow no one under age 18 to register, nor have over 200 guests ever been in attendance in the brief history of Necon. Both of these factors aided greatly in encouraging a more professional interaction between the guests and the celebrities—not just a mass of rabid fans descending upon an unprepared author or artist. In other words, if you wanted to buy your favorite writer or illustrator a drink and bend his or her ear for an hour, you were given every opportunity.

The three organizers of Necon have been Bob Plante, and the husband and wife team of Bob and Mary Booth. According to Bob Booth, this particular convention came about following his work in helping organize the Fifth World Fantasy Convention in 1979:

"We thought there was a shortage of fantasy conventions. So we also thought we'd like to have one that would be in the East every year, so that when the World Fantasy Con goes to the West or the Midwest, people would have someplace to go. So, we created Necon."

Although there was an art show (Jill Bauman was the featured Guest Artist), a dealer's room (where you could buy first editions of H.P. Lovecraft's *The Outsider* and Stephen King's *Carrie*—both for astronomical prices), and feature films presented nightly (such as *An American Werewolf In London*), the main purpose of Necon was its series of celebrity panels. This year's Guests of Honor were T.E.D. Klein, editor of *Rod Serling's Twilight Zone Magazine* (as well as a fine horror writer), and Michael McDowell, a critically acclaimed writer whose latest horror novel is entitled *Katie*. Besides their participating in a Guest of Honor dialogue with Toastmaster Alan Ryan (author of *The Kill*), both Klein and McDowell graciously spent some time talking with us.

Klein, a quietly intense man in his mid-thirties, replied to the obvious question: What were his personal favorite episodes of the television series from which the magazine was founded? "I guess I remember the famous ones that most other people remember as well. I remember the ones that *scared* me the most, such as 'The Invaders' with Agnes Moorhead. And probably—because I was always afraid of ugly faces—'The Eye of the Beholder.'

"One thing that people tend to forget is how *scary* that show could be for young kids.

"For me, what was most special about *The Twilight Zone* was not the stories, it was the presence of Rod Serling as narrator. I think many anthology series have failed, but I think *Twilight Zone* succeeded, not so much on the strength of its writing—which was often very good, but not always—it was that presence of Rod Serling. The avuncular narrator who will step out at the beginning, the end—and often in the middle—to remind you *it's only a story*. I think that's important."

As for Michael McDowell, beginning in January of next year, he will have no less than a six novel epic appearing monthly from Avon. Called *Blackwater*, it will revolve around a large, multigenerational family, the head of which, according to the author, "is not quite human!"

Some of the other panels for discussion included "H.P.L.: A Modern Evaluation," "Trends in Current Fantasy," "Genre Criticism: the State of the Art" (in which yours truly participated; it's a wonderful feeling being someplace where you don't have to explain to anyone what *Fangoria* is), and a slide presentation by Jill Bauman. (In the art show were several of her paintings, including those for the cover of books by Alan Ryan and Charles L. Grant.) But the most controversial panel consisted of Michael McDowell (whose other books include *The Amulet, Cold Moon Over Babylon*), Les Daniels (*Citizen Vampire, Living In Fear*), Kathryn Grant (who, under the pseudonym Les Simons has written *Gila!*), and her husband Charles L. Grant

(*The Nestling, Nightmare Seasons*). Moderated by Douglas E. Winter, columnist for *Fantasy Newsletter*, the topic was: "Horror: the Limits of Violence."

After first explaining how she came up with the idea for *Gila!* as a joke to one of her editors, Kathryn Grant then found her suggestion being taken seriously. And so she wrote the novel for Signet's unofficial "giant bug" series: "Took *Gila!* to the limit. I had all sorts of gore and really explicit sex scenes. But when I went to do my next novel, *Shadoweyes*, which is more serious—it's not a satire—I really drew a lot of limits. I tried to do very little violence that you could see. I just wanted it implied… I thought it would be more powerful that way."

Charles L. Grant shared a similar viewpoint: "I draw the line at clinical description." He then explained how he left out most of the graphic details of a scene he had recently written in which a policeman's arm is torn out of its socket. "Everyone can then fill in the details, and, depending on how imaginative they are, can really get sick to their stomachs or just go 'naaaah.' So I don't do clinical description. That defeats the purpose of horror… In fiction, when you're working on someone's imagination, stopping just short of the actual detail, I think, is sufficient."

Les Daniels happened to look at the limits of violence in his work from the opposite side of the coin: "I write things that I think are pretty outrageous, and realize that people are going to get through them without dying of shock. But I always wonder about this 'leaving it to the imagination' business, though I suppose there's something to be said for that. But I am not the world's leading advocate of 'leaving it to the imagination,' saying that the most frightening things are the things you *don't* see. On the other hand, this could ultimately lead us to the conclusion that the most frightening book ever written was *The Bobbsey Twins: The Secret at the Seashore*—where you don't even know what's happening over the next sand dune!"

Michael McDowell sided with Daniels, stating that if he had the talent to describe scenes of horror in greater clinical detail, he "wouldn't hesitate for one minute! And just for philosophical reasons, I think the tendency in movies to become more graphic is all to the good. I think that television has done a powerful disservice in showing that when people get shot they don't bleed. They don't get knocked back against the wall. They just fall backwards on the floor! And I think this is a terrible thing. And if you have movies showing that it's really *horrible* when somebody gets shot in the head, people are going to be less likely to go out and shoot other people in the head."

Ultimately the panel displayed theories evolving from two distinctly different schools of thought. The Grants believing that "the less you describe, the more terrifying the unknown is," while Daniels and McDowell expressed the catharsis concept, which is basically that, the more graphic the violence is, the more relieved the reader/viewer will feel after being exposed to the pure, undiluted horror of it all.

An unexpected pleasure occurred later that day when a recently successful unknown by the name of Stephen King suddenly appeared on the scene. (Like Daniels and McDowell, he also just happens to be an avowed fan of this publication.) Besides the opportunity to meet with many of his colleagues, King was also here to face the task of signing the limited edition of his most recent book, *The Dark Tower: The Gunslinger*, which publisher Donald M. Grant had personally brought along copies by the box load for that very purpose. King, who later spent many hours in discussion of some of the most recent—and "gloriously bad"—horror films in release, looked in fine health despite his encounters in *Creepshow*.

On the following Sunday morning, the annual celebrity roast was kept a well guarded secret until the actual proceedings were held. Since Stephen King had truly been an unannounced guest to Necon, his being chosen as the victim of the roast was an even greater surprise. Those selected to do the honors—Donald M. Grant, Les Daniels, Douglas E. Winter, Charles L. Grant, and Michael McDowell—each had a specific bone to pick with King, all under the direction of toastmaster Alan Ryan.

Unfortunately, little of what was said in honor—and dishonor—of Stephen King can be mentioned in print, though the rude remarks were always coupled with sincere ones of admiration and affection. Many of the roasters had been to King's home in Maine at one time or another, and this peek into the bestselling author's family life was as revealing as it was hilarious.

When finally given the chance to respond, King graciously thanked everyone concerned, stating that he hadn't really been bothered in the least by their comments. Especially since they were all just "a bunch of no-talent sonsabitches!!!"

The final official event at Necon was an outdoor cookout, before which everyone had one final chance to attend the art show or go broke in the dealers' room. One has to say that what makes this convention such a pleasant experience is the accessibility between professional and fan. There was never that slight sense of hysteria which accompanies some of the more large-scale productions. Rather, Necon was more of an opportunity to make friends with someone whose novels or artwork you have admired from afar, and where an intelligent dialogue could then ensue.

And wouldn't that be just about any fan's dream?

KETCHUM KABOBS

Glenn Chadbourne

PART II
NECON:
THE FIRST 20 YEARS

Red Paint

Red paint dripped
down the canvas
in long thin streams.
Some stopped
along the way.
It was paint,
but it looked
like blood.

Watery redness,
dyed the surface
as it flowed.
Some dripped
off the edge.
It was blood,
but it looked
like paint.

--Jill Bauman

The Hustler, smoking

BY JONATHAN CARROLL

MY FATHER WAS A SCREENWRITER. HE WAS FAMOUS IN HIS TIME; THERE WERE MAGAZINE articles written about him. He almost won an Oscar, made a lot of money but as is true with most screenwriters, he died unhappy and mostly forgotten by the world that had once embraced him so fully. He cruised the Mediterranean on Sam Spiegel's yacht while he and the renowned producer talked about films they wanted to make together. We lived in the country about an hour out of Manhattan. My parents gave parties where famous people came and usually ended up doing blessedly normal things with us, the kids, like throw Frisbees or play baseball. One 4th of July, Paul Newman and I shot off firecrackers in our backyard. One exploded prematurely in my hand. I vividly remember Newman picking me up in his arms and running into our house, shouting for someone to get the medicine! I wasn't hurt, but his concern was so real and palpable that it was the second time in my young life I fell in love with Paul Newman.

The first came in the early sixties when my father and Robert Rossen collaborated on *The Hustler*. It was a great time in my father's career. Rossen specifically chose him to adapt the Walter Tevis novel about a small time pool hustler who had the cajones to go for the big time and challenge the greatest player of them all, Minnesota Fats, to the championship of the world. Icarus in pool hall. Dr. Faustus with a billiard cue.

Because I was so young, really the only thing I remember about Rossen was an intense hunched man who looked like a boxing manager. He smoked constantly and had one of those ripping smoker's coughs that rise from the very bottoms of the feet up into the chest and then out. He had a rumbling voice and accented almost all of his sentences with my father's name thrown hard and sharp like a dart. "No, *Sid*, Fast Eddie can't do that." "Sid, Sid, come on, get sharp on this."

They would sit out on our front porch smoking L & M cigarettes, drinking coffee, and writing notes on yellow pads. How I envy them those great things! The days when cigarettes were okay and delicious and that's what you did when you were writing a movie or a book—you smoked every time you took a break. Or you smoked *and* drank coffee, but didn't feel guilty or worry about how they would affect your heart or your blood pressure or the million things we all know now they ravage. Recently, I read an interview with the ultimate tough guy writer—Norman Mailer. During a break, Mailer offered to share a granola bar with the interviewer. A granola bar from the man who wrote *The Naked and the Dead!*

Paul Newman smoked Salem. Do they still exist? That turquoise and white pack, the horrendously strong menthol stab, like a sword through your chest when you took a drag? That is the first thing I remember about the famous actor.

One day just after filming started, my father took me to the set. I remember the scene they were doing, even after thirty years. Fast Eddie and his manager are driving to Pittsburgh, but they pull off at a roadside bar and grill to have a bite. There's a pool table inside and Eddie goes on to hustle everyone in the place out of their money after fooling them into thinking he's drunk. I remember this because my first vision of Newman was rehearsing how a drunk would take a cigarette out of a pack and light it. He was rehearsing with his Salems, but later they were replaced with some no-nonsense unfiltered brand like Lucky Strike or Pall Mall. Why do I remember those names? He wasn't famous yet, but this film would make him that and more. Newman later became so suspicious about his success in *The Hustler* that he demanded his next two or three films have titles of one name beginning with "H."

Jackie Gleason and George C. Scott were also on the set because they were rehearsing another scene in an adjoining room. Gleason was enormous, did all his own pool shots in the film, and kept up a running banter all the time. When I asked for his autograph, he said "Happily, My Good Man!" as if I was the halest fellow he met all week. I didn't know what autographs were until that day. However, my father insisted I ask everyone for their signatures. I did as I was told. All of them were very kind about it, except for Scott who flat out refused. But because I didn't understand what autographs "meant," I thought he just didn't feel like writing his name on my piece of paper.

A movie set is one of the most boring places on earth, particularly for a little boy who 1. Doesn't understand what is *going* on 2. Has the attention span of a hummingbird 3. Thought he was going to have a fun day with Pop. I was given a chair and a Coca Cola and told to sit there and be quiet for a while. I don't know how long that while lasted, but time got slow and sticky. Naturally, I started to fidget, which was dangerous because they kept shooting the same scene over and over. They couldn't get it right. Rossen kept hollering "Cut!" Then he, my father and the actors would huddle around the pool table trying to figure out how to nail it. Nothing worked. Finally in the middle of perhaps take 15, I said very loudly, "Pop, when are we going?" It could not have been later than ten o'clock in the morning.

Instantly, Newman smiled, walked right off the set and sat down next to me. He reached into his pocket and took out his pack of Salems. There was transparent plastic wrap on it. He took out a cigarette, lit it, then with one eye squinted carefully slid the plastic wrap halfway down the package. Taking the cigarette out of his mouth, he put it to the plastic for a second and burned a small hole. Then he blew smoke into the hole and tapping very gently on the back of the pack, miraculously made tiny perfect smoke rings shoot out, one after another at an amazing rate until the smoke was all gone. I looked at him with all the sudden wonder a child brings to an unexpected magical moment. He nodded to me, as If to say yes, it's true: These things can happen if you know how to do it right.

Unexpected Attraction

BY MATTHEW COSTELLO

I GUESS THE HOUSE—AT FIRST—UNDERWHELMED HER.

Connie took one look at the Revolutionary-era structure, surrounded by overgrown sumac and chaotic brambles that looked on the verge of storming the box-like domicile, and she said, "Puh-lease."

"You don't like it?"

I phrased it as a question, but there wasn't any doubt.

Connie had no trouble communicating her likes…and dislikes.

After I stopped the car, she made no attempt to get out.

"*This* is the best you could do?"

"For the money… yes. It meets a lot of our criteria…"

"Like what … filled with wormwood and dry rot? More animals *inside* than out?"

I turned to her, seeing her pretty face locked into an impassive, fortress-like expression, daring me to mount an assault on her negativity.

"You haven't seen inside. It's amazing. It was built a year after the Revolution."

"By the winners or the losers?"

"And the floors. You love natural wood, and these floorboards are half a yard wide."

"Be still my heart."

I dared to reach out and touch her arm. Touching didn't come so easy for us. That's why we were here, after all. To see if a bit of seclusion could make our marriage work, to get the pieces back into place.

Odds makers in Vegas would have called it a long shot.

There was another reason, though. We were down to one income—hers—and the loft and the city "life-style" had to go. This dilapidated rental was our best, and last shot.

"At least take a look at it."

Only then did Connie turn and look at me. There was no change in her expression. But she was playing fair. I imagine that she felt much as I did… the play was over and this was just the epilogue. Connie and Mark's final breakup.

I pictured the next few weeks, the slow disintegration, the inexorable eroding of the last vestiges of a marriage. It happens. Sure, just like you can find yourself kicked out of Goldman Sachs and absolutely nobody in Wall Street wants you.

This was a mercy mission for Connie. Let's not give Mark all the bad news at once.

Sure, I pictured the next few weeks.

Needless to say, I got it all wrong.

I liked the house. The floorboards were as described (though the cracks between the planks were big enough for one of those plump black ants to crawl through with ease.) And, as I enjoyed pointing out to Connie, structurally the house was in tip-top shape.

"Right—at least it has indoor plumbing," Connie said, in what passed for wit in our Revolutionary abode.

Of course, she expected me to work on the place while she commuted into Manhattan scoring our one pay check.

And I did make some attempts in that direction. I loved the kitchen, dominated by a giant hearth that could easily accommodate a roast pig, were one available. The dining room was a dismal and dark room, and the small oak table that sat in the room looked better suited for deals with Beelzebub than elegant dinners.

It was upstairs that I found myself spending most of my time. The master bedroom was the same size as the other two rooms. "Master" was a completely arbitrary designation.

The upstairs rooms had small windows and screens with gaping holes to accommodate whatever flying insect might like to come in for a visit or a nibble. There was no upstairs bathroom, but there was an oversized linen closet… at least we assumed it was a linen closet.

My head nearly brushed the ceiling on the first floor. Upstairs, my hair *did* actually touch the ceiling… making me feel like one of those amusement park bumper cars clawing at the electricity on the roof.

For some reason, I liked it up there, and not just when I was sleeping.

While waiting for the SNET to come and set us up with phone service, I walked from room to room, listening to the creak of the wood, the sound of my steps, enjoying how wonderfully *old* this place was.

I made plans to paint. To strip some wood. To replace the screens. I did none of it.

Connie came home. We ate quietly together. We talked about her work. And she, after the first week, tactfully avoided any discussion of my day.

What was there to say?

Honey, I looked out the south window and saw two chipmunks racing around. Or, I started a fire in the hearth and, hey, it *works*. We can cook in it. I mean, for those times when we don't want to use the stove. I'll go kill a wild turkey, or maybe I'll trade with the Pompsquatch Indians for some elk meat.

I guess, if I had been able to afford therapy, a trained outside observer would have pointed out the obvious.

You sir, are *de*-pressed. You are down for the count. You are nonfunctional. I recommend daily sessions, and no, you may not call me at home. And by the way, is your lovely wife available for an illicit affair? I mean, since you, quite obviously, can't—

Connie went to bed early nearly every evening. After all, she did have that 6:37 train to catch.

I was up until midnight, sometimes trying to watch the two pitiful Connecticut UHF stations we could get on our TV. (We both had decided that cable was not an option. It was a way of punishing ourselves, or me at least, for having no work and no money.)

By the time I went to bed, Connie was a dark, sleeping (need I say unresponsive) shape in the small dark bedroom.

In a way, it was like living alone.

But like they always say on the *700 Club* . . . you're never really alone.

At least, *I* wasn't.

The first time it happened I was dead asleep.

And I heard something.

Now, we've all heard noises in the night. Some odd sound that wakes us up, stirs us out of the world of dreams and nightmares to that wonderful place known as 2:30 a.m.

First you lie there, waiting. It was nothing, you think. There was no sound.

I can go back to sleep.

That's what happened this night.

And since sleep was the place I felt most content, most at home in the universe, I had no problem burrowing quickly back to REM land.

Which is when I heard the fatal *second* noise. Now, this is, of course, the noise that throws all of one's switches. At the second sound you have to admit that hey, there *was* a noise. And, golly, said noise was loud enough to wake me up. And more... I'll have to listen *very* carefully now, to determine—in a scientific fashion—just what the hell the sound was and where was it coming from.

It's raccoons at the garbage.

Or it's a squirrel on the roof. Or it's the wind, that pesky wind blowing shit at the house. Sure, that's what it is.

Except, with the third sound, I knew that—no it wasn't the garbage, wasn't little feet on the roof. No, this noise was someone walking around downstairs.

Inside the house.

My body felt icy. My assorted limbs seemed to not belong to me.

There was no way they'd move if I gave them the order. No, they'd rebel. Hell no, Captain, we're not moving your lazy ass out of bed and downstairs.

I hoped that there would be no fourth or fifth sound. I could go back to a monitoring state. I wouldn't have to really *do* anything.

But there was another sound, the slow groaning creak of one of those giant floorboards.

The mad killer was downstairs. Soon to come up, where he would slowly torture me while raping Connie... or slowly torture Connie while raping me.

I gave the bad news to the troops.

I slid my legs out from under the sheets, down to the cool floor, wishing I had a baseball bat and a flashlight. And having neither, I slowly made my way to the hall.

My own creaks sang out a warning that, I hoped against hope, would send the mad killer running. God no, the killer would think: someone is coming. And they have feet!

Halfway down the stirs, I devised a plan.

When I was nearly at the bottom, I would call out.

Hey, you. I'm here. You better go. Cause I'm here.

I'd wait then, give the hapless multiple murderer time to run out the back door... so I could get to the phone and call the trusted Connecticut state police.

And that's what I hoped would happen.

I stopped four steps from the bottom. And God, did they make houses dark back then, And why hadn't we put in some night lights... the gloom was positively stygian.

I hesitated. Who wouldn't hesitate. In the manner of an old London bobby, I called out... "Hel-lo..."

Which is when I saw her.

Now, before I proceed to detailing what happened in the next few minutes, a few words of background may be in order.

My relationship with my wife had, for many, many weeks now, perhaps months, been completely free of the shackles of any physical demands. In other words, I was, in a rather diffuse and disoriented way, quite horny.

Did that put me more on edge, make my nerve endings fire a bit too fast in the darkness and gloom of that boxy house? Sure it's possible.

But what happened next, really happened, I assure you.

A woman *appeared*. She was dressed in a flowing gown—of course—a gown which was nearly as sheer and gossamer as her flesh. She glowed like a lightning bulb on a July evening.

And I wasn't scared.

Who'd be scared looking at someone so beautiful. Later, I'd learn her name (Monica) and her sad history. I'd learn how her husband killed her one night for a suspected and falsely accused infidelity... and how she has wandered the house ever since.

But that night, that sweet first night, there was no time for talk. She embraced me in all her firefly brilliance, and, despite a slight chill, I felt her touch. It had been many miles between such caresses.

"I've been watching you," she said. (Yes, she spoke, in a voice that sounded as normal as yours and mine, except for a slight Kathleen Turner huskiness that was, well, absolutely thrilling.)

Her gown rippled behind her as she led me into the living room where, on the aforementioned plank boards, I had an experience, that I'm sure, few have dreamt of.

I was in love. Immediately. And with love, comes complications.

The big complication here was my wife.

The marriage was over, that was obvious. We had even launched a preliminary discussion of how we'd proceed—in a civilized way—to legally ending our relationship. And that all seemed fine for me.

Except for a small problem.

I had no job, no income. I was completely dependent on Connie.

And worse, Connie was now having trouble at work. Her position looked as if it might shortly be excised. She explained that we'd have to leave this revolutionary abode, split up... she probably back to the Big Apple, job hunting, and a life. As for me, where would I go? My Uncle Henry's bee farm in Somers?

As I said, love brings complications.

My paramour, my dream goddess, the woman who now meant the universe to me on a nightly basis, was unfortunately trapped in this house, locked here by some act, some chain of events that we never had time to get into in any detail (at least not in those early, heady days).

And Connie, an organizational juggernaut, proceeded with the plans for the divorce and for our forced imminent departure from the house. During the early evenings, when I'd leave the house to give Connie some "space," I began to panic.

As each night brought new heights of wonder, as skin touched ectoplasm, as I became totally lost in a sea of otherworldly caresses, I told Monica about the problem.

"I'm going to lose you," I said (not once questioning the intelligence of talking to a ghost).

Her face changed. Here was, er, a spirited woman who didn't brook frustration well.

"No," Monica said. "I *can't* lose you. You've become everything to me."

I nodded. Monica was everything to me. But then, I didn't have much. The only difference between Monica and me was that she was dead. Other than that, we were both without any worldly ties.

Except for Connie.

Now, usually in a situation like this jealously might rear its head.

But that wasn't a problem here. No, there was no love between Connie and I ... just my terror that I'd lose the house, and with the loss of the house (and, God, maybe new people moving in) therein lay my terror.

Once, Monica said, "Maybe some nice man will buy the house."

"No," I said. But Monica drifted away. She'd float in the air in the most disconcerting way, a symbol of her sudden change of mood. When she got really annoyed, I'd watch her glow fade, until she was no more than a dusky near-smoke hanging in the room, like air mites caught by the moonlight.

"You will lose me," she said, coldly, matter-of-factly.

Then she was gone, letting me ponder such a fate.

The solution, surprisingly enough, came from me.

"What if," I said only weeks before the house was to be vacated by me... "what if Connie died?"

Now, I had never killed anyone. I was not a cold-blooded person, but you have to understand the adolescent intensity that possessed me. It was, I imagined, what being hooked on crack was like. I'd do anything to keep Monica.

Monica smiled when I mentioned the idea. After all, death held no terrors for her.

"Explain," she said, brushing my longish hair off my forehead, seemingly pleased with my brainstorm.

"Well, Connie and I both have insurance, tons of insurance. What if something happened to her, what if she died?"

Monica drifted closer, the living cloud. Her ghost fingers caressed my cheek, then trailed to my lips.

"Go on, clever boy."

"If Connie died, I'd get the money. We've done nothing to change beneficiaries, not yet."

"And you could buy this house!" Monica grabbed my feverish head in her two cool hands and planted a big kiss on my lips.

(Only then did I think that she seemed a bit too poised to embrace the idea, as if she had thought of it and only had to wait for me to catch up.)

The kiss sealed the idea. Then we needed a plan, and organizing the details of which consumed the next few nights,

... until the fateful evening arrived.

The day of the "event," I took an especially long afternoon walk, all the way to the Gas & Go near the Merritt Parkway. I bought some sugarless gum and a jumbo cup of cafe ordinaire, noir. It was going to be a long evening.

Which began, as most evenings did, with Connie going to bed after a dinner of wilted lettuce and cherry tomatoes drowning in balsamic vinegar and the oil from thrice-squeezed virgins (or so ran my joke, which drew not even a smile from my soon-to-be ex-wife).

And while the idea of Connie's death originated with me, the plan was—mostly—Monica's.

"You live out here all alone," Monica purred. "Such a lonely house surrounded by dark trees. Wouldn't it be terrible if an intruder came one night, knife in hand... someone who'd leave muddy footprints, someone who'd steal some jewelry—"

"And the credit cards!" I improvised. Beautiful Monica nodded. "And you are asleep downstairs... while the intruder makes his way up, to your wife's bedroom..."

"A-and he goes in and Connie wakes up, screams, and—"

"The terrible intruder with a knife panics and—"

Monica waited for me to pick up the ball. But I had a bit of trouble with this part of the story.

Monica repeated… "And he panics and—"

I licked my lips. I nodded.

"And the intruder kills her?" I said.

Monica clapped her hands. "Bravo! And on the way down, you wake up. and now *you* get stabbed too… but only enough to show how brave you were, to deflect any attention."

"You'll take care of that?"

Monica nodded. At that moment, I had the odd feeling that aspects of this set-up weren't actually novel to her. But I was beyond questioning. Outside of the insurance policy, Connie meant nothing to me . . . while Monica meant everything.

That was the plan.

Or—so I thought.

Around two a.m. Monica *appeared*, gliding down the stairs to the living room.

She smiled at me.

"Your wife is asleep," she said.

I nodded. The knife, with a very sharp and very big blade, lay next to me. I wore my winter gloves, puffy mittens that were more suited for skiing than wife-slaying. But they were all I had.

"It's time," Monica said. She leaned forward, her gown seemingly more translucent for the occasion, and as goose bumps rose, she bathed me in surprisingly warmish kisses.

Primed and pumped, she pulled me to a standing position. "Soon there won't be anything to keep us apart."

I smiled.

I started up the steps. Now, the moment became truly absurd… as I became the "dangerous stranger" walking up the steps, murder and mayhem on his mind. The boards on the steps creaked, begging for a gallon or two of linseed oil. I held the knife in my bear-paw mittens. The knife would be deadly… if it didn't slip out of my clumsy gloves.

I reached the hallway.

Monica was right behind me. I could smell her perfume, an intoxicating scent that ebbed and flowed, as if my ghost lover used it as a leash.

I breathed deep. The heady scent fortified me.

I started for the master bedroom.

I'd be less than honest if I didn't confess to some nervousness about phase two of the plan, namely my getting myself gingerly stabbed by the self-same imaginary "intruder." Monica said she'd take care of that, that a ghost can only hurt a living being when they *want* to be hurt (which neatly explained why Monica—who had nothing to lose—couldn't take care of Connie for me).

Still, the idea of getting cut by the same blade that would soon end my unfortunate wife's existence, made me take those last few steps a bit more slowly.

Until—as in the "Tell-tale Heart"—I lingered by the doorway and peered into the black hole of a room.

I smelled Monica behind me.

Then, her lips close to my ear... "Go on..."

I whispered. "I can't see a damn thing."

The lips again, almost nibbling on a bottom lobe. "You *know* where she is."

Sure, Connie would be in the middle of the blackness, wrapped up in the sheets, a lump that would be hard to miss.

"Go on," Monica urged again.

I gave the door a push. And it creaked. I paused, letting my eyes adjust to the darkness, wanting to see if the creak made the lump—only now coming into view—stir. And when it didn't, I gave the door a final push, and the hinges gave out their last warning.

"Now!" Monica hissed.

And I ran into the room, raising the knife, the apprentice killer in action.

I fell, on the bed, jabbing the blade down into the very center, where the lump would be curled unsuspecting.

When the bedroom light came on.

The lump on the bed was only pillows.

I turned.

And there was Connie, standing by the far wall, holding a small handgun aimed right at me. The first question I wanted to ask her was, "Hey, where'd *you* get a gun?"

I realized that this all looked pretty bad... the knife (now enmeshed in the bed springs), the mittens, the skulking around. I wanted to say... "Connie, I have an explanation for everything."

But I didn't have any explanation.

Monica was nowhere to be seen. So I couldn't use her as an excuse.

But I didn't have a lot of time to think about the embarrassing nature of my predicament.

The small gun that was aimed right at me exploded once, and then again. I felt all sorts of weird pain in my chest and midsection. Connie didn't shoot a third time.

I think she recognized that she didn't have to.

I didn't die immediately. I had a few minutes of blurry-eyed consciousness. Which, all things considered, was the only plus of the evening.

And what did I see in those precious few moments...? Something completely amazing and, I must admit, totally unexpected.

Connie stood there, smoking gun in hand, looking ever-so-much like a very noirish 40s gun moll. The gun smoke hung in the air while she waited—I thought—to be sure I didn't need another lead plug to be down for the count.

(I had, up to then, given absolutely no thought as to the reason she seemed, well, *ready* for my entrance, and ready to kill me. But then with two big openings in my body, gushing ye olde vital fluids, I had more important things to think about.)

But in the last few blinks of earthly awareness, I saw the bluish smoke hanging in the air… and then, from the doorway, that gun smoke was joined by something else equally gossamer and smoky. I couldn't turn around, but I could smell it. The perfume was painfully familiar.

And then I did get to see Monica drift close to Connie, wrap her arms around her, pull her close—and final image—give Connie a long, lingering kiss.

I had been set up in a not quite classic lover's triangle. But then the curtains were drawn. For a certain period.

The next thing I saw was the Master Bedroom. It was night. But I immediately knew it wasn't the same night. There was a full moon hanging out the window and, yes sports fans, two bodies in the bed, at rest, I'm glad to say… though I imagined that they might have trysted the night way.

I moved closer to the bed.

My first thought was that it seemed as though considerable time had passed. How did I get here? Was this a dream? There were no bloodstains on the floor. They probably had been cleaned up after the police investigated Connie's quite reasonable charge that her demented husband tried to stab her…

Then I noted how I moved. There was no need for "steps," though my feet did kick and pump.

No, moving was easier… now that I was dead.

I realized why.

I held my hand up to my face—just to be sure. And I saw that my hand wasn't quite opaque. No, I could hold it up to the full moon, and see right through my hand.

I was a ghost.

And having been given this second lease on life, I wasn't about to waste it…

In the stillness of that summer night, I tried my vocal cords to see if they still worked in this new incarnation.

"Good morning, campers! Sa-a-a-y, it's a beautiful evening here in the afterlife, and we're here 24 hours to bring you the very best poltergeist effects that money can buy!"

Connie shot up in bed and screamed.

I guess my reappearance was unexpected. Then Monica, a sister at heart, popped out of the bed like a doughy loaf of bread toasting to a golden brown.

"Go the hell away," Monica snarled, obviously understanding what was happening here.

I shook my head. I glided to the ceiling, and stretched out, face down, right over the bed of my unfaithful spouse. Monica hissed. Connie screamed and threw things—to no avail.

Me, I had a great time… until Connie left days later. My unexpected resurfacing obviously was enough to cool her ardor—and convince her that she didn't want to use the insurance money to buy the old rat-trap of a haunted house.

I was tad disappointed at that...

Until I realized that now I had *eternity* to drive Monica crazy.

And that gave me something to look forward to every night.

The End Of The Line

BY JOHN COYNE

SHELDON BLOCK HAD MANY NEUROSES WHICH HE GLADLY SHARED WITH PEOPLE, soon after introductions or after a few beers, whatever came first. His psych had even given him a list of his minor and major hang-ups. He carried the list in his billfold like an I.D. card. There was little in life which interested Sheldon quite as much as himself.

Among his problems were his mother, Sally, and his girl, Amy.

They all lived together in a beautiful old and dilapidated conch house in Key West along with twenty old cats (some of which they claimed were direct descendants of Ernest Hemingway's six-toed cats), and a gay artist who painted surreal seascapes on varnished driftwood.

Sheldon was a photojournalist. Or sometimes he mustered enough gall to declare he was "into cinematography." Everyone in Key West was into something and they talked about their "profession" a great deal, much like one might daydream over a possible inheritance.

Sheldon sought me out in Key West when he heard I was "into writing."

"How do you do it?" He slipped up next to me at Sloppy Joe's.

"How do I do what?" I was prepared not to be polite. Anyone straight guarded himself against the gays that strolled Dovel Street.

"Get published." He had eager eyes with a tanned face and long curly blond hair, the look of a Raphael angel. He was short and edgy and during a conversation kept moving about like he needed to piss.

I got only a few paragraphs into my story when Sheldon drew the topic back to himself as if he were the host of a late night talk show. Sheldon's solipsism wasn't offensive, for he approached his own life in the third person, and his story was played out in technicolor, on wide screen, perhaps at the local drive-in. His life was comic-tragedy as he'd be the first to admit.

"I was raised without a father." He explained, "and my mother dominated the shit out of me. She wants me to be kosher, to do the right thing."

"And what's the right thing?"

"Well the right thing is best described in a negative. That's the way Sally defines it. The right thing, for example, is not to be a photojournalist. The right thing would be to open up a camera shop because everyone wants to buy a camera." Sheldon shrugged. It was so plainly absurd that it made him weep.

"My other problem is Amy," Sheldon shifted subjects.

"She wants you to open a five-and-dime?" I offered.

"No, Amy's cool. She doesn't give me shit about what I do, just as long as I do it with her. She wants to get married. We've been living together for three years, steady, and she wants to get married. They're in it together, Sally and her." Sheldon shook his head at the conspiracy of women.

There were only two kinds of conversation late at night in any bar in Key West and both were serious. One involved the last-minute, last-drink, negotiations to get some girl to go home with you and the other concerned even a harder nut to crack: one's future.

Sheldon knew his future lay like a skiff on the flats at the edge of the horizon. He could see an image surely, but it was indiscernible. It might be a treasure chest, then again it might only be a hunk of driftwood floating aimlessly towards the entanglement of mangroves. Sheldon was twenty-four, approaching the quarter century of his life and looking for "his place." His was not a new story but to Sheldon it was all that mattered.

Key West was the end of the line. A sign at the bottom of Whitehead Street proclaimed that you were at the southernmost point of the Continental United States. It was here where Sheldon and the hundred others like him had drifted; following the sun until they ran out of land.

At dusk everyday they convened at Mallory Pier to watch the sun set. They came in from afternoons of beaching and deep-sea diving, from itinerant work as waitresses, lifeguards, house painters, and they gathered to the sounds of twelve-string guitars, flutes, and bongo drums.

They were the quintessence of the subculture: the long hairs, the freaks, the acid-heads and weirdoes. They were what the sixties had given to Western civilization.

Here was a grab-bag of fashions: granny dresses, tee-shirts and jeans, sandals with rubber-tire soles. Braless breasts hung like sacks of grain. The nipples made imprints in the thin cloth like trademarks.

And the men were sidewalk pirates: a red bandanna wrapped around the head, open white shirt and pieces of eight hung from the neck, leather black boots laced to the knees, a wide buckled belt. Swashbucklers! Their small children ran among them like gypsies.

They gathered together when a cool breeze picked up for evening and they watched quietly as the orange sun dropped like a tailgate into the Gulf of Mexico. Then they applauded. Near me on a pier a spaced-out head proclaimed, "Far out, sun!"

Sheldon Block met me at Mallory Pier. He had brought along Amy for introductions. Amy was tiny as a fireplug with a wonderful robust body, an hour-glass figure. She was darkly Mediterranean, brown eyed and exuberant. She demanded in a nice way space and our attention, shouldered herself between us like a longshoreman. She had guts and was willing to fight for Sheldon.

"I've got my nails so deep into him," she later declared to me, "that if he left me now he'd bleed to death."

We went for beers at Captain Tony's. She had heard about me.

Her eyes seized on me, waited and watched. Sheldon had been telling stories at home, related my suggestions and advice, and now she was going to deal directly with this outlander.

I meant her no ill. I had behaved only in a Socratic fashion with Sheldon. When he promoted an answer, I questioned the assumption. I was as innocent as an act of nature. But I was in Amy's eyes a bad influence. If she could, she would have kept Sheldon from the bars and away from me. She knew I was out there at Captain Tony's and Sloppy Joe's, waiting like a siren with my Budweiser.

"Have you ever been married?" She asked me on her third or fourth question. She wasn't one to wait around and let my past come slowly out.

"Does it count to say I was engaged?"

She shook her head like a judge.

"Pinned?"

"Have you lived with a woman?"

This was the new watershed mark. No man had credibility unless he had "lived with a woman." We were descending the scale of commitment, soon one could talk knowledgeably about male/female relationships if he had once shaken hands with a girl on a blind date.

I decided it wasn't wise to hang back and let Amy have at me with slings and arrows.

I asked. "Have you lived with anyone else?"

"Yes, in college."

"How long did that last?"

"Four years." She saw the connection and added, "It was just convenient. We didn't have a lot in common. He was from Iowa."

"What was your sex life like?" I pushed the conversation towards the edge of propriety.

"It was very good." She came back without missing a beat. She talked as if a pencil were clamped between her teeth.

"But was not good enough to make a marriage?" I doubled the ante.

"Look I... sex was something we *did*! You know, like sleep! It wasn't the whole relationship. Anyway, it was cheaper to live off campus with some guys than live in a crumby dorm." She was defensive about the affair. "That's all ancient history. Besides, I'm in love with Shel." She slipped her arm into his like a Yale lock.

Sheldon came out of his silence with a declaration.

"I've got to get my shit together." Sheldon's thoughts were never too far away from his problems. But this was a general announcement that made no demands. Still, I wanted to pull him into the conversation. Squaring off with Amy wasn't my notion of a fun night in Key West.

"Have you seen Shel's work?" Amy asked next. "He's getting ready to do a photo essay on the fauna and flora of Key West."

She was as enthusiastic as a press agent.

"I think he's an absolutely fantastic photojournalist!" and with that, she nuzzled up and sealed his fate with a wet sloppy kiss on the check.

Sheldon I know didn't mind all this talk, especially since it centered mostly on him. He listened and watched us as though we were his biographers. Occasionally he did venture a point, a small opinion, edged forward like questionable goods. One could see his comments about himself to gain his point of reference. He used people as mirrors and searched for himself.

All the talk that first evening wasn't monopolized by the life and hard times of Sheldon Block. Amy and Sheldon showed me around.

They took me to their favorite haunts: upstairs at the Whistle, the Bird Cage, out to Louie's Back Yard. It was like my favorite uncle from out-of-town.

Key West is a town on vacation. The snow birds down from the north realize after sunset that the streets offer little amusement except the continual spectacle of themselves. Therefore, the town lends itself to steady and hard drinking, more from boredom than enthusiasm.

We caroused through the night, Sheldon became more expansive with each hour, every new bar, while Amy lost her early brassiness and began to sulk. Her brown eyes filled with shades of melancholy. Amy had her own secrets wrapped away like silver coins in a white handkerchief. She couldn't chance it and tell Sheldon: she had to be strong for him, give him direction and a steady anchor. Sheldon, she knew, was having a hard time growing up.

"What's so terrible anyway about marrying?" Amy asked sometime after midnight. The question had been there all evening, flowing like a tarpon in the shallows of her mind.

We stared at her. Sheldon and I had been discussing permit fishing, something which he had never done, but about which he spoke knowledgeably. Sheldon was a great reader and collector of information. He did not feel the need to do, just to know. One could think of him as a handy resource.

"If you want to marry someone, go find him and get married."

"Jesus H. Christ!" Sheldon's answer had also been smoldering unsaid and needed only the bitchy tone of Amy's lament to pop his composure like a boil.

"I found who *I want* to marry!" she shouted back.

Sheldon slammed the glass of beer and stood back menacingly, though at 5'7" there was little that seemed dangerous. I leaned over and concentrated seriously on the cashews. We were in the Chart Room of the Pier House Motel and the few patrons glanced up at the outrage at the bar and then looked away.

"You're an asshole," Amy whispered.

"Why do you have to always foul things up ... Here John and I were having a fine rap..."

Amy surveyed me with those brown eyes that now had flared into brush fires. She thought of something to say and then thought better.

"Listen Amy, why don't you go home!" Sheldon took another tactic, tried to sound conciliatory. It was, however, the wrong tactic.

"I don't want to go the fuck home!" She measured out the words. Sheldon started around me. Those angelic cheeks had paled and the booze had turned his blue eyes into a steady, dumb stare. Behind the bar, the bartender sensed the coming confrontation and raised a hand in meek bewildered point-of-order.

As Sheldon made his pass, I caught him around the waist and spun off the bar stool myself and wrestled him through the glass doors and into the tropical gardens.

"Let me… goddammit!" He whimpered in frustration and had at me with elbows and arms.

I carried him successfully the twenty-five yards to the pool and then in an unexpected gesture unloaded Sheldon into the mint-green looking water with an outburst of profanity.

Then two tiny fists wacked into the small of my back and my legs slipped away as if I had been clipped by an open field blocker. I tumbled forward, managing a half-assed dive at the last moment, into the cold water. Amy had misjudged the force of her blow or the ease in which she could topple me and when I gave way domino-style she lost her footing and followed us into the pool like the last of the stooges.

The shock of water made us amazingly sober, but it did not sour our good spirits and Amy started giggling at the predicament she had produced. Sheldon swam towards her, shouting threats laced with affection, and touched the shallow end and walked out to search for a towel. Behind me Amy slipped from her dress and disappeared deep into the mint-green water. As she turned, her ass spun into view like a globe.

Sally Block was twenty-five when she discovered in the most elementary way that her husband no longer loved her. "He had my first cousin, Debre, right in our bed. My very own bed! You'd think they'd have had some common decency. And he still had his socks on." Sally Block shook her head and inched closer.

She had me cornered in her house, deep in the pocket of a blue sofa. "To be very honest our marriage would never have lasted. We only got married in the first place because of Sheldon." She nodded and raised both eyebrows.

Sheldon and Amy were in the kitchen "cleaning up." I had been the guest for a home cooked Cuban meal: picadillo, black beans, plantains, flan, cafe con leche. The whole show! The "kids" had volunteered to do the dishes. I didn't trust them out there alone and had a momentary panic that they had abandoned me to Sally. Their voices from the kitchen were distant.

"You're staying long in Key West, Mr. Cohen?" Sally Yiddishified my name and while waiting for an answer she busied herself stacking small pink and blue pillows behind her on the sofa, arranging them like a throne.

Sally was short and rosy plump with a figure maintained, it appeared, by a full armament of corsets. Every joint was creased with folds of fat. It appeared as if a hose had been shoved in her ass and she had been blown up like a balloon.

"My son speaks very highly of you, Mr. Cohen. You've been the talk of our little table every night this week. He's very impressionable, my Sheldon, like his mother." She displayed a shit-eating grin, tiny half-carat blue eyes, and makeup packed like a landslide. I must save Sheldon from all this, I resolved.

"You're an author, Mr. Cohen?"

"Well I write…"

"I've been told myself that I should write down my experiences. They've been, unfortunately or fortunately, very full." She sighed. The sound of it had a certain finality about it, like that of a punctured tire.

"Sheldon wants to be a photojournalist. What do you think of photojournalism… Mr.… John. It is, John, isn't it?" She gained another inch. It was done imperceptibly, a shifting of her haunches.

I could feel the sweat dripping in my armpits. Now there were no longer sounds from the kitchen. Sheldon and Amy had escaped out the back door. It was a conspiracy among them. Those sonsofbitches! All because I had dumped Sheldon into the pool. Never trust anyone under thirty.

I was now in range of Sally's cologne, a mixture of sweat and hair spray, and the aftermath of the hot picadillo sauce. Sally squeezed another sad smile onto her face and from somewhere in the recesses of the sofa conjured up like a magician a black Spanish fan and worked it furiously. It sounded like a tree full of starlings. I began thinking of exit lines.

"I've always been fascinated by authors," Sally announced.

"Well actually, I'm not a real author!" I would give her another inch of sliding maneuvers, and then I'd be off! I might be lonely in Key West, but I wasn't desperate.

"It's practically the same thing. You're both men of words. AND THE WORD SHALL SET YOU FREE!" she suddenly shouted and I glanced at this woman, thinking: This woman is mad!

"Sally, I think I'll be on my way." I sprang from the sofa.

The door of the kitchen burst open and a tiny ageing man carrying a cat in his arms entered and said dramatically, tapping out each word with his bare foot, "For Good God Almighty, Sally, What Is This?"

Thank God I thought. Saved by a queer.

"Elmer, what are you doing sneaking about?" I began edging towards the front door.

"I was just feeding Matthew a little din-din and there was this *rage* from the living room. I wasn't *sneaking about!*" He eyed me appreciatively.

"I was just discussing *literature* with Mr. Cohen. Elmer, come meet Mr. John Cohen. He's Sheldon's new friend you've heard mentioned." She flipped her fan closer and aimed it at me like a pointer.

"John, this is Elmer Todd Netland, one of Key West's leading artists. You've seen his work in the shops, I'm sure."

Sally's voice had lost its sauciness. The moment with me, she realized, was over. I was safely beyond her sofa.

"How do you do Mr. Cohen, sorry to interrupt your party."

"Coyne," I corrected. It was time to claim one's own. I made a move to meet Elmer Todd Netland halfway for a handshake, but Elmer was satisfied with a pearly smile.

"Oh, yes, the writer." He nodded knowingly. Sheldon must have spread my name like Paul Revere. "Well, Key West is full of writers. They're almost as epidemic as queens. Isn't that right, Sally?" And they both giggled at their private joke. Sally fluttered her black fan again, like applause.

"And what is you're particular *genre*, Mr. Coyne?" Elmer lopped the question across the living room floor, arching his eyebrows in the asking. Dramatic eyebrows must run in the household.

"Mr. Cohen writes fiction, Elmer," Sally informed.

"Ah, another Hemingway hero worshipper come to flex his muscles at the shrine of Mr. Machismo."

"And you paint knick knacks I'm told." If this was going to be war, let there be war.

"I work in a variety of mediums." The answer was registered below 32° Fahrenheit. At the moment it was the coldest thing in Key West. "I'm particularly well known for my surreal seascapes." He said this with a certain defiance and pride. "You don't impress me Mr. Coyne, from all that I can ascertain from young Sheldon, as one that would be particularly familiar with painting." It was tit for tat. Elmer stood his ground like a bantam rooster.

"Oh, dears, Elmer!... John! Boys that's enough cattiness. I won't have it in my house!" Sally's voice ranged across a field of octaves. Her fan fluttered.

"My apologies, Sally," I said and, nodding to Elmer, added, making my last remark the final turn of the broken beer bottle to the gut, "I'll look for your handicrafts in town." Then I was off, into the humid night, off to find Sheldon with my new advice.

All week he had been asking me a standard question: what should he do with his life? He talked of his future as if it were a holiday trip. He wanted to settle it all once and for all, get the problem behind him. He wanted his career settled, his girlfriend situation settled. He wanted to come to terms with Sally. He wanted his dreams.

Downtown in the few blocks at the end of Duval the dream lived.

The streets on a February Saturday night overflowed like a minor carnival, though the nightlife had little to offer but warm winter evenings, a few bars trying to parlay an exaggerated fact that Hemingway drank there with sweet rum summer drinks.

The medium age at night was twenty-five, the style of dress shabby and sandled, the drink beer, and the music electric guitar rock and country. This was the territory of the young.

The retired couples who parked their motor homes all day at the end of Monroe Beach and gathered on lawn chairs in the shade and talked about "back North" while watching like spies the freaks sunning in the sand, watched them with their young children, "raising them like squirrels" they condemned, seeing a mother provide for her children out of the back end of a converted van, did not venture into the streets after sundown when the longhairs came out in force: like people from another planet.

Trying to locate Sheldon and Amy among the longhairs was not easy. I roamed the bars awhile, then finally decided to set up shop at Captain Tony's, stood at the bar with a view of the street, and let Sheldon come into range.

I had solved his worries.

"I just can't get a break in Key West!" he had said often over the week. "I know my pictures are good. Everyone thinks so! But there doesn't seem any reason to achieve." The worry in his eyes was like fog.

"You think they're good?"

"Well, sure... I guess. I mean, they're as good as any I see in magazines!" He was defensive.

"Everyone who owns a camera thinks he's an artist"

Sheldon nodded. He knew. It was nothing to declare oneself a photographer, a photojournalist. Where was the proof? In the disposition of one's mind?

"But if they'd give me a chance!"

The theys of the world were keeping a lot of good men down.

"Sally wants me to settle here in Key West." He said that as if there was a squeeze of pain in his side.

He gave me all the reasons Sally had given him for such a move.

She'd back him in business, get him started. He could become a successful businessman. Sheldon sipped his drink and worried. The deal was dangerously inviting. "I could do my photojournalism on the side," he added, relegating art now to hobby.

"It's just a question of how you want to spend your days." That was the kicker. He couldn't get away from that reality. He already felt old, wasting. His days in Key West since leaving college were unproductive. He had survived in his mother's house doing a variety of odd jobs, kept in financial and emotional servitude.

I spotted them on the street, sharing a large box of buttered popcorn and ambling along watching the crowd as if it were a movie.

They weren't talking, but had the look of survivors of a long argument. Seeing me standing at the entrance of Captain Tony's delighted Sheldon. Amy, however, was immediately apprehensive.

"We decided to go for a walk," she hurried to explain.

"Let me buy you both a beer!" I felt expansive. Amy watched me.

"You understand," Sheldon explained in the bar, "sometimes I just can't take her any longer. I have to get away. She goes on and on, like tonight at dinner with that story about the Key West Hi-Rise. I mean, who gives a shit!" Sheldon was now fortified with his beer, my company and the general safety and isolation of Captain Tony's. Sally wouldn't find him there. Amy looked bored. She had heard this story already, all night, I felt sure. "My shrink says it's Sally's need to feel needed, that's why she carries on like that, monopolizing the conversation." He made it sound like a social disease.

"Sheldon," I interrupted, "you can't make it here."

He came up short in his continual explanation; even Amy picked up interest, as if her name had been summoned.

"Can't make what?" she asked quickly.

"Sheldon can't make it here in Key West. *He* has to leave."

"What do you mean he has to leave?" Amy bubbled into irate indignation and began to edge towards me along the bar like a roustabout angling for a brawl.

"You can go, too," I informed before she reached swinging range.

That slowed her progress. She then wrapped her arms smugly about Sheldon and kept her sad brown eyes on me. "In fact," I volunteered. "I think he'd do better with you along." I spread a thick layer of tribute like Jiffy peanut butter.

"Go where?" Sheldon asked innocently.

"Anywhere! But away from Key West! Go some place where you can work on photojournalism." The phrase caught in my throat.

"What about L.A.?" Amy asked. "I've never been to L.A." She was already in the spirit of this new adventure, now that I had okayed her companionship.

"But I don't know anyone in California." Sheldon was lost in the muck of his future.

I kept nodding my head knowingly. The night of wine and beer had made me pleasantly inarticulate.

"In college I had a roommate one year who was from Arizona," Amy informed. "That's close. We probably could stay at her house on the way west. Her father runs a miniature golf course in Tucson." She rambled on.

"California...?" Sheldon questioned and looked at me as if I had suggested the moon.

"No need for California," I found my voice. "You need some experience first. Schooling." Sheldon nodded quickly. "There's a place I know about in North Carolina, way off in the mountains. You could study photojournalism for a year maybe. It would help..."

"Get my act together!"

"Right!"

"Right!"

"I've been to North Carolina," Amy informed, "Winston Salem."

She wasn't letting us get too far ahead of her.

"Amy, for chrissake...!" Sheldon turned on her. Here we go again I thought.

"What's the school like?" He turned back to me, having somehow silenced Amy.

I told him about the place, the easy academics, the chance to do his own thing. I told him I knew the director and could get him into school. I painted a lovely pastoral scene of life in the green mountains of western North Carolina. A journey back to nature. When I finished Sheldon said, "Jesus!" I had taken his breath away.

Amy, too, was impressed enough to keep quiet, to know a good thing when she heard it. When she did speak up it was to ask some practical question about housing. Already she was planning her lair. I was confident that they would cohabitate—"We wouldn't have to pretend we were married?" she asked, as though it were the wildest notion of her mind—and she began to promote the schooling like it was her idea. We spent the evening drinking and dreaming.

After the night of decisions, I wrote North Carolina and got confirming word about his studying. He needed only to appear for the spring term. When the mail arrived I went looking for Sheldon. It had only been a week but Sheldon and I had seen each other in passing, and then we just waved to each other from cars.

Amy and Sheldon weren't out at night; looked for them on Duval Street. I had to keep away from his house, knowing I'd need to be civil to Sally and Elmer; but with the firm word of Sheldon's acceptance, I biked over in the midday heat to deliver the good news.

Sheldon was lounging on the front porch, asleep in the hammock.

No one was about, but the big, sagging house gave off feelings that others were sleeping in the dark. I whispered his name.

"I'm getting married," Sheldon announced when he saw me, still only a blur of shadows in his squinting eyes.

"No photojournalism?" I asked.

"Amy and I are opening up an ice cream parlor on Whitehead. Sally's backing us. We're going to only have the best ice cream, Breyer's, and cater to tourist traffic." He spoke in quick rushes of sentences, as if the information were being relayed by transmitters.

"You'll make a fortune." I tried sounding enthusiastic.

"I guess North Carolina is out..." His voice slid away.

"No problem."

"Thanks, you know, for all the interest." He sounded guilty.

"When's the wedding date?" I shifted topics.

"They haven't said. Soon. I'd like to get that settled. But we have to find an apartment first. Amy wants her own place."

"Can't blame her."

"Sally agrees!" He sounded surprised. "She thinks we should have, you know, time by ourselves."

"That's smart."

"Once I get the parlor set up, I figure I can get back into photojournalism again. The parlor won't take full time, especially since Amy will be working herself."

I kept nodding. Why should I be the one to tell him that soon Amy wouldn't want to work full time, that she'd start talking about starting a family and buying a house of their own, and Sheldon's camera would collect dust from unuse and he'd be planning instead of "getting into photojournalism" to open a second ice cream parlor up the Keys and double his income.

"You're getting your shit together," I said instead.

"Yeah, I think so." A tiny warm smile like an unexpected surprise spread over his face. "You know, it feels good."

Sheldon Black had settled his mind.

A few days later, biking through town, I spotted Amy and waved, giving her a sixties V sign. She waved back with a raised clenched fist and a broad smile of triumph.

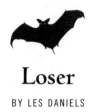

Loser

BY LES DANIELS

SHE HAD BEEN HOME FOR CLOSE TO AN HOUR BEFORE SHE BEGAN THINKING about the orange in her purse. She hadn't forgotten it, really; it had been a vague image in the back of her mind ever since she'd bought it that morning on the way to work. Stupid of her even to pretend to forget, actually since she bought one every morning from the Korean delicatessen halfway down the block from her office on Twenty-Ninth Street.

She liked the idea of the daily ritual, and the way she looked performing it: Today's Woman on the Go, her slim legs eating up the sidewalk with the stride she'd learned as a girl from watching Mary Tyler Moore on television. Flashing all her teeth in the approved Active and Attractive style, she would pick out an orange and toss it up and down in her hand while she paid for it, simultaneously tossing the shining mop of hair that had been tortured into tight curls. She didn't really like the do, which was a pain to maintain, and in her bad moments she told herself that if hair were French fries, hers would be Krinkle Kut. Still, it was The Look of the Nineties, and she wouldn't do herself any good at work by bucking the trend. The decade had hardly started, for Christ's sake, and already everything had been proclaimed The Look of the Nineties, The Book of the Nineties, The Hook of the Nineties. She knew it was a lot of crap, but it was easier to go along than to fight it. For the most part, she emulated the actresses she saw on talk shows when she was alone at night in her apartment. She wore short skirts that displayed her long legs, and boxy jackets that kept her body under wraps. Her shape was nobody's business but her own, after all; although once in a while when she looked at herself in the mirror, she was reminded of those dancing cigarette packs from the stone age of advertising, those faceless female rectangles with the gleaming gams.

She reached into her purse for her Virginia Slims, flicked her Bic, and sucked in some hot nourishment. The orange would wait. She zapped the news with her remote when the sports came on, and picked up on a movie that had started a little earlier on HBO. The heroine was hell bent on revenge, for some wrong presumably done to her during the pre-credits sequence, and during the next eighty-one minutes she killed seven men. They all deserved it.

Then the flick was over, she switched to *Murphy Brown*, a show about a sarcastic career woman with long legs and lots of hair. Recently people had been writing into *TV*

Guide with letters about whether or not it would be okay for this woman to get married. While watching the show, she took out the orange and began to peel it. She wondered if any human beings actually living on the planet had named their daughter "Murphy," and decided that they probably had. Certainly somebody had by now, since the show had been on for a couple of years.

By the time the following show was over, she had the orange peeled. She cleaned up the mess and tossed it in the garbage, then came back into the living room and stared at the nearly naked fruit as it nestled on a saucer of bone-white china. The news was playing again on another channel, and things were tough all over. There were still some soft, stringy bits of white rag clinging to the surface of the orange's juicy segments, and she carefully stripped them away with the sharp plastic fingernails that were glued to her own ragged stumps. When the wet, glistening flesh of the fruit that beckoned to her was absolutely perfect, it was time to take a bath.

She let the square-shouldered box drop from her body, stripped off her silk shirt, let her skirt slip to the floor, and peeled off her all-in-one panty hose. She really didn't need a bra anymore; but it was disappointing, after losing all that weight, to end up not with elegant little ballerina-boobs, but with droopy balloons that looked like somebody had let most of the air out of them. Outside of that, the view as she faced herself in the full-length mirror was satisfactory. She could count every rib, and she could almost get her hand around her thigh.

She didn't really want to turn around for the rear view, but there was no point in kidding herself: her ass was still huge. Even with the cheeks concave and the hip bones clearly delineated, her backside was still the biggest thing about her. In fact, it was the biggest thing in the world.

She thought again about liposuction. To tell the truth, she thought about it all the time, and even dreamed about it once in a while. There was something wonderful about the idea of a kind of vacuum cleaner that could just suck the ugliness out of you, but it was almost too simple. A diet was discipline, not self-indulgence, not just taking the easy way out. Not that liposuction was exactly easy. She remembered the pamphlet she'd read about it months ago. "You care about yourself, and your willingness to endure considerable discomfort and expense proves just how much you care." That made sense, didn't it? You had to care about yourself. Nobody else would love you until you learned how to love yourself. Everybody knew that; it was in all the magazines. And nobody could love fat. It should be drained away, the ugly globs of yellow grease spitting out of a plastic tube into glass jars. It had to be done in secret, of course. Probably keeping it a secret was one of the things you were paying for. Nobody would ever have to know.

She twisted around to stare at her fat ass in the mirror again while she waited for the tub to fill. Why wouldn't it shrink? Everything else was coming along so nicely, but this was still the big pale burden she had to bear. Eventually she stopped looking and crawled into the tub.

The steaming water was as close to boiling as she could stand it: the time she spent in the tub was the only part of the day when she didn't feel cold. That must have been because she had no insulation, but who wanted insulation? Eskimos, that's who. They actually layered themselves with fat. They even ate it. Whale blubber. They couldn't possibly eat it in front of each other, though; they'd have to sneak away behind the igloo or something. *Or* maybe not. They were crazy anyway or they wouldn't be eating all that fat, which everybody knew was a quick way to kill yourself. The North Pole had to be positively crawling with dead, fat Eskimos.

At least they weren't hungry all the time, but that was the price you had to pay for looking good. She knew. When she started college six years ago, she'd been an absolute chubette. Her mother always said what she had was "*just* baby fat," as if it would magically melt away, and in fact during her freshman year she had lost a couple of pounds without even trying. That was when she realized for the first time in her life that she could be in control, and that with a little effort she could be truly free. By her junior year she was almost slim, and things got even better when her roommate showed her that it was possible to eat anything you wanted as long as you puked it up again before it turned into fat. In fact, things got so good that her parents had yanked her out of school and into a hospital for a semester. There she was browbeaten by terms like "anorexia" and "bulimia," but she knew they were just code words that gave other people the right to run her life. Still, she had the sense to fake contrition and puff up enough so she only lost one semester. And when she graduated, she took a job as an assistant editor at a publishing house in New York, three thousand miles away from home.

She'd fooled everyone, and now she was alone.

She'd lost so much weight since she was eighteen that there would have been enough of it to make another person, a person made entirely of fat. Her evil twin. She'd actually had dreams about her, the greasy bitch, a girl made out of yellow jelly who tried to climb into bed with her and wrap her in a flabby embrace. In fact she had a lot of dreams, but it was hard to sleep soundly when you were hungry all the time.

What people didn't realize, though, was that being hungry was a kind of high, not that much different from the speed she took when she was first starting to lose weight. Food made people slow and stupid, but she was light and bright, her mind racing. Sometimes she couldn't shut it off even when she wanted to, and sometimes she got tired, but she worked hard anyway, and once she got home for the night, there was nothing to do but make sure she didn't eat.

Her refrigerator talked to her, and that was the biggest problem with being home alone, almost as big a problem as her rear end. The refrigerator wasn't really talking, of course, she knew that. It was the food inside. She always kept something in there to prove she was stronger than it was, and every second she spent away from the kitchen was another triumph. She was proud of the fact that she hardly ever went into the room at all. On the rare occasions when she weakened, she made herself sick in more ways than one, stuffing her shrunken stomach until she was in agony, then vomiting everything out with her head draped over the rim of the toilet until she was clean again. Such a repulsive, pointless exercise just showed the wisdom of going without instead. Screw the fridge.

She could hear what was there in the cool darkness, clanking and sloshing and chuckling to itself, waiting for the light to go on when the door was opened. Resisting it wasn't always easy, but that was why she bought an orange every day. It protected her, reassured her that she would have something to eat before she went to bed, something to reward her for going twenty-four hours with nothing but cigarettes, black coffee, and a cardboard carton of plain yogurt at her desk for lunch. Without the promise of the orange, the icy siren song of what was in the kitchen would have been irresistible. And if you stuck your head inside the refrigerator, you had to stick it down the toilet. That was the deal.

She stepped out of the tub and shivered as she watched the gray water swirl down the pipes like fat draining away. Wrapping herself in a fuzzy old robe that her mother had given her on Christmas about a million years ago, she padded across the carpet to the living room, the couch, the television, and the orange. It wouldn't do to rush. Everything had to be savored.

She sat down, pulled her feet up on the couch, and hugged her knees. Just for a second, she felt dizzy and lonely and afraid, a little girl unaccountably abandoned to make her way in a city filled with strangers. The room tilted and the walls closed in, but she closed her eyes, gritted her teeth, and waited for the sensation to pass. Then she reached for the remote control.

One of the cable channels was showing an old Katharine Hepburn flick, the one where she dressed up like a boy and confused the hell out of Cary Grant. Of course it was easy for Hepburn, with her bones. Bones made you beautiful. You didn't really have to pretend to be a boy, though—you just had to look like one. No tits. No ass. Period. Or rather, no period either. Not for years but that was just another one of the drawbacks to having a body that keeping thin prevented.

While slowly separating the orange into sections, she wondered vaguely where her Cary Grant might be. Actually, she'd heard that he might have been gay or something. Typical. You couldn't trust any of them. She'd found that out in college, when she got dumped while she was in the hospital. A few of them at work had tried to take her out, for lunch or dinner or something, but of course that was out of the question, and after a while they'd given up. Screw 'em. Or don't. Let 'em stay home alone. They only wanted to jump her bones anyway, and her bones were her own.

While the movie droned on, she finished dividing the orange into separate segments, then arranged them around the plate in a sunburst pattern. She did it meticulously, concentrating on the symmetry so she could ignore the laughing and gurgling that came from what was shut up in the kitchen. The orange was like a crucifix in an old horror picture, keeping the forces of evil at bay.

She was close to nodding off before she convinced herself that it would finally be all right to take a bite. She picked up one piece and bit off half of it, her head hanging over the plate so not a single drop of juice would be lost. The fruit erupted in her mouth, a blast of liquid more sweet and sour than any Chinese dinner. The flavor overwhelmed her, and she could almost feel the rush of sugar cascading through her veins and arteries and capillaries. God! She began grabbing for the pieces on the plate, stuffing them into her mouth, not so hungry for the food as for the sheer taste of it. She knew from past experience that it might go down this way, and always chose a seedless orange. Otherwise, she'd have grown a grove in her gut by now.

Her mind awash in vitamins and carbohydrates, she barely had the self-control to start applying the brakes. Her hands, almost visibly clutching and contracting, pulled away from the plate and gripped her knees while there was still one miserable segment left for her to drool over. And she was still drooling, no doubt of that, with juice running down her chin and pooling on the plate. She dropped her face down and lapped everything up, the white of plate and bones and toilet and refrigerator blending in her brain. Lost in the alabaster blur, she gobbled down the last bit of golden fruit and sat back, trembling. It was not enough. It never was. An orange was really nothing more than a little sugar and water, dammit.

She could hear the tapping and rattling from the refrigerator, and the voice seductively calling out to her:

"You want me. You need me."

It was true, and she knew it. She tried like hell to hang on to the dream of everything ugly draining out of her, gurgling and bubbling away, but she was only human. She had to weaken once in a while. Nobody was perfect, and you couldn't be blamed for slipping sometimes, as long as you followed each failure by puking your guts out.

Tonight was going to be one of those nights when she had to give in just a little. It was okay, really it was, as long as it didn't happen too often, as long as she understood that she couldn't let the all-important orange turn into a mere appetizer. But tonight, that's exactly what it was.

Furious with herself and the world she'd been born into, she headed for the kitchen. It was dark in there. The bulb in the ceiling fixture had burned out and she'd never bothered to replace it. But every unused surface gleamed antiseptically in the shadows. The place was like an operating room, illuminated only by the distant blue-gray glow of the tube, where Hepburn had revealed herself in all her girlish glory.

The dead-white rectangle in the comer bumped and whined.

She hated it, but she hated being hungry even more. She knew what was waiting inside the pale box, and it was everything she had been, everything she could have been, everything she was afraid to be. She pounded on the door with her fists, and sent magnets that held no messages skittering across the polished floor. She was sick and she was sorry, but she wanted what was in there, and it belonged to her.

She pulled open the door, and when the light went on, she saw what she had longed for in its radiance. Everything she had given up was waiting for her, rejected but not abandoned, crying out to her like a lost child.

Each shelf was filled with jars, and each jar was filled with human fat, thick and slippery and yellow. The light from the tiny bulb made it glisten and glow. It was hers, and she needed it.

Her stomach rumbling, she reached for a spoon.

Kisses From Auntie

BY CRAIG SHAW GARDNER

IT WAS THE PUNCH THAT DID IT.

We decided that afterward, of course. There wasn't time to think of anything else when it happened, which was funny. At Auntie's we usually had more time than we could ever use.

"Give us a kiss, Loves," Auntie said, and she smiled with her big red lips. Both Bruce and I closed our eyes and waited. We knew what was coming. If you kept still and didn't squirm, you'd get it over with right away.

I mean, it was bad enough when I had to put on one of my old smelly dresses and then had to let Mom brush out my hair before we went to Auntie's party. And Auntie had parties every week! And then, first thing, right when we got there, Auntie always had to kiss us. A big wet one on the cheek. Absolutely blech!

Auntie had this smell—lavender water, Mom said when we asked her about it. Bruce and I decided that she had to pour it all over herself to smell that bad.

"Oh, you're my special children!" Auntie said when the kissing was over. "If only Uncle were here to see you now. You know, I've watched you grow since you were knee-high to a grasshopper. But you probably wouldn't remember that, would you?"

Bruce and I both shook our heads. "Be polite!" Mom and Daddy always said. For a while we tried.

But I was talking about the punch, half ginger ale and half cranberry juice. It tasted much worse than either one tasted by itself, I mean, absolutely blech. We got it when the grown-ups got their wine or liquor or whatever it was that grown-ups drink. Auntie would go around and ask, "What would you like to drink, Tom?" And Daddy would say, "I don't know, Alma. Maybe a Manhattan." And then Auntie would ask Mom the same question, and Mom would say, "Oh, whatever Tom's having is fine with me." And then she'd ask Gramma and Gramma's other sisters. But never, never did Auntie ask us what we wanted. She just brought us the punch.

Something had to be done about it. Bruce and I both stared at our glasses and frowned.

"Oh dear," Auntie said, bending close so that we could really smell the lavender. "It looks

86

like poor Bruce and Laura have the fidgets. You don't have to stay here, dears, and be bored. Why don't you run upstairs and play until dinner?"

So we did.

Bruce and I decided that everything about Auntie couldn't be that bad, because upstairs was a special place, particularly the door right at the top of the stairs, the place Auntie called the back bedroom. It was full of all sorts of things; Daddy called it junk, but Bruce and I knew better. I mean, there were a lot of dusty green books with gold lettering that nobody would ever want to come and look at, but there also were three big brown photo albums with pictures of Auntie when she was my parents' age, standing in all sorts of places with some man Bruce and I figured must be "Uncle." And there were piles of old *National Geographics*, some of them with pictures of people without any clothes on. There was a big box of old toys that sat in front of the closet door with a lot of dolls and a red metal fire engine and a big bag of crayons, half of them black. When we could get away from the grown-ups, Auntie's back bedroom was all right.

But this time, when we reached the bedroom, the box of toys was gone. I frowned at Bruce. We'd have to look at the pictures again.

"Maybe," Bruce said, "Auntie put it behind the door." He walked over to the closet with me close behind. Bruce turned to me and grinned. It was a door we had never opened!

He pulled the door open as quietly as he could. We were wrong. It wasn't a closet; there were stairs going up.

"Should we?" I whispered. Mom and Daddy might get mad if we didn't come in time for supper, but I'd never seen a real attic!

Bruce hit my shoulder. "C'mon! It's better than going back downstairs to drink Auntie's punch!" The first stair creaked when he put his foot on it. He went up anyway.

I climbed right behind. I had to lift my dress a little so that it wouldn't get dirty on the old steps. They were narrow and spaced wide apart, more like a ladder, almost. It was dark. Something brushed my forehead—a piece of string. I grabbed at it and pulled the light on.

We were in the attic, and we saw the skeleton.

I had turned on two light bulbs with the string somehow. We were under one of them, and the skeleton was under the other—a human skeleton. Bruce grabbed my arm. It got to me too, but I wanted to explore.

"Don't be a scaredy-cat!" I whispered. "Bones can't hurt you." I took a step toward the skeleton. Bruce stayed close behind. It was my turn to be brave.

The walls of the attic were full of shelves, and the shelves were full of jars, all sizes and shapes of jars, each one labeled with tiny handwriting that was hard to read. Bruce squinted inside a particularly big one.

"Aren't those eyeballs?" he whispered.

Honestly! My big brave brother. The first time we get into a strange place, he gets the creepies.

I thought the attic was great. We crept down a narrow path left between the jars on one side and the piles of old furniture and boxes on the other. Bruce started to slow down, but I pulled him after me. We were walking toward the skeleton. The bones hung from a hook in the ceiling, and there as an open space on the floor around them. It was the only open space in the whole attic. On the other side of the cleared place was a big desk, with the biggest book I'd ever seen on top of it. In between the desk and the bones, I could see something written on the floor.

I bent down to take a closer look. There was a big yellow circle painted on the floor, with some kind of black marks scribbled next to it. I tried to see whether the marks said something, but the floor was much too dusty. I rubbed the dirt off with my thumb, but the shape underneath didn't look like any letter I'd ever seen.

I dared Bruce to step into the circle, but he wouldn't do it. He just froze in one spot and stared at the skeleton. What was he afraid of? Brother Bruce, always teasing me, daring me to go places?

I stepped into the circle.

I felt like I was going downhill in a roller coaster, swinging up in a swing, and flying through the air all at the same time. I giggled and danced. I could dance, or jump, or somersault, or fly, or do anything I wanted to. That's how I felt.

My hand hit the skeleton when I jumped.

"How dare you!" I jumped again, and all the happiness left me. Auntie stood on the stairs. "What are you children doing?"

Bruce and I looked at each other. Bruce blurted out something about looking for the box of toys.

"Well, come down from there right away. You could get hurt."

Mom and Daddy were waiting for us in the back bedroom. Daddy looked angry, like he was ready to yell.

"Now, Tom," Auntie said, as she led us both by the hand past our parents. "Don't be too harsh. They're still only children, and I never told them they couldn't go up there. If I move a couple things out of the way they might get hurt with, they can go up there every time you visit."

'Mommy!" Bruce blurted out. "There was a skeleton!"

Auntie laughed. "That's something I'll definitely have to move. Uncle was very fond of it, you know. Part of some research or other. I really never understood it." She steered Bruce and me down the staircase to dinner.

That night, after I got home, I wanted to go back to Auntie's again. I wanted to find out all about the attic and stand inside the circle again. Who cared about my uncle's old skeleton?

Anyway, we went to Auntie's almost every week for what Daddy called "family dinner parties." Daddy called them other things too, but Mom told us never to repeat those. And so we went back to Auntie's pretty soon, even though it seemed like forever to me.

I barely waited for Auntie to kiss us to run upstairs with Bruce before she even got to the punch.

"I don't know if I want to go!" Bruce said as I pulled him up the attic stairs. But he calmed down when we got to the top and he saw that the skeleton was gone. He still looked around nervously, as if he expected it to jump out from the shadows or something. But I told him that Auntie had probably locked it in the back of the attic or hung it in a closet somewhere, and that seemed to make him feel better.

I dragged him straight to the circle and pushed him in. He looked afraid for a second, but then he smiled. I stepped in after him.

Things started to happen. I mean, first it was the same feeling I had had the last time, the flying and all that. Except this time Bruce was flying with me. But then...

Bruce and I looked at each other, really looked at each other so that I saw right inside Bruce's eyes and saw the blue lightning deep down. Bruce told me he saw orange fire deep in mine. And the lightning flashed from Bruce's eyes, the fire jumped from mine, and they hit each other halfway between us. And where they hit, something grew.

I couldn't see what was growing there, not exactly. But I knew that it was there just the same. It grew and rose toward the ceiling.

Then I had an idea. I looked around the room. Jars shook on their shelves; something rattled in an old crate pushed into a corner. Then I saw the book on the desk, that heavy, heavy book that looked like the biggest dictionary I'd ever seen. I pointed to it. Bruce nodded. We stared at it, lightning and fire. The book took off all of a sudden and flew just above our heads. We shrieked and ducked, and the book crashed to the ground.

Bruce and I looked at each other. The lightning and flame were gone. I was happy and scared at the same time.

We heard Auntie's voice call us to dinner.

* * *

The trouble started just as we pulled into Auntie's driveway.

"Laura, darling," my mother said, "and you too, Bruce. Your father and I have been talking. We think you should stay downstairs and talk with the relatives tonight."

"What?" Bruce yelled. "But we have to go into the attic!"

"You don't have to do anything, young man," Daddy said with a frown. "A good part of the reason we come to these silly dinners is for your grandmother and her sisters to see you. So I think you can be polite enough to stay away from the attic for once and talk to everybody."

But we couldn't do that! We had to go to the attic and fly and make everything around us fly! We always went up to the attic!

Bruce started to wail but I shook him and shook my head. Wailing never did any good with our parents. I whispered in his ear.

We ran upstairs before Auntie could even kiss us. We ran into the circle. Jars shook.

The crate rattled and bumped. We'd do what we wanted! We'd show our parents!

Bruce stopped and stared behind me. I turned my head. Auntie was there.

She smiled her big red smile.

"My special children. Your father's very angry at you, you know."

"So what?" Bruce demanded. We were in the circle. We could do anything.

"I told them you'd get tired of your game and come down to dinner eventually. You're both very special to me. I don't want to see anything happen to you."

She walked towards us on old, shaky legs. The smell of lavender filled the room.

"Give us a kiss," she said. For some reason, we let her.

"Now be careful," Auntie said as she walked away. "I don't want to worry your parents."

And she left us alone.

We were still in the circle, and I still felt the fire. It warmed my fingers and toes and ran hot along my spine. Cold lightning flashed in the dusty air, and the fire from my eyes mixed with it, and the thing that came from part of Bruce and part of me grew.

It wanted something. It wanted to be free. It would make us free. We'd never have to do anything that we didn't want to again. No more being polite for our parents, no more kisses from Auntie, no more homework, no more early bedtime. We just had to let it grow, and it would show us how.

The cloud moved away. We heard Daddy's voice echo from the back bedroom.

"Come on kids! Time to go home!"

I looked at Bruce. He shook his head. We couldn't go home now, not now! Neither of us made a sound.

"Come on, you little devils! Don't be so stubborn! You've already missed your dinner! I'm not going to let you miss your bedtime, too!"

We heard Daddy's feet on the stairs.

"Go away!" I screamed. He couldn't come up!

"Nope! Time to go home!"

Blue light flashed in my head. I looked at Bruce. He was right. We couldn't let Daddy get us. Not until we knew.

I concentrated too and could feel the fire meet the lightning, and it grew again. It was stronger than ever this time. I could feel it throbbing in the air.

We pushed it down the stairs.

Daddy said a dirty word. Something fell, bumpity-bump-bump. "Tom!" Auntie screamed.

It was quiet after that. We were scared. What had we done? We only wanted to stay a little while and play.

Bruce went down the stairs first. I came down right behind him. There was no one in the back bedroom. We walked out onto the landing. Daddy lay there, very still. I could hear Mommy on the phone downstairs. She sounded upset.

We walked into the living room as the siren whirred outside. Mommy flung the door open to let in two men carrying some poles. They walked up to where Daddy lay. One of the men felt Daddy's body.

They undid the poles into some sort of stretcher while one of the men talked to Mommy. She nodded, and they put Daddy on the stretcher and carried him outside.

Mommy turned to us. I could tell that she'd been crying.

"Daddy's broken his leg and maybe something else. I've got to go to the hospital with him. Auntie's been good enough to volunteer to take care of you overnight. Don't give her any trouble."

Mommy grabbed her coat and ran out the door.

Auntie smiled her big red smile. "Now, Bruce and Laura, don't be frightened. Give us a kiss."

She put her big wet lips on my check and hugged me tight. I almost choked on the lavender smell. She went over and did the same to Bruce.

Blue flashed in my brain. I blinked. Maybe we could do it now anywhere in Auntie's house. Maybe we could do it anyplace we wanted. We could do anything we wanted.

"You're Auntie's special children." She patted Bruce on the head. "Come into the kitchen. I'll give you some punch."

Bruce and I looked at each other. Absolutely blech.

"And then we can play some games. I imagine you children have lots of games you like to play. We'll have such a good time. And you can stay forever and ever."

Lightning flashed. I could feel the fire. We'd do what we wanted. Nobody—not Auntie, nor our parents, nobody—would ever tell us what to do again.

"Come into the kitchen, children. Your punch is ready."

Bruce and I looked at each other. No more cranberry juice and ginger ale.

It grew.

No more kisses! No more boring games!

The cloud filled the room over our heads. I could really see it now. Spots of orange flame flashed in the darkness. Blue bolts of light stretched to the carpet. No more! No more!

"So soon?" It was Auntie's voice. She could see the cloud too.

The cloud moved toward her. Auntie stumbled against the refrigerator. "Bruce, Laura, you were always my special children. So gifted. When Uncle made his plans I knew…" Her voice trailed off as the first flashes of light snapped at her outstretched hands. She closed her eyes and let the cloud cover her.

The cloud vanished, and Auntie was gone too.

I felt like I hadn't slept in a month. It hit me just like that. The cloud had been too big; it had used up too much of us.

Bruce had fallen on the floor, his eyes closed.

What had we done? What would Mommy and Daddy say when they couldn't find Auntie?

"Bruce?" I whispered, even though there was no one around to hear. "What can we do?"

My brother opened his eyes and smiled. "It's a shame it had to happen so young."

"Bruce?" I asked. What was he talking about?

He rolled over and pushed himself up. He swayed when he stood.

"Still, Uncle will be here soon, and we'll be together forever and ever."

"Stop talking like that!" I backed up toward the kitchen door.

He walked toward me like he didn't quite know how to use his feet. He stretched out his arms to touch me. The smell of lavender was in the air.

"Give us a kiss, Love," he said.

Runaway

BY CHRISTOPHER GOLDEN

KEVIN RAN.

Hot tears cut a shameful path down his cheeks as his legs pumped beneath him, his Pumas slapping the pavement of Fox Run Drive. In some primal part of him, he felt the urge to vomit, but he couldn't. His belly was just ice, a cold counterpoint to the prickly heat flushing his ears and face.

Kevin ran, and the scene that had played out only moments before came back to him in sharp detail. His father had come home late again. Drunk again, or at least with the smell of alcohol on his breath. Jack Murphy wasn't around much. Never had been. He was an attorney who spent too much time with female "clients," and the rest of his time in a bar. He was around for vacations, for the fun stuff, and Kevin could remember a time when he'd been around a lot more, playing ball on weekends or cutting the grass. But it had been a while since then.

It was October, 1978 now, and Kevin was eleven. He didn't think he'd played basketball or even thrown a football with his father since the summer of '76. He remembered, 'cause that was the big Bicentennial year. Everything was red, white and blue, and fireworks, and the Tall Ships came into Boston harbor. He thought his father loved him, then. And he'd loved his dad more than anything.

The hell of it was, he still loved his father. Even now.

Kevin and Jesse had been watching TV on the floor in their parents' room when the fight had begun. Their mom, Aileen, was just tired of it all. The screaming started, accusations flew and were barely denied. Kevin had never heard so much swearing. Jesse, who had turned thirteen only two days before, went into the hall and told Kevin to stay put.

The tears had already started, though, and Kevin was fighting so hard against them that he couldn't respond. Moments later, when the screaming had reached a fevered pitch, and he heard the argument start to move outside, he left his room, went down the hall, and stood at the top of the stairs. Just outside the storm door, he saw his world falling apart.

His mother's face was etched with pain and fury and desperation.

His father cursed her so loudly and angrily that spittle flew from his mouth. Jesse stood on the slate stoop just beyond the door, pleading with their dad to stop it. Just to stop it.

But it didn't stop. It exploded. Kevin's dad started to walk away, reaching into his pocket for his keys. His mom reached out to try to stop him, grabbed hold of his arm, and he shook her off so violently that she stumbled and fell over a bush along the stone walk.

Jesse snapped. He screamed something unintelligible. He leaped onto their father's back, trying to stop him from leaving, or stop him from hurting their mother any more, just to stop him. Just to stop it. But their dad bucked Jesse off his back and swore at him. He didn't even pause as he strode to the old, battered Pontiac in the driveway, pulled out, and tore off down the road.

Kevin went down the stairs slowly, almost as if he were sleepwalking. He'd stopped fighting the tears by then. He pushed the storm door open and stepped out onto the slate stoop, and watched as Jesse helped their mother up off the ground. They were all crying, but she was hurting the worst. Her tears came in huge gasps and sobs, as if everything inside her had suddenly come unhinged. Kevin supposed that was close enough to the truth.

His mother looked at him. Kevin tried to speak to her, but what came out was a wail of pain and sorrow.

Then he ran. Away from it all. Away from the home and the room and the faces that would remind him of the pain that was tearing him apart. He wanted it behind him, all of it. Didn't want to think, ever again. Not at all. Thinking about anything would lead right back home, right back to the wounds in his heart and soul. It was always bad at home, with them. Always had been. But he could handle it.

This, though. This was something else.

The moon and stars shone brightly above, the night sky not that eternal, universal black, but a warm and textured indigo. It was warm for late October, but cold enough that he should have had a jacket over his Captain America T-shirt. There were nine houses on either side of the road going up the hill. At the top, Fox Run Drive dead-ended in a small circle where teenagers sometimes parked to make out or drink or both.

Beyond the circle, there was only the woods. It was a state forest, actually, but that made little impression on the Murphy brothers and their friends. To them, it was a world apart from school and family, a reality all their own. It was winding paths that went on forever through the trees, and hidden gulleys, and huge rocks to climb on. They played army and hide-and-seek, but more often than not, they just explored.

Unless they were building.

Kevin and Jesse and their friends had built three forts in the past two years. The latest and greatest was over a small rise about a hundred feet from one of the secondary paths. It was a tree fort, built in and around four huge oaks, expertly patched together with wood stolen from the new houses being built at the edge of the forest. The fort was twelve feet from the ground and sturdy as anything, with four solid walls and no entrance save for the trapdoor in the floor.

It was there Kevin fled now, forcing his mind to stay numb. He ran half the distance to the top of Fox Run Drive, and then he began to lose steam. At the circle, he slowed to a walk, wiping the tears from his face angrily, embarrassed by them. Yet still they came. Not quite so copiously, but there just the same. As if he'd truly begun to leak, and it was now beyond his power to make the necessary repairs.

He wondered if that, too, might not be close enough to the truth. A single glance back down the hill sent him on his way. It might have been harder if he could have seen his house from there, but there was a curve in the hill and trees as well. If he could have seen the end of his driveway, even, he might have hesitated longer, thought about it more.

Kevin walked to the edge of the circle and entered the dark woods, put off only momentarily by the sounds there, and the way the trees seemed more ominous and closer together at night, and the sense that there was a presence there, some malevolent and grinning entity that was part of the air itself inside the forest.

But that was baby stuff. Kevin knew that.

Eyes front, he plunged into the trees, brushing branches away from his face and careful not to trip over roots and such. Moments later, he broke through onto the main path. It led away to right and left, but Kevin could see very little of it, now that the canopy above blocked out all but the narrowest swath of illumination from the moon and stars. His eyes compensated as best they could, and Kevin turned right, shivering now that the rage and fear had worn off.

All that remained to him was the ache in his heart, the lost, hollow feeling inside of him, and the unformed certainty that at the fort, he could stop. At the fort, he could make the rest of the world disappear. Kevin felt as though he had once been part of something larger but had been torn away, the way some of the shingles had been ripped right off the roof in the tropical storm that had swept through New England the month before. They'd never found those shingles. The storm had carried them away, just as another storm was now carrying him away, off to another place, the world within that forest.

He trudged along in silence, his feet moving along almost without instruction from his brain. A ways along the main path, he turned left. Perhaps sixty yards down that way, and he turned off, blue Puma sneakers buried in wet, fallen leaves as he stepped over a downed tree and then started up the small hill. The forest was dense, there, but he had picked his way through dozens, maybe hundreds of times.

At the top of the hill, he could see the fort.

Though the pain was still there, he didn't feel lost anymore. With a longing he could never have named, Kevin tromped down the hill and stood under the fort, next to the widest of the four oaks. To its trunk they had nailed slats of wood, which could be used as a ladder when necessary. There was a rope as well, thick and strong, and strung from a branch above the fort. It hung down through a hole in the roof, and then further down, through the trapdoor. They could use the rope to haul themselves up, and the slats as footholds to aid in the climb. But when they left, the last one always hauled the rope up and dropped down or climbed the "ladder." Likewise, whoever got there first had to climb up and drop the rope down.

The slats weren't very sturdy. Jesse had said he didn't think they'd hold a grownup. Not a full-grown man, anyway. That setup—with the rope and all—made the fort feel even more special.

Kevin's expression was grim as he climbed the makeshift ladder.

He shivered a little, and his fingers were cold. But he didn't care. Inside the fort, he was sure he would feel warmer. At least the walls would keep out the wind that shook the bare branches all around.

When he reached the top, he boosted himself up into the darkened fort, with only the slightest light coming in through the square windows cut out of each wall. A deep sigh escaped him.

He was there, alone and safe. Everything else was far, far away, and he wanted to keep it that way forever.

At which thought, fresh tears began to bum the corners of his eyes. Their warmth felt good on his reddened cheeks. Not just the warmth, either. The tears themselves felt good. The pain inside was his pain, and being alone with it felt inexplicably good. Kevin felt the sob building in his chest. It would break like a wave on the shore, and spill out of him. But that was all right. He needed that.

He drew a long, shuddering breath, about to cry out.

"You can't make me go back."

The voice, barely above a whisper, came from a shadowy comer of the fort, and Kevin shouted out in fright and scrabbled back into the opposite comer. He narrowed his eyes, trying to make out the figure that sat across from him in the meager moonlight.

"Did you hear me? I won't go back to my parents. You'll have to kill me first."

Kevin could barely make her out. Her eyes glinted in the shadows, reflecting what little light there was as though they sucked it from the air. Wild, black hair fell in a tangle over her shoulders and covered part of her face. Her skin, as well as he could make it out there in the huddle of the fort, looked brown.

He hadn't said a word, stunned into silence by her presence and her venomous tone. Now he realized he had to say something. What came out was not what he intended.

"This is our fort," he told her sternly, sniffling away his now forgotten tears. "You can't be here."

The fort was the solace he had so looked forward to. It had been invaded. Though there were endless questions flashing across his mind, that territorial instinct had come quickly to the fore. Instantly, he regretted it.

For the girl had a knife. He hadn't seen it before, but now the blade twisted in the air in front of her, flashing starlight as it turned in her grasp.

"Who are you?" she demanded.

"You're asking me?" Kevin snapped. growing angry now. Or, at least, covering his fear of that blade by pretending anger. "This is our place, I said. We built it. Me and my brother and our friends. Nobody said you could be in here."

The girl seemed to relax, quite suddenly, sinking back in upon herself, almost disappearing in the corner again.

Kevin heard her crying. His heart went to her, as it would to any girl he heard weeping. He was eleven, but he wasn't one of those boys who thought girls were gross. Not even close. Still, though, the sound of her quiet sobs was like salt in his own fresh wounds, and so his sympathy was dulled quite a lot.

"I'm sorry," she said, at great length. "I thought you were someone else. You're right, this isn't my place. I was running, just running through the wood. And I came upon this place, and I was so tired. I thought I could hide here, just 'til morning, and then I might be safe, or at least not afraid to find my way."

He wanted to tell her to get out. He truly did. But she'd been crying. And she sounded so lost. Lost and empty, just the way he felt. There'd been that knife, sure, but who knew what she was running from. Maybe she thought she needed that knife. What was that she'd said at the beginning, anyway? If he wanted to take her back, he'd have to kill her.

That was serious. Much worse than what had happened to Kevin.

Hell, his mom and Jesse were home waiting for him. They loved him at least. But this girl would rather die than go back home.

"All right, take it easy," he said softly. "You can stay. I just... you scared me, that's all. I didn't expect anyone to be up here and I'm... " His words trailed off, but somehow, she sensed what they would be.

"You've run away, too, haven't you?"

Kevin only nodded, but she must have seen him in spite of the dark, for she slid forward a little, into the moonlight, and looked at him so gently with large, round eyes the color of milk chocolate. He could see now that she looked a little older than he. Though she was smaller, she certainly seemed more mature. In spite of the dark clothes she wore wrapped around her almost like a cloak, he could not help but notice the swell of her breasts.

"Then we have each other, I guess," she said. "I never imagined I'd find a friend in the wood. If we can be friends? My name is Laurel."

"I'm Kevin," he said, automatically.

Everything about her distracted him now. Her name was beautiful. She was beautiful, or as much as he could see there in the gloom. Something else, too. It wasn't "the woods" to her. Or even "the forest." *The wood*, she'd called it, and more than once. Otherwise, she spoke pretty much like other kids he knew, but that was sort of peculiar. Not that he minded. It was kind of nice. It had an odd ring to it, a kind of magic quality that only added to the idea that lingered in his mind that the forest and the fort were a world away from home.

"Kevin," she repeated. "What are you running from?"

Though he knew he would never tell any of his friends, and that he and Jesse might never discuss it more than superficially, he found himself telling Laurel about his family, the pain in his heart, the way his father had thrown his mother and Jesse aside and just gone away. Just left. Before he could stop himself, Kevin found himself crying, and quickly wiped the tears away.

He had never cried in front of a girl before, and he was embarrassed.

"What about you?" he asked, mostly to change the subject, but also because he wanted to know. Wanted to help, if he could. Talking helped a lot. His mom had always told him that, and he'd found it to be one of the truest things she'd taught him.

Laurel laughed, then. It was an ugly laugh.

"My mother treats me like a dog, and my father treats me like a whore. They eat like royalty, and I eat slop. I'm a servant in my own home." She paused then, to wipe at her eyes. But then she lifted her chin high. Her hair fell away from her face a bit, and Kevin saw long golden strands dangling from her ears.

He frowned. Her ears looked almost pointed. "Well no more," she said dangerously. "No more."

"Jesus," Kevin whispered. "I guess… I mean, it was bad, and my father's an asshole, but nothing like… ah, hell, I'm sorry."

For just a moment, he thought that Laurel might have smiled a bit. Then the howling began. Kevin flinched, looking around nervously, so that at first he didn't notice her reaction. Then he heard her whimper, and he looked to see that Laurel sat rigid, blade out in front of her once more, eyes darting from side to side as if someone might be sneaking up on her. Which was impossible, of course. She had the walls of the fort behind her, and just the trees beyond. They were twelve feet up.

"They're coming," she whispered. "I thought I'd be safe here." Kevin frowned.

"Come on. What are you talking about? Your parents have bloodhounds or something?"

It was absurd. But the thing was, it didn't feel absurd. Not sitting up there in the fort in the dark in the middle of the woods—the wood—and Laurel looking like the devil himself were coming for her.

"Go," she said suddenly.

Laurel scrabbled across the wood and pushed him toward the trap door. "They won't dare hurt me, but they'll kill you, Kevin. I don't think I could live with that."

"What?" he scoffed. "Come on, Laurel. You have any idea how that sounds? Who's going to kill me? Your parents?"

She gave him a hard look, then shook her head. "Then I'll go," she said. "It's the only way."

With that, she slid to the edge of the hole in the floor, and then simply pushed off into space.

"Laurel!" Kevin shouted, and stuck his head over the hole to look down.

The girl landed on her feet, knees slightly bent. He blinked, peering into the night, but he didn't think she fell down. At all. Kevin was astounded. He couldn't have done that, and he was bigger than she was. If he wanted to get down without the rope, he'd have held on to the lip of the hole, dangled down, let himself go, and even then, he probably would have had to tumble into a roll when he hit the ground.

With a quick glance up at him, Laurel whispered. "Goodbye, Kevin."

"Wait," he called.

At the sound of his voice, the howling began again. Much closer this time. Kevin shivered, and suddenly needed to pee quite badly. It was like nothing he'd ever heard before, not even the howl of werewolves in old movies on *Creature Feature*. They sounded, almost, as if they were calling out to someone. To each other, maybe, or to Laurel? He didn't know; but that was how it sounded.

And they sounded angry.

"Oh, fuck," Kevin groaned, truly afraid now.

For half a second, he'd thought that he could stay up there, in the fort. But they were coming this way, and if Laurel was going to run, he was going to run, too. If he could catch up to her, they could run to his house. Surely his mom would let her in, at least to get away from the hounds, or whatever. If they could get out of the wood, they could even go to the Levensons, right there at the top of the street. Mrs. Levenson knew him; she wouldn't turn them away. They could call the police.

Fast as he was able, Kevin dropped the heavy coil of rope down through the trap door, and slipped down it, burning his hands a little and dropping the last few feet. He managed to keep his balance, but only barely. Then he was sprinting up the hill and into the trees, branches slapping his face, scratching him deep. He caught his arm on a splintered tree branch and got a good scrape that would leave a thin white scar for the rest of his life.

Still he ran on. The sound was coming from behind him now, and closer. Back there in the dense forest beyond the fort, he could hear them crashing through branches, whatever they were. They growled now, and seemed to roar instead of howling, as though they smelled something good to eat.

"Jesus," Kevin whimpered.

There was something else, too. Something with them. Something big and lumbering. It was a man, he thought. When he glanced behind him, he could just make out a human shape back there. But it moved fast, slamming through the trees, snapping off branches as it went.

Despite the cold, Kevin was sweating. His bladder cramped up, and he wanted badly to stop, but didn't dare. His heart thudded in his chest, and he felt it reverberating all over his body, starting at his ribs, then moving through him like an echo.

He ran. He stumbled over a root. Slipped in fallen leaves. He peered through the branches ahead.

Where's the path?

He should have come to it by now. Before now. Terrified, Kevin knew he had to get his bearings or he might get lost in the wood forever. Those dogs would get him. The man... the man who wanted Laurel back would get him.

They'll kill you, she had said. Suddenly, he believed her completely.

Kevin stopped short, desperate to find his way. He looked back, eyes searching for the hill, trying to place the path in relation to where the ground rose up in front of the fort.

It was there. So were they.

Through a break in the trees, he saw them, standing at the crest of the hill in the moonlight that streamed down through an opening in the canopy above. For a heartbeat, they were silhouetted there. The hounds weren't hounds at all. But what they were, he couldn't have said. They walked on all fours and were covered with fur, but they were the size of ponies, their snouts dangling low to the ground.

What stood between them could hardly be called a man. It was half again as tall as Kevin, a good two feet taller than his dad. It was naked, and its skin looked like leather. It was as broad across as a barn door, and its arms were as thick as a telephone pole, fists the size of a Christmas turkey. It was bald and scarred, and it had a pair of stumpy tusks that stuck up from its lower jaw like a walrus.

That last was what did it. That last was what made Kevin realize that it couldn't be a human being, not even in a circus sideshow.

In that moment, he couldn't breathe. Only that fact kept him from screaming. He was frozen in the dark, and thanking God that he hadn't screamed, when the beasts sniffed him. His silence no longer mattered. They started down after him.

Now Kevin did scream. He turned and fled in the direction he thought the path should be.

It still wasn't there.

He cried—it felt like he'd been crying for days, like there should be no tears left to fall—and he called for his mother, and he felt like his head would split or he might just fall down there and wait for them to get him. A branch gouged his cheek. He held his arms up to protect his face, but still, there was no path.

No path. It was impossible. He should have come upon it way before this.

"Kevin!"

A strong hand clamped upon his arm, and he cried out again, afraid it might break.

"Be quiet, please," Laurel begged, voice hushed.

He turned to look at her, desperate with terror. Her eyes locked on his. She kissed him, quickly, on the lips—the first kiss he'd ever had from a girl, really.

"You were kind to me, Kevin. I won't forget you. But go home, now. Your mother's waiting for you."

No shit, he wanted to say. *What do you think I'm trying to do.*

What came out was "come with me."

"We'd never escape together," she told him. "They only want me back. I'll be punished, but I'll live. You won't. You have to run, now!"

He tried to find the words, though he could hear the man—the thing—crashing through the wood. He couldn't hear the hounds, though, and that worried him even more. They were there, but silent. Maybe too close already.

"Run!" she snarled, and gave him a shove.

Kevin let the momentum carry him, and he ran. Shame built up inside him, and he wanted to stop. She was a girl. He couldn't leave her behind. Even if they didn't kill her, if what she'd told him was true, her life was horrible enough. He had to find a way to save her.

We'd never escape together. I'll live. You won't.

Kevin kept running. He heard the hounds start growling, too close behind him. Heard a thundering laugh that he knew had come from the hunter. That was what he was, too. Some kind of hunter.

If he heard Laurel scream, he'd go back. He promised himself that. If it sounded like she was being hurt, he'd...

I'll live. You won't.

"Oh, God," he whispered.

She had stayed behind to make sure he got away. And all he could do was run. For the second time that night, he wanted to throw up.

Then, suddenly, he burst out of the trees onto the main path, tripped on a stone jutting from the ground, and fell hard to his knees. Kevin's gaze darted down the path to his left, and he knew it immediately. It was the main path at the top of his street. Impossible, of course, 'cause he couldn't have gotten there without crossing that secondary path first. Unless he'd been so scared that he had crossed right through without even noticing.

He peered into the trees for some sign of Laurel, or her pursuers, ready to get up and run. But there was no sign. No sign, no trace, and even stranger, no sound. He could not hear the hounds. He could not hear the hunter. No branches snapped. Just the wind whistling through the naked trees, and the sound of a dog—a real dog, a house pet barking somewhere down on Fox Run Drive.

"Kevin!"

His head snapped to the right, heart thundering in his chest. Then he saw his brother Jesse coming along the path in the gloom. As he got closer, Kevin saw the jean jacket in his brother's hand, and he shivered, longing for it.

"Jess," he said, his voice a croak.

Jesse walked up to him, the pain in his eyes almost unbearable, even in the near dark. Kevin looked away from them. Then he threw his arms around his brother and held him tight, in a way he hadn't done since they were just little boys.

"Mom sent me to find you," Jesse said. "I figured you'd be up here. You go to the fort?"

Kevin nodded. He didn't know what to say. He glanced into the wood several times, but saw nothing.

"Hey," Jesse said, looking hard at his cheek, and his arms. "What the hell happened to you?"

If he'd heard anything at all, then, even the snapping of a twig, Kevin probably would have spilled the whole story, frantic and fearful, even dragging Jesse back into the wood to try to help Laurel. Already, though, what had happened at the fort had begun to seem less important. The girl had a horrible life, that was true. But in that moment, in the here and now, what was happening between them was more important.

"I was running," Kevin replied. "Got a little lost, I guess. I was afraid."

"You're okay now, bro," Jesse said, and threw an arm around his brother.

Together, they started back along the path. Kevin glanced over his shoulder several times, the story right on the tip of his tongue. But somehow, he never shared it. Not with Jesse, or with anyone. He kept it to himself, just as he never told his friends the story of what had happened with his father that night.

When he and Jesse emerged into the circle at the top of Fox Run Drive, Kevin hesitated one last time, thinking of Laurel. He wanted to cry for her, and for himself, but he could find no more tears. They had stopped at last.

"Come on, Kev. Let's go home. Mom's worried for you," Jesse said.

Kevin nodded, and they walked on together. He didn't know what else to do. Laurel's life sucked, that was for sure. But with each step, the things he had thought he'd seen seemed all the more ridiculous. The dogs were just dogs.

Of course they were.

And the hunter was just a man. A big bastard, no doubt. Maybe he'd been wearing a leather jacket with the collar turned up, and Kevin had seen... no, what he'd seen was just ridiculous. It was probably her father. If so, then he figured he was the lucky one. Better to have his father gone than to have a father like that.

Better. Only it didn't feel better.

The ache inside him had been temporarily edged out by fear, and whatever weird hallucinations being in the wood at night had brought about. But it was back now.

Even wearing the jean jacket his brother had brought him, he was cold. Kevin shivered.

"He's really gone, isn't he, Kev?" Jesse asked.

Kevin looked at him in surprise. Jesse was supposed to be the strong one, not him. He was the big brother, after all. But now he saw that pain in Jesse's eyes again, and he knew his brother was waiting for the answer. Waiting for the truth.

"Yeah, Jess. I really think so."

"Do me a favor, Kevin?" Kevin shrugged.

"Don't run away again."

His heart tightened. There was a tiny chunk of ice in his stomach.

Kevin shook his head, vigorously.

"I won't. Not ever. And if I do, I'll take you with me." At that, Jesse smiled.

The Murphy brothers walked side by side down Fox Run Drive.

When they came in sight of their house, it might have been that they walked a little faster.

Undercover

BY NANCY HOLDER

IT WAS A SOMBER NIGHT IN CHICAGO, AND THE SLEET STABBED STAN'S SHOULDERS like daggers—or in his case. incisors—as he ducked into the station house and crammed his umbrella into a stand inside a wire cage.

"Hey, Detective Stepanek," the desk sergeant greeted him. "Man, what a night, eh? It's enough to... Kill... you." His voice trailed off and he went back to his paperwork. His face was a purple blush of embarrassment.

Stan sighed and began peeling off his gloves. Yeah, well, some guys never got used to him. Neither did some women.

He scowled at everyone and no one as he unbuttoned his coat. Twelve months now since his Change. And Leslie wouldn't come near him. Some day he would find the fiend who'd done this to him and pay him back in spades.

Or stakes. Man.

He ran a hand through his hair and pushed through the double doors past the sergeant's desk, and strode down the hall. A couple of beat cops, clad in dripping rain gear, saw him and nodded, but shifted their gazes as soon as they politely could. Frigging cowards.

His teeth hurt. He was hungry.

The black letters on the glass door read, "JACK ZIRES." That was his boss. He rapped hard, waited for the grunt, got it, and went into the small cubbyhole jammed with file cabinets and paper. Tall and bald, Jack was eating a salad out of a Styrofoam container. Six months ago, he had become a vegetarian and ever since then, his cholesterol tap danced near the danger zone and he couldn't bring it back down. It made him cranky.

"Hey." Jack gestured to a seat. He had heavy black eyebrows and a perpetual five o'clock shadow, was bitter about the lack of hair on his head. Took a lot of ribbing for it. Before he became a vegetarian.

"How you tonight?" he asked between bites of salad. Stan had forgotten what lettuce tasted like. Not, he recalled, that it had ever tasted like much. Steak, he missed. Chocolate. Pizza. Not lettuce.

"I'm okay," Stan muttered, straddling the chair.

"Leslie again?" They were close enough to talk about things like that.

"Is it ever anything else?" Stan wiped the raindrops off his head and straightened out his legs. His shoes were soaked.

"Well, yeah, sometimes it is." Jack stabbed a carrot, picked it off the fork, and ate it with his fingers. "Sometimes it's your kids. Sometimes it's your parents. Sometimes it's your fellow detectives and other persons in uniform." As Jack, an unreconstructed chauvinist, referred to the women on the force.

"Jeez. Jack, I'm not a complainer."

"I know." Jack patted Stan's forearm. He was one of the few people Stan knew who would actually touch him. "Listen. Listen hard. I've got something for you, and I'm going to give it to you and you alone. Okay?" He nudged something in his salad, sneered at it, and put down his fork. "Some of these vegetables. I don't know." He touched a paper napkin to his lips and dropped it onto his cluttered desk.

"Okay," he said, and opened a drawer. He reached in and withdrew a plastic bag that contained the remains of a lady's black wallet.

He dropped the bag in front of Stan. Nodded at it. "Check it out."

Stan eyed him, dropped his gaze. Opened the bag and fished out the wallet. "So?" he said, and then saw the fragment of a picture in the inside window, where ordinarily you might slip a driver's license. He gasped and almost dropped the wallet, then held it close and leaned into the beam of light from the crook-neck lamp on Jack's desk.

It was part of a face, but it was a face he suddenly remembered with the force of a roundhouse right. Huge brown eyes, a long thin nose, and a beautiful red mouth that hid her cruel surprise. Yes, he knew it now: it'd been a woman, or something pretending to be one. Dear God.

"How-how did you get this?" He could barely speak.

"Stoolie Bob brought it in. Said he found some broad lying dead on the street. Or so he thought. Took her purse and he was going through it when she stood up and tried to kill him. That's all he said but he hasn't been himself since. I thought of you." Jack winced. "No offense."

"None taken." Stan hadn't been the same since. "Why'd he bring it to you?"

"Wanted me to lock him up for theft."

Stan's heart beat faster. "Got anything else?"

"Put that new guy on finding out where the purse was bought, if possible. I dunno. It's a long shot. Could be somebody else's purse. I mean, does your wife carry pictures of herself in her own handbag?"

"I don't remember," Stan said morosely.

"Aw, man. Women can be so cold." Jack stared down at the remains of his salad and shut the Styrofoam container. "I need a hamburger injection, damn it."

"So," Stan pressed.

"So. I didn't hold Stoolie Bob, and he's waiting for you at The Old Same Place. Wants to talk."

Stan inclined his head. "Thanks, Jack."

"I ain't telling anybody else about this. You got enough problems. Anybody asks you what you're working on, tell 'em special detail, and if they have any more questions to come to me."

Stan reverently put the wallet back in the bag and slipped the whole thing into the pocket of his jacket. "Thank you. If I ever crack this, Jack, I'm buying you a steak."

Jack regarded Stan with sad eyes. "Wish you could eat one with me, buddy." Stan said nothing.

There was nothing to say.

He took his own car to the South Side. The windshield wipers sluiced the gray rain away just in time for more gray rain to take its place. There was hardly anyone on the street; steam rose from the grates. Electric lights were muted, as if the bulbs had filled up with water.

It was not a fit night for man, beast, or those stuck somewhere in between.

But there was one highlight. He pulled into an alley, turned off the engine, and got out, rapped twice on a bright blue door. It opened and a handsome Hispanic woman appeared on the threshold. She was wearing a large, ornate crucifix that bothered Stan not at all.

"Buenas noches." He handed her a twenty. "A usted," she replied. She was a nurse, worked for the university. She left for a moment, returned with something in a brown paper bag. "O positive." He took it. "Gracias." With a barely suppressed shudder, she shut the door. He ripped open the plastic container and scarfed down dinner.

About twenty minutes later, he parked in another alley, behind a Harley, and turned off the engine. Sat for a moment behind the wheel and calmed himself. Stoolie Bob was a real squirrel. He didn't want to spook him, have him clam up. Anything he could tell him about the woman, anything at all, would be the best news he'd had in a year.

He got out and walked around the corner. The Old Same Place was such a dive it didn't even have a nicely hand-lettered sign, much less an electric one. Its clientele consisted of those a buck or two away from homelessness, and looking to make that buck inside The Old Same Place by peddling drugs or other assorted good times, or hustling pool.

Used to be it was okay if he went in there. But now, as he pushed open the wooden door, conversation died away for a moment before it resumed at a higher, more nervous pitch.

He wished he knew what he looked like. But of course, he cast no reflection in the mirror behind the bar.

The floor was cracked linoleum and the barstools and booths were covered in extremely distressed burgundy. Smoke that cast purple cobwebs hung motionless in the air. The place reeked of old cigarettes, mildew, sweat, and cheap perfume. "G'evenin'," he said, and bellied up to the bar.

John Joseph, the grizzled old black proprietor, was washing a glass. A cigar hung out of his mouth. He nodded his reply. "Stoolie Bob in?"

John Joseph jerked his head toward the back corner booth. Sure enough, Bob's signature navy-blue watch cap bobbed up and down like a puppet on *Sesame Street*.

The bartender poured Stan a drink, any drink; it was nice of him to do it when he knew Stan couldn't properly exploit it. Still, Stan blended in better with a fistful to carry around, he guessed. He took the glass and ambled over to Stoolie Bob's booth and stood there.

Stoolie Bob was talking to a young man with scars on his face and neck. Especially his neck. They both saw Stan and the young man whistled through his broken, brown teeth. "It's true," he murmured, awed.

"You mind?" Stan asked harshly.

The man glanced at Stoolie Bob. "Later," he said, scooted to the end of the booth, hesitated, then got up and around Stan as fast as he could.

"I knew you'd come," Stoolie Bob gushed. He made to reach for Stan's hand, stopped himself, "Ya gotta help me. I'm marked now. She'll come back for me."

Stan slid back in his seat and feigned nonchalance. You got more out of Bob if he figured he wasn't going to get much out of you. "She's like you, Mr. Detective!"

"Oh?" Stan yawned.

"Yeah! She's all white, and she's got these teeth!" Stoolie Bob lowered his voice. A vein pulsed below his jaw line like it was sending out a distress call. "I need your help. You gotta tell her to leave me alone. Tell her I'm your friend. That I help you solve cases, alla time. Please." Now Stoolie Bob did grab Stan's hands. His fingers were dry and papery.

"That so."

"Yeah!" Stoolie Bob gripped his fingers.

"And you made her acquaintance at?"

"I was down to the Loop. I was near the Hyatt. I know I'm not supposed to be there, Mr. Detective. But I was hungry." And the pick-pocket pickings were pretty good down in yuppieland, Stan finished silently.

"And she was wearing?"

"I thought she was dead! I wasn't stealing from her!"

"And she was wearing?" Stan repeated.

"Black. All black. Black sweater. Black pants. Black coat." He paused. "Black boots." Stan sighed.

"Where's the rest of her purse? Was her wallet just lying beside her? Was it in her pocket?"

Stoolie Bob hesitated. He let go of Stan and dropped his hands under the table. Stared at the Formica. "Bo-ob, yoo-hoo."

"I thought she was dead." He thrust out his lower lip.

"I'm not going to bust you." Stan folded his hands and leaned forward. "I want to help you 'cause you're right, Bob. She'll come back for you unless I can talk her out of it." A damn lie—well, maybe, how the hell should he know—but what did it matter?

"Okay, okay." Stoolie Bob squared his shoulders. "It was in her pocket."

"Okay, Bob. That's okay. Now, this is important. Was there anything else in her pocket? Think about it. Anything else?"

Bob nodded. "Yeah. Yeah, there was. Book of matches."

Stan's eyes flickered. "Did you keep them? Do you have them?"

Stoolie Bob shook his head. "No. But I read 'em." he said hopefully. "They was from a restaurant. Called something funny. The Zigooner, something like that."

Zigooner. Stan thought. He called to John Joseph, "You got a Yellow Pages?" John Joseph ducked his head under the bar, straightened, and showed him the phone book. Brought it over to the table.

"Thanks." Stan began to flip through it to the restaurant section. Zigooner. Zig. Zigeuner. Bingo. Had to be.

Stan flipped the book shut. He rose, took out his wallet, and gave Stoolie Bob his usual fee of ten bucks. "Night," John Joseph called, but Stan was already out the door.

"Tell her I'm your partner!" Stoolie Bob called out desperately.

Someone else muttered, "J.J. why you let that paste face in here? He make me sick." Paste face. Damn.

The Zigeuner was a Rumanian restaurant near the Hyatt. Bingo. Oh, yes, double bingo and it was all on red, baby. Blood red.

Stan showed the photo to the waiters in white, open-throated Gypsy shirts, trying to keep his voice below the violin music, and they all acted so blind, deaf and orally challenged that he knew he had the right place. Oh, he'd had people freeze up around him— such as his wife—but this was different; this was freezing with a purpose. This was freezing because they knew something.

But they sure didn't want to tell him what it was.

"Listen, I'll leave my card," he told a dark, husky man who kept opening the cash register, counting the money, and shutting it again. "I can be reached here on the night shift." He thought for a moment. "Here's my home phone, too. It's very urgent. If anyone remembers seeing this woman"—and here he held out her picture again, and the man flinched again— "I would really appreciate hearing about it. Really, I would."

He left more hopeful than frustrated. And praying she wouldn't, or hadn't, left town.

Leslie was asleep when he got home. He tried not to wake her, but she had become a light sleeper since his change.

He hadn't touched her in a year. Not even a kiss.

"Hi," she said, as he made sure the curtains were drawn against the windows. "How'd it go?"

"I have a lead." Her expression said she understood what he meant.

"Good."

"Maybe she… maybe I can be…" changed back, he wanted to say, but he was afraid to.

Leslie took a deep breath. "Stan, I filed the papers today. This isn't fair to the kids. I…" She looked away.

"I love you," he whispered. "I would do anything…"

"You can't."

"I have a lead."

She wiped a tear from her eye. Her Adam's apple bobbed.

"It's just that, I, Stan…" She looked at him full on. "I can't help thinking about what you are. What you do to stay… alive."

Her voice broke on that last word. "Please sleep on the couch from now on." She looked away.

Why tonight? he thought. Why, when he finally had a clue? "I haven't hurt anybody," he said.

"You might." She pulled the covers over herself. He started to say more, sensed the futility of it.

Grabbing a pillow and a blanket, he trudged into the living room. Considered. The kids would try to wake him up. She hadn't thought of that. They would see him lying there, staring up at the ceiling like a zombie. Or like what he was.

He got back in his car and drove to a motel. Which was, he suspected, what she wanted all along.

He hoped no one at the restaurant called his home phone. Because all of a sudden, it wasn't home any more.

Sundown, and his eyes popped open.

He called Leslie when he woke up and a man answered the phone. Depressed, he paid a visit to the owner of a pretty shady mortuary and had a snack. So let the guy overcharge on embalming, cut a few other funereal corners.

Man, police work was a dirty job sometimes. Or make that survival. But he had never hurt a soul; Leslie knew that. He had never touched a single living being in the entire hellish year.

He showed up for work at ten, as always. Jack had bent a lot of arms to keep him from rotating shifts; hell, he had broken some arms to keep Stan on the force.

The desk sergeant said, "Some woman called you. Wouldn't leave her name. Did leave a number."

Stan grabbed the slip of paper and ran to his office. Slammed the door. Yes, yes. He screwed up the number and had to punch it in again. Yes, baby, yes.

Jack ducked his head in, brows raised, with a look of eagerness on his sallow, underfed face. Evidently he knew about the call.

Stan looked up at him while the phone rang. Jack was a good friend. "Hello?" Yes. It was a woman's voice, deep and sexy, very nervous. Stan hunched forward. Jack shut the door, leaving Stan in privacy.

"It's Stan Stepanek."

"Ah." A sigh of relief. "Ah, yes. Meet me now. Please, meet me. Alone. Tell no one."

Jeesh, so she could finish the job? He said, "Where are you?"

"No, not here. I can't trust…" She caught her breath. "Meet me in front of the aquarium in twenty minutes." Dial tone.

Stan closed his eyes for a second. The room was whirling. He licked his lips and rose.

The door opened. Jack poked his head in.

"You got any silver bullets?" It was supposed to be a joke, but it fell flat.

Jack replied, very soberly, "No, but I was thinking you could use the tip of your umbrella, if you pushed hard enough. Was it her?"

"Maybe." Better have been.

"What's she want?"

"I don't know." But he knew what he wanted: revenge, an explanation, some help.

"You want backup?" Jack smiled grimly. "Guess not." Without thinking, Stan checked the revolver in his shoulder, felt for his badge. What, was he going to Mirandize her? Bring her in for violating the laws of nature?

"Well," he said, and Jack shook his hand. Swallowed hard, "Good luck, buddy."

Stan nodded, said nothing. Left.

The moon hung low in the sky, casting a silvery glow over the river, and beyond, the vast expanse of Lake Michigan. Over the tall figure who stood on the knoll, watching him advance.

Her face was cast in darkness. He tensed, wishing he had some protection. None of that Bela Lugosi stuff worked—crosses and holy water, no help at all. And he knew what he was talking about.

"Detective Stepanek?" she asked, in that deep, rich voice. It was heavily accented, some kind of East-Europe thing.

"Yes. And you?"

She came forward, into the soft fuzz of a street lamp. He was taken aback. Despite the fact that she was white as chalk, she was the most beautiful woman he had ever seen in his life. Her eyes were huge, and deep, velvet brown; her cheekbones, her nose, her large, red lips blended into a dream that just couldn't be real. Her hair tumbled around her shoulders in soft curls that kissed her neck. Her long, pale, slender neck.

Her photo had not done her justice.

"And you?" he repeated, his voice shaking, maybe not so much with terror as he had expected it to. Maybe with... wow, with he didn't know what—

She jerked. "I'm..." She looked away. "I was Natasha Boranova." When she looked back, tears glittered on her cheeks. "I'm sorry. I didn't know what I was doing. I'm... I'm a stranger here." The tears came in earnest now. They made her look so helpless, so vulnerable.

"Hey," he said softly, walking closer. She was shaking, probably just as... scared... as he was.

"We were here illegally."

"Yeah, I'll bet," he tried to joke. "I don't think Immigration has a quota on—"

"No, before." She cocked her head. "You don't know who I am, do you?"

"Besides Countess Dracula?" he retorted, and was immediately sorry. She jerked as if he'd hit her.

"I was a tennis player. I was here with my coach, Ivan Mazarek? We sought asylum..."

Where had he been? Wrapped up in his Big Problem. He shrugged.

"Sorry. I don't know anything about that. But, ah, aren't we all one big happy New World Order now anyway?"

"So they would all have us think." She threw back her head and raised her fists to her chest. "I'm so sorry. I didn't mean to leave you alive."

Whoah. His hand slipped into his jacket and touched his revolver. Futile, Stan, Futile. He cracked his knuckles and made a fist in his trouser pocket.

The moonlight drained even her lips of color. Even then, she was exquisite. "If you're left alive, you become... what you are now."

"Oh?" he rasped. "I thought it was the other way around."

"No." The beautiful hair waved back and forth, back and forth, as she shook her head in misery. "No, and they knew it, too."

She held out her hands. "Please, help me find the people who did this to me. To us!" And then she ran to him and threw her arms around him. Her lips sought, found his, and she kissed him so hard he staggered backward. It was heaven, pure and simple, especially when you had lived in hell for a year. He felt as it he were floating; he couldn't believe the sensations coursing through him. It was like... it was the way he imagined he would feel if he actually bit someone.

"Oh! I haven't touched another person in five years," she moaned, clinging to him. "Well, except...you know. I've been so lonely, so very lonely. The people at the Zigeuner, they try. But they could never really accept me."

"Yeah," he breathed. They kissed again. And again. They ran their hands along each other, starved, filling up. He tasted her blood on his lips. "You're so lovely."

"Am I?" She beamed at him. "I kept a picture of myself so I could remember what I looked like."

"You look swell. You're even more gorgeous than when you were... the other way."

"Human," she said wistfully, then glanced up at him through her lashes. His knees went weak. Her mouth was swollen and dotted with red, where his teeth had done a little damage.

"But do you know, if we are... together, for that time we are human again." She nodded. "That much they told me. They laughed at me and said I should go make myself an 'Adam.' When they threw me out of the car. After they murdered Ivan."

"Threw you... " But his mind ran back to what she'd said before that. "You mean, if we, um, get intimate, we change back?"

"For a little time only. She saw something on his face, and actually smiled. Her long, sharp canines glittered in the light.

"I understand, however, that you are married."

"What?"

"The desk sergeant told me. We had a chat. I had to make sure you were the right one."

"I am the right one. My wife..." And as sudden as a gunshot, he knew he was leaving all that behind. Wife, job. sunlight, the whole ball of wax, meant nothing while he was in her arms. With her, he could be what he was... and what he used to be. As sure as he stood there, he finally, fully Changed. "I'm a detective," he said. "I know how to find people." He held her tightly, so tightly. "And when we find them, we'll rip their throats out."

"Oh, yes." she said breathlessly, her face buried against his neck. "Yes, my darling, yes, we will."

Sundays

BY JACK KETCHUM

SOMEONE ONCE SAID TO ME THAT IF YOU WANT TO MAKE GOD LAUGH, just tell him your plans. Just tell him who you are.

I lie beside her watching her sleep in the light from the street, watching her face and her breasts rise and fall and think how she and I are not one person but so many, both of us and all of us for that matter each uncertainly housed in a single wrap of flesh, and memory intrudes like thick smoke from a wood fire and surrounds us in our bed.

My father Bradford Collier was a squirrel hunter and a good one. I remember him sitting rocking in the shade of our porch his Sunday afternoons off with his old .22 cradled in his lap and watching the stand off our grouped tall black oak trees far across the field which the squirrels would naturally favor for their rich crop of acorns and we inside would hear the short flat bark of the rifle maybe half a dozen times over an hour and then his boots moving slowly down the wooden steps. There'd be silence and then we'd hear the boots again and Anne and Mary Jo and I would rush out from the kitchen to find him working on the five or six he'd shot, pinching the loose skin of the back to slit with his knife and inserting his fingers to tear and peel it away like a too tight glove, cutting off head and tail and feet and slicing the belly open to flip out the tiny entrails.

Should he decide a hike was the order of the day there was another stand of six hundred-year-old oaks down by the brook about half a mile away. He'd disappear down there for a while.

They were clean kills nearly every time though like any other hunter he'd had to slit a throat or two. But what my father shot normally didn't suffer much. And my mother's stews were fine.

My father considered squirrels vermin, though. Pests. Even if they did make for good eating. So that it was a surprise to all of us when in the summer of 1957 when I was just turned eleven and my sisters Anne and Mary Jo were twelve and ten my father returned from the stand of oaks with five dead eastern greys in one hand and in the other, one that was very much alive, held by the scruff of the neck and trying hard against all hope to bite him.

"Must've fallen out of a tree," he said. "And fallen long and hard. See? Front paw's broken. Danny, you get on into the kitchen and ask your mother for some string and good thick twine. Girls, get a couple of those popsicles you been suckin' on all summer long out of the freezer. Eat 'em fast or run 'em under the water, I don't care which."

He lay the five dead greys out on the porch and we did as we were told. My mother came out to join us and take hold of the squirrel by the scruff of the neck and the base of the tail while we watched my father cut and loop the twine around his jaws and snout in an expert bowline knot so he could bite no longer and once that was done had her turn him over on his side. He used his hunting knife on the popsicle sticks stained pink and orange and cut a length of string. The squirrel chattered and scrabbled at the wood but could gain no purchase.

"Hold him tight now, Marge. This will hurt."

But seeing those two big gloved hands coming toward him must have frightened the squirrel to such degree that he stopped resisting entirely and simply rolled his eyes. Even when my father took his delicate paw and forearm and gave them a sharp jerk apart he just jumped once and then lay still and panting. My father splinted the leg with the popsicle sticks and wrapped it tight with string.

"Take that twine and make me another bowline, Danny. We'll collar him and tie him off to this post here and see what happens. If he doesn't go into shock on us he might be fine in a week or so."

"Shock?"

"From pain. Or what we just did to him. Either one could kill him."

And once we had him sitting up dazed and baffled and leashed to the support stud with his makeshift muzzle removed my father did an astonishing thing. *He took a glove off and ran his hand across the squirrel's back.* Just once. *Bradford Collier* did that. A man who never had use for animals in his life unless they were working animals, a cat who was a good mouser or a guard-dog maybe, and who considered the greys nothing more than fat rats with furry tails. Who happened to taste good and were cheap at twice the price.

"Husk some walnuts, kids. Put 'em nearby and then leave him alone awhile. That's one scared animal."

In time my father actually allowed us to name him. It took some spirited wrangling between the three of us but we did. We named him Charlie after Steinbeck's *Travels With Charlie.* My older sister Anne's idea. I thought it was dumb to name a squirrel after a dog but Mary Jo sided with her and that was that.

Charlie took to the easy life right away. A bowl of water on the porch in front of him and all the acorns and walnuts he could eat. He never again tried to bite. In a couple of weeks my father determined he'd healed and removed the splint and though he ever after favored the leg he got around well enough and was quick enough so that once we let him off his leash you had to be careful opening the screen door or the next thing you knew he'd be inside, barking and chattering at the furniture and climbing it too.

There was nothing he couldn't get into. No cabinet or drawer was safe. But he never made much mess except somehow to *displace* things. A fork in my father's socks-drawer, my old cat's-eye marbles mixed in with the spoons. So after awhile we tolerated him inside and got used to his invasions. My mother bought mason jars to protect the beans, rice and macaroni. My father, who was as good with woodworking as he was with the wrench down at his garage, even went so far as to cut him a small hinged trap at the base of the door to the porch so Charlie could come and go as he pleased.

He never once went back to the stand of oaks across the field. Not that we knew of. In fact we observed that he wasn't much for trees in general anymore. He seemed to prefer to stay in or around the house, under the porch or in the tall field grass and the low scrub beyond. Maybe it was remembering that fall, that height, that sudden break. He'd climb the bookshelves or the bedposts or the banister up to our rooms handily enough—my mother was forever polishing the tiny scratch-marks he left behind with wood-stain. She didn't seem to mind. She said Charlie was just antiquing her furniture. But the trees he mostly left alone.

He climbed us too.

He seemed to know not to go for a bare leg or arm but if you were wearing pants or jeans or especially a jacket—he liked to rummage through deep open pockets—he'd be up and over you and riding your shoulder in a matter of seconds. You could walk around with him that way and he'd just hold on perfectly balanced like some strange furry added appendage.

Only my father wouldn't tolerate it. Like the rest of us he'd feed Charlie a walnut now and then but *that* far he refused to go. He was almost as fast with his hands as Charlie was on his feet and would pluck him off like an annoying bug and drop him soundly to the floor. Charlie was persistent, though. It was almost as though my father were the one he *really wanted* to climb and the rest of us were just amusement. Walking monkey-bars. Finally it got through to him that he just wasn't wanted but I'd still catch him watching my father sometimes, that nervous sidelong glance, chittering, nose twitching, and was never quite sure that someday, sometime, damned if he wasn't going to try again.

My father still continued to hunt. Twice a month, maybe. Across the field or down by the shady brook.

And I sometimes wondered what Charlie thought if he thought anything at all of the scent of squirrel-meat steaming in our stewpot. I look back on it now and how we could actually eat the stuff with him running around underfoot is something I'll never understand. But we did.

As I say, we're not one thing, we're many. We're capable of all kinds of balancing acts in our heads. Until something or someone tips the balance.

The way my wife beside me's tipping it now.

That winter was a cold one in northern Jersey and the snow fell thick into five-and-six-foot drifts against the house and mostly Charlie stayed indoors. He liked the mantle over the fireplace which I always thought unnatural since wild animals are supposed to be afraid of fire or even the scent of fire but for Charlie the hotter the fire in the grate the better. He'd fall asleep up there basking in the updrafts.

Come spring and he was using the trapdoor again and using it a lot, his comings and goings according to some design unknowable to us but clearly urgent to him. He'd either be flying through the trap constantly back and forth or else he'd disappear for hours at a time. We suspected sex of course, though only Anne and Mary Jo and I would talk about it and only in private. Parents weren't comfortable talking with kids about sex back then.

"I wonder how squirrels do it," said Mary Jo.

"With their penises, silly," said Anne. "Just like everybody else."

"Charlie's gettin' some!" I laughed. They ignored me.

"Anybody ever see Charlie's penis?" asked Mary Jo.

"Not me."

"Ugh," said Anne. "Spare me!"

I rarely went along with my father on his Sunday excursions down to the brook and never once in memory shot from the porch at all. At an age when most boys would shoot at most anything that moved with rifle, bow or slingshot I had no taste for bloodspots.

One afternoon in May he asked as he often did though and this time I accepted. I think I was angry with Anne for some reason and felt the need to get out of the house that day. Anne could be bossy or else she and Mary Jo would side together against me in an argument and that could make me furious. Whatever the reason, I went.

My father and I never talked much and didn't that day either. I followed him through the tall field grass into the woods and found his well-beaten trail down to the brook, both our .22s held at port arms. I had no intention of using mine. It was there because my father wanted it to be. I was a miserable shot and my father knew it but it was a formal thing with him. You didn't go hunting unarmed. It simply wasn't done.

His habit was to walk first to the brook and then approach the stand of oaks from there, the fast-running water masking whatever sounds we might make along the dirt embankment. It had rained the day before, the brook swollen with water the color of coffee with a dash of cream. I could never have found the exact spot to cut up to the trees from there amid the tangled foliage had I been alone but my father had no problem and I saw that he'd worn a path of sorts there too barely noticeable amid the scrub. I could see the six tall trees about forty yards away up a gentle slope.

We walked twenty of those yards and stopped at the edge of the clearing and knelt each of us on one knee and my father started firing, small sharp cracks in that wide open space that could have been branches breaking and the first squirrel slammed against the tree-trunk twenty feet up as though a hand had pushed it and then fell and my father worked the bolt and chambered another round and fired as another raced across the high branches of the same tree and tumbled bouncing from limb to limb. By then squirrels were racing barking across the ground and pouring down off the trees but my father took his time and squeezed off two more rounds. I saw one big grey somersault across the ground and another skitter and roll just as it reached the bushes. He missed with the fifth round but the sixth caught another where the bole met the root system of a second tree and flipped it on its back, the .22 round going through the squirrel entirely and chipping at the green wood behind him.

"Five's enough," my father said.

It had taken just moments.

We stood and he took the canvas sack off his belt and we went to harvest them.

"Good shooting."

"Thanks."

"Five out of six and they were really *moving!*"

"They were, weren't they."

I wasn't nearly as excited as I was trying to sound but something told me my father expected it. The greys were still barking angrily at us yards away in the safety of heavy scrub. My father moved slowly and methodically, prodding them with a stick to make sure they were fully dead and wouldn't bite and then picking them up by the scruff of the neck with one gloved hand and shoving them into the sack.

"Uh-oh. Damn."

"What?"

We had four of them in the sack and were walking toward the scrub. My father suddenly picked up his pace considerably, the closest I ever saw him come to running.

"The one I shot at the edge here. I think he's gone."

We got to where the grey ought to have been and wasn't. "Maybe you missed him."

"I didn't miss him. Look here."

He was looking at a cluster of ferns. I could see blood speckling the leaves, glistening in the sun. Behind them the scrub was all thick briers. The day was hot. Neither of us was wearing much. A short sleeve shirt for my father, a tee shirt for me.

"We've got to find him. You can't leave an animal like that. Come on. He couldn't have gotten far."

We plunged carefully into the scrub, my father plucking the stems away and holding them back for me with his gloved fingers while I did my best to keep them at a distance with the barrel and stock of my rifle.

The briers were thickest down low so we couldn't try to follow a blood trail. We'd have cut ourselves to shreds trying. We might have had more luck splitting up but he knew I needed him to hold back the briers for me. We searched for well over an hour. By the time my father gave it up my skin felt like it was crawling with small biting insects and my arms and face were streaked with sweat and blood. I washed them in the brook and we headed home.

My mother and sisters had gone to town shopping so the car was gone and the yard was empty. We crossed the field of waving grass in silence. I remember glancing at my father and that his face was grim. He hated losing that squirrel.

I don't know how it was that I should be the one who saw it first because only a year or so later I'd be wearing glasses and my father's vision was 20-20 and we were walking side by side. We were about eight feet from the porch. I remember thinking he *should* have been the one and not me. I don't know why I felt that way but I still do. That somehow it wasn't right.

I think I came close to falling then. I know I staggered, that it felt like somebody had pushed me suddenly hard in the chest and that was what had forced the gasp out of me like a silent call for help, my body calling for help where there was none.

"What?" my father said and then looked where I was looking at the blood-trail leading up the three porch steps to the landing, smeared across the landing as with a single long stroke of a half-dry paint-brush all the way to Charlie's trap door, a direct and determined line to that door he'd painted with the very life of him.

I knew what we'd find in there, that it was impossible for him to have come this far bleeding this much and still be alive and when my father flung open the door and we saw him on the rug, lying on his side and shot in the very same shattered shoulder that once had housed a broken leg, I saw that I was right, though we'd missed him by a matter of minutes only. His body was still warm. I touched him and looked into his glazed open eyes and tried hard not to cry. We knelt there.

"He came home looking for us," my father said quietly.

I don't know why I said what I did. It wasn't anger or accusation and it wasn't just sadness either but it came out of me like a fleeing bird and it was true.

"He came home looking for you, dad." I said. "Not us. You."

I'll never forget the look on my father's face that day.

I remember it better than the look on any face I've ever seen before or since except maybe this one here on the pillow in front of me, sleeping now but only hours ago curled in on itself and nearly unrecognizable in anger and hurt which is the face I'll remember when she leaves tomorrow, not this familiar face but that one. She told me early on even before we were married that the one thing she couldn't handle was if I were unfaithful because that's what her father was and that was what I was and what I was again and since she knows it now she will leave. She's as good as her word.

My father never hunted again. The rifle went into the basement to rust away.

Something in him changed after Charlie. He went out with my mother more on Sundays for one thing. We were old enough to fend for ourselves by then. And then later he began to drink more. And later still, once we were in college, stopped drinking. And when he was old and sick became a bitter man.

We're many things, all of us, blown by so many unexpected winds. And I have to wonder, who am I now and what will I be tomorrow?

What have I done?

And what will I do with my own Sundays once she's gone?

—*For Anush and Misty*

THE OLD DUDE'S TICKER
Richard Sardinha

The Old Dude's Ticker

BY STEPHEN KING

In the two years after I was married (1971 -1972), I sold nearly a dozen stories to various men's magazines. Most were purchased by Nye Willden, the fiction editor at Cavalier. Those stories were important supplements to the meager income I was earning in my two day jobs, one as a high school English teacher and the other as an employee of The New Franklin Laundry, where I washed motel sheets. Those were not good times for short horror fiction (there have really been no good times for genre fiction in America since the pulps died), but I sold an almost uninterrupted run of mine—no mean feat for an unknown, unagented scribbler from Maine, and at least I had the sense to be grateful.

Two of them, however, did not sell. Both were pastiches. The first was a modern-day revision of Nikolai Gogol's story, "The Ring" (my version was called "The Spear," I think). That one is lost. The second was the one that follows, a crazed revisionist telling of Poe's "The Tell-Tale Heart." I thought the idea was a natural: crazed Vietnam vet kills elderly benefactor as a result of post-traumatic stress syndrome. I'm not sure what Nye's problem with it might have been; I loved it, but he shot it back at me with a terse "not for us" note. I gave it a final sad look, then put it in a desk drawer and went on to something else. It stayed in said drawer until rescued by Marsha DeFilippo, who found it in a pile of old manuscripts consigned to a collection of my stuff in the Raymond Fogler Library at the University of Maine.

I was tempted to tinker with it—the seventies slang is pretty out of date—but resisted the impulse, deciding to let it be what it was then: partly satire and partly affectionate homage. This is its first publication, and no better place than Necon, which has been the best horror convention since its inception, folksy, laid-back, and an all-around good time. If you have half as much fun reading it as I had writing it, we'll both be well off, I think. I hope some of Poe's feverish intensity comes through here . . . and I hope the master isn't rolling in his grave too much.

—Steve King

YEAH, SPOOKED, I'M PRETTY FUCKIN' SPOOKED. I BEEN THAT WAY EVER SINCE I came back from Nam. You dig it? But I'm no section eight. What happened over there, it didn't screw up my head. I came back from Nam with my head on straight for the first time in my life. Dig it. My ears are like radar. I've always had good hearing, but since Nam... I hear everything. I hear the angels in heaven. I hear the devils in the deepest pits of hell. So how can you say I'm some kind of fuckin' psycho case? Listen, I'll tell you the whole story. Think I'm crazy? Just listen to how cooled out I am.

I can't tell you how I got the idea, but once it was there, I couldn't shoot it down. I thought about it day and night. There was really nothing to pin it on. I had no case against the old dude. I dug him. He never short-dicked me or ranked me out. Yeah, he had bucks, but I'm not into that. Not since Nam. I think it might have been his... yeah, his eye. Jesus, like a vulture's eye. Pale blue, with a cataract on it. And it bulged. You dig what I'm saying? When he looked at me, my blood ran cold. That's how bad it freaked me. So little by little, I made up my mind to waste him and get rid of the eye forever.

Okay, now dig this. You think I'm nuts, okay? And crazy people don't know anything. Run around with drool slobbering out of their mouths, stabbing wetbacks like that guy Corona, stuff like that. But you should have dug me. You should have seen how cool I was. I was always one step ahead, man. I had that old dude jacked up nine miles. I was super-kind to him the whole week before I killed him. And every night, about midnight, I turned the knob of his door and opened it. Quiet? You better believe it! And when it was just wide enough for me to stick my head in, I put in this penlite with the glass all taped up except for one little place in the middle. You follow? Then I poked my head in. You would have cracked up to see how careful I was, poking my head in. I moved it real slow, so I wouldn't roust the old dude. It took me an hour, I guess, to get my head in far enough so I could see him laying there on his rack. So tell me... you think any section eight would have been able to carry that off? Huh? But dig this! When my head was in the room, I turned on the penlite. It put out one single ray, and I put it four-oh on that vulture eye. I did that seven nights in a row, man, seven nights! Can you dig that action? I did it every night at midnight, but the eye was always closed and I couldn't get it on. Because it was the eye. And every morning I went right into his bedroom and clapped him on the back and asked him how he slept. All that good bullshit. So I guess you see he would have to have been some heavy dude to guess that every night I was checkin' him out while he was asleep. So dig it.

The eighth night I was even more cooled out. The minute hand on my watch was trucking along faster than mine was. And I felt... sharp.

You know? Ready. Like in Nam, when it was our turn for night patrol. I was like a cat. I felt ace-high. There I was, opening the door, little by little, and he's laying there, probably dreaming he's balling his granddaughter. I mean, he didn't even know! Funny? Shit, sometimes I laugh until I scream, just thinking of it. I started to laugh at the idea. Maybe he heard me, because he started to move around. Probably think I split out of there, right? No way. His room was black as a cat's asshole—he always drew the shutters because he was afraid of junkies—and I knew he couldn't see through the door, so I kept pushing it open, a little at a time.

I had my head in and I was getting ready to turn on the old penlite when it knocked against the side of the door. The old guy sits up in bed, yelling, "Who's there?"

I stayed still and kept my mouth shut. You dig it? For a whole hour I didn't move. But I didn't hear him lie down, either. He was sitting up in bed, scared shitless, just listening. The way I used to get sometimes in Nam. A lot of guys used to get that way, thinking those guys in the black pajamas were coming, creeping through the jungle, through the dark.

I heard him groan, just a little one, but I knew how scared he was.

It wasn't the way you groan when you just hurt yourself, or the way old folks sometimes groan at funerals. Uh-uh. It was the sound you make when your head is totally fucked up and you're starting to blow your circuits. I knew that sound. In Nam, at night, I used to get that way sometimes. Nothing wrong with that, a lot of guys did. Nothing section eight about it. It would come up from your guts like acid, getting worse in your throat, scaring you so bad that you had to put your hand in your mouth and chew it like a chicken drumstick to keep from screaming. Yeah, I knew the sound. I knew how that old dude was feeling and I felt sorry for him, but I was laughing, too, inside. I knew he'd been awake since the first sound. He'd been getting more and more scared. He was trying to, you know, blow them down, but he couldn't do it. He was saying to himself, "It was the wind around the eaves. Or maybe a mouse. Or a cricket. Yeah, it was a cricket." You dig? He was trying to cool himself out with all kinds of shit. But no good. Because Death was in the room with him. Me! Death was sniffing right up his old man's nightdress. Me! He was feeling that. He didn't see me or hear me, but he dug me.

After I marked time for a long while without hearing him flop back down, I decided to give him the light. So I turned it on and that single ray shot out from the masking tape and landed square on that fucking eye.

It was wide open and I got more and more pissed off, just looking at it. I saw every detail of it. This dull dusty blue with that gross-out white stuff over it so it looked like the bulging yolk of a poached egg. It froze me out, man, I kid you not. But, see, I couldn't see anything else of his face or body. Because I held the light straight on that goddamned eye.

And didn't I tell you that what you call crazy is just how together I am? Didn't I tell you how sharp my hearing has been since Nam? And what came to my ears was this low, quick noise. You know what that sound was like? Have you ever seen a squad of MPs on a parade ground? They all wear white gloves, and they all carry these little short sticks on their belts. And if one of them takes his stick out and starts tapping it into his palm, it makes a sound like that. I remember that from Nam, and from Fort Benning where I trained, and from that hospital where they put me after I came home. Sure, they had MPs there. White gloves. Short sticks. Slapping those short sticks into those white palms... white, like the cataract on the old dude's eye. I knew what that sound was, there in the dark. It wasn't any GI head-bopper. It was the old dude's ticker. It made me even madder, the way beating a drum will make a GI feel ballsier.

But I still kept cool. I hardly breathed. I held the flashlight still. I tried to see how steady I could hold that one thread of light on the eye. His heart was beating even faster. I could hear it, are you digging me? Sure I could. Quicker and quicker, louder and louder, it got so it sounded like a whole regiment of MPs beating their sticks into their palms. The old dude must have been scared green! It got louder, you dig what I'm saying? Louder every second! You follow me? I told you I'm spooked, and I am. And in the middle of the night, in the creepy quiet of that big old house, that sound really got to me. But I still held off. It got louder… louder! I thought his ticker would bust wide open. And then I thought, "Hey, dig it, the neighbors are going to hear it. They got to. I got to shut him the fuck up!" I let out a yell and threw the flashlight at him and went across the room like O.J. Simpson. He screamed once, but that was all. I dragged him onto the floor and yanked the bed over on top of him. Dig what I'm saying. I started to grin at how good it was going. I could still hear his heart, but that didn't get on my case, not at all. No one was going to hear it, not with that bed on top of him. Finally it quit. I pushed the bed off and looked at the body. Yeah, he was dead. Stone dead. I put my hand on his ticker and held it there for five, ten minutes. Nothing. His eye wasn't going to bother me anymore.

If you still think I'm a section eight, dig on how cool I was getting rid of his body. The night was getting on, and I worked fast, but I kept it quiet. Quiet was the password. You got it? Quiet. I cut him up. I cut off his head and arms and legs.

I pried up three of the planks on the bedroom floor and stuffed the pieces of him down inside. I put the boards back so carefully that no eye in the world—not even his—could have spotted anything wrong. There was nothing to wash out, not a single bloodstain. I was too cool for that. I cut him up in the shower, you dig it? Ha! You dig that scene? Ha! Ha! Far fucking out, am I right?

By then it was four in the morning, still dark as midnight. The doorbell rang. I went down to open it, and I was feeling good. Why not? It was the fuzz. Three of them. They were cool. One of the neighbors had heard a yell.

Sounded like someone had been cut or something. The guy called the cops. They had no search warrant, but would I mind if they took a look around?

I grinned. I had no worries, right? I told them to come on in. The scream was from me, I said. Bad dream. Had a lot of them. War veteran, and blah-blah-blah. You're digging it, I see you are. I said the old dude had gone up to his country house for awhile. I took them all over the house. Told them to look anyplace they wanted. No sweat. After a little while I took them into his bedroom. I opened his desk, showed them that the cash he kept in the lockbox was still there. Also his watch, and the cat's eye ruby pinky ring he wore sometimes. Nothing touched, nothing even out of place. I dragged in some chairs and told them to sit down and rest their feet. Me, I was really flying. I was ace-high. Dig this. I put my own chair right over the spot where the old dude had gone to pieces, you might say. Ha! Ha!

The piggies were satisfied. They were getting my good vibes, I think. They sat and we shot the shit, where was I stationed in Nam, oh is that so, we were there, how many years were you in, man, what a bitch, you know the scene. I was everything a good Boy Scout is supposed to be, brave, reverent, cheerful. But before too long I started to crash out and wished they'd split. My head was starting to ache, my ears ringing. The way I was when they shipped me back stateside, back to that hospital. Combat fatigue, they said. Fuck that bullshit! And they just sat there, the cops, I mean, shooting the shit, Dong Ha, Saigon, Da Nang, all that creepy crap. The ringing in my ears got sharper. Even sharper. I talked more and more to get rid of it, but it was getting more and more together, more and more like... like it wasn't in my ears at all.

I could feel myself getting pale. But I talked even faster, and louder, too. Yet the sound got louder. It was this low, quick sound... like a bunch of MPs slapping their night-sticks into their white-gloved palms. I was having trouble catching my breath, but the cops didn't seem to notice. I talked more quickly, but the sound got worse. A whole battalion of MPs now...whap! whap! whap! Jesus! I started arguing about all kinds of small shit with them, which hill was where, who commanded what, I don't know. The noise still got worse. Why didn't they just get the fuck out? I started pacing the floor, stamping up and down, as if something one of the cops said had pissed me off—but the noise got worse. Oh, Christ! What could I do? I raved. I swore at them. I told them their mothers were whores, that their uncles were also their fathers. I started whirling the chair I was sitting on, grinding it on the boards, but I could still hear it in spite of all the noise I was making. A meaty, pulsing sound, like nightsticks whacking into palms covered with white duck cotton gloves. It got louder— louder—louder! And the cops just kept on smiling, shooting the shit. You think maybe they didn't hear it? God! No, no way! They heard it!—they suspected!—they knew!—they were putting me on!—I thought that then and I think it now. Nothing could be worse than the way they were smiling at me! I couldn't take it! If I didn't scream I'd die!—and I could still hear it, MPs, like the ones stationed at the hospital, the hospital where they took me after I scragged the lieutenant, the place I crashed out of—MPs—millions of them—short sticks— whacking—whacking—louder—louder—white cotton gloves—that dull quick meaty sound—louder—

"Stop it!" I screamed at them. "Stop it! I admit it!—I did it!—rip up the boards!— here, here!—its his heart! It's the beating of his hideous heart!"

Statement taken August 14, 1976. Investigation has confirmed that the suspect, going under the name of Richard Drogan, is in fact Robert S. Deisenhoff, who escaped from the Quigly (Ohio) Veterans Hospital on April 9, 1971.

Freddy And Rita

BY G. WAYNE MILLER

THE MISSILES FALL AT NOON ON A PERFECT AUGUST DAY. NEW YORK, WASHINGTON, Houston, Los Angeles—all gone, instantly. Springfield, Massachusetts, a small city west of Boston, has the misfortune to be spared. The nearest hit is the attack-submarine base at New London, Conn., 50 miles south. Before they sign off, the emergency people on the radio and TV say it will be eight hours before the cloud reaches Springfield. Plenty of time, they predict, to evacuate north to Vermont where only one weapon, an errant one that failed to detonate, has dropped into a pasture.

It is six-twenty p.m.

Freddy is hungry. Freddy has a weight problem and he's almost always hungry. He strolls Merchants Mall rifling through the trash barrels, as is his wont, for something good to eat. Usually, he is rewarded—half a hot dog, a Chicken McNugget, the soggy bottom of a Baskin-Robbins ice cream cone, his favorite treat—but today the pickings are slim. He moves down the mall, working the barrels, humming a tune whose words he's never learned. In Angelo's Department store, the window-display TVs are still on, but only silver static fills the screens. On the street corners, the traffic lights continue through their cycles: red to green to yellow and back to red. Smoke curls from a small fire in the alley behind Burger King. It is quiet.

Freddy is alone.

Six or seven hours ago (or was it more? time is such an elusive concept), the mall was mobbed. When the announcement came, there was a moment of silence. You could see something new, something terrible, in the faces of the shoppers and bankers and secretaries on their lunchtime strolls. Like someone had died or the president had been shot. It didn't last, that strange silence. Soon there was screaming, and people running, and cars racing, and horns blaring, and then there was a traffic jam that didn't unclog. When most everyone had gone, the looters moved in. Freddy found shelter in a doorway and watched. It was kind of funny, what they went after. Not the TVs or jewelry or even the money in the banks, as near as he could tell. Things like flashlights and transistor radios and cans of soda. Freddy even saw one guy with a bag of canned hams come tearing out of the deli. Freddy went to get one for himself, but by the time he got there, they were all gone, along with all the cheeses and bologna and chicken roll.

Today is Freddy's 42nd birthday.

This morning, with Mother's help, he dressed in his madras shorts and that green shirt with the alligator over the pocket that she gave him last Christmas. He put on white knee socks and sneakers and, lastly, his Red Sox cap. He's never been to Fenway Park, but you don't have to, to get one of those caps. You can buy them right inside the sports department at Angelo's, and Freddy did, his last birthday, right after Mother's check came in. When he gets home tonight, she's going to have a special meal for him. Hot dogs, and potato salad, and chocolate ice cream with fudge sauce and whipped cream from a can for dessert.

He continues up the mall. Now and again, he looks at the sky.

It is still cloudless. He doesn't know what the cloud they say's coming will look like: a normal fluffy white cloud, or maybe a dark cloud, like before the thunderstorm or the hurricane that September weekend a few years back. He doesn't know what will drop out of the cloud, if anything at all.

Freddy finds Rita at the fountain.

The colored water isn't squirting out today, but there's plenty left in the pool, and she's sitting next to it, her head cocked toward the sky, her sunglasses on. Cool. It's like she's getting a tan, except her skin is already shiny and dark and delicious, like a freshly unwrapped Hershey bar. Freddy's seen Rita a hundred times before. She's a prostitute, and the skirts she wears are always very short and bright, her blouses very tight. She's always looking at men, always walking like she's itchy or something. And she never wears a bra. If the sun's shining the right way, you can sometimes see her nipples, even darker and thicker than Hershey Bars. Freddy fights with himself to turn away at times like that, but he's not always successful.

Rita hears him coming. She's surprised to see anyone, what with the panic that spread through the city starting with the first TV reports. Her own crowd piled into Dino's Cadillac hours ago. When they got nailed in that crazy traffic jam that's still there except no one's in the cars and busses anymore, Dino started firing his pearl handled pistol into the air. When that didn't get them anywhere, they abandoned the car, just put it in park and left the engine running, and went running off on foot like everybody else. Before she got buzzed, Rita wondered just how long it would take them to get to Vermont, anyway. She's never been to Vermont. Never had any reason to. Never had the slightest desire.

"What you still doing here?" she says to Freddy. It almost sounds like she's glad to see him, but he can't be sure. She's never been glad to see him before, and she sees him almost every day. Like the rest of her friends, especially Dino, the bald guy who drives the white car with the dark windows, she calls him Tard-O and tells him to get the fuck out of here. But she doesn't call him that today. Doesn't tell him to get the fuck out of here.

"So what you still doing here?" she repeats.

"Walking," he says, stopping, but not daring to sit next to her or anything. Her skirt is way up on her thighs and he can't help but get a glimpse of white cotton near where her legs disappear into a V. "They say the world's going to end. Do you believe it?"

Freddy shrugs his shoulders.

"They say we gotta go to Vermont. I hate Vermont. Too much cowshit. How 'bout you?"

Freddy shrugs his shoulders again.

"Shit, ain't no escaping something like that cloud. Not if you go to the moon. That's where I'm at with the cloud. May's well fry here at home as up there with that cowshit."

Freddy is silent.

"What's the matter, cat got your tongue?"

"Birthday," Freddy finally says, adjusting his cap, his voice all nervous and his mouth dry. An ice cream cone would take that dryness away, he figures. An ice cream cone would be very nice right about now.

"What?"

"Birthday."

"Today?"

He nods.

"Shit. Sure picked a hell of a day to celebrate your birthday," she says. "How old are you?"

"Forty-three." He holds up his hands, four fingers extended on the left one, three on the right.

"You be putting me on!"

"Nope."

"You look 20."

"Forty-three."

"Shit! I be goddamned!"

There's a silence and Freddy's even more nervous than at first. Mother's always told him to stay away from women like Rita, no good ever came from hanging around them, but there's something exciting about being so close to her. Something getting him all worked up. He can feel it inside him, almost like a crackling you can hear. He's never been this close to a woman like her. Never been alone with one.

Rita reaches into her purse and withdraws a Bic lighter and a cigarette. It isn't a regular cigarette. It's wrinkled and funny shaped. Freddy knows what it is. Mother's warned him about them. It's a marijuana cigarette. A joint. He looks behind him nervously, thinking the police will come running. But there is no one there. Just Freddy and Rita and a cloudless sky.

"Want some?" she says.

"Uh-uh."

"What's your name, anyway?" she says, lighting the joint and inhaling.

Not Tard-O, he thinks. "Freddy," he says.

"You know what I am, Freddy?" she says, blowing the smoke out. It envelops his face.

Freddy coughs. Then he nods yes.

"A prostitute. A *hooker*. You give me money, I give you me. Any part of me you want. *All* the parts, you got the money. That's America," she says, giggling a marijuana giggle. "Supply and demand."

He nods.

"You ever have it, Freddy? With a woman?" He averts his eyes.

"Well?"

"No," he mutters.

"Shit. I didn't think so. Ever have it with an animal?" She laughs. "German shepherd or a sheep?"

"No. "

"You want sex with me, Freddy? For free. For your birthday. To celebrate the end of the world!"

He's light-headed now. Thinking he ought to leave, and wanting desperately to stay. If Mother ever saw him… But Mother couldn't possibly see him, not today or any other day. She can't get that wheel chair out of their apartment, never mind all the way down here to the mall.

"Come on, Freddy," she says. She gets up and walks over to him. She drops to her knees and starts rubbing him down there. She doesn't bother to take her sunglasses off. It feels good, what she's doing, better even than when he touches himself down there in the dark in the middle of the night when Mother's asleep. She starts to unzip his fly. Because she's bent over, her breasts dangle almost out of her blouse. They look like the ones in those dirty magazines he sometimes fishes out of the trash, big and smooth and shaped like torpedoes. He could touch them if he wanted to. He knows she wouldn't mind. He's getting hard. But only for a moment. The second she reaches inside, he goes soft. He's scared. It's not right, what she's doing. Not right, where she's doing it, wide out in the open by the fountain that isn't working today. Naughty.

He pushes her away.

"What's the matter?" she snaps. "You a fag?"

He tries to think fast. That's a terrible thing to be called, Fag, worse even than Tard-O. No one wants to be called Fag, especially when it's not true.

"Ice cream," is all he can manage.

That catches her off guard. "Huh?" she says, her enthusiasm waning.

"Hungry," he says.

"Jesus, you're weird," she says, standing. "Shit."

Enough of that. Creep's beyond her help. Freddy zips his fly back up, careful not to catch himself in the zipper like sometimes happens when he's finished going to the bathroom. He feels better now. Much better. He always feels better when he's honest and just comes out and says what's on his mind. That's what Mother says, always tell the truth, and she's right.

"*Chock-lit* ice cream," he explains.

"All right, all right," Rita says, annoyed. But not terribly.

She's got a wicked case of the munchies, too, and ice cream might really hit the spot.

"Come on," she says, gesturing for him to follow.

He does. They move down the mall, Rita in the lead. She's smoking another joint and wobbling a bit, but she's basically okay. They go past the drug store, its windows smashed.

Past the benches, empty except for the pigeons. Past a dog digging through a Dumpster. Past the body of a man who's been shot and killed, probably by one of the looters, Rita says. When they get to the body, Freddy bends down to get a closer look. He's never seen a dead body before. Never seen so much blood. It looks like it came out of the back of his head and flowed in a little river along the sidewalk to the curb and down into the street, where it finally found a gutter. "Gross," says Rita. "Really gross." Freddy's fascinated. The blood is gooey now, thickened up like molasses or the grape jelly Mother used to make a long, long time ago when they lived in the country and Daddy was alive.

A breeze is beginning to tickle the tops of the trees, but there are still no clouds.

Baskin-Robbins is on the corner of Main and Elm.

"All the ice cream you ain't never gonna eat!" Rita says, laughing hysterically. Freddy doesn't get the joke, if that's what it is. He often doesn't get the joke.

They go inside. The looters passed right by here, and the shop's just as those smiling people in their white uniforms and funny hair nets left it: clean, fluorescent-bright, the nuts and jimmies and dry cones and plastic spoons in their proper places, all the ice creams neatly arranged in cardboard tubs in the glass-covered freezers. The freezers hum. With all the people gone, and it is so spooky quiet, you can actually hear them. Somehow, power is still getting to the city.

"Goodie!" Freddy says, his face lighting up. Mother's only given him enough money a couple of times to actually come into Baskin-Robbins, including once on another birthday way back when, and so this is a treat. A major treat. Rita doesn't seem that excited, but she's definitely hungry. She goes around to the other side of the counter and dishes herself a scoop of chocolate-chip, which she devours in about half a minute. Then she looks at Freddy. He's still standing there, staring through the glass, smiling, overwhelmed by all the flavors.

"What'll it be?" Rita says. Freddy isn't so bad, after all, she's decided. Just a harmless Tard-O. It could be worse. She could've gotten stuck with Dino when he was loaded on Angel Dust. He'd be beating her up by now.

"Well?" she insists.

"Sundae," he says.

"What kind of ice cream?"

"Chock-lit."

"That's right. All the fixin's?"

"Yep!" he beams.

Rita ties an apron around her waist, takes the largest plastic dish she can find and loads it with huge scoops of chocolate ice cream. She buries the ice cream with fudge sauce, butterscotch, strawberries, marshmallow and whipped cream. She sprinkles nuts on top, then tops it off with a red cherry.

"The works!" she says.

"Thanks."

"No charge! Everything's free today!"

She hands the sundae across the counter to Freddy, who's never seen one that big in his life. It dribbles onto his hands and onto the linoleum floor as he carries it over to a table. He doesn't worry about the mess. He knows there's more where that came from. All the ice cream in the world today.

He eats in silence as Rita reaches into her purse, takes out a Ziploc bag, pours the white stuff inside it on the Formica countertop, rolls a dollar bill, puts it inside her nose and snorts. When her ears are pleasantly ringing and the powder's gone, she moves to the cash register, opens the money drawer, and takes out the fistful of tens and twenties inside. Laughing, she sets them on fire with her Bic lighter. Tiny ashes fill the shop.

Freddy has three sundaes. Rita prepares each of them with a different ice cream base. She can't believe he can eat so much. Even a stupid fat Tard-O like him. She wants to see how many more he'll have before he tosses his cookies and she's going to move along. Maybe she'll go to Vermont, after all. Track down Dino. Maybe it wasn't such a good idea telling him to fuck off, even if he is bad news when he's flipped out. And was he ever flipped out today. Firing his pistol and screaming like that.

All of a sudden, a scowl appears on Freddy's face. Oh, God.

He's forgotten all about Mother. All about the special dinner—the hot dogs and potato salad and chocolate ice cream. He's forgotten all about the clock.

"Time?"

He knows it must be getting late because the shadows are thickening and it's getting cooler. He fingers his Red Sox cap nervously, staining it with chocolate ice cream.

"What difference does it make?" Rita says. "Shit."

"Gotta go."

Rita laughs. "Where's to go?"

"Mother."

"You be kidding."

"Mother," he repeats, more urgently. "Home."

"Why? You gonna be dead tomorrow. Next day, at the latest. We been nuked, pumpkin-pie!"

"Time?" he repeats.

"If you must know, it's eight-ten."

"No. No! NO!"

Freddy is panicked now. Even in a wheelchair, Mother can administer a mean licking. He wipes his face with paper napkins and goes to the door. Rita goes with him. They look outside, at the sunset. It is brilliant red, but down close to the horizon there is a thin band of gray. Beneath the gray, there is an even smaller band of black. Clouds, whipped along by a fresh wind.

"Why don't you come with me?" Rita says.

"Gotta go," he says. "Mother."

Rita laughs—a rising laugh that follows Freddy as he walks off, down the mall, under the thickening dark clouds.

"Shit," says Rita, reaching into her purse for her last joint.

The Lake

BY KATHRYN PTACEK

"IT WAS SO COOL, HON—I SAW SWANS FLYING OVER OUR HOUSE YESTERDAY," Maggie Stevenson said to her husband, who was busy stirring green peas into his mashed potatoes.

"Those weren't swans; they were white geese," David replied without looking up, fork halfway to his mouth,

"You don't know that!"

"I do. Why would swans be flying around here?" His tone faintly mocked.

'There's a conservancy down the road, and I've even seen swans on the lake there."

"Swans. Yeah, right." David dropped his napkin on his plate and stood up, the legs of his chair scraping across the brick floor.

The noise knifed through her. She watched as he stomped out of the kitchen and into the living room. Seconds later canned laughter blasted into the room. He had the TV turned up really high—high enough that she wouldn't be able to say anything more to him.

Gritting her teeth, Maggie gathered the dishes. As she washed up, she gazed out at a bird splashing in the birdbath in the backyard. Another typical night. A meal where they barely spoke, and if they did, he sneered at everything she said; then afterward he buried himself in a newspaper or magazine or cranked up the TV so loud they couldn't talk.

Somewhere in the last year or so their marriage had begun failing, Maggie knew now, but she'd missed all the obvious signs. He came home late from work; they never went anywhere together; he barely spoke to her with any amount of civility, much less affection.

As for lovemaking… that had ended months ago. She almost chuckled aloud with each excuse he offered when she put her arms around him and whispered she wanted some loving: "I've got a headache," "C'mon, Mag, we just ate a big meal," "I've got to get up early in the morning," "I'm not in the mood tonight."

David was never in the mood, though; not for sex, not for cuddling, not for talking, not for… anything.

It wasn't like she was unattractive. Only weighing five pounds more than when they married thirty years ago, she worked out regularly; she kept her graying hair nicely coifed and dyed; she was always ready with a laugh or a word of encouragement. She never nagged. She never did this or that, or anything she thought would somehow repulse him. And yet…

The signs had been there, but she'd been too busy with her job as a sought-after architect, too preoccupied with her own problems to see the strains. Plus it had not been a good year for her: her mother had died after a prolonged illness, her father had gone in a nursing home, a childhood friend had stopped talking to her without explanation, and she'd entered that natural state of the older woman, menopause.

Any one of these would have proved stressful enough, but combined… sometimes she'd had to focus on just forcing herself to get out of bed and get dressed in the morning. But she had persevered, and now she was through the worst of it. Or so she thought until she realized their marriage was in deep trouble.

So, if he was so unhappy with her, she wondered, why didn't he ask for a divorce? For that reason, why didn't she? She wasn't sure she wanted one. But then she wasn't sure she *didn't* want one.

She finished the dishes, wiped her hands on a towel, then opened the sliding glass doors to the patio. She stepped outside, pulling the screen door shut behind her; no sense in letting in any insects. David would be screaming about the moths or some poor late season bee buzzing around harmlessly.

She didn't understand what had happened, either. During her mother's illness, Maggie had turned to David, supportive as ever. He'd helped take her mother to the various doctors month after month, had sat with Maggie in the hospital room that final night. He had gone with her to half a dozen different nursing homes to interview the staff when it was apparent her father could no longer care for himself.

It wasn't all the strain of the past year, was it? They'd been through strains before— God knows, their friends used to joke about the ups and downs of their lives. Shortly after their wedding, David's father had died, and then not long after that his sister died, followed within two years by his mother. A few years later David had been fired from a job he'd held for years. In their tenth year together, they moved cross country, uprooting after decades in the same place. Up and down, up and down… a regular roller coaster… that was their history together, but most couples had ups and downs. That was the way marriage was—hell, that was the way *life* was.

It was a childless union, but that had been by choice. Once, early on, she'd gotten pregnant, a mistake, and panicked, not knowing what to do. Did she want the child? Did she want an abortion? Before she could even make up her mind, she'd suffered a miscarriage, and she had mourned for the child she'd lost, the child she hadn't wanted—and yet somehow did. After that, David and Maggie had been particularly careful about birth control.

Now, she was nearing sixty; birth control wasn't something she had to worry about. At least she didn't think so, she told herself dryly. But that concern had been replaced with another: the feeble state of her marriage.

A faint breeze had sprung up, and she shivered, wishing she wore a heavier top or one with longer sleeves. She rubbed her forearms. She was damned if she would go back inside right now.

Even so, for mid-September, it was a bit warmer than usual, the trees just now being touched here and there with scarlet and gold. Everything was winding down... the flowers fading, leaves slowly drifting down... It was her favorite season.

Something rustled behind Maggie, and she glanced over her shoulder. David stood there, on the other side of the screen. He wouldn't come out onto the patio, even though she'd designed it for him. Too many bugs, he said; he preferred staying within the house's sterile confines.

"What did they sound like?" he demanded.

"What?" She blinked.

"The swans." he said impatiently. "Those swans you thought you saw."

"Well, I heard this honking, and I stopped—I was bringing the groceries in—and looked up, expecting to see Canada geese—but I saw three swans overhead. They were so close, too, and honking."

"Geese then, just like I thought. Swans don't honk."

"Well, you don't know what they sound like while they're flying." She hated that slightly indignant tone creeping into her voice. She sounded so defensive. She doubly hated *that*!

"They hiss."

"I *know* that, David. I've read about swans, but they don't hiss while in flight."

He practically glowered at her, and had she not known it was David she wouldn't have recognized him. "Geese. You saw geese, not swans. Damn it, Maggie, can't you get that through your fat head? Why do you have to be so Goddamned stupid about some things? Can't you just admit you're fucking mistaken?"

She stared at him, then tears stinging her eyes, walked across the yard and out the gate. She didn't look back. She didn't want him seeing her crying. She dashed at her eyes with the heel of her hand and took a deep, ragged breath.

That was new, too—the swearing at her—something she'd noticed within the last month. David had never been a prude when it came to cursing, but he had never ever directed those words toward her. Now, he did. She was a "damned fool," "stupid bitch," "fucking idiot," and worse.

Sometimes Maggie thought she didn't know her husband any more.

It was like the man she loved for so long had been snatched away by aliens one night and replaced by an imposter. Preposterous, of course, but...

She realized then she'd walked past the convenience store on the corner and circled back. She had several bucks in her pocket to buy some day-old bread. She'd go to the lake and feed the waterfowl. Maybe she'd feel better doing that.

As she headed down the road toward the lake, she tried to figure out why her husband had changed.

David had a tumor. Something malignant pressed on his brain, making him say things he didn't mean. Except that when they were around friends, David was just as nice and affable as ever. He was unpleasant only with her. In fact, their friends had noticed; she could tell from the way they looked at him, then her.

David was going through male menopause. Could be. He was her age—58. He was ready to retire from his corporate job in a few years. He went to the doctor regularly, and surely the physician would have said something, given him something to take. Surely.

David wasn't really her David. He was someone else, a stand-in, an evil clone, an alien. She muffled a giggle at that one.

David had simply gone nuts. It did happen, could possibly happen. Some chemical imbalance occurred or something snapped inside the brain or...

Or David was having an affair.

Oh, Maggie, she told herself, that makes absolutely no se—

She stopped abruptly, puffs of dust rising up from the road, and her cheeks flushed as she realized the truth.

He arrived home late most nights. He made numerous phone calls from his corporate cell phone—calls that he had to make from another room. One day while doing laundry she'd found a handful of calling cards in his pants pocket. With calling cards there'd be no incriminating record on the monthly phone bill. He had no time for her, for the things they had done together. He had no desire—nothing—for her. One plus one equals... two having an affair.

Maggie found it hard to breathe right then. She forced herself to relax, to stay calm. She didn't want to have a heart attack here in the middle of the road. She didn't know for sure David was having an affair. She wasn't 100 per cent sure. Just ninety-eight per cent.

That had to be the explanation, and yet she couldn't completely accept it. David had never strayed throughout their long marriage.

Never.

Or at least he'd never been caught, one tiny voice inside pointed out.

At the lake now, she found a large boulder near the water and sank down onto it.

Wrong, wrong, wrong, Maggie told herself. David wasn't having an affair; he had never had affairs before. He had been completely faithful to her.

Then why had Fiona, her longtime friend, stopped talking to her?

Why did David stop mentioning Fiona?

All those so-called business meetings throughout the years... all those times when he came home late... drinks with the guys... a late night client... a phone call from overseas that he had to wait for... In the beginning he'd been careful, late only here and there. It was recently, within the last year, that he'd grown sloppy. Or perhaps he just didn't care to hide things from her any more.

Maggie put her head in her hands. Yet no tears came. She was dry, a husk, with no tears left. She told herself she must be mistaken, but she knew she was right. He was having an affair, had had others. And she was the absolute last person to know.

A splash nearby made her look up. A brown duck had landed in the water and was swimming toward her.

She remembered the loaves of bread she'd dropped on the ground when she sat down. She got up and retrieved one.

The birds must have smelled food, because suddenly she was surrounded by a handful of Canadian geese and several ducks and smaller birds, too—robins who hadn't fled south yet for the winter, several kinds of sparrows, a few talkative blue jays, and a cardinal couple. She was amazed at the variety of the birds back east; when she and David had lived out west, she hadn't seen many—sparrows, crows, hummers, a couple of others. Here she'd spotted dozens of species: flickers, red winged blackbirds, goldfinches, catbirds, juncos, mourning doves, red-tailed hawks, more. She had feeders scattered throughout the yard, making it a veritable avian smorgasbord, as well as a few hummingbird feeders at the kitchen windows for those rare appearances by the tiny birds. Every morning she made sure the birds all had clean fresh water to drink and bathe in.

Originally David had delighted in the creatures, just as much as she, but lately he'd been making wisecracks about them as well.

In fact, she thought nothing in her life was safe from his sarcasm now.

He ridiculed her job—even though she made as much money as he did and was a respected member of an old architectural firm. He made biting comments about her friends. He sneered at her hobbies, at anything she did now or said.

When had he become such a disagreeable person?

She tossed several pieces of bread toward the birds, and there was a great commotion as they eagerly snatched the morsels. She started tearing apart another slice of bread and noticed her hand trembling again. She clamped down on it with her other hand and closed her eyes, willing the tremor to go away.

That was something she had noticed during the summer—how her hands trembled ever so slightly. The shaking had grown more distinct since then. Nerves, she'd told herself, but now she wasn't so sure. She had to go to the doctor, but was afraid of what he would say. Afraid it would be Parkinson's, afraid it would be worse. She hadn't told David; now she'd be damned if she'd let him know.

She fed more birds, then watched as a pair of majestic swans glided across the lake.

"Ah, the royal couple approaches," she said aloud, nearly laughing when a cardinal backpedaled at the sound of her voice.

The trees around the lake remained mostly unchanged, although here and there red and yellow peeked out from behind green. Sunlight glinted on the surface as she watched a few dragonflies hovering nearby. She caught the scent of wood fire from somewhere. A camper or hunter perhaps.

It was so serene. She should come here more often. Maybe this was what she needed: a place to get away from it all. It didn't matter that she lived only a mile or so away. A retreat. Where she could sit and look around and think or not think, as the case may be.

A place to heal.

Something nipped at her jean-clad leg and she looked down. The brown duck, grown impatient for more bread. It hadn't broken the skin or drawn blood; in fact, it had just pulled at the material.

"You guys sure are greedy." Somewhere a mourning dove cooed in response.

She tossed more bread to her circle of feathered friends, making sure the swans got some, too.

The sun hung low on the horizon now; it would be dark within the hour. They'd eaten early today, what with both of them being home, and no doubt she should go back. But why?

It wasn't like David would miss her. In the past he would have been concerned, worried if she went away for hours without telling him. Now she didn't think he would even notice she was gone.

She felt a heaviness in her chest at that, and her hands trembled more. She tore bread apart, flinging it as far away from her as she could.

Suddenly the male swan hissed.

"I thought I'd find you here."

Her teeth clenched, and her shoulders hunched upward. David.

The bread bag still clasped in one hand, she turned around.

"Feeding your little feathered friends? Telling them your little sob story?"

The sun was at Maggie's back so she could see his expression all too well, while David had to squint to see her. He edged closer to the water, so he'd be at a different angle.

The second swan hissed.

"Well?"

"Well, what?" she asked, crumbling more bread and feeding it to the birds. Another duck grew bold and swiped a piece from her hand. She smiled and held out more.

"Oh, isn't that precious? Saint Maggie of the birdies."

"Are you trying to be funny or what?" She was nearly finished with the one loaf; time to open the second one. Overhead a raucous seagull, miles inland from the coast, wheeled in tight circles.

"I thought you'd want to talk about things. You always do. Talk and talk and talk and rehash and run things right into the ground until I'm sick of you flapping your gums. You've become a real motor mouth, you know."

The hand inside her chest squeezed, but Maggie forced herself to look into his pale eyes. "Talk about what, David? You're having an affair. You've had them before. You'll probably continue to have them until your pecker falls off inside someone's slimy hole."

He looked absolutely stunned. Good! She'd shocked him; he'd never heard such language from her. He had not expected her to confront him; no doubt he imagined she was completely ignorant of his peccadilloes. Well, she had been until this afternoon. And in truth, she was also surprised by her own language and tone.

A Canadian goose honked, and Maggie flipped a piece of bread its way. She dropped more crumbs by her foot, and the sparrows fluttered around.

David recovered quickly, as he always managed to do. "So, what do you want to do, *sweetie pie?"* He smirked at her. She'd never heard an endearment sound so obscene.

Pressing her lips together, Maggie pitched bread at her husband.

The slice landed at his feet; instantly a blue jay pounced on it.

"Watch it!" David said, stumbling back slightly. "That bird almost touched my shoes!"

"Afraid those expensive shoes might get messy? Gosh, we can't have that, can we? Those leather loafers are so much more important than your wife's silly feelings, right?"

Maggie hurled a piece of bread at David, and it bounced off his arm. Another blue jay flew up, grabbing the scrap before it hit the ground.

"Don't!"

"Oh, David, stop whining." She half-smiled to herself. She knew he'd rehearsed this in his mind on the way down here, and these were his words; she wasn't supposed to say them. "Be brave. Keep your chin up. Everything will work out." She laughed now.

"What's so funny?" he asked, scowling.

The birds gathered around David as she tossed more morsels toward him. He backed away, and she watched in amusement as he slipped in a patch of mud and suddenly his shoe was underwater.

Cursing, David leaped away from the lake. His actions startled the birds, causing them to fly away. Only the swans remained, softly hissing.

"Look what you've done now!" he said, taking his shoe off and shaking the water out. "You've ruined it!"

"No, David," Maggie said calmly, "you've ruined it. It's time you take responsibility for your actions. You've ruined your shoe. You ruined your life. You ruined mine."

"My life isn't ruined."

Maggie's smile widened. "It will be by tomorrow when I call your boss."

"And tell him what?"

"That you're screwing his wife." A wild guess, and by the way David's eyes opened she knew she'd hit the target.

"You don't have proof."

"I don't need it, *sweetie pie*. Think Bill is going to be thrilled at seeing you toddle into work tomorrow? I'm sure he's had some suspicions all along. My phone call will only solidify those fears."

"You don't want to ruin me!"

"Wanna bet?"

The birds were flying back now, looking for more handouts. Maggie fed some crumbs to a robin, then gave more to several ducks and a Canadian goose. A handful of crows squawked for a handout, while just beyond David grackles and starlings fought over a crust.

"Oh, Maggie, c'mon, honey, you know it wasn't anything serious," he said, his tone wheedling. "I promise to walk the narrow and straight from now on. Really. You can depend on me!"

She shredded more slices and flung them at David as hard as she could, her anger and frustration boiling up. The selfish bastard hadn't changed, wouldn't change, she knew, and that he was trying to con her infuriated her. He backed away. He was so upset, she noted, he didn't realize water lapped at his heels.

"You're not the woman I married," he said accusingly.

Maggie sighed. "No. I'm not. Nor are you the man I married. The man I exchanged vows with loved his wife, behaved honorably, and would never have gone sneaking around her back and lived a lie for God knows how long."

A duck plucked at David's pants leg. More startled than anything, he yelled, stumbled, falling back and down into the water. There was a cracking noise as he landed on a submerged rock, and David screamed, clutching his leg. The swans hissed as they moved closer.

Maggie spread more bread around for the gathering birds,

"Help me up, Mag. I'm stuck in the mud here, and I've hurt myself." Tears of pain ran down his face.

Maggie smiled at her husband, then opened the third loaf, ripping up the slices and throwing them toward David. A chipping sparrow with its little copper cap hopped onto the man's knee to peck at bread there. A starling swiped the bread from the sparrow, its wing grazing David's chest, and he recoiled.

"Sorry, David. I'm all out of help today."

She loomed over him now and dribbled bits and pieces of bread on him. He was trying to get up now, but it was obvious he couldn't maneuver into the right position with his hurt leg. The mud sucked at his hands and feet, keeping him mired. He swatted constantly at the birds, but they kept coming back to him to eat the bread.

Three robins and a solitary catbird perched on his knees and head now. The starlings paused at the edge of the water and gazed, unblinking at him. He slapped the robins away, and a grackle dive-bombed him. He ducked his head, just missing being pecked.

David glared at her. "C'mon, Maggie, this isn't funny any more."

"Really? When did you finally realize that, David?"

The ducks waddled closer and grabbed his pants leg, shook their heads when they didn't taste bread. One leaned forward and quacked, while a goose responded noisily.

Suddenly Maggie thought of a phrase she'd heard years ago: "nibbled by ducks." It described all the little things getting at you, bit by bit... the way she had been feeling lately. No, the wording wasn't quite right. Nibbled to... nibbled by... what was it now?

The swans skimmed closer, hissing louder now, and she thought how mysterious they looked in the light of dusk—those dark eyes and black masks. But they were so beautiful with the long graceful necks, the elegant wings. Incredibly wonderful creatures. As David fought to get out of the mud, the swans lunged and bit him.

David howled. Maggie dropped more bread on him, and watched him struggle frantically against the starlings and waterfowl, while the crows, like black arrows, aimed for his head. He struck the birds with his flailing hands, and that enraged them even more. More birds attacked.

As the birds pressed around her husband, biting and nibbling and tasting, Maggie remembered the phrase.

"Nibbled... nibbled to death by ducks," she said aloud and laughed, although she doubted David could hear her with all that screeching, coming from bird and man alike. She turned her back and walked away as the geese and crows and ducks swarmed onto David, completely engulfing him.

A few yards away she paused and watched as he fell back into the water, the ducks ripping at him, the swans biting into flesh, the goose bobbing its head in triumph over a prized tidbit. She watched until the crows and starlings and grackles, seeing no more food, flew off to find roosts for the night. The ducks and geese waddled toward a rotting log in search of insects, while the swans floated serenely away, specks of crimson dabbing their white feathers.

Still chuckling about the phrase, Maggie turned into the darkness and headed home.

The Last Performance of Kobo Daishi

BY ALAN RYAN

"READY," THE JESTER SAID.

One of the king's servants hurried down the corridor to where a small door opened into the great hall behind the place where the king sat. The jester watched, his face impassive, as the man stooped, then disappeared through the doorway. The clatter of dinner and voices rattled from the great hall. Kobo took a deep breath.

Takama, his servant, fussed around him, smoothing the yellow cloak across the old man's narrow shoulders, plucking invisible threads from the cloth, settling the hanging folds for the best effect.

The great double doors to the hall swung silently open. Takama stepped quickly out of sight. Kobo remained standing in the doorway, head bowed, hands joined before him. He waited for the king's word as a tree waits for the breeze that stirs it.

Word was whispered in the king's right ear.

He sat up straight, leaning back from the low table, and clapped his hands together sharply, louder than the clatter of cups and bowls. It was enough. The hall fell silent.

Without raising his voice, he made it ring across the open space at the center of the hall. "As so many times before," he said, "I am pleased to welcome you here. You do me honor by gracing my court."

All around the hall, the guests bowed their heads in acknowledgement. Among them were the sons of two kings of distant courts.

"And to entertain you, I am pleased to offer Kobo the Jester. It may be that his name is known to you."

The king paused and once again the guests bowed in acknowledgement.

"May it please you," the king said, using the traditional form to honor his visitors.

He clapped his hands again. Once.

Around the perimeter of the hall, behind the low tables, guests shifted, sat straighter, tucked legs more comfortably beneath them. A crinkle of straw mats rattled around the room. Servants silently backed up to the walls, sank to their knees, and sat back on their heels to watch. No one would call for more food or drink while Kobo performed. The servants counted themselves blessed; they had seen him perform more often than any of the king's guests at court all through the years. The hall was silent. All eyes swung toward the open doorway.

Kobo was a small man, not so old as his parchment skin declared, but with the tracks of accumulated memory beginning to line his face and thin his hair. He stood with arms folded now, his hands—the hands of the magician—tucked inside the full sleeves of his yellow robe. He waited while the wave of silence swept across the hall and coiled around him in the doorway. Then, eyes still lowered, as custom demanded, he walked forward to the center of the hall and turned to face the king.

Kobo the Jester. Yes, his name was familiar to the guests, even to those who had traveled farthest. Despite their properly placid expressions, their eyes shone bright with anticipation.

Kobo let his arms drop to his side and all eyes followed the movement. Then—slowly—he raised his right arm before him, closed the fingers—slowly—into a fist, extended one finger slowly—toward the king. All eyes followed the line of the arm and the pointing finger.

From the doorway, Takama rapped one note on a drum. In the same instant, a green flame shot from the tip of the jester's finger. It danced momentarily in the air an arm's length in front of him, then leapt up and hovered twice a man's height above the floor, a flickering, dancing tongue of emerald fire.

While all eyes watched the green flame, the jester raised his left arm, his left hand, and—slowly—uncurled one finger and pointed it toward the king. A red flame leapt forward, danced ruby-red, hovered, rose to join the green.

Both fingers pointed now at the king. The jester held the position for a moment, then suddenly crossed his outstretched arms in front of him. Tongues of bright yellow flame sprang forth from his fingertips. They danced about to a rhythm of their own, then rose to join the red and green.

The jester swung his arms rapidly back and forth in front of him, fingers spread apart, and the air before him was filled with dancing tongues of flame of every color: green, red, yellow, and icy blue, plum purple, pink of cherry blossoms, flickering, phantom colors as flames danced together for an instant, then flew apart, merged, blended, and danced away again. Kobo swung his arms above his head and the ball of flames swung upward in rhythm. He swept one arm down and the tongues of flame slid sideways in a dazzling arc through the air. He whirled around and the flames swooped with him, veering out in a great circle over the heads of the king and his guests.

King, guests, and servants alike stared wide-eyed, fearful to blink lest they miss a part of the miracle.

The tongues of flame swirled about like a great floating disc of jewels, radiant, brilliant, with the light of a dazzling sun shining through their gleaming facets. It floated above the jester's head while he stood still, face still immobile, arms upraised, palms flat toward the tiny gem-like flames.

He moved his fingers. SNAP.

Instantly the flame shivered, shimmered, flowed together into a flickering smooth surface of flame, colors darting among colors, rearranging themselves again and again, and at last formed into a living canopy of airborne color above his head...

SNAP.

The sheet of shifting colors flowed downward and gracefully draped itself over the yellow robe on Kobo's shoulders, hung there for a moment and...

SNAP.

...disappeared.

The jester bowed low before the king, face still solemn, then slowly turned all around the hall and finally back to the king.

The king inclined his head slightly. It was high praise.

Kobo paused, stood stock still, then slowly moved again. He raised his hands before him, palms out flat. He moved his hands sideways through the air. And where he moved his hands there was a patch of color, deep ocean blue from the right hand, rich forest green from the left. Then as if painting a wall with the flat of his hands, he extended the area of color in the air. His hands moved faster and in a few moments had constructed a wall of color. He turned, made another wall, then another, then a whole upright box of color, solid except for an area at the level of his face in the king's direction.

Inside the box he turned and looked out at the king. Then his hand appeared at the opening, moved quickly, and a rainbow of color, like bamboo slats in a window, flipped into place and sealed off the box completely. There was a moment of perfect stillness. Then one panel of the box, the one facing the king, slid aside like a door. The jester stepped out, slid the door of color closed behind him... and bowed once again to the king.

The king smiled, leaned forward. It was a terrible breach of tradition, but an unparalleled and unforgettable compliment. The jester, bowing, bowed a little lower.

Then Kobo straightened up and stepped aside, extending one hand toward the box, the other toward the king. He inclined his head in invitation. Nothing happened. He inclined his head again. Then the king understood. He leaned forward, eyes fixed on the box of color that stood in the center of the hall, then—after glancing quickly at the jester and away—clapped his hands together sharply. The box of color winked out of existence.

Kobo bowed once more, then backed from the room before the bowed heads of the court. None could see his face, for their heads were kept low in admiration and wonder. Only the eyes of two servants followed him, the king's guards, whose charge it was never to close their eyes. Finally, when Kobo had backed out of the hall and the great doors had swung on him, one of the servants lightly touched the king's elbow. Tradition observed, the king looked up instantly, his eyes darting toward the great double doors, but they were closed already and the jester was nowhere in sight.

Kobo staggered back against the carved panels of the door. He raised one trembling hand to his face. Instantly, Takama was at his side.

"Master, are you all right?" the servant asked anxiously.

"I am exhausted," the jester gasped through white lips. "Please, Takama, help me outside."

Takama fumbled to support him as Kobo leaned heavily on his shoulder. The jester was a small man but he had no strength left in his body and his whole weight was in the arm he threw clumsily across the servant's back. Slowly they made their way through the bare corridors, footsteps shuffling on stone, until they reached an outside door. The king's guards they passed on the way stepped aside respectfully but none offered to help. Their eyes and hands were for the king alone.

Takama elbowed open the last door and they were outside. The cool night air made Kobo shiver. He stopped, leaned back, steadied himself with one hand on the servant's shoulder and the other against the rough stones of the wall. He was trembling. He closed his eyes.

"Master?"

Kobo nodded weakly, "I am all right," he said. "Wait just a moment, let me catch my breath."

The servant hovered nervously about. He could hear the jester's labored breathing. Two moons shone in the night sky but their light was not enough to erase the tired lines from the old man's face or to paint a healthy color in his pale cheeks.

Finally the jester's breathing slowed, eased, and his body relaxed back against the wall. He licked his dry lips.

"All right, Takama," he said. His voice was paper thin. "Please help me home now."

He still leaned heavily on Takama's shoulder as they crossed the open court, taking care with the slippery stones, passed between the high towers of the gate, and made their slow way through the moonlit streets the short distance to his dwelling.

When Kobo awoke the next morning, Takama was sitting cross-legged on the floor beside his sleeping mat, waiting for him. "I greet the day," the jester said.

"I greet the day," the servant repeated.

The jester closed his eyes, opened them again, stretched his tired body, and sat up.

"Your fingers are burned," Takama said, his voice flat.

Kobo glanced down at his hands. White watery blisters swelled at his fingertips. "Why, so they are," he said. "How careless of me. Takama, please bring me some tea."

The servant rose and in a moment returned with a bowl of tea already prepared.

The jester took it gratefully and raised it to his lips. He held it between the palms of his hands, carefully keeping his blistered fingertips away from the hot bowl. Takama watched him.

The room glowed bright with morning sunshine. It was a pleasant room, its colors—straw and polished wood—warm and natural, its floor mat-covered, the sliding wall-panels painted by the king's finest artists with scenes of Kobo's favorite places on Edo-planet. He had spent long hours, years before, describing to them the places he had visited before coming to the court of the king. In those days he had traveled widely, welcome wherever he went, and had seen much of Edo-planet. Some said he had even traveled to other planets but, though it was widely whispered, none knew for certain; of that Kobo spoke not at all, not even to the king.

Kobo lowered the artfully lacquered cup from his lips and handed it to Takama. "Perhaps…" he said. Takama took the cup and rose to refill it.

The servant had been with the master since his first arrival at the court. He had come in supplication as an apprentice. Kobo had labored patiently with him for years—judging his spirit worthy and capable of the minor levels of the art—but never had Takama been able to learn anything of the jester's secrets. Once, it was true, he had succeeded in making an unlit candle flicker to life across the room. But never again, There was only that one guttering flame for him to remember, and even so he sometimes wondered if the jester had not himself performed the trick—for it was nothing more than that—in order to encourage him.

Kobo finished the second cup of tea in silence, then set it down on the floor beside him. He raised his hands and pressed his knuckles gently against his eyes. Then he looked to the servant.

"The king has sent a message," Takama said.

Kobo nodded. "Ah."

"He offers his usual congratulations and a gift to show his appreciation."

Kobo nodded again.

"The gift is twice the number of jewels he usually sends."

The jester nodded still again but this time his gaze flicked away from Takama.

"He also sends word that he would speak with you."

"Does he name an hour?"

"No, master. It was a brief message and the servant who brought it seemed puzzled himself."

"Well, then," Kobo said slowly, "we must await the king's pleasure. There are more important matters for a king's attention than business with a mere jester."

* * *

Kobo spent the day as he spent most days, instructing his three pupils in the art of calligraphy. When he was done with the third and the pupil had bowed himself out of the master's studio, Kobo arose from his knees and walked to the quiet garden in the back. The garden, like the house and the painted wall-panels that enriched it, had been a gift of the king. An artist like Kobo, the king had said, must have a place suitable for the meditations of a great spirit. Indeed, the garden was modeled on that of the king himself, but few knew that for few had ever seen the king's garden. Such privileges were reserved for those to whom the king wished to show special favor. It was many years now since Kobo had first been invited there.

The garden was not large but was subtly designed to suggest a feeling of openness. Here in this corner to the right was an arrangement of irregular rocks set in a smoothly raked bed of gravel. There to the left was a tiny pond laced with mosses. At the far end was an artful slope of rocks and plants down which cascaded a fall of crystal water. And beside the pool into which the water flowed grew the one thing that, beyond all others, made Kobo's garden unique. At the top of a tall, sturdy green stem, a large, flat disc of a flower trembled in the afternoon air. And around and around the silky surface of the disc swirled red and purple pinwheel circles. The colors spoke with a loud voice in the hush of the garden.

Word of the flower had long ago reached outside Kobo's house, carried by the king's workmen who had constructed the garden. Horrifying bad taste, some said when they heard. Sacrilege, other murmured. Still others put it down to the whimsical and unpredictable ways of all artists everywhere. Others smiled, said nothing, and understood. As for Kobo himself, the flower pleased him. True, he had contemplated many days, while work on the garden progressed, before settling on this flower. Then it had been some while before a lush and perfect specimen could be found. It was one of the rarer varieties, seldom seen in this part of Edo-planet, and all the more shocking because of that. But Kobo liked it. It helped his meditation. A garden like this—fit, obviously, for a king's meditations—must also be suited to the individual. In that way, a closer approach might be made to a perfect contemplation of one's own heart and its nearness to the impenetrable harmony of the world. The flower's brightness, its swirling colors, echoed the brightness of the jester's art amid the quiet contemplation of his life. It suited him. The garden, with its single passionate flower, was in harmony with his life.

Kobo seated himself on a stone bench beside the flowing water and the dazzling flower. He was tired. Sharp pain shot through his knees and his back arched from bending forward all day on the floor, endlessly repeating the brush-strokes his pupils must learn to imitate. First they must imitate, repeating the strokes exactly, before they could hope to go on and add the strength of their own characters to the ancient patterns. Normally this pleased and satisfied Kobo; he was honored to pass on the traditional art. But today he was exhausted.

I am growing old, he thought. He turned his hands palm up and studied the blisters on his fingertips.

The performance last night had left him drained and weak. It had gone, indeed, exactly as planned, all the effects falling into place as intended. And the cloak of flames was a great success; he had seen, from behind his own unmoving gaze, how its triumph shone in the eyes of the court. But it was also a subterfuge and he wondered if any had realized that. A hovering blanket of flickering color was a lovely thing to behold, but it had also been meant to distract the audience from the relative simplicity of the rest of the performance. The box of color was itself an old device, done this time with a new variation, the sliding door. It was good variation, Kobo knew, one with logic, a light-hearted sense of order, a tasteful symmetry. It was surprising but inevitable and therefore pleasing. But it was, in essence, a refinement—one of questionable value—of his art, rather than an advancement of artistry. But the line of thought was getting tangled now. Kobo shook his head. Yes, he thought again, I am growing old.

He sat very still and focused unblinking eyes on the red and purple pinwheel circles of the flower. It swayed gently in a soft breeze. Its colors shimmered and spun in the light of late afternoon.

For a long while he sat very still and waited.

He had long ago disciplined his body as well as his mind, and when a blue-grey shadow fell across the flower Kobo did not move.

A moment's silence hung in the air. Finally, a familiar voice spoke behind him. "Master magician," it said. "Jester."

Kobo inclined his head. "Please be seated," he said to the king.

There was just room on the bench for one other person. Kobo did not rise or change his position as the king sat beside him. This was his garden, the garden of the artist, and even the king would acknowledge that.

An alien thought flickered for an instant through the jester's mind and he carefully suppressed a wan smile. Poor Takama, he thought, he must be so nervous.

But what did the king want? Why had he come? It was unfitting to think the king would come personally to offer a compliment. Besides, he had already sent his compliment and his gratitude that morning, as custom demanded. But then perhaps—as Kobo had been thinking all day—this visit was for some purpose outside custom.

"Why is my garden honored by your presence?" he asked in a soft voice. It would have been too presumptuous, not knowing the king's thoughts, to suggest that he himself was honored.

Now it was the king's turn to remain silent. When at last he spoke, his voice sounded troubled.

"I wish to speak to you," he said, "about your art." There was only a moment's pause before he continued. Kobo could hear the pain mixed in the tone of the king's words and, perversely, it eased his having to hear them.

"Age is a beautiful thing, a thing worthy of all honor," the king said slowly. "It refines. It polishes. It softens that which should be soft and strengthens that which should be strong. But what it refines in some ways, it weakens in others."

Kobo watched the flower sway with the air's caress. "A blade, for example" the king went on, his voice steady. "With continued honing, the blade grows sharper and finer, a better cutting tool, a better blade. But the more it is refined, the thinner it grows. Whether it is a fine war sword or a mere kitchen knife, all the refinement serves only, in the end, to make it more brittle. Such, too, is the fate of art."

The red and purple pinwheel circles spun in the warmth of the light.

"Your art is the finest we know," the king said. "It shall be a measure for all others. And it is time now for you to think of passing it on. Just as you are a great artist, so you will be a great teacher. Kobo, you must teach your art lest in the future it be lost. To this purpose,

I honor you now with the name *Daishi*."

Silence behind the whisper of a breeze.

"I already bear an honorable name," Kobo said quietly. "This title is already linked to one of this name, whose echo rings still after many centuries."

"It is done" the king said. "I honor you Kobo Daishi."

At last the jester bowed his head. But after a moment he spoke again.

"It is not an art that can be taught," he said. "Only those who have visited the Heart of the Edo-planet have those powers. And of those only a few have the spirit to turn the power to an art."

"Just so," said the king. "But Kobo Daishi your art is like no other. Lesser men have gathered favor and fortune with lesser art. True, the power comes from the Heart of Edo-planet, but the art itself is yours alone." The king's voice was stronger now, more determined. "Once more, after a while, I would have you perform before the court. Beyond that, I would have you bend every effort to lengthening the shadow of your spirit."

Kobo Daishi stared long at the red and purple pinwheel circles of the flower but the king did not go on.

At long last, the jester raised his head and, with unprecedented boldness to match this unprecedented conversation, looked directly into the eyes of the king.

"My art is such?" he asked quietly.

"Yes, Kobo Daishi," the king answered, meeting his gaze, "your art is such."

Kobo Daishi held his eyes steady for a moment, then said quietly, with a hint of relief, "As the king wishes."

Then the two men, jester and king, turned back to a lengthy contemplation of the bright-voiced flower as the garden quietly slipped into evening darkness and cloaked their bowed heads in silence.

A full day passed before Kobo Daishi spoke to his servant of the king's visit. When at last he did, Takama was relieved.

"I had thought it—forgive me, master—some displeasure. Great men are often unpredictable."

Kobo Daishi smiled at that. "Great men," he said, "are often all too predictable. If I myself were a wiser man..." But he did not complete the sentence.

He then told Takama of his conversation with the king, of his title of Daishi, and of the king's wish. "Therefore," he concluded, "I take it as the king's meaning that I should wed and, in due course, father a child."

Takama's eyes did not waver from his master's face. "It will not be easy to find a suitable bride," he said. "Unless you have someone in mind?" He raised his eyebrows.

Kobo Daishi smiled again. "No, Takama," he said, "I have no one in mind. You yourself must know that. Therefore I wish you to undertake this task for me. I regret the burden it places on you but I think it will be better this way. If I were to seek a wife myself, it is possible that more than one would be offered…"

Takama opened his mouth to speak but Kobo Daishi continued on.

"… and if more than one were offered, it would then be necessary to choose among them. And since only one may be chosen, others so I flatter myself—would be disappointed. And it would be improper for Kobo Daishi to disappoint any. There is also the question of stature. Some may feel their families too low to wed the king's jester. Some may feel too exalted. It will be hard to judge these things, since there is little custom to guide us on this path."

Few jesters had ever married. True, Kobo Daishi in his earlier travels had met several who had wives and many who had lovers. But it was understood that a jester's art ranked higher than any other thing and married jesters were few in number.

"I give you responsibility in this matter, Takama. I know you will settle it satisfactorily, for I know how much you love me."

The servant bowed his head to hide a look of mingled pride and sorrow. Kobo Daishi, understanding but knowing that the moment outweighed words, lightly brushed his servant's arm with gentle fingers.

* * *

It took Takama two months to find a suitable bride for his master.

During that time, Kobo Daishi continued instructing his pupils in calligraphy and twice he was invited as a guest to the court. Each time, he was given a place of honor at the tables, on the king's right and not far away from the king's own seat.

The girl's name was Mistu. She was young, one-third the age of Kobo Daishi, and lovely. She had large, dark eyes, as black as the color of night on Edo-planet. Her figure was girlish, gently proportioned, and she moved with the unconscious grace of a beautiful woman.

Her father was a trader who, like Kobo Daishi, had traveled widely over Edo-planet and knew the jester's reputation as a man of great art and a spirit of great sensitivity. He himself was sometimes a guest at the court of the king. He counted it an honor that his daughter should be so chosen. Mistu, whose feelings in the matter her father sought, declared herself pleased also. Takama had chosen well.

On the appointed day, father and daughter came to the house of Kobo Daishi. The jester welcomed them and, in short order, the marriage was agreed upon. Then Kobo Daishi took the girl alone to the garden at the back of the house. While they were gone, Takama served tea to the father. None ever knew what passed between the jester and the girl during that time in the garden—and none ever inquired, but when they returned to the girl's father, both seemed content. Afterward, Kobo Daishi told Takama that he was well pleased and that he himself could not have made a finer choice.

A date was settled for the wedding ceremony and on that day Kobo Daishi and Mistu were married and Mistu went to sleep henceforth in her husband's bed. Takama continued his former duties, both household obligations and personal service for his master.

Mistu became a pupil of Kobo Daishi and made rapid progress in imitating the master's subtlest brush-strokes. It was a source of great joy to both of them. Never had Kobo Daishi taught a young pupil whose hands perform such miracles of balance in proportion with the brush. And when Kobo Daishi went forth from his house, Mistu always accompanied him. It was almost unheard of for a woman to go about so freely in this part of Edo-planet, but Mistu was so pleasing and Kobo Daishi so well respected that none were inclined to find fault.

About the time Kobo Daishi and his young wife became aware that Mistu had conceived a child, the king departed on a long journey through distant parts of Edo-planet. Through the months of the king's absence, Kobo Daishi continued to instruct his pupils and Mistu continued to perfect her calligraphy. It seemed almost that the life within her gave life to the brush she wrote with. And finally, when it came near time for Mistu to deliver her child, word reached the court that the king was returning.

The day after the king's return a messenger arrived at the house of Kobo Daishi. He brought word of a gala celebration in honor of the king's return and in honor of the foreign guests who had accompanied him. And would Kobo Daishi honor the court by performing? The event was set for five days hence.

"Takama," Kobo Daishi said at once, "please send word to my pupils that I cannot see them until after the king's celebration."

Takama, when he sent word after, did not say when Kobo Daishi would be able to resume the lessons. They would be informed, he told them.

That afternoon Kobo Daishi went into the garden and seated himself on the bench by the flower and the cascade of water. It was some hours before he stirred. When finally he lifted his head, Takama appeared at his side with a steaming cup of dark green tea. The jester took it and sipped gratefully.

"You are tired," Takama said.

Kobo Daishi nodded. "I am."

"The king would understand if you asked to be excused from performing."

"The king would understand, yes. And forgive. But, Takama, if I do not practice my art, I do not live."

"You could perform another time."

Kobo Daishi smiled. "When I am less tired? No, Takama, I will never be less tired. And my powers will never be greater. Nor will I ever be better prepared than I shall be for this occasion. I will perform for the king and this performance shall be my last and my finest. It is time."

Takama hesitated but his desire to speak won out. "But, master, you can perform for many years yet. The king did not forbid that. You must only husband your powers."

"No," the jester said. "Powers are not to be husbanded. Powers are to be used, spent if necessary. Look at this flower, Takama. Look at its shining disc, its whirling colors. The flower does not husband its powers."

"Nor does it bloom all year," the servant said gently.

"Ah, but the point escapes you, Takama. It does bloom all year. True, it does not have this lovely flower all year, but it blooms even in between the times of flowering. For when there is no flower, no red and purple pinwheel circles, there is green, living green. And in the green, in every atom of the green, in every moment of the green, there are red and purple pinwheel circles, red and purple that are perhaps even more brilliant than these red and purple we see now."

The servant shook his head sadly. "I have no doubt of what you say, master, for if you say it, it must be so. But I do not understand."

Kobo Daishi smiled gently. "In time, Takama," he said. "In time and very soon."

The jester spent the days until the king's celebration in silent meditation, seated on the stone bench by the flower in the garden. Then, shortly before the appointed time, he prepared to leave the house. Takama stood ready to accompany him, carry the yellow performance robe and the drum that he himself would strike but once.

When Kobo Daishi went to his young wife, he found her in pain. "Shall I remain here with you?" he asked at once. He knelt beside her.

"Oh, no," Mistu said. "You must go and perform for the king. I will be all right." She smiled weakly and her husband wiped her damp forehead. "Women have borne children through the ages."

"But never have you borne one."

"And never have you performed as you will tonight. It is fitting, is it not?"

Behind the jester's back, Takama exchanged a look with the woman who served Mistu. She shook her head slightly. The secret was beyond them.

Kobo Daishi bent forward and kissed his wife. He let his cheek rest for a moment against hers. Then he hurried from the house and, with Takama at his side, walked quickly up the hill toward the castle of the king.

Kobo Daishi, the great jester, took his position before the great double doors of the king's hall. From inside, the sounds of dinner just reached his ears. A servant of the king hurried toward him.

"The king says he is ready at your signal."

"Ready," said the jester.

The servant hurried down the corridor.

As Takama gave the yellow robe one last tug into place, he let his hand linger for a moment on the master's back. Then he stepped out of sight, ready with the drum.

The great doors swung open on the sudden silence of the hall. The court awaited the jester.

He walked slowly to the center of the hall, feeling the eyes upon him, touching him like fingers of hope. He kept his face composed. It was not his face or expression they were meant to see.

He bowed before the king. The drum rapped once.

In a swirl of motion, the jester threw his arms upward, flicked his fingers upward, and the air was filled with apples, glowing red, and with peaches red and yellow, stems taut— stretched from unseen but visible branches, swaying, blown, tossed by a wind unfelt but known. The air was dizzy with the sweet scent of an orchard in flowering bloom. Then again he flicked his fingers and among the apples and peaches were oranges and limes and a tangy scent. And again, another flick of the fingers, and a torrent of fat red cherries cascaded through the air, endlessly falling, and the hall was filled with their perfume. And he flicked his fingers again and the apples and cherries were gone, with their colors and scents, he snapped his fingers with a crack and in his hand was a blazing red pomegranate and he tossed it in the air, caught it, tossed it again, caught it—convinced them of its solidity—then threw it across the room and at the top of its arc snapped his fingers crack and though it winked instantly out of existence all eyes still followed its flight.

Before held breaths could be expelled, he whirled about again, arms above his head, and there were three red flowers and they hung in the air at three points around the room. He moved again, moved arms, fingers, again and there were three blue, then pink, then purple, then orange, lilac, until the room was encircled by a whirling ring of brilliant flowers. The jester whirled in a circle, arms outstretched, fingers yearning outward, and the ring of flowers rushed together, spun together, to the center of the hall, colors crashing, smashing together, and in the blaze of color there was only one flower, one flower, a whirling disc of red and purple pinwheel circles, spinning, spinning, spinning.

Careful not to obscure the king's view, the jester sank to his knees before the flower, then sat back on his heels with his hands resting calmly on his knees. He watched the flower, watched its red and purple pinwheel circles. The hall was hushed with held breath.

Then slowly, so slowly that at first none were aware of it, the flower began to dim, fade and finally... it... was... gone...

All around the hall, eyes stared at the spot where it had been. The jester was the first to move. He stood with infinite slowness and ceremoniously bowed before the king. The king did not move but only bowed his head until his chin was touching his chest. And Kobo Daishi, honored by the silence, backed from the room.

A serving boy waited at the door as Kobo Daishi and Takama approached. He ran forward as soon as he recognized them in the night.

"The child is born," he cried breathlessly, as soon as they were close enough to hear. Kobo Daishi stopped, stood still.

"Mistu is well," the boy said hastily. The jester said nothing.

"And the child is... She is well," the boy answered. "She..." Takama looked quickly at his master.

"Just so," the master said. "I am content."

Mistu had a chamber of her own for her confinement. When Kobo Daishi awoke the next morning, Takama, as usual, was waiting beside him.

"I greet the day," the jester said.

"I greet the day," Takama repeated.

Kobo Daishi sipped the tea. When he was finished, he looked at the servant.

"All are well in the house," Takama said.

Kobo Daishi smiled warmly. "I know that," he said, "for you have said nothing to the contrary. I know too that there is no message from the king."

"That is true, master."

"There will be," Kobo Daishi said quietly.

And late in the afternoon a messenger did arrive from the king. He brought no word, only a small wooden box which the king had bid him deliver only into the hands of the jester. Kobo Daishi took the box and thanked him.

Then he asked Takama to follow him and carried the box to the room where his wife lay with the baby girl in her arms. The servant stopped in the doorway while Kobo Daishi went to his wife.

Watching his face carefully, Mistu asked, "Are you happy, Kobo Daishi, that the child is a girl?"

He knelt beside her. "I am," he said. And smiled.

His face was alight. He said, "See what the king has sent." And he opened the box and drew forth from it a long gold chain and, hanging from the chain, a small flashing figure, intricately worked: a gleaming, jeweled disc, a flower of flickering gems, red and purple pinwheel circles. He held it up before the eyes of his wife and child.

"You see," he said, "the king himself is pleased."

And he swung the glittering jewels back and forth and the colors of the flower made the mother smile and the baby made a sound that could have been a laugh. And from that day forth, the day following the last performance of Kobo Daishi, the jeweled flower never died and the baby's eyes flashed fire and her laugh was the color of peaches and her smile the aroma of apples.

On the Last Night of the Festival of the Dead

BY DARRELL SCHWEITZER

". . . then all things which have been begun shall be finished."
—The Litanies of Silence.

ON THE FIRST NIGHT OF THE FESTIVAL OF THE DEAD, THEY WERE LAUGHING. All the capital rang with mirth; fantastic banners and kites festooned the towers and roofs of the City of the Delta. The streets swarmed with masked harlequins bearing copper lanterns shaped like grotesque faces which sang through some trick of flame and metal. That was a kind of laughter too.

On the first night, Death was denied. Children crouched by the canals and floated away paper mummies in toy funeral-boats. Black costumed skeletons ran from house to house, pounding on doors, waving torches, shouting for the living to emerge and mingle with the dead. Revelers swirled in their shrouds, their death-masks revealing their ancestors, not as they had looked at the close of life, but with rotten features hideously, hilariously distorted.

That was the joke of it, that everyone was masked and no one knew who anyone else was. All gossip and insult and roguery might be done with impunity. Nothing mattered. Death itself was a jest. Surat-Hemad, the crocodile-headed Devourer, god of the Underworld, could be mocked.

But it was nervous laughter. Inevitably, even on the first night of the festival, some of the restless dead actually returned from their abode in Tashé, that shadowy country which lies beyond the reach of the deepest dreams. So the possibility was always there, however remote, that the person behind the mask, either speaking or spoken to, might actually be a corpse.

If not something far stranger.

"Is this the house of the great Lord Kuthomes?" the person who had knocked at the door said, holding out a small package wrapped in palm fronds.

That was all the two servants who answered could remember: the soft voice, the diminutive messenger with long, dark hair; probably a child, gender uncertain. The mask like a barking dog, or grinning jackal, or maybe a bat. Plain, scruffy clothing, maybe loose trousers or just a robe; probably barefoot.

They'd merely accepted the package and the messenger ran away.

Their exasperated master took it from them and ordered them to be beaten.

Lord Kuthomes tore the fronds away and held in his hands a small wooden box, cheaply made of scrap materials, without any attempt at ornamentation.

The box vibrated slightly, as if something inside it were alive, or perhaps clockwork.

Thoughtful, ever on guard against the trick of some enemy—for he was a great lord of the Delta and he had many enemies—he carried it to his chamber. As he entered, living golden hands on his nightstand lifted a two-paneled mirror, holding it open like a book.

Kuthomes sat on a stool, a candle in one hand, the parcel in the other, gazing at the reflections of both in the black glass. The hands shifted the mirror, showing the image in one panel, then the other.

As he had so many times before, Kuthomes searched for some hidden clue which might reveal treachery or useful secrets. He was a magician of sorts, though not a true sorcerer, wholly transformed, reeking of poisonous enchantment. His art sufficed to unravel such lethal puzzles as one Deltan lord might design for another. In this mirror, he had often learned the weakness of some rival. Once he had even reached through the glass and torn out a sleeping man's heart.

He hefted the box. It weighed perhaps two ounces. But he had an instinct about such things. He sensed strangeness, and in strangeness, danger.

But when he held the box up to the mirror, even with the candle positioned to shine through the delicate wood, he saw only his hands, the box, and the candle's flame. The depths remained inscrutable; they did not even reflect Lord Kuthomes's silver-bearded face.

The box stirred, humming like one of those metal lanterns the harlequins carried. For an instant, Kuthomes was furious. A festival night *joke*? He would have crushed the thing in his hand and hurled it away. But that same caution which had made him a great lord of the Delta again prevailed.

He placed the object down on the night stand, took a delicate calligrapher's knife, and, by candlelight, began to chip away at the thin wood. There were no envenomed needles. no springs, no magic seals waiting to be broken. The fragments fell away easily.

Inside was a sculpture about two inches high of a laughing corpse-face, its head thrown back, gap-toothed mouth stretched wide. Inside the mouth, a tiny silver bell rang of its own accord. Kuthomes touched the bell with the tip of his knife and the ringing stopped.

Outside, the mob laughed and roared. Drums beat faintly, muffled, far away.

He laid the knife down on the table top, and the ringing resumed. It wasn't a matter of a breeze or a draught. He placed the whole object under a glass bowl and the bell still shivered.

He knew, then, that this was no thing of the living world, but a death-bell, manufactured in *Tashé* itself by dead hands, then borne up, like a bubble rising from a deep, muddy pool, through the dreamlands of *Leshé*, until it was present, very substantially, at the doorstep of Lord Kuthomes of the Delta. It was a token, a summons from the dead.

"Whoever has sent this," he said aloud, "know that I shall find you out and wrest your secrets from you, though you be already dead. You shall learn why Kuthomes is feared."

He rose and prepared himself, performing the four consecrations, forehead, eyelids, ears, and mouth touched with the Sorcerer's Balm, to shield him from illusion. His midnight-black sorcerer's robe came to life as it closed around him, its delicately glowing embroideries depicting a night sky never seen over the City of the Delta; the stars of Death, the sky of *Tashé*.

He regarded his reflection in the mirrors, only the robe visible in the darkness, like some headless specter.

The original owner of that robe, he recalled, had been headless toward the end, but well before he died, before others carried the remains away and finished the unpleasant, perilous business. He knew that to kill a sorcerer is to become one. The contagion flows from the slain to the slayer. Therefore a sorcerer must be disposed of carefully, by experts, not such dilettantes as he, who might occasionally require that the serpentine motif on a jade carving come to life on cue, or a sip of wine paralyze the will, or the face of one man be temporarily transformed into that of the other. These were stock-in-trade for any lord of the Delta, to be applied as deftly as a surgeon's knife.

But no, he was not a sorcerer.

Therefore he also carried a curious sword in a scabbard underneath his robe, its strong blade inlaid with intricate, ultimately mystifying silver designs. It was the weapon of a Knight Inquisitor, one of those fanatic warriors from the barbarian lands across the sea, a sworn enemy of all gods but the Righteous Nine and especially of the Shadow Titans, who breathe sorcery like a miasma into the world. The sword was proof against all the magical darkness.

But Kuthomes, merely a man, had strangled the Knight Inquisitor with a cord, years ago, when he was younger and had the strength for such things.

He put on the jeweled, brimless cap of his rank and took up the death-bell in his hand, then passed silently through the halls of his own house in vigorous, graceful strides. He crossed the central courtyard. Up above, someone hastily closed a shutter. Even on such a merry night, it was ill luck to look on Lord Kuthomes in his sorcerer's aspect.

A single lamp flickered in the atrium. There were still palm fronds on the floor, and a stain where the servants had been beaten. That would be cleaned up on his return, or made larger.

He slipped out into the street.

By now the night was almost over. Stars still shone overhead, but the sky was purpling in the East. He found himself in an utterly dark street, without a single lantern hanging from a doorway, a channel of featureless exterior walls. Higher up, the balconies were empty, the shutters invariably locked.

He stretched out his palm and held the death-bell up level with his face. It laughed at him, but slowly now, the faint tinkling interspersed with silence.

Several streets away, someone shouted. A horn blew a long, trailing blast that began as music and ended in flatulence. Something fell and broke, probably crockery. Then silence again.

He walked confidently along that dark street until he stumbled, cursing, over what looked like an enormous, long-legged bird left broken and sprawling.

But Kuthomes did not fall. He regained his footing, crushing the death-bell in his hand. The thing felt like a live wasp, scraping to get free. Hastily, he opened his hand, then stood still, gasping.

Gradually he made out an inert reveler in some absurd costume: trailing cloth wings, tatters and streamers, a crushed and shapeless mask.

There must have been stilts somewhere, or else a crowd had carried the fool aloft.

In his younger days, Kuthomes might have given the fellow a kick to the ribs, but now he merely spat, then continued on his way.

He tried to follow the delicate voice of the bell, turning where it seemed to ring louder or more frequently. But his ear could not actually tell. He wandered through the maze of streets, once or twice passing others, who hurried to get out of his way.

In a market square, he faced the East. Dawn's first light sufficed to reveal the solitary figure standing there: very short, clad in shapeless white, arms akimbo, bare feet spread apart, face hidden behind some cheap animal mask.

"You there!" Kuthomes dropped the insistent bell into his pocket and stepped forward, but the other turned and ran. For an instant he thought it was a dwarf, but the motion was too agile. A child then. He couldn't tell if it was a boy or a girl.

He pursued until his breath came in painful gasps and it seemed his chest would burst.

Again and again he saw his quarry, near at hand but out of reach, vanishing around a corner at the end of an alley, on the other side of a courtyard, or gazing down on him from a balcony or from a bridge over a canal.

"Do not dare to trifle with me!"

Bare feet padded on cobblestones. Hard boots clattered after.

But in the morning twilight Kuthomes could go no further. He had to sit down on a stone bench and lean back against a wall, gazing out over the central forum of the city. All around him the temples of the major gods faced one another. The rising sun made the rooftops and the many statues gleam. Divinities, kings, and heroes lining those rooftops and perched on pillars and ledges seemed momentarily alive, gazing down benevolently or wrathfully, each according to their nature. Yawning peddlers opened their stalls. A flock of pigeons stirred, murmuring on the steps of the temple of Bel-Hemad, the god of new life, of springtime, and forgiveness. But the house of Surat-Hemad, the lord of Death, was still a mass of shadows and black stone, the eyes of the carven crocodile head over the doorway aglow like faint coals with some mysterious light of their own.

Kuthomes half-dozed, exhausted, enraged that he had been the object of a joke on the first night of the Festival of the Dead. He set the death-bell in his lap, and still it rang, a far more serious matter than anybody's joke. He laid the sword of the Knight Inquisitor across his knees, and the ringing stopped. When he put the sword away, it resumed.

He couldn't think clearly just then, weary and angry as he was, but he was certain that he was proof against illusion, and that there was an answer here somewhere, in the haze and dust and fading shadows. If he concentrated hard enough, he would have it, and his revenge, later.

Was he not Lord Kuthomes, feared and respected by all?

Eventually he fell asleep on the bench and dreamed, strangely, that he, the feared and respected Lord Kuthomes, had ventured alone into the city at night, and that the city was empty. All the revelers, soldiers, courtiers, even the Great King himself had fled before him, and Lord Kuthomes's heavy footsteps echoed in the empty palace, even in the vast Presence Hall where he mounted the throne with the double crown of the Delta and Riverland on his head.

He sat still and silent in his dream, the crown on his head, crocodile-headed scepter in his hand, gazing into the empty darkness, until he heard the sound of the tiny death-bell approaching.

Someone shuffled and emerged from behind a column. Kuthomes stiffened and beheld a tall, cloaked figure approach the throne slowly, tottering like a very old man; no, swaying side-to-side like a crocodile reared up, imitating a human walk.

The thing opened clawed hands when it stood at the foot of the throne. The face beneath the hood was indeed that of a crocodile. In the open hands, nothing at all.

Here was one of the *evatim*, the messengers of Surat-Hemad, whose summons may never be resisted or denied. Kuthomes shrank back in his stolen throne, knowing that all his magic and even the silver sword were useless.

But the other tore off a crocodile mask, uncovering a laughing corpse face identical to that which held the death-bell, head back in a paroxysm of hilarity or terror, mouth agape. In the unimaginable depths of its throat, a tiny bell rang insistently. Then the apparition breathed laughter, neither harsh nor exactly gentle, impatient, with a touch of petulance, and at last a voice spoke from those same black depths, soft, definitely feminine, a young woman's voice, maddeningly familiar.

In his dream, it was too much effort to recall. He almost recognized the voice, but not quite.

"Do you not know me?" the other said.

"No," he replied.

"Ah, but you did once, long ago."

"How long ago was that?"

She only laughed for a brief instant. Then the laughter was gone and the bell rang.

Lord Kuthomes shook himself out of his dream and found himself on the bench at the edge of the dusty forum, in the blazing mid-day sun. The bell, in his lap, still rang. No one had dared to disturb him, of course. Those who gaped in wonder suddenly turned their faces away, pretending not to have seen.

He took up the bell again and lurched to his feet, shouting for an old woman to fetch him a litter. When she had done so, she held out her hand for a coin. He patted his pockets, found nothing, then scowled and spat, tumbling into the litter, drawing the curtain behind him. The bearers set off, the litter lurching, swaying. Kuthomes felt sick by the time he reached his house.

Inside the atrium, the palm fronds and the stain on the floor were still there.

Later. There would be time for that later.

On the second night of the Festival of the Dead, they were dancing.

This was a more somber time. The streets and rooftops echoed with stately music. Paper masks from the first night floated in the canals or littered the streets. Now people wore beautifully carved and adorned wooden masks, ageless, ideal visages which did not so much hide the identity of the wearer as abstract it, like a name written in intricate, illuminated letters.

Musicians, clad in dark cerements and masked in imitation of the evatim, moved slowly from house to house, to palace and hovel alike, excepting no one, summoning the inhabitants to dance, to mingle in the wide forum before the temples of the gods. On this night the dead would truly return in great numbers, out of the dreams of *Leshé* and the darkness of *Tashé*, climbing up from the Great River and the city's many canals to walk among the living. It was a night of portents and revelations, of sorrows and bittersweet joys, reunions, secret dooms, and frequent miracles.

Lord Kuthomes had rested and bathed. He had pored over such books of sorcery as he owned and could read, unable to find any answer to the riddle before him, but still certain some enemy had laid a trap.

He would be ready. Once more he anointed himself four times and put on his sorcerer's robe. Once more the silver sword pressed against his thigh. This time even he wore a mask, beautifully wrought, set with gems and feathers until the features of Lord Kuthomes had been transformed into some fantastic, predatory bird.

When the revelers reached his door, he gave them such coin as custom required, then stepped out into the throng, moving along the dark and crowded streets, into the forum where moonlight shone on the roofs of the temples and the many bronze and golden statues. The gods seemed to be watching him alone, waiting for something to happen.

Even the Great King, Wenamon the Ninth, was there with all his lords and ladies, all of them masked, to do homage to Death. Kuthomes took his rightful place in the great circle of their dance. Once he held the warm hand of Queen Valshepsut, who nodded to him, and he to her, before he yielded to the King.

Around and around dancers turned, as the musicians followed, pipes skirling, drums beating stately, muted time. Acolytes with lanterns or torches pursued their own paths at the periphery, the intricate revolutions imitating the cycles of the universe. In the center, priests of Death stood motionless in their crocodile masks.

Or were those perhaps the true faces of the evatim?

The fancy came to Kuthomes that many of the faces around him, in the royal circle, in the crowd, were not masks at all.

In the midst of them was one who did not dance, who clearly did not belong: some scruffy urchin in a paper mask that was probably supposed to be a fox, in shapeless white trousers and shirt, bare feet spread apart, arms this time folded imperiously. He could see the figure clearly.

He broke through the dancers. "You there! Stop!" But the boy was gone.

Then someone, whose touch was very cold and dry, whose grip was like a vise, took him by the hand and whirled him back into the dance. He hissed, "Who *dares?*"

But the other merely bowed, with both arms spread wide, then straightened and stepped back, in a half-formed dance step. He discerned a slender lady in rotting funeral clothes, but that meant nothing on this night. Her mask was plain and featureless white, with mere round holes for eyes and mouth.

Now the rhythm of the dance changed. The music slowed and the circles broke apart. Dancers clung to one another, drifting off in pairs into doorways and alleys, beneath canopies, there to unmask.

The stranger led Kuthomes into the darkness beneath a broken bridge, far from the crowd, into silence. They stood on a ledge above the black water of a canal. The other lifted Kuthomes' mask off and made to throw it away, but he snatched it back and held it tightly against his chest. She twirled her own white mask out over the water, where it splashed, then drifted like a sparkle of reflected moonlight.

"Do you not remember me?" she said, speaking not Deltan but that language universal among the dead, yet known only to sorcerers among the living and never uttered aloud. Kuthomes could make out enough: "... your promise long ago. Our assignation. Complete what you began."

He cried out. He couldn't break free of her arms. Her breath was foul. Her filthy hand pressed over his mouth.

When she let go, he managed to gasp, "Name yourself... "

"Remember poor Kamachina... "

Then she was gone. He heard a splash. The black water rippled.

He stepped out of the shadow of the bridge, into the moonlight and stood still, amazed and afraid.

The absurd thing was he didn't know any Kamachina. It was a common female name in the Delta. There must have been hundreds of servants, daughters of minor nobility, whores, whoever. He searched his memory for a specific Kamachina. No, no one. He tried to laugh, to tell himself this was another, tastelessly misconceived joke, that even the dead could blunder.

But then he got the death-bell out of his pocket and held it on his palm. The bell still rang.

On the third and final night of the Festival of the Dead, those who had received special signs assembled in silence on the steps of the black temple of Surat-Hemad, who created the crocodile in his own image.

The temple doors formed the Devouring God's jaws. Bronze teeth gleamed by torchlight. Within the great hall, two red lanterns burning above the altar were the all-seeing eyes of Death.

In the vaults beneath the altar, in the belly of Surat-Hemad, dead and living commingled freely, and the waters of dream, of *Leshé*, lapped against the shores of the living world those of the land of the dead. On this night, of all nights, the borders were freely crossed.

The doors swung wide. Twenty or so pilgrims entered. Dark-clad, bearing the death-bell and his sword, but unmasked, Lord Kuthomes filed in with the others, circling thrice around the altar and the image of the squat-bellied, crocodile-headed Surat-Hemad, then descended into the deeper darkness of the vaults. He walked among stone sarcophagi containing the mummies of great or wicked men, who might return at any time they chose to inhabit such earthly forms.

He placed his hand on the carven effigy of some lord of centuries past. The mummy within stirred and scratched.

His mind was clear, though he had not rested after the second night. He had searched his books and gazed into his mirror for long hours, coming up with no revelation at all. He knew, then, that he could only confront the dead and allow them to speak. His fate, perhaps, was no longer in his own hands.

All things return to Surat-Hemad, so the prayer went. Yes.

Still he could not remember a specific Kamachina. He didn't know who the boy was either. The child's significance, in particular, eluded him. He did not fit.

All things—

He had even consulted a true sorcerer, an ancient creature deformed and trans-formed by the magic within him, who walked in swaying jerks like a scarecrow come alive in the wind, whose head flicked constantly from side to side like a bird's, whose nose-less face was a mass of scars, whose metal eyes clicked, whose hands were living fire. The sorcerer laughed slyly in a multitude of voices, and turned away.

A priest of Bel-Hemad had merely shaken his head sadly and said, "By the end of the third night, you shall know who this lady is. I am certain of that."

Kuthomes had offered a fantastic sum of money, enough to startle even the priest.

"What is this for?"

"Help me escape. There must be a way."

The priest had merely shrugged, and Kuthomes stalked away from the priest's house, muttering to himself, striking people and objects in blind rage, pacing back and forth to fill the hours until the sun set and the third night of the Festival of the Dead began. The waiting was the worst part.

Dread Surat-Hemad, may all things be completed and finished and laid to rest, the prayers went. Lord Kuthomes did not often pray.

Now he walked among the tombs of the ancient, sorcerous dead, the carven, laughing corpse-face in his hand, the tiny bell in its throat tinkling. Like all the others, he followed the sputtering tapers held aloft by the masked priests of Death, until all had gathered in an open space before a vast doorway.

A priest touched a lever. Counterweights shifted somewhere. Stone ground against stone, and the doors slid aside. Cold, damp air blew into the musty crypt, smelling of river mud and corruption.

Here was the actual threshold of the world of the dead. Beyond this door, he knew, down a little slope, black water lapped silently. Funeral barges waited to carry the dead—and the living—into Leshé, where madmen, visionaries, and sorcerers might glimpse Lord Kuthomes passing through their dreams.

Kuthomes hoped they would know and remember whom they had seen.

At the threshold, the tiny death-bell stopped ringing. Kuthomes threw it away, certain it was of no further use.

He reached under his robe and drew out the silver sword.

"You won't need that." A warm, living hand caught his wrist. The voice was soft, but not feminine, speaking Deltan, accented very slightly. The boy.

Kuthomes slid the sword back into the scabbard. "Who are you?"

"One who will guide you to your trysting place. Lord Kuthomes, the Lady Kamachina awaits."

"Explain yourself, or die."

"If you kill me, you will never know the answer, will you?"

"There are slow methods, which inspire eloquence... "

"But hardly worth the exertion, Lord. Come with me, and all will be made clear."

Kuthomes hesitated. Slowly, the other pilgrims crossed the threshold. What could he do but follow? The boy was waiting.

Hand-in-hand, the two of them passed through the door and into absolute darkness, where not even the priests with their tapers dared accompany them. The only sound was the sucking of boots in the mud.

The boy seemed to know where he was going. Kuthomes allowed himself to be led. They groped their way into a barge and sat still, among many other wordless pilgrims.

Then they were adrift, and gradually stars appeared overhead, not those seen over the Delta on any summer night, but the stars of Deathlands, of *Tashé*.

He discerned crocodile-headed things in the river, thousands, floating along like a great mass of weed; but their bodies were pale and human, like naked, drowned men. These were the true messengers of Death, the *evatim*.

Someone in the company shrieked, stood up, and did a frantic, whirling dance, hands waving and slapping as if in an attempt to fend off invisible hornets. He fell into the river with a splash. The evatim hissed all as one, the sound like a rising wind.

Someone else began strumming a harp. A song arose from many voices, a gentle, desolate lyric in the language of the dead. From out of the air, from far beyond the barge, more voices joined in.

Many wept. Kuthomes was unmoved, impatient, tensely alert.

The boy took his hand again, as if seeking or offering comfort. He couldn't tell which.

They were deep into Dream now, and the visions began. Some of the others cried out from sudden things Kuthomes could not see; but *he* was able to behold vast shapes in the sky, half human, half-beast, like clouds moving *behind* the stars, pausing in some incomprehensible journey to glance down at those in the barge below. These might have been the gods, or the Shadow Titans, from whom all sorcery flowed. Kuthomes had no idea. He did not choose to ask the masked boy beside him, who, he was certain, *did* know.

From *Leshé*, Dream, as they passed over into the realm of Death, the rest of the adventure was like a dream, inexplicable, without continuity.

Once it seemed that he and the boy sat alone on the barge. The boy closed and opened his hands, and blue flames rose from his scarred palms. Kuthomes removed the boy's shabby mask, tossing it out among the evatim. By the blue light, he could see a very ordinary face, soft, beardless, with large, dark eyes; a man-child somewhere in the middle teens, with tangled, dark hair. Part of one of the boy's ears was missing. That struck Kuthomes as merely odd.

"Who *are* you?" he whispered in the language of the dead.

In that same tongue the boy replied, "A messenger."

"One of the *evatim* then?"

"What do you think?"

"You seem alive."

"Death, also, is a kind of life."

In another part of the dream they walked on water, barefoot because the river would not hold up Kuthomes as long as he wore boots. Ripples spread on the frigid surface. They walked through a dead marsh in wintertime. Among the reeds, skeletal, translucent birds waded on impossibly delicate legs.

Later still, the sky brightened into a dull, metallic gray, without a sunrise, but with enough suffused light that Kuthomes could see clearly. He and the boy walked for hours through sumptuous dust, until they both were covered with it. A wind rose. Swirling dust filled the air. By tricks of half-light and shadow, in the shifting dust, he seemed to make out buried rooftops, part of a city wall, a tower. But all these crumbled away when he touched them, then reformed again somewhere nearby.

Sometimes he saw faces on the ground before him, or in walls or doorways. He made his way through the narrow streets of a city of dust. The boy led him by the hand.

Here was the silently screaming dust-face of Lord Vormisehket, stung by a thousand scorpions; and here Adriuten Shomash with his throat still cut, sand pouring out of the nether mouth beneath his chin. Lady Nefirame and her three children confronted him. She had hurled herself into a well with the children in her arms. So many more, faces and bodies sculpted out of transitory dust, forming and reforming as Kuthomes passed, dust-arms and hands reaching out for him, crumbling, reaching again.

He saw many who had been useful to him for a time, then inconvenient: Akhada the witch; Dakhumet the poisoner, who hurled tiny, darts fashioned like birds; even the former king himself, Baalshekthose, first and only ruler of that name, whose sudden ascent and descent both Kuthomes had brought about.

The boy dragged him on, pulling at his arm, completely plastered with the gray dust so that only his eyes seemed alive.

Kuthomes felt indignant anger more than anything else. Why should these phantoms accuse him? Such deeds were the stuff of politics. Those who wielded power must be, by the nature of that power, above the common morality.

It was only when they came to a halt by a broken bridge over a dust-choked canal that Kuthomes recognized where he was. Here, in dreams and dust and ash, was a replica, shifting and inexact but a replica nevertheless, of the City of the Delta, of a disreputable district where, many years before, he had promised to meet someone by that bridge.

In this place of dreams and death, amid the dust, the memory came back to him, clearly, like a book opening, its pages turning.

She was waiting for him, tall and slender in her dusty shroud. He knew her even before she spoke, before the caked dirt on her face cracked and fell away like a poorly-wrought mask to reveal empty eyesockets and bare bones.

Her voice was gentle and sad and exactly as he remembered it. She spoke in the language of the dead.

"Kuthomes, my only love, I am your beloved, Kamachina, whom you once promised to marry and make great."

He could not resist her embrace, or her kiss, though both revolted him.

"I never knew what happened to you," he managed to say at last.

He had been seventeen, an upstart from outside the city, youngest of many sons, driven out of his village with few prospects, ridiculed by the great ones of the Delta, desperate for recognition, for a position of any sort. He had dallied with a girl, the daughter of a minor official. Already he was precocious in the ways of the court, though he had yet to set foot inside a palace. His lies had the desired effect, with hints of plots and of suppressed factions soon to rise again; with the implication that Kuthomes was not who he seemed at all, but perhaps a prince in disguise, whose true name would make the mighty tremble. With this and more he secured introductions, a position. In exchange for the favor of the girl Kamachina, he promised to make her family great.

Later, when she pressed her claim and became inconvenient, he put her off, all the while whispering that she and her father were both mad, obsessed with absurd plots. At the very end, there had been the assignation at the bridge. The two of them would exchange marriage vows but keep them secret until the time was right for the revelation.

"But you never came," she said. On that final, sacred night of the Festival of the Dead, when uttered vows are binding forever, he had betrayed her, and, in her grief, she had flung herself into the canal and drowned.

"I truly loved you," she said. "You were my every, my only hope."

"I... did not know."

"I was great with your child. Did you know that?"

"I... had not seen you in several months."

"I could hardly confess such a thing in a letter."

"Someone might have intercepted it," he said.

She dragged him to his knees, then lay by his side in the cold dust.

At last he broke free, stood up, and brushed himself off.

"But all this was almost *forty years ago*. How can it matter now?"

She reached up and took him by the hand. "Among the dead, time moves much more slowly."

He looked around for the boy and saw him crouching nearby in the dust, hands folded over his knees, watching dispassionately.

"Is that your son?"

"I have no son," said Kamachina, reaching up for Kuthomes. "My child is still within me, waiting to be born." Once more she dragged him down into her irresistible embrace, pressing her corpse-mouth against his.

Kuthomes screamed. He fought her, drawing his silver sword, striking her again and again, slashing her head off, hacking her body to pieces.

But it was no use. She merely reconstituted herself, a thing of dust and dead bones, sculpted by some magical wind.

She caught his wrist in her crushing grip and made him throw the sword away.

"I'm sorry," he said. "I did what I had to do. I didn't know... If I could help you, I would, but it's too late..."

"What is begun on the last night of the Festival of the Dead," she said, embracing him once more, "is sacred, inviolate, and must always be consummated."

So it was that Lord Kuthomes came to dwell in the country of the dead with his Lady Kamachina. He was mad with the terror of it all for a long time. It seemed that he sat on a throne, and ruled as emperor among the corpses, but slowly, subtly, they turned from him, perverting his every command, until at last he was cast down, reviled, trampled into filth. He shouted that he was a great lord, that he was alive and they mere corpses, but they only laughed at him.

Dead hands tore his entrails out of his body, lifted his bleeding heart up before his face; dead lips drank his blood and devoured him. So it seemed, in his madness, though each time he awoke, he found himself whole.

He tried to bear all this in the manner of a great lord, silently plotting his revenge, but that was absurd, and before long he too was shrieking aloud at the hilarity of the idea.

"How shall I be revenged against myself?" he asked the ghosts. "How?"

They could not answer him.

All the while Kamachina was with him, touching him gently, whispering of her love. She alone did not mock him, nor injure him in any way, but her love was the worst torment of all.

In his madness his mind opened up. The speech of gods and of the Titans poured into him. There were many revelations, passed through Kuthomes into the dreams of men who awoke in the living world.

Gradually his pain and his madness lessened, and it seemed he had merely backtracked along a path he had once taken, then set out on another. His old life became the dream, the fading memory. Now he came to see himself dwelling, not in dust, but in an austere palace of massive pillars and black stone, there waited upon by ghosts, while his wife's belly swelled with his child.

"Is it not the duty of a lord," she said, "to provide for the comfort of those beneath him?"

He supposed it was. He didn't know anymore.

He sat with her in her garden of leafless trees and brittle stalks, listening as she spoke or sang softly in the language of the dead. He learned to play a strange harp made of bones as delicate as strands of silk. He came to behold the growing life in that dead garden, the nearly invisible leaves and blossoms like sculpted smoke, and he ate of the fruits of the trees, which tasted like empty air, and was sustained by them. After a while, he could recall no other taste.

She was delivered there, in the garden. The mysterious boy appeared once more, to assist the birthing.

"Who are you?" Kuthomes asked. "Can you not tell me at last?"

"I am the sorcerer Sekenre," the boy said.

"But, but, one so young—"

"For sorcerers too, as for the dead, time moves differently. I was fifteen when my father caused me to slay him, filling me with his spirit, and the spirits of all his victims, and the victims of his victims, all united in one, who must sometimes struggle to remember that he was once a boy called Sekenre. My voices are like a flock of birds. We are many. But for three hundred years and more, my body has not aged. I have learned and forgotten many things, as you, Kuthomes, have learned and forgotten."

"I too have a hard time remembering who I am sometimes," said Kuthomes. "We are alike."

"You are the loving father of this child." The boy Sekenre reached into Lady Kamachina's dead womb and lifted an infant girl out in his hands. Kuthomes thought his daughter looked more like a delicate carving than a child: skin translucently white, eyes open and unblinking, the expression severe.

Sekenre passed the baby to Kuthomes, who rested it in his lap.

"The world shall fear this one," Sekenre said, "but not for any evil in her. She is a mirror of the evil in others. In a hundred years' time I shall need her as my ally, against an enemy yet unborn."

"Therefore you have directed all these things, my entire life, to your own purposes."

"Yes, I have," said Sekenre.

Kuthomes shrugged. "I suppose one has to do such things." He felt, vaguely, that he should be angry, but there was no passion left in him.

Kamachina smiled and took the child from him.

Ghosts gathered around them, whispering like a faint wind.

On the last night of the Festival of the Dead, Lord Kuthomes emerged from the vaults beneath the temple of Surat-Hemad in the City of the Delta. He had grown very old. His once tall, vigorous figure was bent, his silver beard now purest white. No one knew him, or the bone-pale girl he led into the world.

His daughter clung to his arm, her eyes dazzled even by the gloom of the inside of the temple; amazed at everything she saw, whispering to him, for comfort, then out of excitement, chattering softly in the language of the dead. The grave-wrappings she wore had partially fallen away, revealing almost transparent skin. She seemed more to float on the air than to walk.

Outside, she had to cover her face from the starlight. Kuthomes found a discarded mask for her.

They walked through streets he remembered now only from his dreams. She had so many questions he could not answer. He took her tiny hand in his and led her to a place he had dreamed, where a certain magician was waiting. This man would nurture her for five years before an enemy killed him, bore her off, and came to regret the prize.

But these things were Sekenre's business.

Kuthomes departed without even bidding his daughter farewell, then hurried back to the temple of Surat-Hemad, and descended into the vaults, so that what had been begun on the last night of the Festival of the Dead could at last be finished.

The Exercise of Faith

BY LUCIUS SHEPARD

FROM MY PULPIT, CARVED OF EBONY INTO A LONG-SNOUTED GRIFFIN'S HEAD, I can see the sins of my parishioners. It's as if a current is flowing from face to face, illuminating the secret meaning of every wrinkle and line and nuance of expression. They—like their sins—are an ordinary lot. Children as fidgety as gnats. Ruddy cheeked men possessed by the demons of real estate, solid citizens with weak hearts and brutal arguments for wives. Women whose thoughts slide like swaths of gingham through their minds, married every one to lechers and layabouts. Yet for all their commonality, the congregation is remarkable in that their sins mesh, are wholly compatible with one another. For every potential pederast there is a young boy in the first flush of his deviancy, for every violent urge a seeker of pain, and for every bitter widow a lust of knitting-needles sharpness with which to mend the piecework of her days. This has always seemed to me a circumstance worth exploiting, though until recently I had no idea as to how that should be done.

Not only can I see my parishioners' sins, I am able to experience them, both talents visited upon me by, I believe, the church. It is an ancient house of worship, its white plaster walls and black beams emblematic of the Puritan rigor whose sanctity it was built to guarantee, and it is graced by twelve stained-glass windows, each depicting a beast framed by a border of grape leaves. Legend tells that its cool dry air seethes with the caliginous spirits of old killed witches, most of them dead at the hands of the first pastor here, one Jeremy Calder, a man gone bloody with the love of God. However, I doubt his astral presence or that of his victims is responsible for the inception of my psychic gifts. No, rather I feel these gifts are a product of the essence of the place and time, for that, it strikes me, is the nature of all extremes of reality, be they good or evil: that they are bred from the interaction of a thousand ephemera, the conjunction of congruent normalcies that together act to compound an anomaly... But I was going to tell you how I experience my congregation's sins.

This morning as I stand on the steps in my surplice after the eleven o'clock service, with the red and yellow leaves of the sycamores and birches that line the street bristling and flashing like semaphores under the high sun, I greet each by name and shake their hands, and with every touch a vision opens in my brain. Take Emily Prideau, now. Child of Bess and

Robert. Sixteen years old; nubile; sweet. Her breasts molded into prim curves by the pink starched decorum of her Sunday dress. Yet from her fingers courses the vision of a midnight wood, where cross-armed she lifts her sweater and those heavy breasts bound free, globed pale and perfect by the moonlight, and next, smiling, she looses her wraparound skirt, proving underwearless, erecting the dry-throated boy who gazes dumbstruck at her curly secret. "Do me first," she says, and as he kneels to her, I feel the jolt of pleasure triggered by his tongue.

"Wonderful sermon, Reverend," she says, parroting her dad, and I am forced to restrain a laugh, amused not by the incongruity of the compliment in relation to her thoughts, but by the fact of the compliment itself. My sermons are mild and cautionary nothings, annotated with announcements of bake sales and raffles, and do not attempt salvation. For what purpose should I save them? Heaven? That curdled fantasy has long since fled my brain, and God's absence is everywhere... although I have sensed a scrap of His divinity floating in the belfry, as flat and black as a shadow, and know that he only waits the proper summons to return transformed into a God suitable to the times. That, you see, is the core principle of the divine, that we must pour It full of sins—as, indeed, I have been filled during the six years of my ministry—and kill It, and then resurrect It in new form, a vessel suitable for the shapes of contemporary wrongdoing.

Purse clasped to her belly, Emily strolls off 'twixt Bess and Robert into the myth of her virginity, and I am confronted by the banker, Miles Elbee, a sapless twig of a sinner gone gray at forty, weathered and wrinkled as a man half-again his age. From his perfunctory shake I have a glistening of leather, a whip crack, and an exultant scream. He always withdraws his hand so quickly. I wonder if he knows I see his passion for submissiveness and is ashamed. "Fine morning," he says, and with a tailored smile, he joins the menfolk on the walk to discuss the NFL. And here, Marge Trombley extends her white-gloved hand. Auburn hair and a pale face so delicately engraved with thirty years of suffering, it seems as exquisitely wrought as a cameo. Ah, Marge! Your sin is the sweetest fellow to my own. From the pressure of your fingertips I am blessed with the sight of you and me coupling in the choir stall. And something else beneath that sight, a dark knurl of more-than secret sin (Have I mentioned that locked in every heart is the knotty shape of the last and greatest evil of which we are capable?). I return the pressure, letting it linger a moment too long for propriety, infusing those lovely features with a blush.

"I am hoping to see Jeffrey one Sunday," I say. This initiates a litany between us. Jeffrey is the ne'erest of ne'er-do-wells, given to weekend binges and wife-beating; he has never set foot in St. Mary's, and our exchanges concerning him rarely vary.

"He's been sick," she says. "And he's depressed about his job." A smile breaks the lock of suffering. "I'll try to bring him along next week." Then, leaning close, a whisper. "I must talk to you, Reverend."

I respond that unfortunately I'm off to a church conference for the week—a lie— but that the Saturday evening after my return will be free. If she would care to stop around sevenish...? She would, indeed. Marge, Marge. Is this to be our flowering?

And so it goes, one Episcopal life after another: neatly decked-out shells enfolding a chaos of frustrations.

Once they have all made their way homeward or to lunch or tennis, I sit in the back pew, drinking the last of the communion wine and staring at the animals in their light-stained, grape-bordered universe. They stare back from the windows, trembling with life. They are alive. I mean this not in the ordinary mystical sense, but in one common to a grander age, the age of Jeremy Calder and his witches, who knew the truth that life is an idea. Every bubbled imperfection in the glass holds a germ of principle, the lead mullions flow with the conception of rivers, and as I watch, the bear lifts his snout from a golden honeycomb and grumbles a prayer for my salvation; he is the holiest of the lot, a gentle monster whose last red meal was so long ago that he has forgotten the call of the blood and now passes the hours in monastic contemplation. The owl, persnickety old darkness, nods judgmentally; the lamb gambols, beckoning me to sin with flirtatious wags of its bobbed tail. They each have some comment to make on my performance, my life… all, that is, except the lion. He has never moved or spoken in these six years, and because he is the most beautiful of them, the noblest, he withholds much commentary that I long to hear. I wonder for what stimulus he is waiting. I've heard that Jeremy Calder often carried out private interrogations of the witches beneath this particular window, and that at times the cries of pain issuing from the church were indistinguishable from cries of womanly pleasure. Could this have silenced my lion? And did Jeremy go probing after Satan, risking the very extent of his manhood in scourging those vessels clean, or like me, was he merely lustful? The intent once mattered, I suppose. But no more. This age suppresses the importance of intent, and what is valued is effect, result, profit.

I swallow the dregs of the wine, and pulp catches between my teeth. I'm pleased, seeing in this an omen, because it's the pulp of life I'm always seeking in the thin wine of existence. The palpable, the chewable. Difficult to minister without some knowledge of those wilds, for we live in a universe of black rules and rudderless stars, and how can one navigate without grounding oneself in the depths of that medium? Thus it is I must indulge my needs from time to time… though in truth I need no excuse for indulgence. I'm a hale man in my early forties, my wife is dead, and I have met no suitable replacement, unless good Marge Trombley were to unshackle from her Jeffrey. Sigh. Would that it were so! I gaze at my warped reflection in the bottle glass. Its emptiness is my own. But not for long. A sense of purpose has lately begun stealing over me, less an emotion than a physical condition, yet embodying qualities of both. Perhaps it will come clear at the "church conference."

Two-hundred-and-eight miles from Fallon, where St. Mary's bides in whiteness, lies the town of Corn River, and on its southern outskirts stands an old brick house, home to the beautiful Serena de Miron (nee Carla DiLuca) a purveyor of Greek, French, and various Third World nationalities so exotic in character that not even the Bible was sufficiently wise to warn against them. Other girls live in the house, but it is Serena I fancy… Serena who knows well the muscular analogues of my spiritual requirements. Black hair, pale unblemished skin, the face on an angel by Degas, and as fine a set of warheads as these eyes have ever seen.

All coupled with a gum-chewing, airhead mentality. The perfect tour guide to the pulp of contemporary life. She is waiting for me in a room whose walls show as veins of a cream-colored mineral seaming a bedrock of posters, most depicting depraved-looking men with guitars. "Frankie!" she squeals, coming to her knees and bouncing on the bed. "Where you been?"

"Sales trip," I say, shrugging off my jacket. Franklyn is, indeed, my Christian name, but I have told Serena that I'm a traveler in costume jewelry, and on each visit I present her with some bit of gaud as proof. From my trouser pocket I remove a pair of long rhinestone earrings that twist and twinkle like gemmy worms. Serena snatches them, holds them to her ears, pulling back her hair to let me judge the effect... a witchily beautiful effect. Good thing for you, Serena, that old Jeremy has not come in my stead.

Some hours later, lying face to face, still joined, I mention my problematic attraction to Marge Trombley. "Ya like her, huh?" she says.

"Like?" I mull over the quality of my feelings. "Let's say I'm drawn to something in her, something I can't quite fathom."

Serena gives me a chummy internal squeeze. "You're so sensitive, Frankie. I wish you was a younger guy."

This inspires me to prove that age has not entirely drained my vitality, and we do not continue the conversation for another hour.

"I don't know what to tell ya," she says. "What's she alla 'bout?"

I have little more than intuition to draw on as regards Marge's character, but I make a stab at analysis. "Quiet, conservative," I say. "On the surface, at least. Repressed. And that's the thing I want to know in her. Whatever's buried under those years of repression."

"And her husband beats her?"

"Habitually."

"Y'know," Serena says, "Sounds to me she ain't sure what she wants. I mean she is sure but she might need convincin'. Like maybe gettin' beat up alla time... well, she probably don't enjoy it or nothin'. But she's probably used to bein' forced."

"I don't understand."

"Yeah, you do." Serena squirms, and I respond. She giggles. "Ooh, I like that!"

"What were you going to say?"

"'Bout what?"

"Marge... convincing her."

"See"—a crease mars Serena's brow, and her tone grows earnest, knowing—"she's gonna go right to the edge with ya, and then she's gonna need a push, y'know. To make her fall."

"A push?"

"Serena laughs. "Y'gotta be masterful, Frankie. Y'know how to be masterful, don'tcha?"

On cue, I become masterful.

Between bouts with Serena, I wander the brothel. It, too, is a place of worship, one with a more comprehensible god than that scrap of darkness who inhabits St. Mary's and as such I find its lessons apt. Standing in the gloomy corridor, listening to cries of pleasure both fraudulent and unfeigned, I remember my wife's cries of pain as the thing that ate her from within gnawed closer and closer to the quick. How I loved her, yet at the same time how I resented her unsightly dying. Sometimes I could scarcely determine whether my urge to put her out of her misery was funded by mercy or by an irrational murderous impulse. Those months of watching her die, of trying to soothe her agony, unhinged me, set me on a canted course from which I have not yet and perhaps never will recover. . . .Does it surprise you that I'm aware of my deviant sensibilities? Perhaps it is surprising; however, I've lived too long within my own cracked shell to be confounded by the eerie slants of light that penetrate and color thought. In any case, to be mad in this age is a form of wisdom, a lens through which one can view its oblique truths and gain knowledge by which to apply what is learned. So, though madder than most, I am also wiser, more capable of action, and the action, or rather the confluence of actions, that occurs to me while standing in the hallway strikes me as being the zenith of my mad wisdom. Why haven't I seen it before? It should have been obvious! Marge and our Saturday evening tryst, the compatible congregation of sin, Serena's advice, the traditions of the church, and on and on. Everything points to the fact that like any good shepherd I shall have to lead my flock by example, steer them onto the path of righteous wickedness, and bring forth the fire of a new god from the embers of the old. By example … and by the word that will spring from that example. Yes, yes! Finally a fit topic for a sermon, a fit occasion to commemorate. Smiling, my clouded sense of purpose in focus at last, I fling open the door to Serena's room, startling her. She rolls on her back, her Naughty Girl nightie riding up over her thighs.

"Geez, Frankie," she says. "You look …" She tips her head to the side, searching apparently for an appropriate term or word. "Different or something."

Could my illumination have worked a physical change? Anything is possible, I suppose. I study my reflection in the mirror backing the door, but see nothing out of the ordinary… except in the measure of my self-regard. I realized now that for months I have avoided mirrors, not wanting to view the hapless soul shriveling in my flesh. But that soul is not in evidence. In my mirror image I perceive confidence, a lion's-worth of confidence. And intent. Oh, I am ripe to bursting with intent.

"What you see before you," I say, turning to Serena, "is man grown suddenly great with conviction."

Serena giggles and pats the mattress beside her. "Well, don't waste it Frankie. Come on over 'fore it shrinks back to normal."

Saturday night, the last pallid light of an ashen day illuminating the stained-glass windows, and candles burning steadily on the altar, flanking a silver cross of a size suitable for the crucifixion of a small child. Separated from Serena and the Church of Fleshly Delights, my conviction—as Serena playfully intimated—has shrunk. I am nervous, full of doubt. Yet my intent remains firm. Doubt-ridden or not, I will do the deed. And as Marge enters through the front door, I slip the bolt into place, securing us within an unknown country, one whose boundaries we are soon to defame. The snick of the bolt makes her jump, but I smile reassuringly. "Burglars," I say.

"Or mischievous choirboys." She smiles in return, relaxing.

With a sly wink toward the lion, I lead her back into the rectory, which is attached by a corridor to the choir's dressing room, and I sit her down on the red velvet sofa. Her hair is sewn with glints by the dim track lighting, her lips are redder than the velvet, gleaming curves, and in the cleavage of her frock I spot an inch of lace. One button more than usual undone. The final signal, Marge. I will not fail you.

I offer wine, she demurs, I insist. The wine is the same pale red of her hair, and as she sips, I enjoy the conceit that she is tasting her own substance. I sit beside her, not too close, not too far. A seductive distance, yet I disguise a tempter's propinquity with sincere concern, listening to complaints about her Jeffrey.

"He's been gone almost two weeks this time," she says. "And he swore he wouldn't be back.

Thank you, Jeffrey.

"He'll be back." I say, stroking her arm. "Don't worry." Not a flinch from Marge, only a shy glance.

"I know you're right," she says. "But…"

"Yes."

"This will sound awful, Reverend, but…"

"Franklyn," I say, "Please call me Franklyn."

"All right." Wan smile. "Franklyn." She sighs, and a curve of white flesh swells above the lace. "As I was saying, this will sound awful, but I'm not sure I want him back."

I pretend to be in a deep study. "It's not awful in the least," I say. "You've endured too much from him already."

She stares into her wine glass as if seeking an oracle. "I don't know."

"Marge," I begin.

She looks at me, startled.

"Forgive my familiarity," I say, drinking in those delicate features. "It's just I feel close to you, in your confidence."

"No, no. It's all right."

"Marge," I continue. "You've been married how long… almost ten years, isn't it?"

A nod.

"To stay and suffer more abuse would be foolhardy."

"I suppose, but it's not so simple a question. I'm afraid I might be leaving him for the wrong reason." This last accompanied by a flush.

"I see." And I do see: Marge is close to an admission. I pretend awkwardness. "I... uh." Clear my throat. "May I ask if there's someone else?"

She lowers her head, and this time the nod is almost imperceptible. "You have strong feelings for this other man?"

"Yes."

"Love is nothing to be ashamed of Marge. Not in your case, not given the loveless circumstance of your house. You have to seize what joy you can, you have to obey the imperatives of your heart."

I have planned a long drawn-out seduction, but fired by my own words I shift closer, our thighs nearly touching, and lean to her. "Marge," I say. "I know, I know."

She tries to harden her face, but melts. "I can't," she says. "I'm not sure." But her mouth opens to me. I undo a button, and she arches beneath my hands. Inch by inch the frock divides, and my palms glory in the weight of her breasts. I whisper, telling her of my long desire. I slide one strap of her slip off her shoulder, bury my face in softness. Feel her tense.

"No!" she says, pushing my head away. "No, please."

"Don't be afraid," I tell her, and burrow in again.

"No!" She yanks at my hair, beats a fist against my shoulder, and I realize that we have reached the point that Serena in her wisdom predicted. Now is the proof of conviction, the honing of intent into action. I rip away the last buttons, and Marge screams, tries to claw me. But I beat her hands aside, and drag her from the sofa and into the bedroom.

"Go ahead," I say, panting. "Scream. No one will hear. You're going to get what you came for, witch!"

The venom in my voice astounds me, as does the epithet. It hardly seems that it was I who spoke. But I put it from mind and address her in a gentler fashion.

"It'll be sweet, Marge. You'll see. After tonight there'll be no regrets, no recriminations."

All the while, I'm lashing her wrists and legs to the bedposts with four lengths of rope. Odd... I don't recall having cut them. Ah, well. In some fugue I must have foreseen the determination underlying her recalcitrance. "Witch," I realize, is a most fitting term. For though I have seen her form by day, humble and gentle, sightly to the moral eye, even then I glimpsed the hidden form that now confronts me: a voluptuous figure that might adorn a Tarot card, with hair and rags blown to cover her nakedness by a wind that no one but her can feel. She looks at you—as Marge is looking at me this moment—with terror and anxiety, and you know her name is Woman, frail and sweet, demanding guidance. Yet penetrating that glaze of fear, you make out another eye, blue and calm, regarding you with measured appraisal, and you understand that the name of this interior self is Reason. Oh, she has many names, and none are wholesome, for all are funded by that last interior creature, that fuming golden thing with eyes as blank as suns, who stands in the scorched circle of the Devil gaze, exposing to him the charms with which she seeks to govern all men, and it is she who is the Great Lie, the embodiment of intoxicating and corrupting principle, and her name the men speak with awe and longing, unaware of its enervating effects, her name is Love...

I feel a touch of dizziness and pinch the bridge of my nose in an attempt to stem it. The tenor of my thoughts disturbs me, yet I chalk them up to the extreme nature of my actions, the conflict between their necessity and the disciplines instilled in me at the seminary; it would be surprising if I were not somewhat disoriented. I stare down at Marge. Lashed tightly in the remnants of her clothing, heaving up from the bed, she is a pretty sight, and while I undress, I talk to her... No, I make purring, rumbling comments that are less speech than animal promises. Then, kneeling between her legs, I find that despite her protestations, reduced now to whimpers, the witch is ready for our consummation.

After I'm done, I sit naked with pen and paper at my writing desk and, unmindful of Marge's pleading, begin the creation of my next day's sermon. I have never felt so capable, so filled with thunderous verbal potential.

"I won't tell," says Marge. "I won't tell anyone. Just let me go."

In the half-light, her breasts gleam pale, inspiring me further. I choose my text and scribble a brief introduction.

"I swear," says Marge, and breaks in to sobs.

Exasperated, I let out a sigh and set down my pen. My duty as lover must pre-empt my priestly duty for awhile; I must finish Marge's instruction, bring her wholly into the realm of the senses, unravel that dark knot in her breast that I have only begun to loosen. "Darling," I say as I enter her again. "This, too, shall pass."

Though she twists her head aside, though she affects revulsion, her cry is of pleasure not pain. She cannot fool me. I am expert in these matters.

I alternate bouts of lovemaking and sermon-writing. The two pursuits, I understand, are linked, and I come from each renewed and eager for more of the other. Marge tries every ploy to deny her feelings, to cousin me into releasing her. For a time she pretends to pretend enjoyment, thinking to tempt me into untying her, not knowing I perceive her true ecstasy, her absolute involvement, her delight in the bonds. I let her know that I am not persuaded by instructing her in several of the exotic practices I have picked up at the brothel in Corn River, disciplines foreign to Marge, yet ones to which she swiftly adapts, growing ever more silent in contemplation of the new sensations she experiences. And in that silence, the dark construct of her secret sin starts to lose conformation, to send out threads through her flesh and spirit. By first light she is all but its embodiment, and had I another hour before the service, I would be able to complete the work I have begun. But both it and she will wait. I check her bonds, kiss her on the brow, look onto her staring eyes, wide-open in the study of that internal unraveling. A bit vacant I think. But her color is good, she will mend. Yes, the witch will bless my name for this night of liberation.

Eleven o'clock, and showered, serene and in a freshly starched surplice, I stand behind the griffin's ebony beak, gazing out over the congregation, listening to thunder, watching the rainy light penetrate the segments of stained glass, spreading a gray gloom over all. My flock seems edgy, no doubt the result of my minute-long consideration of the words I am about to speak. Soon, though, they will be relaxed as never before, freed from the bonds of propriety to enact their sly wishes. I smile, nod, and they glance nervously at one another. It may be that—as do I—they sense some vast imminence. At last, resting my hands on the griffin's head, I begin.

"The first part of my text for today," I say, "is taken from the French poet and playwright, Atonin Artaud."

This causes a general stirring . . . not that Artaud and his cabalistic creed are known in Fallon, but it unsettles them that I should stray from my usual course.

"Do evil," Artaud says. "Do evil and commit many sins. But do no evil to me." I allow no time for a reaction, but launch into the body of the sermon. "This direct instruction might be taken for a misstatement of the Golden Rule, but in truth it implies the essence of the rule, it gives a new reading of that truth appropriate to our time. For we are all evil, are we not? Whatever good resides in us, it is mediated by a quantity of evil, and locked together these two forces intertwine and darken in us, until in the end one and one alone establishes dominion. We may by force of habit effect good works, love a good life, sin only minimally, yet mostly we are not impelled to behave thus by the empowering radiance of good, but rather by the fear of admitting to evil, of facing it and giving it its due. We have been taught that to master evil we must suppress it. And this is wrong. The act of suppression twists us. We become vessels filled with repressed desires and needs that without light grow into gnarled and mutant shapes."

Rustling everywhere. Women whispering together; men sitting expressionless, refusing to confront their discomfort; a child giggling.

"This," I go on, "brings me to the second part of my text, a quote from the magus Aleister Crowley. 'Do what thou wilt be the whole of the law.'"

The rustling increases, but I pay it no heed.

"Crowley was not advising us to rape and murder, to do unnatural deeds. Rather he was encouraging us to liberate our evil natures, to give vent to sin before it can grow great and malignant. And Artaud: . . . 'do no evil to me.' This bespeaks a comprehension that evil thus vented rarely involves a crime with a victim, that it expresses itself in mild forms such as lust. Once expressed, then our good works—when we attempt them—become the products of a true saintly intent and not fear."

The word "lust" might have been a needle thrust into the bony rump of every old woman in the church, for they all sit up straight, fully attentive and unanimously grim. My fingers clench the griffin's skull, and I feel a force surging through the black wood. The stained glass animals twitch in their rectangular confines. The moment is near. I lean forward, becoming folksy, gentling my tone.

"We of St. Mary's are much blessed." I nod, imbuing the gesture with a thespian measure of sagacity. "Much blessed. For our sins, though multiplicitous and diverse, have each a complement among our body. And so we need not venture out into the world and risk humiliation in order to express our desires. We need only do what we have always done, and that is, trust in the fellowship. Here amidst friends and neighbors, we can bare our secrets … and not merely bare them, but indulge them with those whose secrets are partner to our own. Here we can share joy and pleasure free from spying eyes and moral judgments, and in so doing find the new meaning of God."

Indignation and anger are creeping into their expressions, but I am not concerned. The truth will set them free.

"I know your sins," I say. "I know them as you believe only you know them. There is no reason for shame in this place. Here you may admit and openly engage those forbidden pastimes of which you have long dreamed. Join me now in an act of liberation, empty yourselves of the vile. Taste and touch and know the flavors and textures of freedom." I pause to let them absorb my meaning, to let them prepare for what will come. "I have chosen this day to introduce you one to the other, sin to compatible sin, desire to desire. This morning we will initiate our adventure in the prurient, and bring God's bud to bloom in an exaltation of joyous camaraderie."

I favor them all with a loving gaze; their agitation and discomfort compels me to cut short my preamble. I will not allow them to suffer more the imprisonment of joy. "Miles Elbee," I say, "meet Cory Eubanks. Submissive meet dominatrix." A gasp from the back row where pretty, plump Cory sits with her husband. "No need for alarm, Cory," I cry. "No need to hide those black leathers and spike heels in the closet any longer, for in Miles you have one who will bleed for you, who will crawl to kiss the braided tip of your whip."

Miles jumps to his feet, sputtering, and the stunned pale faces of the rest are fixed on me.

"Emily Prideau," I say. "Meet Billy Taggart, Joey Grimes, and Ted Dunning. Their dream, like yours, entails a three on one, the Holy Trinity made flesh."

Emily ducks her head into her mother's arm, but the boys smirk and nudge one another.

"Carlton Dedaux," I shout above the growing babble. "Meet little Jimmy Newly. Look into each other's eyes and see the wet imprint of your kindred lusts."

They are all standing, shaking fists, berating me as I continue to make my introductions. My voice falters. Could I have been wrong? It seem so. How can I have misjudged their temper, their readiness for the new?

Miles Elbee strides to the base of the pulpit. "You son of a bitch!" he screeches. "The bishop's going to hear about this! I'll …"

Anger forks through me, and I lean down to him. "Go ahead," I say. "The bishop's underwear is the same brand as yours, only his lace trim is a bit more provocative."

Miles glances to his waist to see if anything is showing, then backs away, cursing at me. Other men, Emily's father among them, are being restrained from attack by their fellows, and the women are streaming out the door. Children are laughing, playing tag around the baptismal font. The entire concept of spiritual advancement is in disarray, the revolution I have envisioned is overthrown before it is begun.

They bunch at the front door, looking back at me, and as the last of them exits, hopelessness takes the place of my anger. A rock splinters the window of the old bear, shattering for once and all his search for a honeyed philosophy. Someone calls to me, accusing me of evil as if evil were something I have avoided confronting. They did not hear a single word I spoke.

I step down from the pulpit, walk along the aisle and slump into a pew beneath the lion, whose expression now seems one of disapproval or—at least—of stern judgment. He is right to think badly of me. Not only have I failed in my intent, I have lost my sinecure. What, I wonder, awaits me? Will I join the homeless, wandering the streets, my possessions in a Hefty bag? No, no, it will be worse than that. There's Marge to consider, after all. I doubt she will be forgiving in the face of my failure to enlist the congregation. An asylum, perhaps. Possibly jail. I think I would prefer the penitential solitude of jail to the gibbering complexities of straitjackets and Thorazine and electroshock.

Outside, the gray light darkens, and the eyes of the lion grow balled and leaden. Thunder, the scent of ozone as lightning cracks the sky with a ripping sound, starting me from my morose reverie, alerting me to a change in the atmosphere, in—it seems—the very fabric of reality. Steam is billowing from the griffin's snout, the walls are trembling, and except for the lion, all the stained-glass animals are pacing in their windows. I jump up, amazed. This is what I expected at the culmination of my sermon, at the conjoining of my flock. How can it be… I have failed, have I not? And then comprehension dawns. I see it clearly now. My sermon was not the event essential to provoke this change, or if it was, it was only the spark and not the true burning. And I see, too, that I have not failed. Oh, my flock will publicly disavow what I revealed, will disparage me. However, after the scandal dies down, they will look around at one another, recalling my list of sins and compatibilities, and slyly at first, then more openly, they will seek each other out for the purposes in which I have instructed them. But what of the burning that must take place before this can come to pass? Suddenly dismayed, I sit back in the pew. Maybe I am seeing things, maybe nothing will happen, maybe griffin is not writhing, tossing his ebony-feathered head, and maybe … A noise behind the choir stall, a white shape moving in the shadows.

Marge!

Naked, with shreds of rope trailing from her wrists and something shiny in her hand.

On spotting me, she freezes, then starts forward, haltingly at first, but growing more assured with every step. Her eyes are black, no whites showing whatsoever, ovals of griffin-color, and as she descends from the altar to the aisle, she raises a shining knife high.

For an instant I am afraid, and I start to come to my feet, thinking to run to take the weapon from her. But a moment later understanding banishes fear. Of course, of course! Everything is plain to me. As with the birth of every new religion, a sacrifice is necessary. I've been a fool not to anticipate this, and now that my fate is at hand, I rejoice, because I also understand that for me death will be liberation. That it has ever been the one means by which I might elude the gravities of the ordinary. Marge is speaking to me in some pagan tongue, some evil parlance, drooling spittle, and from this evidence and that of her pupilless eyes, I reach a further understanding. I have been hasty in debunking the myth of Jeremy and his victims, short-sighted in assuming that the supernatural would play no part in the infinite congruency of events and moments essential to the creation of divinity. It's an obvious truth that every fleck and fragment of the past must be represented in this seminal act. Marge's aspect is unshakeable evidence of witchy possession, a spirit given purchase by the trauma of rape, (perhaps this was the knot within her, no real thing itself, but rather a nest in which an incubus could lodge); and recalling my venomous abuse of her, seeing in new light the particular definition of my madness, it is apparent that Jeremy and I are more closely connected than by tradition alone.

Marge stops beside me, the knife trembling above, and with her sweaty breasts heaving, her deep sin unraveled and leaking forth, never has she seemed more beautiful; an object of pure license, pure chaotic principle.

"Ah ... ah!" she says, seeking to translate the dictates of her Satanic duty into words I will understand, unaware that my understanding is at last complete.

"Do what you must," I say, fixing my gaze on the lion. Why does he refuse to bless me with his powerful knowledge? Soon it will be too late.

Another incoherent gasp from Marge, a spit-filled sound that seems to me redolent of frustration, of some internal struggle.

"No reason to feel remorse," I say.

Our eyes meet, our darknesses co-mingle, and I turn away, rapt in contemplation of my release, yet not wanting to witness the downward arc of the instrument of release. Several seconds slip by and I begin to worry that some human weakness is restraining her.

"Hurry, Marge," I tell her.

"You... uh..." she says, her hand scrabbling at my shoulder. "You!"

She needs encouragement, needs to know that I welcome this ending, that I comprehend the requirements of divine resolution.

"Marge," I say, "You have never seemed so desirable as now. How much I truly love you."

A shriek breaks from her lips, and I feel the force of her firmed commitment in the instant before the knife sinks home. The pain is sharp, the shock all-absorbing. Yet there is sweetness in the pain, in the strength it dredges up, the profound confidence it rips loose from the recesses of my being. I refuse to fall, I want to savor every instant of my passage, to know everything left to know. The griffin howls, a long keening note, and I feel wetness on my chest. Truth is everywhere, the church is black with God. I am not dying, I realize. In some element of that dark force, I will continue. Like Jeremy, I will go on, the shadow of a shadow, the hint of a spectacular possibility. Marge strikes again, weakness overwhelms me. My heart—though pierced—is glad, my soul at peace. And as I topple sideways on the pew, looking up to the window glowing with supernal light, the stained-glass lion—always my favorite—lifts its head and roars.

Erotorium

BY STEVEN SPRUILL

A SENSE OF LOSS SETTLED OVER CHEMOSH AS HE WATCHED THE CELEBRANTS WRITHE together on the couches and carpets of the Erotorium. Here and there, the flash of a creamy thigh or a moan of pleasure would pique his interest, but he got no real charge from it, no sense of power, no arousal. In fact, he found it boring—which, in turn, depressed him. Some of the females were quite beautiful, indistinguishable from women of his own species…

To the eye.

But what else mattered in sex?

However love might enrich the act, few if any of these citizens were in love, at least with each other, and look at them roll and grapple, nuzzle and stroke, moaning, arching, getting drunk on their bodies the way nature intended.

With a goodly boost from Anat, goddess of fertility.

Having lit the celebrants' erotic fires on behalf of the goddess, who was unable to do so herself because she didn't exist, he might at least draw some heat from the spectacle, but no. For the best, no doubt, but still it left him feeling cheated.

His next stop tonight would not be boring.

No, you must not think about that now.

At once, Chemosh blocked from his mind the burgeoning desire that would be so dangerous while he was attuned to blood. Instead, he occupied himself with counting the celebrants. A good turnout, over three hundred, making thirty or more pregnancies likely. The population of the sister cities would continue to grow, while the tax remained constant, reducing the burden on each citizen. Good for all concerned.

Continuing to engorge those blood vessels which would keep the crowd burning with sexual frenzy, Chemosh turned away, gazing out the window of arching stone. Other great towers of the city rose to the east and west. The nearest—the tower of Astarte—spilled light like molten gold into the moonless night. Faint cries of climax carried across from the celebrants in that tower, as they revelled under the Influence of the phage priest Baraqel. A good crowd there, too, from the sound. It would be interesting to know whether the phallic towers and the female rounding of most of the windows in the city had any real pre-stimulative effect on the populace. Abezi-Thibod, the principal phage architect of the city, touted the high turnout at the nightly celebrations as vindication of his designs, but it was enough for Chemosh that the shapes were graceful and pleasing in their own right.

A beautiful night, warm but not too hot. North of the city walls, the sea murmured and sighed. Wishing to see it better, Chemosh willed blood into the capillaries that fed the specialized receptors in his retinas. His eyes prickled faintly and the sky lightened from dull black to a lovely cobalt blue with swirls of emerald. Now he could see the silvery phosphorescence of starshine rippling across the waves. A sea breeze billowed the curtains around the open arch, bringing him the scents of salt and kelp, the teeming organic richness of the sea. In the gardens below, crickets chanted their mad, breathless poems, soothing to his ears.

And yet he felt uneasy.

Studying the sky, he searched for clouds that might not be clouds. Why was he so on edge? Part of it was his condition, of course. He was depleted, physically parched. But it was also Balberith's fears, he knew. He was letting his general's paranoid counsels work on his memory and imagination, even though three hundred years had passed since a destroyer attack. Surely Uziel and his legions, appalled by their own wretched excesses at Atlantis, had forsaken their murderous raids for all time. Memories of that terrible night, mercifully blunted by the centuries, were still sharp enough to catch in Chemosh's throat. A civilization destroyed, because of Uziel's delusions of grandeur.

I saw him weeping, Chemosh thought, after he had exterminated my people. Staring in horror at the bodies of children floating on the ocean, he covered his eyes and fled, with all the rest of them ....

The nape of Chemosh's neck tingled. There—at the horizon, rising from the sea? No, just a small cloud formed by a humid updraft.

A woman's shriek jerked his attention back to the chamber. One of the celebrants had, in a paroxysm of lust, twisted his mate's head around. Sorting quickly through the lines of control, Chemosh found the offending male and dilated his jugulars. As the blood dumped from his brain, the man slumped over, unconscious, his fingers slipping from the female's hair. She shoved him off her with a curse. Chemosh calmed her with a rush of blood to the pleasure center of her brain; she gave an enraptured laugh, pressing her hands to her cheeks. The celebrants around her, who'd turned in concern, smiled and went back at each other. Chemosh felt a small satisfaction. They were his wards, these people, and if he could feel no physical attraction, maybe it was because they were, in a very real sense, his sheep and he their shepherd. He protected them, gave them the pleasure they loved even more than food, kept order among them while allowing them more freedom than most kings, increased their numbers and asked only a just return, a commitment made willingly by most since it need be made good by only a few.

Gazing over the Erotorium, he realized that several of the celebrants were sweating profusely; faces had turned dangerously red. Time to end this session, before someone's heart burst.

As Chemosh eased his influence from their veins and arteries, the feverish activity began to slacken. Moans gave way to sighs, hands turned back to service their own bodies, patting disarranged hair back into place, wiping away sweat, searching the floor for fallen clothes. A murmur of laughter and conversation arose. Their sated smiles pleased him. A good celebration. They began to file toward him and the door. Rising from his divan, Chemosh descended to the mosaic, taking up position in the center of the stylized moon. Each citizen bowed as he passed, and Chemosh made sure to touch each outstretched hand, to give each lowered head an affectionate pat.

God, made real.

But he was not a god, no. Just a priest king for gods invented by men—the safest kind. Best always to keep that in mind.

When the crowd was gone, he allowed himself to feel again the excitement that would have been too dangerous during the fertility celebration. Hurrying down the steps, one hand trailing along the slight curvature of the wall, Chemosh exited halfway down, striding across the top of the Astarte gate, past the temple of Asherah and into the tower of El, where he spiraled back up. He knew he would arrive well ahead of the new acolyte, who must present him or herself exactly at midnight, but need made him hurry anyway.

The phage on duty at the temple of El opened the great double doors for him and closed them behind him without a word, rather than risk irritating him in his edgy condition. Chemosh checked his reflection in the glassy surface of the cleansing pool, blessing the remarkable body that, even as it neared depletion, neither sweated nor panted—both unseemly for a representative of the gods.

If physically unruffled, he must still compose himself emotionally. The elect were often accompanied by family members, a husband or wife, and he must let none of his eagerness show, only the gravity of the great occasion. Taking a flaming brand from beside the pool, Chemosh circled the vast chamber, igniting the torches that brought each section of the Mural of Changing to light. A true masterpiece, superior even to the one Douma had painted in the now sunken temple of Atlantis. When all the torches were lit, Chemosh stood in the center of the chamber, turning slowly to admire the mural as it progressed around the temple. To the left of the door, where it began, the pair of acolytes looked small and entirely human, their heads bowed in worship. In each successive section, the man and woman straightened, and their plain robes took on the embellishments of the priesthood, as they grew in stature and beauty, until finally at the right hand of the door, they became hemophage priest-kings of El.

It had a certain power, this painting. If interpreted as metaphor, it wasn't that far from the truth. A transformation from human to phage would take place here tonight, one of life and death significance.

The gong outside the door sounded its deep, shivering tone, and Chemosh opened the round portals that let the light of the torches lance out in brilliant shafts. The guard would wait ten seconds from this impressive signal, he knew, giving him plenty of time to step back to the center of the room and occupy the moon circle in the great mosaic. Chemosh turned to face the doors again, his chest full, the air humming sweet in his lungs.

His anticipation dipped as the doors yawned open and he saw that General Balberith was with the two normals waiting outside. What was wrong with him, now of all times?

The normals held a deep bow as Balberith swept past them to the circle.

"What are you doing?" Chemosh whispered in a voice too low for any normal ears.

"Sorry, but I need to speak with you."

"It will have to wait."

Balberith frowned. "It can't."

"Yes, it can. I'll be quick."

Balberith's dark, handsome face softened in belated understanding. "All right. I'll wait outside."

What could he want at a moment like this? Chemosh wondered with irritation. More alarmist prattle about the Destroyers? The possibility chilled him and he nearly called Balberith back, but the general was already outside again, and the normals, rising from their bow, had entered.

Chemosh's heart quickened, and he forgot everything else. A graybeard in a rough robe who looked to be in his mid-forties led a woman of perhaps thirty to the outer band of the moon ring and bowed again.

"Welcome," Chemosh said in a voice that was both magisterial and kind, and not in the least excited. "Which one of you is coming to join the gods?"

"Her," the man said. "My niece. Her name is Hannah. I'm Ephriam. She drew the white coin last lottery. It has this date and time on it."

"May I have it?"

The woman fumbled the coin from the folds of her robe and presented it to him. He saw that her hand trembled. Fear? He steered the blood to her pleasure center, and saw her shoulders lift in a quick intake of breath. Ephriam seemed grim as well, so Chemosh gave him a little push, too, and he smiled, his eyes filling with tears of pleasure. "Ah," he said. "This is a great day, your worship."

"Indeed it is, Ephriam. I congratulate you and all your kin. You understand that Hannah must enter the ring of the acolytes now, and must remain unseen by her kin and all citizens for ten years or the gods will destroy her and any who defile her with their gaze?"

Ephriam's smile slipped, but only a little. "Of course, your worship."

"And after she is purified and instructed in the ways of the gods, she will gain our priestly powers and become a ruler of the kingdom."

"Yes, worship." Ephriam bowed, and so did Hannah.

"You may embrace her if you like, and say your goodbyes." Chemosh turned his back, not just to give them privacy but because his eyes burned now with tears. This was the moment he dreaded each time. A lump rose in his throat. To himself, he uttered the words that were the religion's only real truth: *This is the way it has to be, not just for my sake but for all the thousands out there. I didn't choose it, and I am at its mercy as surely as this woman.*

Turning again, Chemosh saw that Ephriam still lingered. "You had a question?"

"Is... there any chance the gods will allow Hannah to serve them here in our city when she has finished her transformation?"

"You know that's very rare."

"Yes, but will…" The man swallowed. "Will you pray for it?"

He'll die of old age before the ten years is up. "Yes, Ephriam."

The man backed out, bowing. "Thank you Father. Goodbye, Hannah, goodbye."

The guard closed the doors on him.

Mindful of Balberith waiting outside, Chemosh hurried past the woman and threw the bolt on the door. As he turned, Hannah looked up at him. She was attractive, he saw, with lovely brown eyes and a fine, oval face. He pushed the realization away.

"Your worship, I'm so hon—"

He dilated her jugulars at once, before she could finish the sentence that he knew would only tear at his heart. Her knees buckled and she fell sideways, her head hitting the mosaic with a sickening crack. Chemosh verified that her heart was still beating, then stripped off his robes to spare them and fell on her, sinking his teeth into her throat, tearing at the arteries. The blood, bright and rich, smelled of dark bread soaked in wine. He tore at her, in thrall to his own frenzy now, elated as the blood coursed down his throat, and the strength flowed into him. Rising from her corpse, he danced around the circle, rubbing her blood on his chest in an ecstasy he could not control, a part of his nature he could no more escape than breathing.

When the euphoria had passed, he knelt beside Hannah's body and took her cooling hand in his and thanked her, for giving him the blood that would stop him from relapsing into the horrible, starving sickness no phage could escape if he did not feed. *I was like you once,* he told her tenderly. *Long, long ago. And then, in my thirteenth year, the sickness came upon me. I'm sorry I had to do this. But order is the salvation of your people as well as ours. When we prey on you without giving anything in return, we descend into evil wantonness and many more of you die. This way there is restraint for you and some honor for us. We fight off the rapacious Canaanite kings who would kill many more of you than we. None of your kind can stand against us in battle. We defend you, protect you, give you all we can. You have flocks of your own, you carry the lambs in your arms, you love them as much as you dare, but some must always die to keep you alive.*

If there is a true god, may he receive you now.

And may he forgive me—or take this hunger from me.

Chemosh washed quickly in the basin at the side of the circle and put his clothes back on. "Ready," he said. A small door at the rear of the chamber opened and Apheus, who had fed only a night ago, came in to remove the body for burning and to clean up, a favor he, himself, would perform here tomorrow night.

Balberith, pacing up and down in the anteroom, wheeled to face him. "You're finished?"

"Yes."

"We have problems."

Chemosh, still drunk with well-being on the blood, tried to look suitably grim so Balberith would know he was paying attention.

"Two strangers were seen in the city," the general said. "Tall and beautiful."

"So?"

"They went to the house of a malcontent whose wife has been trying to sow dissension about the lottery. Her name is Orna, I believe. Her sister drew the coin over ten years ago, and when the time was up she and her husband came to the temple asking to see her. They were told she had gone to another city, but it didn't satisfy them, particularly the woman."

"Are people listening to them?"

"No," Balberith said almost reluctantly. "In fact, the family has become something of a joke."

"Then what is our problem?"

"When these two strangers came to their house, their neighbors saw them going in and they gathered outside. As I said, the strangers were good looking, so the crowd started inviting them to come out and join a celebration they were headed for. Orna's husband came out and offered his daughters, instead."

"I don't think I like this family," Chemosh said with distaste.

"Disgusting," Balberith agreed, "but let me finish. The man barred his door and the crowd, offended by this, made a good-natured rush up the steps, as if to break in and ravish the guests. At that point, they were all struck blind."

"What?" The afterglow of feeding drained from Chemosh and he stared at Balberith in shock, feeling punched in the stomach. Only two creatures on the face of the earth had the power to blind normals with Influence—phages and destroyers.

"Remember Atlantis?" Balberith said. "The destroyers had agents in the city for days before the attack. They're back, Chemosh. I was right. This proves it."

Chemosh felt cold. He tried to think what other meaning the blinding could have. Maybe the two strangers were phages from some far place ....

Footsteps floated up the stone stairwell, growing rapidly louder. Balberith turned as one of his lieutenants entered the anteroom. The phage nodded at Chemosh then said, "Orna and her husband and daughters are leaving the city. The two strangers ushered them to the gates."

Balberith's face paled. "Those traitors." He turned back to Chemosh. "What do we do?"

"Have you kept the strangers in sight?"

"Yes."

"Have your agents approach with care and deference. If the two permit them to come close, tell them I must see them."

"What good will that do?" Balberith asked.

"We've got to negotiate, while there's still time."

Balberith scowled. "I say if they let us get within range, strike them down with

Influence and take them hostage, make that murdering bastard Uziel—"

"We don't know this is Uziel."

"Who else? He's the one who believes he's an angel and has convinced his followers of the same. The left hand of God he calls himself. I know you think he regretted Atlantis, but that won't stop him if he thinks his god has spoken to him again."

"If you're right, hostages will do us no good either. Our only hope is to persuade him of the good we've done here."

"He won't see it. He thinks we're the spawn of the devil, wanton with lust, and that we've made depraved heathens out of everyone in the kingdom, that we've turned them to false gods."

"Their gods were here when we came."

Balberith made a dismissive gesture. "Yes, but we've made them more real for our own purposes. Uziel does not care that we must drink blood or die horrible, lingering deaths. He cares only that we drink."

"But in return—"

Balberith held up a hand. "You don't have to convince me. The point is, you'll never convince Uziel. We must fight."

"'How? Their Influence reaches further than ours. They can simply stay out of range and hammer us, like last time. We'll never get close enough."

"Maybe we will, if we can take the two 'strangers' hostage. That might lure the legion in close for a rescue attempt, where we at least have a chance."

"Look!"

Balberith's lieutenant pointed out the window. Chemosh saw the cloud and froze in dread. Red, roiling around the edges, it swept toward the city with terrifying speed.

"Too late." Chemosh's voice came out in a broken whisper. A vast, bitter anguish filled him. Hurrying to the window, he leaned out and looked down at his city for what he knew would be the last time, at the distant temple of Baal the storm god, second only to El, at the graceful towers of celebration, jeweled with light, the arching gateways and fountains, drowsing peacefully while doom swept in.

"I'm taking my fighters into the towers," Balberith said. "Maybe some of the destroyers will dip too close."

Chemosh waved a hand distractedly, barely hearing the clatter of their footsteps receding down the stairs. The cloud blocked out the horizon to the north now, and he could almost make out the individual destroyers, their great wings of energy flaring together in a slow, rhythmic beat, deadly and bewitching. Anger began to burn in him. Climbing from the window, he hooked his fingertips into the seams between the stones and scaled the remaining hundred feet of the temple of El, running across the rooftop to the northern edge. This was the highest spot in the city. He would stand here and wait for Uziel, dare him to come down. Maybe they could yet talk, and the kingdom, with its two great cities, could be spared.

If not, Chemosh thought, I will kill him.

But he knew with a scalding frustration that it wasn't likely, probably impossible. Come on, come on!

The last minute was nearly unbearable, watching the cloud blot out the night, hearing the cries of alarm in the city below as people woke to the sinister, red glow dancing on the walls of their bedrooms. They must think it was simple fire, frightening enough, but they could have no inkling of their true fate, only seconds away now.

Warm air blasted Chemosh's face, combing his hair straight back, the shockwave of heat pushing ahead of the cloud. There at the head of them all he could see Uziel now, the great wings blazing with their own light, the mane of red hair, the eyes, blue as glowing sapphires, his snowy robes.

Then the cloud swept over and white bolts stabbed down, a thousand times the power of lightning. The top of the tower of Anat shattered into a fountain of burning stones that turned like giant rubies against the night before showering down and igniting the streets below. The smell of sulfur scorched Chemosh's nostrils.

"You!" cried a voice above him, in three different pitches, pure as trumpets.

Looking up, he realized Uziel had dropped down from his legions and now hovered only a hundred feet above, glaring at him with those terrible eyes, now black as oil from lid to lid. "Why couldn't you learn?" Uziel cried. "You have defiled them again. Lured them into debauchery and sin. Their souls are on your head."

"Murderer," Chemosh cried, and saw Uziel flinch. The thought flitted through his mind that he, too, was a killer, but not on Uziel's scale. Only Uziel slaughtered whole cities in a night.

"'I'm no murderer," Uziel shouted. "I follow God's command."

"Every man, woman and child? All the innocents?"

"There are no innocents, thanks to you."

Enraged, Chemosh struck out with Influence, grappling for the arteries in Uziel's neck and shoulders, and for a second, the avenging angel wobbled in the air, but there was no fear on his face, and as he broke free and pulled away higher, his face showed a strange, momentary regret. But then he pointed down with his left hand. Knowing what was coming, Chemosh defiantly ripped apart his robes of priesthood, baring his chest.

"Go ahead, kill me too." But he knew he would find no release tonight.

The bolt hit him, and excruciating pain flung him down squirming against the stone roof, and then the stones shattered around him, and he glimpsed the great mural of Douma as he hurtled down through the temple, each floor melting beneath him with the hideous heat from Uziel's left hand, until he crashed among the burning stones at the bottom.

His skin seemed to burn, but he knew it was only the nerves, the vestiges of the body he'd been born with, warning him to run. He did run through the burning streets, trying to find someone to save, but he was far too late, passing bodies by the hundreds, burned crisp in the postures of running, or reduced to ash, flowing down the molten streets.

And then he passed through the arch of the city's south gate, flinging off the burning stones as they fell on his shoulders, staggering onto the plain. Sobs tore at his throat. "Let me die too," he screamed, but there was no one to hear.

He ran down the road away from the city, half out of his mind with grief, hearing the rumble behind him, feeling the ground shake as the heat spread below ground, as it had in Atlantis, shaking the pillars of the earth itself. A crack split the road ahead. He leapt it with a curse and kept running, clapping his hands to his ears, but the roar of the earthquake churned inside his skull. The mountain at the foot of the sea beckoned and he turned off the road toward it, running tirelessly, powered by the blood of Hannah. As he loped up the first foothill of the mountains, he saw ahead, the fleeing family of Orna, the only ones to escape the carnage. Chemosh stopped and stared at them, the man and three women working their way up the mountain trail, traitors to the slaughtered thousands behind them. Was it really possible that this lone woman, refusing to give up her sister, had drawn Uziel and his destroyers to her?

I will kill her, Chemosh thought.

He ran after the departing family, scrambling straight up the rocks to cut them off. He could see them plainly now, the man, old but spry in his fear, was in the lead. The two younger women—the daughters he had offered to his neighbors—kept up with him, but the older one, Oma, lagged behind. Chemosh was almost within range now. His breath tore at his throat, not from exertion but from grief and rage.

And then the woman turned, gazing out over the burning city, and Chemosh saw a vindictive pleasure in her face. With a growl of fury, he struck out at her, finding the motor areas of her brain and draining them of blood. She had time for one scream—a man's name, her husband no doubt, and then her muscles locked, freezing her where she stood. Unable to expand her chest, she suffocated, still staring out over the burning city.

Reaching her side, Chemosh looked for her husband and daughters. There—still hurrying away up the mountain path. Look back, and I will kill you too, he thought. But they did not, and in that moment, his fury crumbled under the weight of all his grief and he knew he would let them live. Maybe they would suffer as he knew he would, or maybe not, but there had already been far too much killing tonight.

Turning back to Lot's wife, Chemosh saw the distant flames dancing in her dead eyes—Sodom and another spot of red light, made smaller by distance, which he knew must be Gommorrah. Weeping, unable to turn as she had, Chemosh watched the lights until they had died out in her eyes.

Response From a Surprised But Pleased Recipient

BY PETER STRAUB

Dear MarketAmerica, Inc.:

We are not supposed to get mail from anyone but our families and legal representatives in here, but the envelope containing your questionnaire got stuck in with a batch of indignant letters from the Brewster Gladden Gilroy LLP secretarial staff and passed through the system unnoticed. My heartfelt thanks go out to the dozing Mailroom officials, to those amusingly irate young women who so dependably rise to the bait provided them by a fellow seeking only to fill the empty hours, and—above all—to you!

In enumerating my responses to your lively and oft-times intriguing questions, I have omitted the aforesaid questions themselves on the grounds that you folks at Market-America, Inc. undoubtedly have an intact list somewhere or other on the premises.

Here goes:

1. Deep River, CT.

2. March 16, 1960, and you know what? I may not be a household name, but I'm the most famous person ever born on that particular day!

3. Let's just say, A large, ugly, impersonal facility entirely at one with its location within the brown, bleeding hills directly northeast of Durham, NC, not to mention the awful gullies, ravines, culverts and freeway underpasses characteristic of that area, which are one and all so hideous you want to break down and weep just at the sight of them. Or, you could say, Undisclosed For Reasons of Security.

4. Unmarried, at least at present.

5. Jefferson Blaine, 22; Tiffany Ronette, 20; Thornton Blaine, 18; Acey-Deucey Colt, 17; Springfield Blaine, 15; Runt, 13; No-Count, 12; L'il Stretch, 10; Other Tiffany, 8.

6. Amherst College, BA (Withheld), 1991.

7. Freelance Consultant; Freelance Website Designer; Financial Advisor; Massage Therapist; Bouncer; Bodyguard.

8. Presently, zilch. In my best years, upwards of, say, $200,000 per annum, and I'm being very conservative here.

9. *Time, Newsweek, The American Mortician, Forensic Science Monthly Updates, TV Guide.*

10. Iceberg Slim, William Burroughs, Poppy Z. Brite, Algernon Swinburne, the Almighty.

11. I'm pretty eclectic: Liberace, Roy Rogers and the Sons of the Pioneers, The Clash, the Ramones, Peter Nero, Toto, Abba, the New York Dolls, Paul Anka, Robert Goulet, Glenn Gould, Chet Baker, Rat Scabies, Elton John. It's about sensitivity, whatever the style.

12. I hope this question is a joke. No, I hate Jerry Seinfeld. What a whiny, smirky, soulless creep, what a monument to self-satisfaction. If they ever put me alone in a room with Jerry Seinfeld, they'd have to wash what was left him down the drain with a hose.

13. The old guard, the unsung heroes—Edmund O'Brien, Rondo Hatton, Lon Chaney Jr., Sheldon Leonard, Dan Duryea, Lionel Stander, Peter Lorre, guys like that, guys you could take to the bank and walk out with a sack full of money.

14. *Sweeny Todd* and *Assassins*, hands down.

15. Did you ever take a good look at the Second Amendment? Every man, woman, and child, not to mention every numbskull, pervert, retard, lunatic, and moron in this country has the right to bear arms, I don't care if it's a piddly little .22 or an AK-47, that's their God-given right. Ignore it at your peril, because once Justice is done, I sure as hell won't.

16. Shirley Temple. According to my counselors at BGG, I can say no more than that. If I could, you'd get an earful, believe me. Wowee, Shirley Temple! Man oh man.

17. To the best of my recollection, I never cast a vote in a national election. If I did, I hope I came down in favor of some lame-brain, scum-sucking loser, because the rest of those guys will steal you blind the second your back is turned.

18. None of your business. Well, okay. It happened when I was looking at a picture of a severed finger in *True Detective*. Kooky, huh? I can smile about that now.

19. That I never had the privilege of serving in the Armed Forces, and I place my right hand over my heart as I write these words, awkwardly, with my left.

20. Another thing I'm not allowed to tell you, but it sure tasted good the one time I was able to try it, I can tell you that. Sort of like a cross between free-range chicken and prime horse-meat, mmmm hmmmm.

Nocturne

BY THOMAS TESSIER

IN THE CALM OF HIS MIDDLE YEARS, O'NETTY MADE IT A POINT TO GO FOR A WALK at night at least once a week. Thursday or Friday was best, as there were other people out doing things and the city was livelier, which pleased him. Saturdays were usually too busy and noisy for his liking, and the other nights a little too quiet—though there were also times when he preferred the quiet and relative solitude.

He enjoyed the air, the exercise, and the changing sights of the city. He enjoyed finishing his stroll at a familiar tavern and sometimes seeing people he knew slightly in the neighborhood. But he also enjoyed visiting a tavern that was new to him, and observing the scene. O'Netty was by no means a heavy drinker. Two or three beers would do, then it was back to his apartment and sleep.

O'Netty went out early one particular evening in September and found the air so pleasant and refreshing that he walked farther than usual. A windy rainstorm had blown through the city that afternoon. The black streets still glistened and wet leaves were scattered everywhere like pictures torn from a magazine. Purple and grey clouds continued to sail low across the darkening sky. Eventually he came to the crest of a hill above the center of the city.

He decided it was time to have a drink before undertaking the long trek back. He saw the neon light of a bar a short distance ahead and started toward it, but then stopped and looked again at a place he had nearly passed. The Europa Lounge was easy to miss. It had no frontage, just a narrow door lodged between a camera shop and a pizzeria. The gold script letters painted on the glass entrance were scratched and chipped with age. But the door opened when O'Netty tried it, and he stepped inside. There was a small landing and a flight of stairs—apparently the bar was in the basement. He didn't hesitate. If it turned out to be something not for him, he could simply turn around and leave, but he wanted at least to see the place.

The stairs were narrow and steep. The one flight turned into two, and then a third. O'Netty might have given up before descending the last steps, but by then he saw the polished floor below and he heard the mixed murmur of voices and music. The bottom landing was a small foyer. There was one door marked as an exit, two others designated as rest rooms, and then the entrance to the lounge itself. O'Netty stepped inside and looked around.

The lounge could not have been more than fifteen feet by ten, with a beamed ceiling. But there was nothing dank or dingy about the place. On the contrary, at first glance it appeared to be rather well done up. It had a soft wheat carpet and golden cedar walls. There were three small banquettes to one side, and a short bar opposite with three upholstered stools, two of which were occupied by men a few years younger than O'Netty. Along the back wall there were two small round wooden tables, each with two chairs. Table lamps with ivory shades cast a creamy glow that gave the whole room a warm, intimate feeling.

There were middle-aged couples in the back two banquettes but the nearest one was empty, and O'Netty took it. The bartender was an older man with gleaming silver hair, dressed in a white shirt, dark blue suit and tie. He smiled politely, nodded and when he spoke it was with a slight, unrecognizable accent. O'Netty's beer was served in a very tall pilsner glass.

The music playing on the sound system was some mix of jazz and blues with a lot of solo guitar meditations. It was unfamiliar to O'Netty but he found it soothing, almost consoling in some way. He sipped his drink. This place was definitely unlike the average neighborhood tavern, but it wasn't at all uncomfortable. In fact, O'Netty thought it seemed rather pleasant.

After a few minutes, he realized that the other people there were speaking in a foreign language. He only caught brief snatches of words, but he heard enough to know that he had no idea what language it was. Which was no great surprise. After all, there were so many European languages one almost never heard—for instance: Czech, Hungarian, Rumanian, Bulgarian and Finnish. O'Netty concluded that he had come across a bar, a social club run by and for locals of some such eastern European origin. Before he left, perhaps he would ask the bartender about it.

Although he couldn't understand anything the others said, O'Netty had no trouble catching their mood. Their voices were relaxed, lively, friendly, chatty, and occasionally there was some laughter. It was possible for O'Netty to close his eyes and imagine that he was sitting on the terrace of a cafe in some exotic and distant city, a stranger among the locals. He liked that thought.

Some little while later, when O'Netty was about halfway through his second glass of beer, he noticed that the others had either fallen silent or were speaking very softly. He sensed an air of anticipation in the room.

A few moments later, a young man emerged from the door behind the bar. The music stopped and everyone was still and quiet. The young man came around to the front of the bar. He could not yet be thirty, O'Netty thought. The young man swiftly pulled off his T-shirt and tossed it aside. He was slender, with not much hair on his chest. He kicked off his sandals and removed his gym pants, so that he now stood there dressed only in a pair of black briefs. The other two men at the bar had moved the stools aside to create more space.

The young man reached into a bag he had brought with him and began to unfold a large sheet of dark green plastic, which he carefully spread out on the floor. He stood on it, positioning himself in the center of the square. Then he took a case out of the bag, opened it and grasped a knife. The blade was about eight inches long and very slightly curved. The young man's expression was serious and purposeful, but otherwise revealed nothing.

What now, O'Netty wondered. Let's see.

The young man hooked the tip of the blade in his chest, just below the sternum, pushed it in farther, and then carefully tugged it down through his navel, all the way to the elastic top of his briefs. He winced and sagged with the effort, and he used his free hand to hold the wound partly closed. Next, he jabbed the knife into his abdomen, just above the left hip, and pulled it straight across to his right side. He groaned and dropped the knife. Now he was hunched over, struggling to hold himself up, and he could not contain the double wound. His organs bulged out in his arms—liver, stomach, the long rope of intestines, all of them dry and leathery. There was no blood at all, but rather a huge and startling cascade of dark red sand that made a clatter of noise as it spilled across the plastic sheet. The young man was very wobbly now, and the other two at the bar stepped forward to take him by the arms and lower him gently to the ground. The young man's eyes blinked several times, and then stayed shut. The other two carefully wrapped his body in the plastic sheet and secured it with some tape they got from the bag. Finally, they lifted the body and carried it into the room behind the bar. They returned a few moments later and took their seats again. Conversations resumed, slowly at first, but then became quick and more animated with half-suppressed urgency.

After a while O'Netty finished his beer and got up to leave. No one paid any attention to him except the bartender, who came to the end of the bar for O'Netty's payment and then brought him his change.

"By the way, sir, in case you don't know. You can use the fire exit. There's no need to climb all those the stairs."

"Ah, thank you," O'Netty replied. "It is a lot of stairs."

"Good night, sir."

"Good night."

The fire exit opened onto a long metal staircase that brought him to a short lane that led to a side street just off one of the main avenues in the center of the city. It was already daylight, the air crisp and fresh, the early morning sun exploding on the upper floors of the taller buildings. O'Netty stood there for a few moments, trying to regain his bearings and decide what to do.

Then he saw a city bus coming his way, and he realized it was the one that went to his neighborhood. It must be the first bus of the day, O'Netty thought, as he stepped to the curb and raised his hand.

Night Deposits

BY CHET WILLIAMSON

YOU ALMOST GOT TO KNOW ZANE KAYLOR TO APPRECIATE THIS. COURSE YOUNG as you are you probably wouldn't. You might recall, though, seeing Zane on the street. A big, tall, skinny fella he was, built like a fence post a rough wind split in two. Jesus, but he was thin.

Wasn't always like that, though. Hell, I remember him back in the thirties being really stocky like. That was when he owned the mill. Big wood mill, everybody in town got their lumber there, back before wood got so dear nobody can afford it no more. Course too that was before the Martin boy's accident. That was what made Zane so thin. And what made him finally start making those queer night deposits of his at the bank.

Must've been '34 or so when it happened. There wasn't much call for safety things back then, and there was a great big band saw Zane had at the mill. Now it would've been all right if Zane had grown men who knew what the hell they were doing on that saw. If he had, I doubt the sheriff ever would have said a thing. But Tommy Martin was working it after school, since Zane hired boys like that rather than pay his regular men overtime after four.

Well, Bill Painter—he was sheriff then—comes in to pick up some planks and sees Tommy Martin working on that big old saw without no blade guard or nothing, and he tells Zane that he's a fool to put a kid on that machine and if he's going to do it he'd better goddam well put a blade guard on it, or maybe Painter'll take a close look at some fire regulations that Zane wasn't paying all that much attention to.

This pisses Zane off something awful, but he don't want to get on Painter's wrong side, so he says real sulky that he'll get a guard on it and not to worry. Tommy Martin hears all this, but he don't pay no attention to it much. Hell, a quarter an hour was damn good for a high school boy then, and it's fun sawing them boards up.

But Zane, he's pretty tight with money anyway, he looks for the cheapest way to make a blade guard, so he solders together a few tin can halves, and bolts them onto the housing. A couple days later Painter comes back and looks at the guard and tells Zane it looks like shit. Zane gets pissed and says a guard is a guard and it'll hold up, and Painter doesn't push it any. A week later, though, he wishes he would've.

It's like that fella's law, says if something can go wrong, it will?

Sure enough, the mill's open late Friday night, it's about ten o'clock, and Tommy

Martin's dog tired. He's pulling a big four by eight off the saw for Glenn Weidman when he loses his balance and falls on it. Those tin cans get knocked against the blade and it just whips them apart, shooting them into the air like knives. A piece caught the kid's face, Glenn said afterwards, and it sliced his right eye open like a grape. But that wasn't the worst of it.

The boy fell right across the blade then, and it started to chew into him at gut level. He pushed himself off, but fell back for a second, and that was when it got his hands. Both of them. Must've gone through the wrist bones slicker than shit through a goose. By the time Glenn and Zane got to him to pull him away, he was bleeding like anything. Wasn't screaming because he'd gone into shock. They called the county ambulance first, then Doc Lindemuth. The boy lived, though. It was a miracle how, Jesus, both hands and the eye. What made it a double shame is that he was the best goddam pass receiver the high school'd had for years.

Well, that was over, of course, and so was Zane Kaylor's mill.

When Sheriff Painter heard about it he actually arrested Zane and locked him up. He got out on bail the next day, and the county didn't press any criminal charges, negligence or whatever. But Painter told Roy and Esther Martin—they were Tommy's parents—to sue Zane, and that he'd back them up.

They had the sympathy of everybody in town over Zane. Oh, folks liked Zane well enough, but we all knew he was a cheap bastard, and it was plain to see that if he hadn't been cutting corners so close, this all wouldn't've happened.

So the Martins got a real good lawyer from over in Harrisburg, and Zane hired John Moyers here in town. County judge found for the Martins. After Bill Painter and Glenn's testimony, there wasn't much doubt that'd happen. I don't recall what exactly Zane had to pay, but it was a heap. And because Tommy was a kid, Zane hadn't paid no worker's compensation for him. That was just like Zane, though, always wanting to take a chance rather than spend an extra buck.

It hit him hard. Had to sell the mill and even that wasn't enough for what the judge had ordered, so he borrowed the rest from the bank and just got himself into awful debt. He stayed at the mill as a workman for Homer Johnson, who bought it from him, but he didn't stay long.

Three months after the accident, Tommy Martin killed himself.

Pulled the shotgun trigger with his toe. Doc said it was a helluva mess—worst he'd seen in thirty years. The Martins moved away soon after, down south to Florida. Zane started drinking then, coming to work late, sneaking away early, until Homer Johnson told him he'd better find another job somewhere, that being in the mill just wasn't good for him. Truth was, aside from the drinking, Homer was afraid Zane would hurt himself. Sometimes Homer'd come in and Zane would just be standing staring at that big band saw. Made Homer feel all creepy.

So he fired Zane, and Zane had to look for another job, which wasn't easy in the middle of the depression. He just kept drinking and not doing much of anything until his payments to the bank fell way behind and they had to foreclose on his house. That was the last straw for his wife. She took their little girl and went upstate to live with her folks. They got a real divorce a couple years later.

Her leaving sort of brought Zane around. He got two jobs then—both ones nobody else much wanted. Days he worked out at the rendering plant—isn't there no more—and nights he was over at the White Horse doing everything the bartender and the waitresses wouldn't: cleaning spittoons, keeping the john red up, taking the garbage out from the kitchen till midnight, when he went to bed in the room they let him have above the kitchen. Then he'd get up at six to go to the rendering plant.

He did that for years, until his debt was paid off. The house hadn't brought enough to pay the bank completely, and he was paying the rest of it with what he made off the White Horse. Every Friday night after he got paid he'd cross the street to the bank and put money in that night depository chute. I seen him do it many times. My rooms are still where they were then, over the furniture store catty-corner from the bank. Those days I could howl till midnight or later, and lots of times I saw Zane drop his money down that chute. None of us ever thought he'd get that debt to the bank paid off.

But he did. I guess it was in the early fifties, around the time my sister's boy died in Korea, that Zane stopped making those night deposits. We found out from Harry Becker, who worked at the bank, that Zane's debt had finally been paid.

Well, that night some of the boys decided to throw a little shindig in the White Horse for Zane to celebrate—a surprise like. I said I don't know if it was all that smart, that maybe Zane would just like to forget all about it. But you know what guys're like when they have a few drinks, so Wally Lovinger—he was bartender then—sends Zane up to Heisey's store for a case of club soda, claiming he's run out. The boys go across to the five and dime and buy streamers and balloons, and when Zane comes back everybody's cheering and yelling. He's confused at first, and then one of the boys tells him it's to celebrate his getting out of debt. His face goes white then, and everybody stops laughing.

Then he says, "I'll never be out of debt." Just like that, real quiet and whispery, but everybody in the room hears it, and he walks out and doesn't come back that night at all.

He quit his job at the White Horse the next day and took his clothes and things out of the room above the kitchen and moved in with the Koser sisters over on Oak Street. I saw him a few days later in the park and asked him how things are, and he says the Koser sisters are real good to him, and he even has his own bathroom and a hot plate and can use their refrigerator.

So the years go by, and when the rendering plant shuts down about fifteen years back, Zane goes on the social security and it's enough to get by on, but just barely. I don't think the Koser girls ever raised his rent in all those years. They must've figured he'd had enough trouble. Course when Emma died a few years back I guess Miriam was glad for the company.

It was just last year that his mind starts going on him. You'd say hi to him on the street and he'd just sort of smile like he didn't really remember who you were, and when you told him he'd just nod so that you knew he really didn't recognize the name any more. Miriam Koser looked after him all right, even though she's almost eighty herself now. But even she didn't know what was happening near the end.

Zane never went to a doctor. Never. After his first trouble he couldn't afford it and I guess he got out of the habit. But most of us could see that more was going than his mind. He started to walk funny like, as if he'd got arthritis bad, or his legs was going on him for some other reason. Limped at first—end of the summer it was—and finally had to use two canes, one in each hand, by the time fall came on. I talked to Jane Garber about him one day and she thought as how it was arthritis, as he even had trouble holding his canes come winter, especially with those big thick mittens he wore.

He had so much trouble getting around come Christmas that we hardly ever saw him out on the street at all. That's one reason it was such a surprise to me when I saw him through my window late one Friday night.

It was around midnight, and I'd gotten up to take a leak—that's what happens when you get old—when I looked out the window and saw Zane hobbling up the street. Course I wondered why in hell he was out at such an hour on such a cold night, so I just stood there and watched him. He goes right up to the night depository, pulls it open with his cane handle sort of fumbly like, and shoves an envelope down the chute. Then he turns around and walks back toward Oak Street.

Now I'm confused. I know damn sure he doesn't have to do that any more. Miriam Koser takes care of his social security checks. But even so, there's nobody in that bank. It's clean empty.

This was about six months after they opened the new building up on the ridge and locked the old one up. Tore it down this spring to put up those apartments. So Zane's making a deposit in a bank that's not even open for business and never will be again. Right then and there I know he's crazy, but I start to wonder about what he's putting in that night depository slot. I hoped it wasn't any money because he sure as hell can't afford that. I figured pretty easy that he's going back in his mind in time, you know, making those deposits to pay back the bank like he did for so many years.

I didn't mention it to anybody. Nobody's business but his, really, and I didn't think he was hurting anything. Miriam kept tight enough watch on his money that he wouldn't put much down there, if any, and if he did drop a dollar or two down, well, like I said, his business. I thought if it made him happy, fine.

I'd sort of forgot about it by the next Friday night. It wasn't until I'd gotten up about four or so to visit the john that it crossed by mind. So I looked out the window, never really expecting to see Zane out there at that time, just one of the things you do, and I see this mound of white in front of the night depository.

It'd been snowing earlier, but had stopped. The streets were all covered with it, and there was just this mound of white lying there. And I knew right away what it was, that it was Zane Kaylor. So I pulled my clothes on and called Doctor Barnes before I went out, even though I knew that if it wasn't Zane I'd look goddam stupid, but I was sure it was.

Then I went out and across the street and brushed the snow off him, and it was him, lying there curled up like a baby, looking as if he was sleeping, and there was a little smile froze on his face. Doctor Barnes came up shortly after, and young Bob Darkes, the cop, was with him. They saw right away he was dead, and Doctor Barnes started feeling over him to see how long he'd been there. I could've told him since midnight, but he didn't ask.

Anyway, the doc pulls off one of Zane's mittens and just yells, real frightened like. Bob Darkes and me look down at Zane and see what's scared the doc so.

Zane's hand's got no fingers on it.

Then I know everything. I know why Zane started limping last summer, and I know why it got worse as the weeks went on. I know why he kept his mittens on, even inside stores, when fall came. And I know that it hasn't been money he's been dropping down the mouth of that night depository every Friday midnight.

The twenty white envelopes Bob Darkes found in the cellar of the old bank proved me right. Even when the money was all paid to the bank, Zane Kaylor had to start paying off his debt to Tommy Martin.

Next morning the sun melted the snow on the sidewalk, and I found something Bob Darkes hadn't. It was an old bankbook. I don't know where Zane had got it, but he'd scratched his name on the first page. The rest of it was blank. Two days later I slipped it into Zane's coffin at his funeral, but not before I wrote paid in full smack dab in the middle of the last page.

Demonsong

BY F. PAUL WILSON

"HO, OUTLANDER!" CRIED THE BURLIER OF THE TWO MEN-AT-ARMS WHO STOOD BEFORE *the city's newsboard. His breath steamed in the chill post-dawn haze. "You look stout of arm, poor of cloak and lame of brain—this notice from the prince should interest you!"*

"He'd have to be an outlander to be interested," his companion muttered through a gap-toothed leer. "No one from around here's going to take the prince up on it."

The first scowled. "The prince ought to go himself! Then maybe we'd get a real man on the throne. Musicians and pretty-boys!" He spat. "The palace is no longer a fit place for a warrior. Wasn't like that during his father's reign."

The other nodded in agreement and the pair walked off without a backward glance.

The outlander hesitated, then approached the elaborately handwritten notice. He ran long fingers through his dusty red hair as he stared at it. The language was fairly new to him, and although he could speak it passably, reading was a different matter. The gist of the notice was an offer of 10,000 gold grignas to the man who would undertake a certain mission for Prince Iolon. Inquiries should be made at the palace.

The outlander fingered his coin pouch; a few measly coppers rattled within. He didn't know the weight of a grigna, but if it was gold and there were 10,000 of them... money would not be a problem for quite some time. He shrugged and turned toward the palace.

Kashela was the commercial center of Prince Iolon's realm and its streets came alive at first light. Not so the palace. It was well nigh midday before Glaeken was allowed entrance. The huge antechamber to the palace was empty save for an elderly blue-robed official sitting behind a tiny desk, quill in hand, a scroll and ink well before him.

"State your business," he said in a bored tone, keeping his eyes on the parchment.

"I've come to find out how to earn those 10,000 grignas the prince is offering."

The old man's head snapped up at Glaeken's unfamiliar accent. He saw a tall, wiry, red-headed man—that hair alone instantly labeled him a foreigner—with high coloring and startlingly blue eyes. He wore leather breeches, a shirt of indeterminate color girded by a broad belt that held a dirk and long sword; he carried a dusty red cloak over his left shoulder.

"Oh. A northerner, eh? Or is it a westerner?"

"Does it matter?"

"No... no, I suppose not. Name?"

"Glaeken."

The quill dipped into the well, then scratched out strange black letters on the scroll. "Glaeken of what?"

"How many Glaekens do you have in this city?"

"None. It's not even in our tongue."

"Then Glaeken alone will do."

There was an air of finality to the statement that caused the official to regard the outlander with more careful scrutiny. He saw a young man not yet out of his third decade who behaved with an assurance beyond his years.

A youth with oiled locks entered the antechamber then. He was dressed in a clinging white robe and gave Glaeken a frankly appraising stare as he sauntered past on his way to the inner chambers.

"Captain of the palace guard, I presume," Glaeken said blandly after the epicene figure had passed from sight.

"Your humor, outlander, could cost you your head should any of the guard hear such a remark."

"What does the prince want done?" he said, ignoring the caveat.

"He wants someone to journey into the eastern farmlands and kill a wizard."

"He has an army, does he not?"

The official suddenly became very interested in the scroll. "The captains have refused to send their men."

Glaeken mulled this. He sensed an air of brooding discontent in the palace, an undercurrent of frustration and hostility that was perilously close to the surface.

"No one has tried to bring in this wizard then? Come, old man! The bounty surely didn't begin at 10,000 gold pieces."

"A few squads were sent when the problem first became apparent, but they accomplished nothing."

"Tell me where these men are quartered. I'd like to speak to them."

"You can't." The official's eyes remained averted. "They never came back."

Glaeken made no immediate reply. He fingered his coin pouch, then tapped the heel of his right hand against the butt of his long sword. Finally:

"Get a map and show me where I can find this wizard."

* * *

Glaeken dallied in one of those nameless little inns that dot the back streets on any commercially active town. His seat was by the window. The shutters were open to let out the sour stench of last night's spilled ale and the late morning sunlight glinted off the hammered tin goblet of cheap wine that rested on the table before him. The harlot in the corner eyed him languidly… this foreigner might prove interesting. It was a little early in the day for her talents, but perhaps if he stayed around a little longer…

A commotion arose on the street and Glaeken peered out the window to find its source. A squat, burly, misshapen hillock of a man with a square protruding jaw was trudging by, a large, oddly shaped leather case clutched with both arms to his chest. Behind him and around him ran the local gang of street youths, pushing, shoving and catcalling. The wooden heels of their crude boots clacked as they scampered about; all wore a makeshift uniform of dark green shirts and rough brown pants.

"Ho, Ugly One!" cried a youth who seemed to be the leader, a wiry, black haired adolescent with a fuzzy attempt at a beard shading his cheeks. "What have you got in that case? Give us a look! It truly must be something to behold if you're clutching it so tightly. Give us a look!"

The man completely ignored the entire group, but this only incited them to greater audacity. They began pummeling him and trying to trip him, yet the man made no attempt to protect himself. He merely clutched the case closer and tighter. Glaeken wondered at this as he watched the scene. This "Ugly One" certainly appeared strong enough to handle the situation, having a heavy frame and arms that were long and thickly muscled. Yet the well-being of the leather case seemed his only concern.

The leader gave a signal and he and his followers leaped upon the man. The fellow kept his footing for a while and even managed to shake a few of the attackers off his back, but their numbers soon drove him to the ground. Glaeken noted with a smile of admiration that the man twisted as he fell so that he landed on his back with the case unharmed. It was only a matter of a few heartbeats, however, before the case was torn from his grasp.

With the loss of his precious possession, the little man became a veritable demon, cursing, gnashing his teeth and struggling with such ferocity that it took the full strength of eight of the rowdies to hold him down.

"Be still, Ugly One!" the leader commanded as he stood near Glaeken's window and fumbled with the clasps on the case. "We only want to see what you've got here."

As the last clasp gave way, the case fell open and from it the leader pulled a double-barreled harmohorn. The shouts and scuffling ceased abruptly as all in sight, rowdy and bystander alike, were captured by the magnificence of the instrument. The intricate hand-carving of the harmohorn glistened in the sun under countless coats of flawlessly applied lacquer. A reed instrument, rare and priceless—in the proper hands, it was capable of producing the most subtle and devious harmonies known to man. The art of its making had long been lost, and the musician fortunate enough to possess a harmohorn was welcomed—nay, sought—by all the royal courts of the world.

The squat little man redoubled his efforts against those restraining him.

"Damage that horn and I'll have your eyes!" he screamed.

"Don't threaten me, Ugly One!" the leader warned.

He raised the instrument aloft at if to smash it on the stones at his feet. In doing so he brought the horn within Glaeken's reach. Until now the outlander had been neutral, refusing to help a man who would not help himself. But now he knew the reason for the man's reluctance to fight, and the sight of the harmahorn in the hands of street swine disturbed him. The horn switched hands abruptly.

The leader spun in surprise and glared at Glaeken.

"You!" he yelled, leaning in the window. "Return that before I come in and get it!"

"You want to come get it?" Glaeken said with a tight smile. "Then by all means waste no time!"

He grabbed the youth by his shirt and pulled him half way through the window.

"Let go of me, red-haired dog!" he screeched.

"Certainly." And Glaeken readily replied, but not without enough of a shove to ensure that the youth would land sprawled in the dust.

Scrambling to his feet, the leader turned to his pack. "After him!"

They forgot the man they were holding and charged the inn door.

But Glaeken was already there, waiting and ready.

He smiled as he met their attack and laughed as he darted among them, striking and kicking and wreaking general havoc upon their ranks. But these youths were hardly novices at street brawls and when they realized that their opponent, too, was well experienced in this dubious art, they regrouped and began to stalk him.

"Circle him!" said the leader and his followers responded with dispatch. Before the menacing ring could close, however, the pack found itself harassed from an unexpected quarter.

"Ugly One" was upon them. Having regained his feet and sized up the situation, the little man charged into the pack with the roar of an angry bull. He was enraged to the point of madness and a smiling Glaeken stepped back to watch as the street youths were hurled and scattered about like jackstraws. A complete rout seemed inevitable. It was then that Glaeken glanced at the leader—and saw him pull a dirk from within his shirt and lunge.

The blade never found its target. For Glaeken had moved and the pack leader felt himself yanked to the ground; the knife was pulled from his grasp and his neck was extended over the red-haired outlander's knee. All fighting stopped as everyone watched the tableau of Glaeken and the pack leader.

"You should be slain outright," Glaeken said, toying with the dirk over the terrified youth's vulnerable throat. "And no one would miss you or mourn you if you were."

"No!" he cried as he saw the cold light in Glaeken's eyes. "I meant no harm!"

Glaeken used the point to scratch an angry, ragged red line from ear to ear across the leader's throat.

"A good street brawl is one thing, my young friend, but if I ever see you show your steel to the back of an unarmed man again, I'll finish the job this scratch has begun!"

So saying, he lifted the youth by his hair and shoved him toward his companions. The green-shirted pack and its frightened leader wasted no time then in leaving the scene.

"Ugly One" turned to Glaeken and extended his hand. "I thank you, outlander. I am called Cragjaw—although I assure you I was not given that name by my parents."

"No thanks are called for," Glaeken said, clasping the hand firmly. "A street brawl at midday is a good spirit-lifter." He did not offer his own name in return.

"I'm quite sure I can find better ways to amuse myself," Cragjaw muttered as he stooped to pick up the empty leather case.

The bar master was sheathing a dirk of his own as they entered.

The contested musical instrument lay on the bar before him.

"I guarded the harmohorm well while you were out on the street!" he shouted.

"And what would you have done with it if he hadn't been able to return to claim it?" Glaeken asked with a knowing grin.

The bar master shrugged and eyed the horn as Cragjaw replaced it in the case.

"I suppose I would have had to sell it to someone... I have no talent for such an instrument."

Glaeken threw a coin on the bar. "That's for the wine," he said and turned toward the door.

Cragjaw laid a hand on his arm. "At least let me buy you another cup before you go."

"Thanks, no. I'm riding the East Road and already I've tarried too long."

"The East Road? Why, I must travel that way, too. Would you mind a companion for a ways?"

"The roads are free," said Glaeken.

* * *

Glaeken's mount, a stallion called Stoffral, took his eastward from Kashela at an easy walk. Cragjaw ambled beside him on a chestnut mare.

"You're a Northerner, aren't you?" the shorter man observed. "In a way, yes."

"You never told me your name."

"It is Glaeken."

There was a pause before Cragjaw spoke again.

"Stories circulate among the wine cups in the back rooms of the court of Prince Iolon—in whose service I am presently employed as a musician—about a man named Glaeken. He's said to live in the Western Isles and is supposedly young and flame-haired like yourself."

"Interesting," Glaeken remarked. "And what are these tales?"

"Well, he is called Glaeken-the-Laugher by some and it is said that he once led the dreaded Nightriders who pillage vast areas of the Western Isles."

Glaeken nodded for his companion to continue.

"I only know what I've heard, but 'tis said that each of these raiders rides a monstrous bat with a body the size of a horse and wings like ketch sails that sweep the night. The tales tell of an evil king named Marag who was the favorite target of the Nightriders and who sent many champions against them with the quest to bring back the head of the Nightrider lord. But shortly after each was sent out, a monster bat would fly over Marag's hold and drop the latest champion's body into the courtyard.

"Finally, a man named Glaeken—who had refused to be the king's champion for many years—was called into Marag's court. And there, in a steel cage suspended from the ceiling, was the damsel in whose company this Glaeken had been often seen of late. Now, they say that Glaeken had no serious future plans for the young lady but felt somewhat responsible for her present predicament. So he traveled to the pinnacle fortress of the Nightriders and challenged and beat their lord in a contest of swords."

"And did he bring the head to Marag?" Glaeken asked.

"That and more, for it seems that by tradition the Nightriders must claim as leader the man who fairly defeats the reigning lord. This Glaeken returned with his new followers and taught Marag a grisly lesson." Cragjaw glanced at his companion. "Could you be that Glaeken?"

"It's a good tale, my friend, but how could I and this bat-rider be one and the same? How could I be pillaging the Western Isles at night and ride the East Road in Prince Iolon's domain with you today? Quite impossible."

"Not so," said Cragjaw with a sly grin. "For it is also said that after a year or two with the Nightriders, the man named Glaeken grew restless and dissatisfied. He left them to their own devices and no one knows where he travels now." The squat little man made a point of clearing his throat. "Where travel you now, Glaeken?"

"To Elder Cavern in the eastern farmlands."

"Elder Cavern! Why that's in the very center of the plague area—there's nothing out there but dying farms and…" Cragjaw's voice faded as he remembered something. "Oh, I see. You must have answered the Prince's notice."

Glaeken nodded. "It seems that the mystery of the region's inhospitality has been cleared up. They've discovered that a sorcerer named Rasalom—a giant of a man, I'm told—entered the cavern nearly two years ago and it was not too long thereafter that the crops, the cattle, and the farmers in the area began to sicken. Rasalom has been neither seen nor heard from since, so the Prince's advisors feel that he's still in the cavern."

"So the infamous Rasalom is behind it all," Cragjaw muttered. "We've long thought it to be a plague of some sort, released from the cavern after eons of sleep."

"The prince's advisor's were rather vague about the plague," Glaeken said. "Do you know what it's like?"

"Stories vary, but most agree that the victims complain of a throbbing in the head and ears and slowly begin to lose their strength, becoming very lethargic. Soon they cannot get out of bed and eventually they waste away and die. But what puzzled the court physicians was the curious fact that all victims seem to improve and recover when moved out of the area. No one could give a reason for this… but sorcery explains it well: Rasalom has laid a curse of some sort on the region."

"So it would seem," Glaeken agreed.

"But what purpose could he have? Why would he want to lay waste the eastern farmlands—for not only people sicken and die out there, but cattle and crops as well."

Glaeken shrugged. "That is not my concern. I admit that I'm somewhat curious, but my task is merely to bring back Rasalom himself, or some proof of his demise, such as his Ring of Chaos, whatever that may be."

"It's rumored to be the most potent focus of power for black sorcery this side of the Netherworld. You will have to slay Rasalom to gain it, and that will not be easy." He shuddered. "Not only does that wizard have the black arts at his command, but he is said to stand half again as tall as a tall man, and be three times as broad in the shoulders. No wonder Iolon has to send an outlander! No local man would set foot in Elder Carvern! I hope the prince is paying you well."

"I seldom take on a gainless task." Glaeken replied quietly.

"If that's true, then why did you aid me against those street thugs?"

Glaeken smiled. "I was quite willing to let them have their fun with you until I saw the harmohorn. I have a weakness for music and consequently respect for musicians."

They came to a crossroads and Cragjaw turned his horse to the north. "We part here, Glaeken," he said. "I go to the prince's summer quarters to prepare entertainment for the arrival of his entourage tomorrow. I would bid you ride south and have no further thought of Elder Cavern, but I know you'll not heed me. So instead I bid you luck and hope to see you at the summer palace soon with either Rasalom or his ring. One word of warning though: travel quickly. Few who venture into that land nowadays are ever seen again."

Glaeken waved and headed east. He did not quicken his pace.

* * *

The land was arid and vegetation generally scarce in Iolon's domain, but as Glaeken penetrated into the eastern farmlands he became aware of an almost total lack of greenery. Bark-shedding trees lifted their dry, stunted, leafless branches skyward in silent supplication for surcease of—what? And the further east he moved, the darker became the sky; grey clouds slid by. twisting, churning, writhing and roiling as if suffering from an agony of their own as they passed over the region.

Long-rotted cattle carcasses dotted the fields on both sides of the road; the hides were dried and matted and loose-fitting in death, perfectly outlining the skeleton within. Glaeken saw no evidence that scavengers had been at the carrion, and then realized that he had not seen a single trace of beast or fowl since he entered the region. Even the vultures shunned this place.

The motionless air became thick and heavy as he pushed on and his lungs labored at their task. Evening consolidated the grey of the sky to black and Glaeken was glad to dismount. He found a spot not too far off the road between a dead tree and a large stone where he built a fire. Stoeffral was given free rein to find what nourishment he could in the lifeless, desiccated grasses nearby but the horse seemed to have lost all appetite. Glaeken, too, felt no hunger, unusual after half a day's ride, but managed to force down some dried beef and stale wine.

He was strangely tired and this gave him some concern. He had never been one to believe in sorcerers and evil magic, considering them little more than tales designed to frighten children. The only magic he had ever seen had been the work of charlatans. Yet for a man of his age and fitness to feel so lethargic after a mere six hours on horseback was decidedly unnatural. Maybe there was something to this curse after all.

He moved away from the heat of the fire and sat with his back against the rock. The silence was oppressive and made him uneasy. The night bugs were quiet. He glanced about... there were no pairs of feral eyes reflecting the firelight from the darkness around his little camp. That, too, was unusual. Slowly, his eyes grew heavy. Against his better judgment he allowed himself to doze.

... the sound grew in his brain by imperceptible degrees, a horrible, keening, wailing cacophony of madness that assaulted his sanity with murderous intensity... and as the volume increased there appeared wild, distorted visages of evil, countless blank-eyed demons howling with mindless joy, screaming louder and louder until he was sure he must go mad...

Glaeken found himself awake and on his feet, sweat coursing along his skin in runnels. The fire had burned down to a fitful glow and all was quiet. He shook his head to clear it of the dream and glanced around for Stoffral. Gone! He began shouting the horse's name. Glaeken was fully alert to danger now—Stoffral was too loyal a beast to desert him. His third shout was answered by a faint whinny from behind the rock. Glaeken cautiously peered into the darkness and saw the dim form of his mount on the ground. He ran to its side and made a careful check. The horse had suffered no harm and Glaeken concluded that Stoffral must be a victim of the same lethargy that was currently afflicting his master.

He slapped the horse's flanks in an effort to rouse the beast back to its feet but to no avail. Stoffral's strength seemed completely drained. Glaeken remembered the cattle carcasses along the road and swore that his steed would not suffer a similar fate. He stalked to the fire and lifted a branch that had been only partially consumed. Fanning it in the air until the tip glowed cherry with heat, he applied the brand to Stoffral's right hindquarter. There was a whiff of singed hair, a hiss of searing flesh, then the horse screamed in pain and rose on wobbly legs.

Glaeken could not help but cast a fearful glance over his shoulder as he steadied his mount; horses were rare and highly valued creatures in the land where he had been raised, and any man caught doing harm to one was likely to be attacked by an angry mob. But pain or not, scar or not, Stoffral was on his feet now and somewhat revived. That was all that mattered at the moment. And the horse instinctively knew that the act had been done without malice.

Replacing the saddle on Stoffral's back, he packed it with everything but the jerked beef, the water skin, and the half-dozen torches he had fashioned before leaving Kashola. Then he shouted and slapped the horse's flanks and chased him back down the road. Hopefully, Stoffral would await his master beyond the zone of danger. Glaeken waited a moment, then shouldered his pack and began walking in the opposite direction. It would have been

preferable to wait until morning... travel would have been easier then. But Glaeken's doubting attitude about the supposed curse on the eastern farmlands had been thoroughly shaken.
He was no longer quite so sure there wasn't something truly evil afoot in the region. For all
he knew, morning might prove too late if he waited for it. So he traveled in darkness.

* * *

Dawn lightened the perpetual overcast as Glaeken stood before the high arched
entrance to Elder Cavern. He felt as if his eyes had been torn out and replaced with heated
coals. His head buzzed and hummed; his sword had become a drag anchor. The very air
weighed down upon him like a stone. He stood swaying, questioning the wisdom of entering
the opening before him. His strength had been traveling in a steady decline the entire night
and he was now so weakened that he seriously entertained thoughts of abandoning his mission.

Everything seemed so hopeless. With barely strength enough to stand, it would be
insane to challenge a giant in stature and sorcery such as Rasalom. But turning back would
be equally suicidal, for he would never make it to the crossroads; he would end up like the
rotting cattle he had passed the day before.

Glaeken staggered forward into the cavern maw. Perhaps he did so because it was
his only real alternative and there might be a slim chance he could outwit Rasalom in some
way. Perhaps he was thinking of the reward Iolon offered, or perhaps he was determined to
find out what was behind the curse that lay upon this region like a plague. And perhaps he
went forward because he was possessed of that curious perversity that afflicts all men who
stand out from their fellows: the drive to carry a task through to its finish.

As he was engulfed by the darkness within, Glaeken paused, removed the tinderbox
from his sack and ignited one of the torches. The growing flame flickered light off the walls
and made marching armies of the stalactite and stalagmite shadows as he moved. His scuffling
feet kicked up smelly clouds of dust that irritated his nose. He knew the odor well—bat
dung, and none of it fresh. Even the bats were gone.

The tunnel sloped downward and the walls and roof closed in on him until he had
to walk in a slight crouch. The walls glistened with moisture as he plunged deeper and deeper
into the earth and his torch would hiss as it brushed against them now and again. The odd,
persistent humming in his brain grew louder as he moved and distracted him uncomfortably.
He could only hope that the tunnel would lead him directly to Rasalom.

The passage broadened into a wider, higher chamber and Glaeken cursed as the
torchlight revealed the problem he had hoped not to meet: three other tunnels opened into
this same chamber. As he slumped against the wall in near exhaustion, his torch sagged and
dipped into a brackish puddle. In total darkness he fumbled for the tinderbox to light a fresh
torch, then froze. The faintest hint of illumination was trickling down the tunnel to the right.

Glaeken forgot about torch and tinderbox and crept down the passage toward the
beckoning tendrils of light. Rounding a corner, he found himself in a dim, long-shadowed

room. The walls were smooth and bare except for a few oil lamps flickering here and there. A huge, throne-like chair rested in a dark corner. Otherwise, the room was empty.

Wary, Glaeken started to draw his broadsword as he moved further into the room, but the weight of it seemed so enormous to his weakened muscles that he let it slide back into its scabbard. He rested his hand instead on the handle of his dirk.

Cut into the wall to his right was what appeared to be a massive door. Glaeken approached it with eyes darting constantly about the room. There was no latch, no ring, no handle, but the acute scratches on the floor before it were proof that the door did in some way swing open. Yet try as he might, he could not see how.

A voice rasped behind him: "There's a hidden latch."

The nape of his neck tingled with fear and surprise. Glaeken wheeled and peered closely at the massive chair in the corner. The seat was totally immersed in stygian shadow. He moved closer and faintly made out a human outline. Grabbing an oil lamp from the wall, he held it high.

The shadows receded and Glaeken saw that he faced a lank-haired skeleton of a man dressed in a robe once richly embroidered but now tattered and torn, foul and filthy.

"You must be a strong-willed man to have come this far," said a voice from the seated figure, a voice like rats' feet scurrying over dried corn husks.

"Who are you?" Glaeken demanded.

"I am called Rasalom."

"You lie! I've been told that Rasalom is a giant of a man, not a mere bag of bones!"

"I am he, nevertheless," Rasalom replied with a grin that was horrible to behold.

"You no doubt started on your journey with visions of a terrible struggle against a huge sword-wielding wizard. You foresaw a mighty battle with the flash of steel and shouts of fury. Yet look at us now: you can barely stand and I have not the strength to cast the most elementary of weirds." He barked a harsh laugh. "What comedy we play! We face each other like two impotent, senile gods come to blows at last on some backwater Armageddon!"

But Glaeken could see no humor in the situation. He spoke with desperate determination.

"I've come in the name of Prince Iolon to put an end to this curse you've laid on the land!"

"I know all about Iolon and his reward," Rasalom snarled. "He wants you to bring back Rasalom or his ring." He fumbled within his robe and withdrew a large ring of intricately worked gold. It was set with a small, spherical black stone, so black that it seemed to absorb all light, appeared to be a rent in the very fabric of existence, a tiny portal to the nothingness beyond. The ring dangled from a golden chain.

"You wish the Ring of Chaos?" he said. "Here… take it. It no longer fits me and I have no further need of it."

Glaeken stiffened visibly at the offer.

Rasalom smiled again. "No trick, I assure you. For why should I want to keep the mere Ring of Chaos when I know that I'll soon be an integral part of Chaos itself?" The warlock's eyes began to glow as he spoke. "I, Rasalom, have called forth the twelve hundred idiot demons of the Amphitheatre! It took two years to complete the task. Each of the twelve hundred had to be called forth by a separate spell, and each spell took its toll. I was once as you were told—a huge, robust man. Look at me now! But I care not... Eternity is mine!"

Glaeken's expression mirrored his doubts about Rasalom's sanity.

"You think me mad? Beyond that stone door you tried so futilely to move lies the Amphitheatre of Chaos, and therein are assembled the twelve hundred idiot demons... the Choir of Chaos. They exist only to sing. There is no curse on the land... only their singing. For they sing to Chaos itself and the vibration of their song strikes discord in the life processes of all living things!"

"But you—"

"I am protected, for I am performing The Task. And what a task it is! The Lords of Chaos are wise. They know that to extend their domain they must ever be ready to accept new blood into their ranks. But the newcomer must prove beyond all doubt that he is worthy. So The Task was set, an ordeal that only a sorcerer of the greatest skill and stamina could hope to accomplish. For each of the twelve hundred demons of the choir sucks a little bit of life from the one who calls it forth. I have raised them all and yet I still live! I am wasted but I have succeeded!

"And within the Amphitheatre the embryo of my new form gestates, slowly incorporating my being into its own as it matures. The time for parturition draws nigh. I shall soon be eternal and all this world my domain!"

Glaeken remained unconvinced. "Your sorcery has wasted your mind as well as your body, Rasalom. Lift your curse and give me the ring and I shall leave you to your delusions. Refuse and my blade will end everything for you."

"You fool!" the wizard screamed. "You doubt my word? I tell you there is no curse! The Choir of Chaos sings and its song is slow death to all within reach of it! You are dying at this very moment, my foolish interloper. And do not threaten me with death for that would only accelerate the embryo's progress. I would welcome death at this moment—it would bring my rebirth that much closer!" He pointed to the door. "Go! See for yourself! Pull the handle on the lamp by the door. The passage leads to the Amphitheatre. View the Choir of Chaos and die!"

Wordlessly, wearily, Glaeken shuffled to the door. If Rasalom were mad, this would prove it. If sane, then Glaeken's life—nay, his whole world!—was in grave danger.

He pulled down the lamp handle. It moved easily. Behind the wall he could hear the clank of weights as they were released. Slowly, the door swung open and revealed a narrow passage lit with oil lamps similar to those in the room. A faint throbbing hum reached his ears. Glaeken moved into the passage and saw another stone door at its end. This one was equipped with a ring latch. He grasped the ring and pulled on it, doubting very much that he had strength left to budge it. But the hinges were perfectly balanced and the stone slab swung toward him. He repeated this procedure with the three identical subsequent doors and each time the hum increased in volume until at the final door it had risen to a muted scream. This door was doubly thick and vibrated with the intensity of the sound behind it. But it swung as easily as the others when Glaeken pulled on the ring.

The sound was a physical thing, washing over him with a volume and intensity that drove him to his knees. He was on the edge of a precipice and before him lay the Amphitheatre of Chaos, an inverted cone, mistily illuminated by light that filtered up from the unguessed depths below. Carved into the rounded walls that sloped upward to the pointed roof were twelve hundred niches, and in each of those niches crouched one of the twelve hundred idiot demons. Blank-eyed and mindless they were, shaped in every deformity imaginable and unimaginable. Their faces suffused with an insane, malignant glee, they howled and caterwauled in tones that ranged from far below to far above those audible to the human ear. No two tones harmonized, all was discord and conflict. Glaeken now knew the origin of his dream the night before… the Choir of Chaos was assembled and at work.

His gaze, however, was drawn from the howling demons to the ebon sphere that floated in the center of the Amphitheatre. It appeared to be a thin-membraned ball of inky fluid, suspended above and before him by no visible means. And the eyes of each of the twelve hundred were fixed steadily upon it.

There was a slight swirling movement within the sphere and Glaeken recoiled as he caught a fleeting glimpse of a dark, nameless shape and two glowing malevolent eyes.

The embryo of Rasalom's new form! It floated there in its inky amnion, suspended on a placenta of sound from the Choir of Chaos. Rosalom was not mad—he had been telling the truth!

Suddenly, Glaeken, too, began to sing. Perhaps it was inspiration, a feeble effort to counteract the effect of the sound that pressed down on him with such ferocity… perhaps the glimpse of those eyes in the sac had pushed him to the brink of madness and the song offered a tenuous link to sanity.

He sang the hymn of praise to the goddess Eblee, a sweet simple song known the world over. And his effort did not go unnoticed. The demons of the Choir pulled their gaze away from the amniotic sac before them and glared at him with unrestrained fury. It seemed that the merest trace of coherent melody within the Amphitheatre could disrupt the gestative process. Even now there was a slight ripple coursing over the membranous surface of the sac. The twelve hundred increased their volume and Glaeken was knocked flat. Vision and consciousness blurred as every fibre of his being screamed in anguished protest. Still he sang, clinging to the melody as a last thread to sanity; but he was fading, losing his grip on consciousness. His hoarse tones grew lower as the Choir of Chaos attacked him with unwavering vocal fury.

Glaeken's voice was suddenly augmented. The dulcet tones of a harmohorn had joined him in song. Blinking his eyes into focus, he turned his head and there behind him was Cragjaw. The squat little man, eyes closed, bathed in sweat, was leaning against the wall and blowing a perfect modal harmony to Glaeken's song. Glaeken found new strength then and redoubled his vocal efforts.

Something was happening in the Ampitheatre. The acoustics were flawless and the new sound permeated the huge chamber. If a touch of coherence had proved slightly disruptive before, the harmony of man-made instrument and human voice was now having a shattering effect. The twelve hundred demons were agitatedly thrashing in their niches, their voices faltering. And this in turn was having its effect on the embryo. The membrane was being tortured and stretched by the roiling convulsions of the thing within. The glowing eyes pressed against the sac wall in unearthly rage.

There came a weakening, a tiny puncture, a rent—the membrane ruptured and its contents spilled out into the air. The sac, its fluid and partially formed occupant fell silently and abruptly into the mists below.

The howling scream of agony went up from the Choir of Chaos.

The idiot demons ceased their song and flew into fits of rage, hurling themselves against the walls of their niches and finally over the edges and down. One by one, then in groups, and finally in a hellish rain, they followed the embryo.

* * *

Silence.

Glaeken had almost given up hope of ever experiencing it again. He remained prone and reveled in the lack of sound as strength and sanity surged back into his body.

"Ho, Cragjaw," he said finally, rising to his feet. "What brought you to this concert?"

Cragjaw sighed exhaustedly as he slipped the harmohorn back into its case. "I owed you a service so I came after you. Seems it's a good thing I did."

Together they stumbled back down the passage to the antechamber.

"We are more than even, my friend," Glaeken said. "I did but aid you in a street brawl—and enjoyed it, too. You risked your life just by entering this region."

They arrived then in the antechamber and found Rasalom stretched out on the floor halfway between the throne-like chair and the doorway. He was dead. Glaeken reached into the withered sorcerer's robe, pulled out the Ring of Chaos and snapped the chain.

"That cannot be Rasalom!" Cragjaw exclaimed. "And where did he come from? I didn't see him when I passed through!"

"It's Rasalom, alright. The curse is broken but I suppose Iolon will want to have the ring before he gives me the reward." Cragjaw started to speak as they headed for the surface, hesitated, then started again.

"Ah, Glaeken, I fear I bring bad news. When I reached the summer palace I learned that Iolon had been overthrown by his army. There will be no reward, I'm afraid."

Glaeken took this news in silence and continued walking. Receiving no reply, Cragjaw continued.

"I, too am out of work. The generals have no liking for the harmohorn. Their tastes in music are a bit coarse for my skills, running more to naked girls with tambourines and bells. Knowing they would not honor Iolon's promise of a reward, I traveled to warn you that you would be imperiling yourself for naught. I found your horse on the way—he is well—and thought you might be in some danger, so I rode my own horse nearly into the ground and ran the rest of the way on foot in an effort to catch you before you entered the cavern. I was too late. But I heard this awful caterwauling within and followed the sound. You know the rest."

Glaeken nodded appreciatively. "But what made you bring the harmohorn?"

"You don't think I'd leave it unguarded, do you?" Cragjaw replied indignantly. "It never leaves my side!"

"I suppose you sleep with it, too?"

"Of course!"

Glaeken laughed and tucked the Ring of Chaos into his belt. "Ah, well, the quest has been rewarding in one way if not another. I may not come away a rich man but at least I've found a friend among these strange easterners."

"Strange easterners, are we?" Cragjaw said with a gleam in his eye as they reached the mouth of the cavern. "Then you must be from the Western Isles after all!"

With the late morning sun warm on his face, Glaeken gave only a good natured laugh in reply.

NECON PROCEEDINGS
Cortney Skinner

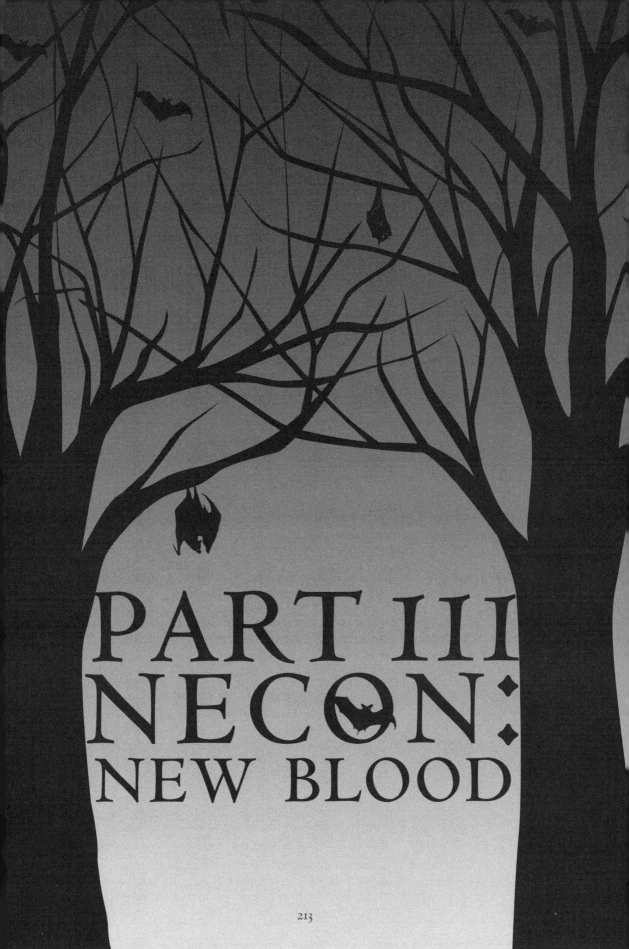

PART III
NECON:
NEW BLOOD

A Death In The Day Of

BY GARY A. BRAUNBECK

"And God had him die for a hundred years and then revived him and said: 'How long have you been here?'
'A day or part of a day,' he answered."
—KORAN, II, 261

NANCI LIEBER ROLLED OVER AND SAW HER BROTHER STANDING IN THE DOORWAY
of her bedroom, a 7.65 caliber Deutsche Werk pistol in his hand. She squinted in the darkness,
trying to catch a glimpse of the expression on his face, but could make out nothing.

"Who wants it?" she said.

"Mom." There was an edge of surprise in his voice. "She asked me to bring it down
before I went to bed."

Nanci looked over at her clock. It was almost four in the morning.

"You just get home from work?"

"Yeah," said her brother, Russ, looking down at the weapon he held.

"What is it?"

"I figured we were done with this," he said. "I mean, after last time I thought—"

"There's no such thing as the *last* time," said Nanci. "Not around here."

Russ gave a slow nod of his head, jacked a bullet into the chamber, and offered her
the gun. "Will you take it to her? Her and Dad are sitting in the kitchen."

"I think you should."

"C'mon, Nance! I'm tired."

"So are they."

"I don't want to."

"Tough shit. Do it." Her eyes had adjusted to the darkness now, and she could see
her brother glaring at her, his anger and confusion joining hands as they danced around his
reason. When he spoke again his voice was hesitant, quavering.

"Please, Nance… I just can't—"

"Give me the goddamned thing," she said, climbing out of bed and coming toward
him. "It only makes things worse when you wait. You should know that by now." Standing
in front of him she could see the weariness starting to etch its way into his features; the bags
under his eyes, the tiny marks on his cheek, the lattice-work lines of age that knew no patterns
or sympathies.

"You look terrible," she said.

"The shift was a bitch." Nanci reached out and gently took the pistol from his hand. His skin was warm but calloused, heavily calloused, calloused far too soon for a kid who should have been figuring out who he was going to ask to the homecoming dance instead of working swing on the weekends. Russ was too young to be this tired and beaten.

She leaned in and kissed him on the cheek.

"How come we don't fight more?" he said. "I always thought a brother and sister were supposed to be at each other's throats all the time."

"I don't know," said Nanci. "Maybe we'll work on it." But that was a lie. Nanci knew very well why she and her brother never really fought, never engaged in the sibling rivalry that was supposed to be the earmark of children belonging to a healthy nuclear family.

Fighting was destructive, and around here, destruction was redundant.

"Go to bed," she said. "I'll take care of things."

Russ gave her a smile and then shuffled into his room, not bothering to turn on any lights.

Nanci put on her robe and went downstairs, pistol in hand. Russ needed his sleep, and she had to be getting up in another hour anyway to get ready for work, so...

Mom and Dad were sitting at the table. Nanci's mother turned and smiled at her daughter.

"I'm tired," she said.

"I know," said Nanci. Dad said nothing, only gave her his usual half-smile while his fingers drummed solemnly on the side of his metal lunch bucket.

They were both dressed for work.

"Did you get the towels out?" said Nanci.

"Oh, dear me, I knew I forgot something," said her mom, rising from the table and going to the bathroom. "I was trying to put some Band-Aids on my fingers. See here?" She offered her hand, and Nanci looked down at the series of deep, ugly scratches that decorated her mom's fingers.

"They got me working with a different kind of cable this week, and the terminals are so small. Those edges are the sharpest things, I swear."

"I can imagine," said Nanci. Her mom was a cable assembly worker at a place in the Cedar Hill Industrial Park that manufactured all-night banking machines. The machines allowed for customers to make deposits or withdrawals any time of the day or night.

The work only withdrew, day in, day out. And Mom had cuts on her fingers to prove it.

Nanci told her to sit at the table, then removed two thick towels from the cabinet in the bathroom.

"How come Russ didn't come down?" said her dad.

"He was pretty tired."

"Who ain't?"

Nanci closed her eyes tightly, took a breath, then opened her eyes again.

Tired, tired, tired.

The Lieber Litany, performed daily, with special matinees on selected Sundays.

She draped a towel around her mom's shoulders so the bulk of it lay against her back, then did the same for her dad.

"Will these be thick enough?" asked Nanci.

"Don't matter," said her dad. "I'm wearin' such a dark sweatshirt nobody'll notice."

Nanci smiled at her father, remembering a line from some poem she once read, a poem that spoke of a house's chronic angers and glories, of a man's quiet sacrifice for his family, and the chill of a wintry Sunday morning; but most of all, she remembered, it had spoken of love's austere and lonely offices, and how little a person could ultimately know of such places.

She kissed both her parents and then handed the pistol to her mom.

"Remember," said her dad, "you put it in your mouth and press it hard against the roof."

"I remember," said her mom.

Nanci went into the living room until they both had used the pistol, then came back and wiped up each parent with their respective towels, all the while wondering how she was going to find all the little pieces there were to be recovered.

Most of Mom was on the microwave.

Dad had landed in the sink.

Mom's pieces went into her towel, Dad's into his. Nanci then picked up the gun and checked to make sure it was empty.

It was.

Good boy, Russ, you remembered to put in only two.

She took the gun back upstairs and put it in the hall closet, then knocked on her brother's door.

"Russ?"

"I'm awake." She edged in through the door and darkness, made her way over to his bed, and sat at the foot.

"What now?" he said.

"I'll go back down in a few minutes and see how things are." She felt his calloused hand reach out and take hers.

"Are you okay?"

"I'm fine," she said, lying.

No one here was ever fine. Ever. Not with the bills and the godawful hours and the unions threatening strike; not with age creeping up, a blade in its hand, always ready to cut you down when you walked into its path; not with all the backaches and headaches and cuts on your fingers; and not with morning approaching. Never with morning approaching.

"Were you listening to Dad the other night?" asked Russ.

"I heard a little, not much." She could sense the tears welling in her brother's eyes;

there was never any need to actually see them.

"He was talking… about maybe trying to retire at sixty-two, you know? But he figured that he'd only get something like a hundred and twenty-eight bucks a month from his plant pension—"

"He's only been there twelve years," said Nanci.

"But he's sixty-one years old! The last place fucked him out of all his pension when they closed down! He worked there almost thirty years and got left with nothing."

"It's the way things go."

"I know, I know, but… *goddammit*… it's not fair."

Nanci pulled her hand away. "Don't talk to me about *fair*, Russell, don't *even* use that word."

"But it's not—"

"Stop whining! It's not going to do any good, so just stop it. There is nothing we can do, you hear me? We just get on with it."

"Aren't you tired of all of it?"

"Yes, I'm tired! And don't think I don't hate it as much as you. I am very tired. I get sick of looking at it. Jesus! You go to school so you can get a decent education, you make plans, you go out to work and make money so you can see those plans through and then… something happens. It happens every time, Russ, it does."

"What? What happens?"

Nanci felt an odd pressure in the back of her throat; all these years, so many times, and this was only the second occasion where she could remember feeling her own sorrow.

But she quickly swallowed it.

The blissful numbness returned.

"Things don't work out. It's one of the rules. You work your whole life long so your family can have some of the finer things, but you end up only being able to afford the nice things. Sometimes not even that. You get swallowed up, Russell. It happens. Maybe every once in a while you want to go… I don't know, out to eat or something like that, a really nice restaurant where a waiter will pull out your chair and offer you a wine list and make you feel like something special…"

"… yeah?"

"… except it's a little out of your range. And maybe it's kind of silly, but it might've been nice, so you settle for the pipe-dream of *might've* and just take the family out for hamburgers, but even that breaks you."

There was a sound from the kitchen. Nanci rose. "I really do love you, Russell, but you've got a lot to learn."

"I'm sorry, Nance. I just don't see—"

"No one ever does, Russ. You just accept things. Then you get on with it." She smiled at him through the darkness, then left his room and went downstairs.

In the kitchen her mom was making coffee while sticking tiny pieces back into the hole made by the pistol.

Dad was in the bathroom, trying to comb his hair so it covered up his hole.

Nanci went over to the sink, saw one of her dad's pieces, and tried to pick it up.

It was too small and too slick. She went into the bathroom, excused herself, and took a razor blade from the medicine chest.

"Didn't mean to get in your way," she said to her dad.

"Typical goddamn Monday," he said, but managed to smile at her when he said this.

Nanci went back to the sink, scraped out her dad's piece, then took it to him.

"You missed one," she said.

"Shit," he said, taking the piece and tucking it in. "And I just got my hair right, too."

She went back to the kitchen and poured herself a cup of coffee.

"You look tired," said her mom.

"I am, just a little."

Her mom smiled and kissed Nanci's cheek. "I'm riding with your father this morning, we have to get going. Would you please toss the towels in the wash before you leave for work?"

"Sure thing."

"You're a good girl, Nanci. When you get older you'll understand how things are a little better."

"I hope so."

Her dad came out of the bathroom and grabbed his lunch bucket. "We gotta get movin' now. I don't wanna be late."

"Yes, dear," said her mom. Then her parents stood next to her.

"Do we look all right?" asked Mom.

"Turn around." They did.

"You both look fine," said Nanci.

They kissed her good-bye, told her how much they loved her, then left. Nanci stood at the door and watched them drive away to their jobs, wondering how they managed to do it.

They had their little secret.

And, when she got older, Nanci knew she'd understand.

She finished her coffee, dressed, then tossed the towels into the washer.

She checked her purse to make sure she had everything, then sat on the front porch and waited for her ride.

Her shift started in twenty minutes.

She didn't want to be late.

And We'll Be Jolly Friends For Evermore

BY P.D. CACEK

"...WAS REAL DARK SO THE BOYS COULDN'T SEE THAT THE WOODEN BOARDS covering the top of the well were rotten... it had been a real hard winter and wet spring and one of the boards had cracked all the way through. But the boys didn't know that. They lived in different towns and only got to see each other in the summers when they came to stay with their grandparents, so they didn't think about looking at the boards because that's where they played 'King of the Hill' every year. They'd raced to the well and the first one to reach it jumped up on top. They always did that, every summer... and it looked okay, y'know?"

Bennie went quiet then and peeled a few more lines of bark from the willow twig in his hand while he studied his audience, just like his grandpa did whenever he told a story. Dean, sitting well within the warm yellow circle of light from the campfire, nodded solemnly and hugged his knees in closer to his chin. His family had only just gotten television, so he was still more used to hearing stories then watching them. Bennie envied him a little... but only just a little. There was a smudge of charcoal on his cheek and a speck of white in the corner of his mouth—the remnants of the last marshmallow he'd roasted—that twitched every time his buck teeth chewed a little more dried skin off his bottom lip. Which was every few minutes or so. Dean was hooked good and proper, caught in the story like a lightning bug in a bottle.

And with just as much chance of escaping.

Bennie pulled off another sliver of bark and fed it to the fire before looking over with a secret smile at his bestest friend in the whole world. Spit and blood brothers forever. And ever.

Stevie was sitting with his back against the stones of the abandoned well, so far away from the campfire that only a tiny glimmer of the light reflected off the whites of his eyes. He'd heard the story before and Bennie could tell he was bored hearing it again.

"Two boys with one shadow" was what their parents said each summer when either his or Stevie's family drove the five-miles over washboard roads to the other's farm. Insepa-rable was another term their folks used, which Bennie had looked up in his grandfather's big dictionary and knew meant "incapable of being separate."

And it was true. Had been true ever since the first summer they met, three years ago this summer. Three summers and no winters, with Bennie forgetting all about his friend once the cold started creeping down from the hills and his parents started packing up their summer things into the Rambler's trunk. He never thought about Stevie in the autumn or winter or spring, never once cleared a space in his brain already overburdened with football scores and Saturday morning westerns and evil mysteries of long division to think about his friend during their nine months of forced isolation.

But once the air got warm enough to fill with the sound of mosquitos, Stevie was all he could think about.

It was funny how that worked.

Bennie fed another strip of bark into the flames. It really was funny.

"So what happened?" Dean asked in kind of that whiny way he had. "Come on, finish the story."

"Yeah," Stevie said, "finish it."

Bennie nodded and tossed the twig into the flames. It sizzled for a second then curled into the shape of a lazy capital C.

"The wooden top was solid enough," Bennie repeated, to keep them on track, "so when the boy jumped up on it, it held him, just like it always did every summer. It even held him when he started pounding on his chest like Tarzan of the Apes, y'know... ."

Bennie was going to try and imitate Johnny Weissmuller's famous yell, but thought better of it when a gust of barbecue-scented wind swept through the clearing. Although the well was almost dead center of his grandfather's apple orchard, it wasn't that far away from the farmhouse. If he yelled now, even though he knew it would raise a full flock of goose-bumps along Dean's backbone, at least one, if not all the adults still sitting around the picnic tables would saunter out into the orchard to see what the ruckus was all about.

Bennie knew from experience that adults didn't like any sort of ruckus, and that would have ruined everything. He wouldn't be able to finish the story and Stevie would be even madder at him. It seemed like Stevie was mad at just about everything lately.

"Come on, Bennie-beans," Stevie mumbled, "finish the story."

He took a deep breath and nodded. "Okay, okay. The boy didn't hear the board crack because he was really good at doing Tarzan... but all of a sudden, there was this other sound, louder, y'know, and his friend jumped. But the boy on the well didn't, he didn't hear it because he was still yelling. His friend tried to tell him, tried to get him to jump down but the boy just kept pounding his chest and yelling and laughing... he was laughing at his friend, I guess, because he looked scared... and then the board split in half."

Bennie clasped his hands together just like he did during school assembly and looked into the fire as hard as he could. He could still see Dean—hunched forward, chin resting on his knees, eyes wide—on the other side of the flames. Stevie was so far back he was nearly invisible. Nearly.

"Golly," Dean said. His voice was soft and hushed like he was in the library or church or something, and that made Bennie feel good.

Unlike Stevie who was his best-ever friend, Bennie had only met Dean a week ago when his family had pulled into his grandfather's driveway asking directions to the new KOA Campground two miles down the road, but only a quarter-mile through the orchard. Bennie's grandfather mentioned that to Dean's parents—how close the campground was— if he got bored with camping and wanted some company. His grandfather had even made Bennie offer Dean his hand and say how he'd be pleased to show him around the farm.

And such.

Since then, Dean's father had walked him over to the farm each morning and come back for him each afternoon. And Stevie had gotten angrier and angrier over being replaced even though Bennie promised he hadn't been.

But he did calm down a bit when Bennie told him this was Dean's last night. His family would be leaving the campground in the morning, bright and early, crack of dawn, which was why Bennie's grandparents had decided to throw a barbeque for his new best friend's family.

That was the part that made Bennie mad. He didn't want a new friend, and especially not a new best friend. He had Stevie and Stevie had him and that's all either of them needed.

Two boys with one shadow.

At least for the summer.

"Come on, Bennie," Stevie's voice whispered through the growing dark, "his folks'll want to get going soon. Finish the story."

"So what happened, Bennie?" Dean added. "Come on."

Bennie shrugged one shoulder. "The boy's hands were still up against his chest when he fell. Maybe if they hadn't been, he might have be able to grab a root or something on the way down... there were a lot of roots down there, from the apple trees, and that's what made it so hard to get his body out. There's not too many now... they had to cut most of them away, y'know."

"Wow." Dean's eyes shifted toward the well, reflecting the dying light. Stevie leaned to one side, his white cotton tee-shirt scraping softly against the stones. "And... he was dead, right?"

Bennie waited until Dean looked back to nod.

"Uh-huh," he said. "The well's deep... my grandfather's father dug it out and it goes down a long way. There's still supposed to be some water in the bottom, but it's too murky to drink. Only the boy never made it to the water... one of the roots... Doctor said his chin mustta caught one of the roots on the way down and snapped his neck."

"Ouch," Stevie said.

Bennie shrugged the other shoulder. "Better'n drowning, I guess."

Dean's head went up and down slowly. Stevie yawned.

When a barn owl suddenly hooted somewhere beyond the trees, Bennie and Dean jumped like scalded cats. Stevie rolled his eyes.

"And his ghost is still there," he prompted when his eyes made the full circuit, then let Bennie continue playing story-teller.

"And his ghost is still there," Bennie said, pointing to the well's worn rim just above Stevie's head, "haunting the well."

Dean's eyes made their own slow slide to the well and back again. "Really?"

"Yeah."

"Nah-uh."

"UH-huh."

"Wow."

"You want to see him?"

Another gust of wind blew through the clearing, stirring the leaves on the lower boughs. The lightning bugs had come late and gone early, because of the drought his grand-father said, and Bennie missed them. Telling the story, even with Stevie there, always gave him a case of spook-cooties and being able to look up and watch lightning bugs blink like Christmas tree lights helped.

A little.

Unless Stevie saw what he was doing and laughed. Like now.

"Hahhahhah!"

Stevie was still and always would be his best friend, but sometimes Bennie wished...

"You want to see him?" Bennie asked, scrapping one toe of his Keds sneaker against the dirt as Dean's body went rigid.

"You mean n-now?"

Bennie nodded as Stevie stood up, brushing off the seat of his dungarees and moving around the well to the opposite side. The firelight didn't reach that side at all and turned Stevie into just another shadow. Bennie tried to rub the spook-cooties off his arms without anyone noticing, and blushed when he heard the familiar chuckle.

"Jeeze-Louise," Stevie giggled, "next time I'm gonna tell the story."

Be my guest, Bennie wanted to say back. But didn't. Never had, never would, because they were best friends. Two boys with one shadow, just like their parents said.

"Yeah," he said instead, getting to his feet and walking over to the fire-lit side of the well. "Come over and say hello."

Dean was even slower than Bennie had been to stand up, and even then he didn't move. "I—Jeeze, was that my mom? It was really nice of your grandparents to invite us over but my dad wants us to get an early start in the morning so I really better get back so we can go and maybe we can come back next year and then I'll—"

He was talking so fast Bennie's ears had a hard time catching up, but the minute Dean paused to take a breath he managed to slip in one word... the word that horrified ten-year-old boys more than any ghost ever could.

"Chicken."

Dean was smaller than Bennie, about the same size as Stevie, but he pulled himself up as if his bones had suddenly attached themselves to wires hanging from the stars.

"Am not," he shouted and then seemed to remember they were standing next to a haunted well and got quiet again, "I just don't want to get into trouble, you know? When my dad says he wants to leave early he means it."

"Yeah," Bennie agreed, "I know, but it won't take long. See, he's… the ghost of the boy likes company. I guess he's kinda lonely… being trapped in the well and all."

Dean's sneakers, less worn and beat up than his or Stevie's, left furrows in the dirt as he scuffed his way toward the well. Back to the fire, his shadow rose up and slipped over the rim to the darkness below. "You ever… you know, see him? The ghost, I mean."

"Yeah, every summer. And I bring him things, y'know, to play with."

That must have peaked Dean's interest—or curiosity about what a ghost would play with—because he took another step closer.

"What kind of things?"

"Checkers," Stevie said and leaned forward, letting his arms dangle into the well's gaping mouth. Bennie's stomach always twisted up inside him when his friend did that.

"A box of checkers and a board," Bennie clarified, just so Dean wouldn't think he hadn't given some thought to it, "and comic books… *Archie* and *The Fantastic Four* are his favorites."

"Mine, too," Dean said, joining Bennie at the well. "Does he, I mean, did he like *The Green Lantern* or *Captain America* best?"

"Thor," Bennie answered before Stevie could.

Dean finally worked up the nerve to look over the edge, just a quick peek and real fast, but Bennie's stomach tightened up another notch.

"What else do you throw down there?"

"A baseball and playing cards and I once threw down my transistor radio but it hit the side and broke before it reached the bottom." Bennie turned and pressed the quivering muscles of his belly against the cold stones. Stevie looked up and smiled. Winked. "It probably wouldn't have worked anyway, the reception would have been really bad that far down, but I thought he'd like to have some music or listen to the World Series. He liked baseball a lot."

Dean's shoulder pressed against Bennie's as he looked down into the well. "Jeeze, can't see nothing down there."

"Nope."

"You throw anything else down there?"

Bennie licked his lips and was rewarded with the ghostly taste of oven-baked beans and charred burgers. It had been a really great barbecue, one of the best he could remember, in fact.

"You gonna tell him, Bennie-beans, or am I?" Stevie asked.

"Yeah… like I said, he gets real lonely, you know, being out here all year when I'm back home and he has no one to talk to, so I started bringing him pets… and stuff."

"Huh?"

"First it was dead birds I found and y'know, raccoons and rabbits that got smooshed on the road." Bennie shrugged and felt Dean jerk back when their shoulders touched. "I thought, it'd be okay, since he was dead, too, but it wasn't. They were just dead things, y'know, no ghosts... so I had to throw down... y'know live things so their ghosts would be trapped in the well with him."

Dean's voice sounded real funny when he asked, "Like what?"

"A couple of chicks, first off, but chicks are really kind of stupid. Then I found a kitten and then a puppy and I thought it'd be enough... but he's still lonely."

"Needs someone to talk to," Stevie prompted.

"Yeah, he needs someone to talk to... and play ball with. Y'know?"

"Wow... cooooool."

Dean lifted himself onto the toes of his sneakers and leaned forward until his face was hidden in shadow. The knot in Bennie's stomach tightened into a perfect sheepshank, like the one he'd finally mastered for his Boy Scout merit badge. He had to swallow real hard to keep the ghost of his dinner from joining all the others in the well.

"Jeeze-beans," Stevie grumbled and flicked a pebble off the rim. Bennie counted all the way to nine before he heard the hollow plunk when it hit the water. Dean jumped, but only a little.

"Do you think that was the gho—"

Dean was a lot easier than the puppy had been. The stray mongrel had been squirmy and twisty and almost too heavy for Bennie to lift... and once the puppy figured out what Bennie was about to do, it scratched and clawed at his belly so badly that Bennie'd had to wear a tee-shirt for the rest of the summer, even when he went swimming.

The puppy howled on the way down and the sound had echoed up from the darkness so loud that Bennie thought sure his grandfather or someone over at the KOA would have heard it. But they didn't, no one did... no one ever did.

Dean didn't make a sound except for sort of a gasp when Bennie grabbed the hemmed cuffs of his pants and tipped him over.

Bennie forgot to count before he heard the meaty thud echo up from the dark. He and Stevie stared down into the well for what felt like a long time, listening to the soft twisting of leaves and crackle of the fire, and letting the night settle itself.

"Think he's dead?" Bennie asked. He hated the idea of anything—kitten or chick or boy—alive and suffering down there alone in the dark. "I don't hear anything. I think he musta broke his neck before he hit bottom, don't you?"

He jerked back like he'd been lightning struck when Stevie suddenly grunted. It wasn't the sound Bennie hoped to hear from his friend.

"What?"

Stevie's elbows were jabbed against the rim, chin firmly set into the V of his open hands. He didn't look happy.

"I bet he doesn't even know how to play checkers," he said, looking down into the dark pit, "or Crazy Eights. And I bet he'll cry and get all pouty if he loses."

"He didn't when I played with him," Bennie said and instantly regretted having let that slip out. Stevie didn't like him playing with anyone but him. Ever. "Grandpa got me a new Monopoly game," he added quickly. "I could throw that in, too."

Stevie's eyes met his across the dark pit.

"I only like playing Monopoly with you," he said and Bennie felt the cold come creeping up under his skin despite the campfire warming his back. He knew what Stevie wanted, had wanted ever since he'd fallen down the well and died. Bennie was his bestest friend and bestest friends were supposed to stick together no matter what. Two boys with one shadow, just like their parents said.

But that'd been easy when Stevie was alive.

Bennie shook his head as he backed up. "I'm sorry, Stevie, but Dean's a good guy... you'll like him once you get to know him. Really. You'll have a lot of fun together, you'll see."

Stevie sighed—or maybe it was just the wind again. "It didn't hurt, Bennie, just a little right at the end... when my neck broke, but only a little. Come on, Bennie-beans, we'll have lots of fun, just like we always did. Please?"

Bennie didn't take his eyes off his friend until the fire was between him and the well and Stevie was just another shadow... just like he was supposed to be.

"You got Dean now, he'll be fun. I gotta go and... y'know, before they come looking for us. I'll tell 'em it was another accident, like what happened to you."

"But we're friends, Bennie. You and me."

Bennie shook his head and even though he couldn't see Stevie anymore, he knew his friend was still watching...

"It was just a little pain, Bennie-beans."

... still waiting for him to stop being chicken...

"Tell Dean I'm sorry, okay?"

... and would still be waiting for him the next summer and the next and the next...

Becoming Men

BY DOUGLAS CLEGG

SHADOWS FLICKERED AROUND THEM, THE DARKNESS ITSELF ILLUMINATED BY a brilliant moon grown hazy with the canvas that stretched above their heads. The smells were sweat and farts and hidden tears—the fear was in all their mouths, in their nostrils, like smoke from a catching fire. The bunks and cots were shadowy with the other boys, some of them moaning in real or imagined pain, others huddled together like the small group Ralph found himself in, a circle of boys sitting up on two cots and sprawled on the wood floor of the Hut.

A match lit, the tiny yellow flame illuminated the circle of boys, casting their faces in flickering. It was like camp, that's what Ralph thought, it was like camp only it wasn't camp, it was the nightmare of what camp was to children much younger than them. Part of him felt as if he were still four years old and he'd been left all alone at the playground, his mother had not come to get him after school, and all the other children were gone, no one needed him enough to be there. No one wanted him enough. No one cared. But he was older now. He had to let the memory of that turn to ash. He needed to tell what had happened. He had to break the silence so the other boys around him could break theirs, too, so they could find relief from this night.

Ralph went first, his breath coming slowly because he still hadn't recovered from the way they'd held him down, his asthma had kicked in slightly and they'd taken away his inhaler so he had to be careful. Slow, deep breaths. His eyes hurt just from the memory of the interrogation's bright lights and then the bitter tears that followed his confession. Was he still crying? Even he wasn't sure, but he tried to hold it in as much as possible, to hold in the little boy inside him who threatened to burst out and show the others that he was what he'd always feared himself to be: a weakling. The darting matchlight slapped yellow war paint on all of their features. They were Indians in a sweat lodge. He closed his eyes and began, "I had just barely gotten to sleep—halfway in a dream and it was all kind of like a dream when I heard all the shouting, it was my dad, he was shouting like crazy."

Jesus DeMiranda, the smallest boy of thirteen that Ralph had ever seen, said nothing, but his eyes widened, and he had a curious curl to his lips like he was about to say something, even wanted to, but could not. There was something compelling to his face, something withdrawn yet very proud. Ralph tried not to only look at him, because it made him feel little and ready to break down crying again, so he laughed like it didn't matter, "And my dad is such a loud son of a bitch."

Jack jumped in, "My dad didn't say a word. The bastard."

Hugh coughed. "My dad went nuts, he was just shouting, and my mom was crying, but even when the big guy grabbed me—"

"The big black guy," Jack added, then glanced at the others. The match died. Another one burst to life immediately; Ralph and his matchbook again.

"A big white guy," Marsh said, slapping Jack across the top of the head.

"Yeah, a big white guy, wearing camouflage shit and his face was all green, it was freaky, I tell ya," Ralph continued, holding the piss-colored fire in his hands like a delicate small bird in front of the others so they could all see their own fear, "and I was so scared I pissed my underwear and my dad, when I saw him, he was practically crying but since I could tell they weren't beat up I knew somehow that they had something to do with this, and it had something to do with that thing with my cousin from three days before and maybe with the fire that burned down this old shack, but I never really thought they'd do something like this, I mean, shit, this kind of Nazi bullshit—"

"It's scary," Marsh said, and his voice seemed too small for his six-foot tall frame. He grasped his elbows, leaning forward on his knees. "I just smoked some pot. That was it. Not half as much as my friends."

"What did you do that got you sent here?" Ralph asked Jack.

A silence.

Match died.

"Ralph," someone said in the dark, Ralph wasn't sure who it was, but he waited in the dark for a moment because the ghosts of their faces still hung there, photographed by the last light of the match.

Scraped another one against the matchbook.

Marsh continued, "With me, I thought they'd killed my folks and my sister and they were gonna do something terrible to me. And then I wished it was a dream. All of it."

"They hit you hard?" Hugh asked, nodding towards him.

Marsh shrugged. "They hit me. That's all. I barely felt it by then. I just figured they were gonna kill me. I figured if I just concentrated or something it would all happen and then it would be over. I thought it was because of the time I bought pot and got more than I paid for. That's what I thought. I didn't even think. I just figured that was it. It was over."

"And it's worse than that," Jack said. "You know what I heard my mother say when they put the blindfold on me? I heard her say—"

"No one cares," Ralph spat. "They all lied."

The boys fell silent for a minute.

"I thought it was gonna be like Tough Love or something."

"They sold us up a river."

Jesus opened his mouth as if to speak, but closed it again. Fear had sealed his lips.

"They did it because they love me," Jack said, but he was crying, he was fourteen and crying like a baby and Ralph decided then and there that he didn't care what the others thought. He leaned over and threw his arm over Jack's shoulder. It reminded him of when his little brother got scared of lightning or of nightmares, and even though Jack was his age, it seemed okay, it seemed like it was the only thing to do. Jack leaned his head against Ralph's neck, and wept while the others watched, not shocked, not confused, but with longing for someone to let them cry on his shoulder, too.

Jesus DeMiranda wept, too, softly. Ralph asked him why, and he said it was because he was afraid of the dark. Ralph gave him one match to keep. "For an emergency," he said, and all the boys watched as the little DeMiranda boy put it in his pocket, as if the match were hope and someone needed to keep it.

Ralph kept lighting his matches as other boys gathered around in the darkness and told their stories of woe, and wept, and gave up what fight they had in them.

By the time Ralph's last match had died, morning had come, and with it, no sound until the foghorn blasted its wake up call.

* * *

TO BE A MAN
YOU MUST KILL THE CHILD
YOU MUST BURY THE CHILD
YOU MUST GROW UP
YOU MUST ACCEPT RESPONSIBILITY FOR YOUR ACTIONS
YOU MUST TAKE ON THE RESPONSIBILITIES OF OTHERS
YOU MUST BURN
YOU MUST FREEZE
YOU MUST GIVE YOURSELF TO US

The words were emblazoned on the side of the barrack wall, and every morning, Ralph knew, he would see those words, every morning, no matter how hard he tried to resist them, they would enter his soul. In the line up, they had to shout out the words, they had to shout them out loud, louder, I can't hear you, louder, over and over until it seemed as if those words were God.

"Number one!" the big man named Cleft shouted so loud it rang in their ears, pounding his chest hard as if he were beating it into his heart, "I am your priest, your father, your only authority, understand? I am Sergeant Cleft, and my colleagues and I, your superiors in every way, are here to drill you until you break. We are not interested in bolstering your gutless egos. We are not interested in making men out of you. You are the worst kinds of boys imaginable, every one of your families has disowned you, and we intend to break you down as far as is humanly possible to go. Then, if you have what it takes, you will build yourself up from the tools we give you here. Right now, this is Hell to you. But when we are through grinding your bones and spirits, this will be heaven. I don't want any quitters, either. You never give up, do you understand me, grunts? Never ever give up! This isn't a camp for sissies and pansies, and you aren't here because you been good little boys! You got sent here because you are headed for destruction! You got sent here because you couldn't cut it like others your age! You got sent here before someone sent you to jail! Before you destroyed your families! Before you could keep up your stupid anti-social ways!" His barks sailed over them, for by dawn, even the terrified ones were ready to put up some resistance, even Ralph's tears were dry and he spent the time imagining how to escape from this island in the middle of nowhere, how to get a message out to the authorities that he'd been kidnapped against his will, and then he was going to sue his parents for kidnapping, endangerment, and trauma. He looked at Cleft with cold eyes, and wished the big man dead. Cleft was musclebound, large, a baton in his belt strap, pepper spray too, and something that looked like a stun gun looped at his back. Ralph glanced around at the others, the twenty-three boys, all with dark-encircled eyes, all looking scrawny from a night of no sleep and dreadful fear, and he shouted inside his mind. How could they do this? How could all these parents do this to their children? What kind of world was this?

Morning had come too soon, and they'd been roused and tossed in the open showers (like the Jews, Ralph thought remembering the show on the History channel, like the Jews being thrown in showers and gassed, or hosed down before they started on their backbreaking labor, treated not like people but like cattle), and then they all had been given uniforms, and the boys had complied. It struck Ralph as strange how everyone accepted it all; as if this was the Hell they were all consigned to, and there was no way around it. The uniforms were brown like shit, that's what Cleft had told them, "Like you, you are shit, and you will look like shit until we make men out of you!" Then no breakfast, but barrels of water just outside the showers, and each boy, if thirsty, had to stick his head in the barrel like an animal and drink. Some didn't, but Ralph did. He wanted water badly, he wanted to drink the entire barrel despite the other boys' spit he saw floating in it, and the insects that had fallen in. The bugs were everywhere, from sucking mosquitoes to huge dark winged beetles that flew at the screen door on the barracks. And what kind of island was it? Where? Was it the Caribbean? Ralph thought it might be off the coast of Mexico somewhere, something about the light of the sky, something about the water, but his experience was limited. He knew the island was flat where they stood, raised like a plateau. There were cliffs diving down to the sea, he'd seen them when the helicopter had brought him in the night, when the blindfold had slipped slightly and he'd glimpsed the rocky cliffs and the crashing waves far below.

"Grunt!" Cleft shouted, and Ralph looked up. Cleft pushed his way through the front line of boys in their shit-colored uniforms, and found him. Cleft looked like a parody of a marine, a steroid joke, a pit bull-human love child, and when he stood right in front of Ralph, Ralph wished he would wake up. Just wake up, he told himself. It's a dream. It has to be a dream. Piss your pants. Roll out of bed.

Cleft barked, "You worthless sack of owl dung, you keep your eyes on me, you understand? I seen a lot of boys come through here, and you are the sorriest ass piece of shit I ever saw. You hear me?"

Ralph kept his gaze forward, staring at a place just below Cleft's eyebrows, not in the eyes, but between them.

"I said, you hear me?"

Ralph trembled slightly, feeling his knees buckle. Hunger grew from a place not in his gut, but in his extremities, his fingers, toes, the top of his head, it was like a spider tingling along his skin, squeezing his nerves. His mouth felt dry.

"I hear you like to set fires, Pig Boy," Cleft almost whispered, but a whisper that boomed across the heads of all the other boys. "I hear you did something really nasty to another boy back home. I heard you—" Ralph shut his eyes for a second and in his mind he was flying over all the others, he was going up to the cottony clouds. He felt hunger leave him, he felt tension leave him, he felt everything fly away from his body.

With a sickening feeling, he opened his wet eyes.

Then Cleft glanced down from Ralph's face to his chest, then his crotch. Cleft laughed, a nasty sound. "Baby Pig Boy here has pissed his panties!" Cleft clapped his hands together. "He's pissed his panties like a big Baby Pig Boy, haw! You can put out a lot of fires with that piss, can't you Pig Boy?"

Then, Cleft shoved him hard in the chest, so hard Ralph fell backwards on his ass. He looked up at the big man, the bulging muscles, the sharp crew cut, the hawk nose, and gleaming teeth. "Let me show you how to put out a fire, men!" Cleft laughed as he spoke, unzipping his pants and Ralph screeched at first, like an owl, as the piss hit his face. Cleft continued shouting, telling him that to be a man, one had to first prove himself worthy of manhood, one had to accept humiliation at the hands of one's superior, one had to take what one deserved whether one liked it or not, one had to know one's place—"You like to set things on fire, grunt, but you need a man to put out the fire inside you!"

Just kill me, Ralph thought. Just kill me.

We are just like the Jews in the concentration camps, Ralph thought, glancing to the others who still had their eyes forward, their lips drawn downward, looking scrawnier and weaker than boys of thirteen to sixteen should look, looking like they would all have been happy to not have Cleft pissing on them, happy that Ralph was the first sacrifice of the day, happy to just die.

Just die.

It became a routine that they neither looked forward to, nor complained about, and the others who had sat up with Ralph the first night never spoke together again. Ralph would give Marsh a knowing look, and Marsh would return it, but for a millisecond before his eyes glazed over in what Ralph came to think of as "Clefteye." It was the zombie-like way they were all getting, Ralph included. When he lay asleep in his lower bunk, he could hear Hugh weeping in his sleep, then whimpering like a puppy, and sometimes Ralph stayed up all night listening for Hugh to cry, and it would help him fall asleep if only for an hour or two. Food got better, but not good. From the first two days of water only, they went to bread and water. By the end of the first week, they were having beans, rice, water, bread, and an apple. By the second week, it was beans, rice, water, bread, milk, apple, and some tasteless fish. Ralph noticed that his diarrhea had stopped by the third week, as did most of the boys'. The labor was grueling, but Ralph didn't mind it because while he hacked at the logs, or while he chipped at stone with what seemed to be the most primitive of tools, he remembered his family and home and his dog, and it was, after awhile, almost like being with them until the workday was over. The maneuvers began at night. Cleft, and the six others who ran the camp, had them running obstacle courses in the stench of evening when the mosquitoes were at their worst, when the mud was hot and slick, when the sweat could almost speak as it ran down his back. Wriggling like snakes beneath barbed wire, climbing ropes to dizzying heights, leaping from those heights into mud, running across narrow, stripped logs, piled end to end, it all became second nature after the initial falls and screams. Foghorn, as they called a large boy in Hut D, fell and broke his leg the first day of the obstacle course, and Jesus, the little boy that Ralph had never heard say so much as a word, got cut on the barbed wire, badly, across his shoulders, and then got an infection when it went untreated. After the third week, none of the boys saw Jesus anymore. Some said he'd been sent back home. Some said he'd died. Some said he'd run off. Some said it was all bullshit and he was probably back with his dad in New York City, lucky bastard, with a scar on his shoulder, and an excuse for not being in Camp Hell.

Rumors circulated that Jack and Marsh had been caught jacking each other off. The next time Ralph saw them, he also noticed bruises around their eyes and on their arms. Boys had ganged up on them, but Ralph didn't want to know about it. He was somewhere else. He didn't need to be among any of them, he was in a place of family and fire in his head, and although his muscles felt like they were tearing open when he lay down in his bunk at night, he knew that he was growing stronger both inside and outside.

And then, one day, Jack came to him.

"Got any more matches?"
Ralph opened his eyes. It had to be four a.m., just an hour to First Call.
The shadow over him gradually revealed itself in the purple haze of pre-dawn.
"What the—"
"Matches?" Jack asked again. "You're like the fireboy, right?"
"No."
"Liar. Come on, wake up. We have something to show you."
"I don't care. Leave me alone." Ralph turned on his side, shutting his eyes.
"He pissed on you. Don't you hate him?"
Ralph kept his vision dark. If he didn't open his eyes, it might all go away. "I don't care."

"You will care," Jack said. The next thing Ralph knew, it was morning, the horn blasted, the rush of ice cold showers, the sting of harsh soap, the barrels of water and then chow. Out in the gravel pit, shoveling, someone tossed pebbles across Ralph's back. He looked over his shoulder.

"Leave me alone," Ralph spat, the dirt sweat sliding across his eyes; he dropped his shovel, looking back at Jack.

"You set fires back home, I know that," Jack whispered. "We all know it. It's all right. It's what you love. Don't let them kill that. We need you."

"Yeah, well, we all did something. What did you do to get you sent here?"

Jack said nothing for a moment.

Then,

"We found Jesus," Jack said, and tears erupted in his eyes. Ralph wanted to shout at him not to cry anymore, there was no reason to cry, that he was weak to cry, just like Cleft said—

Ralph asked, "Where is he?"

"Dead," Jack said. "They killed him. They killed him and they hid him so we couldn't find him. Did you know he was only ten years old?"

"Bullshit," Ralph gasped. "He's thirteen."

"Ten years old and his father sent him here after he left his mother. His father sent him because his father didn't give a damn about him. You, Ralph, you set fires. And me, I maybe did some stuff I'm not real proud of. But Jesus, all he did was get born in the wrong family. And they killed him."

Ralph closed his eyes. Tried to conjure up the vision of his family and home again, and the beautiful fires he had set at the old shack in the woods, the fires that had made him feel weak and strong all at once and connected with the world. But only darkness filled his mind. Opened his eyes. Jack's face, the bruises lightening, his eyes deep and blue, the dark tan bringing out the depth of the color of those eyes, a God blue. "Dead?"

"Yep." Jack said this without any hostility.

We are all zombies here. "How?"

Jack glanced over at Red Chief and the Commodore, the two thugs disguised as Marine-types who stood above the gravel pit, barking at some of the slower boys. "Keep digging, and I'll tell you, but do you know what I think we're digging?"

Ralph cocked his head to the side, trying to guess.

"Our own graves."

"Me and Marsh been trying to find a way out every single night. We wait till three thirty, when the goons are asleep with only one on watch, and we get mud all over us, and we do the snake thing and Marsh and me get away from the barracks until we go out on the island, and we see that there's no way anybody's getting off this island without killing themselves, that's why security ain't so tight. It's a nothing island, maybe two square miles at the most, with nothing. The thugs' huts are in the east, and between those and ours and the work pits, there ain't a hell of a whole lot. But we find this thin crack opening between these rocks just beyond the thug huts, and we squeeze in—that's all the bruises—"

"I thought you got beat up."

Jack held his temper. "That's what we said, dumbshit, so nobody would know."

"I thought you two…"

Jack cut in. "We spread that story, fool. So we squeeze through the opening, and it's too dark to see, and this cave that we're hoping will take us out ends within six feet of entering it, only we feel something there in the dark, we feel something all mushy and stinky and only when Marsh falls on it and screams does he realize it's a body."

* * *

It was Jesus DeMiranda, the littlest boy at camp, dead not from an infection but from something that smashed his hands up and his knees, too. Ralph heard the rest, tried to process it, but it made him sick. "Where the fuck are we?" he whispered, leaning in to Jack.

"All I know is, I think we're all dead."

"All?"

"I think," Jack said. "I think they're going to just kill all of us. I don't think any of us are leaving." Jack stuck four small rocks in the back of Ralph's shorts, and then put some in his own pockets. Ralph looked at him, but Jack betrayed nothing in his eyes. "Later. They'll be useful," Jack said.

"Just like the Concentration Camps," Ralph whispered, and then Commodore shouted at him, and he returned to shoveling while the blistering sun poured lava on his back.

"I said get up here, you worthless Pig Boy!" Commodore yelled.

By the time Ralph made it up from the pit, crawling along the edges, he had scraped his knees up badly, and he was out of breath.

"Something you want to share with the rest of us?" Commodore said, his eyes invisible behind his mirrored sunglasses. His head was completely shaved, and he had green camouflage make up striping across his face. "I saw you chattering down there, Pig Boy."

"Don't call me that," Ralph coughed, his breathing becoming more tense.

"Something wrong?"

Ralph covered his mouth, hearing the balloon-hiss of air from his lungs. "Asthma," he gasped. "I don't have…my inhaler…"

"It's all in your tiny brain, Pig Boy, you don't need some inhaler like a mama's boy, you just need to focus. You need to be a man, Pig Boy." Commodore laughed, and shoved Ralph down in the dirt. Ralph felt his windpipe closing up, felt his lungs fight for air. He could not even cough. His eyes watered up, and he opened his mouth, sucking at air.

Commodore lifted him up again, bringing his face in line with Ralph's. Eye to eye,

Commodore snarled, "Breathe, damn you!"

Ralph gasped. He knew he would die. He knew his lungs would stop. His vision darkened until all he could see were the man's brown eyes. He thought of little Jesus, dead, his hands smashed into bloody clay. Dust seemed to fill his mouth.

"Breathe!" Commodore continued, and reached over, pressing his hand down hard on Ralph's chest. "You want to be a man, Pig Boy, you breathe like a man, open up those lungs, make 'em work," and suddenly, air whooshed into Ralph's mouth, he gulped, gulped again. The darkness at the edge of his vision erased itself into the light of day.

Ralph sucked at the air like he was starving for it.

"There," Commodore said, and pushed Ralph back down in the dirt. "You boys, you think you can create the world in your own image. That's your problem. You think you can keep from growing up. Well, growing up means accepting the burden just like the rest of us. Accept it, accept the truth, and you'll thrive. Keep doing what you've been doing, and you'll die."

Ralph sat on the ground, staring up at the man. The air tasted pure. He gulped it down, feeling his lungs burn.

* * *

TO BE A MAN
YOU MUST KILL THE CHILD
YOU MUST BURY THE CHILD
YOU MUST GROW UP
YOU MUST ACCEPT RESPONSIBILITY FOR YOUR ACTIONS
YOU MUST TAKE ON THE RESPONSIBILITIES OF OTHERS
YOU MUST BURN
YOU MUST FREEZE
YOU MUST GIVE YOURSELF TO US

They shouted it in the morning, still shivering from the icy waters that erased their dreams, standing in the shimmering day, a mirage of day, for in their hearts, they never felt dawn. At night, Last Call, the bells ringing three times, running for the piss trough, running for a last cold shower, running for two minutes in the latrine, and then Light's Out.

"He's under the Hut," Jack said. He'd gathered Hugh, Marsh, a boy named Gary, a boy named Lou, and Ralph wanted to see, too, to see if they were telling the truth about Jesus. At three a.m., they all hunkered down, crawling like it was another maneuver under barbed wire to get out of the Hut unnoticed; then under the Hut's raised floor, down a narrow tunnel that might've been dug out by jackals. Jack and Marsh had dug an entrance that led down into a larger hole, and there, in the dark, they all felt Jesus' body, smelled it, some vomited, others gagged. Ralph reached into the dead boy's pocket and drew out the last match, the one he'd given the little boy the first night they'd met to keep him from the dark.

Ralph struck the match against a rock, and it sputtered into crackling light.

They all looked at Jesus, at the rotting, the insects already devouring his puffy face, the way his hands were bloody pulps, his kneecaps all but destroyed.

"Holy—"

"—Shit"

"They did it," Jack said.

"Mother—"

"Yeah—"

"Holy—"

"Is that really him?" Gary asked.

"It has to be," Marsh said.

"Who else?" Ralph said, and then the last match died.

Sitting in the dark, the stink of the boy's corpse filling them, Ralph said, "If we let this go, we all are gonna die. You all know about concentration camps in World War II. You all know what happens. This is just like it."

"Yeah," Lou said. "They killed him. Man, I can't believe it. I can't believe my mom would send me here. I can't believe..."

"Believe," Jack said. Ralph felt Jack's hand give Ralph a squeeze. "Maybe our folks don't know what they do here. Shit, I doubt Jesus' father even knows."

"I can't believe it either," Ralph said. "They're monsters."

"They aren't human, that's for sure," Marsh added.

"What are we gonna do?" Jack asked the darkness.

"What can we do?" Ralph countered.

"Someone should do something," Gary moaned.

Then, they crawled out of the ground, up to their Hut. The diffuse moonlight spattered the yard, lit the barracks and huts and showers and the boy's faces were somehow different in the night, flatter, more alike than Ralph had remembered them being. Before they went inside, Jack turned to Ralph and said, "Too bad you wasted that match. We could've set fire to this place with it."

Ralph said almost to himself, "I've never needed a match to set a fire."

In the morning, a quiet permeated the camp, and when the boys trooped out to shout their pledge of allegiance to the dawn, their mouths stopped up as if their tongues had been cut off.

On the side of the barrack wall, the words:

TO BE A GOD
YOU MUST KILL THE ENEMY
YOU MUST BURY THE ENEMY

YOU MUST NEVER GROW UP
YOU MUST BURN THEM
YOU MUST FREEZE THEM
YOU MUST GIVE YOURSELF TO THE CAUSE OF JESUS

There, besides the hastily scrawled revision, written in rough chalk, the body of Jesus DeMiranda, held up by barbed wire twisting like vines around his limbs and torso.

Ralph glanced at Jack, who laughed, and then to Marsh who had a tear in his eye. Behind them, Cleft came striding, whistle in his mouth, wearing a green baseball cap and green fatigues.

"Into the showers, you pansy ass bitches!" Cleft shouted, blowing the whistle intermittently, and then seeing what they'd done, the writing, the body, — the whistle dropped from his mouth. He reached up and drew his baseball cap off, dropping it.

And then the rocks. Jack had made sure there were enough, just enough, for ten of the boys, Ralph included and they leapt on Cleft, stronger now, their own biceps built up from weeks of labor. Cleft tried to reach for the pepper spray, but he had to raise his hands defensively to ward off the blows. Cleft was like a mad bull, tossing them off to the side, but the rocks slammed and slashed at his face, tearing his hawk nose open, a gash above his eye blinding him with blood flow, and as the red explosions on his face increased, Ralph felt something overpowering within him. He became the most ferocious, ramming at Cleft with all his weight, cutting deep into Cleft's shoulder with the sharp edge of a rock, loving the smell of the man as he went down on his knees. Ralph grabbed for Cleft's belt, tearing it off the loops, holding up the pepper spray and stun gun and baton. Tossing the gun and spray to others, he lifted the baton in the air and brought it down hard on Cleft's skull.

It hit loud, a crack like a break in rock when a pickaxe hit, and blood flowed anew. And then all of the boys fell upon Cleft.

"YES!" Ralph shouted, high-fiving Jack, running like a pack of wolves with the others, across the muddy ground, through the steamy heat, rocks held high, Cleft's pepper spray in Ralph's left hand. Jack held the stun gun, and Marsh, the fastest runner of them all was in the lead, waving the baton that still had Cleft's fresh blood on it. They shrieked the words of rebellion, twisted from the Wall. Several of the boys had taken down the body of Jesus DeMiranda and were carrying it like a battering ram between them as they flew to the sergeants' barracks. They caught the masters in their showers, mid-coffee, shaving, cutting at them with their own razors, scalding them, beating them, until two more were dead, and the others unconscious. But the last thing Ralph remembered was the feeling of all of them, all the boys together, moving as one, storming the island, like lava overflowing a volcano. The rest was nothing to him, the hurting and maiming and all the rest, all the war cries and whoops and barbaric ki-yi's that stung the air—it was nothing to him, for his mind was overflowing.

When it was all over and night covered them, Ralph leaned forward to Commodore—the man was tied to a chair, his great muscles caught in wire. Ralph held out a cigarette lighter—a souvenir from a downed sergeant. Stepping forward to Commodore, Ralph struck the lighter up, the flame coming forth.

"Arsonist, murderer," Commodore said, his eyes bloodshot, his face a mass of bruises.

"Shut up or I'll cut out your tongue," Jack laughed. Ralph looked back at him, and wondered if, like Jack, he was covered with blood as well. He heard the shouts of the other boys as they raided the food supply.

"We didn't kill that little boy, you dumbfuck," Commodore said.

"Okay, here goes the tongue," Jack said, coming up to the bound man, clippers in hand.

"Liar," Ralph said, twisting the lighter in front of Commodore's face.

"One of you must've done it, " Commodore spat, but it was the last thing he said, for Jack had the clippers in his mouth. Ralph couldn't look, it wasn't something he enjoyed, but Jack had that glow on him, his whole body radiated with his joy.

The man didn't even try to scream.

Ralph looked at the blood on Jack's hands.

"Jesus, Jack," Ralph said, feeling the spinning world come back to him, the world of sanity that had somehow gotten out of control. "Jesus, Jack."

"What?" Jack laughed, dropping the clippers, clapping his red hands together.

Ralph looked back at the man, his mouth a blossom of bright red.

The man's eyes did not leave Ralph's face.

Ralph was amazed that the man didn't cry out in pain, that he kept his eyes forward, on Ralph, not pleading, not begging, but as if he were trying to let some truth up from his soul.

"Jack," Ralph went over to his friend, his blood-covered friend, his friend who had helped him get through this time in Hell. "Was he lying?"

"Yep," Jack said, averting his gaze. The blood ran down his face like tears. "He's one of them. They always lied to us."

"You sure?"

Jack closed his eyes. "Yep."

Then, "Did you and Marsh kill Jesus?"

Jack opened his eyes, staring straight at him. "If that were true, would it change anything? Jesus is dead. He came here. They did all this."

Ralph felt his heart stop for a moment, and then the beating in his chest became more rapid.

"We're just like them," Ralph whispered, mostly to himself.

"No," Jack grinned, blood staining his teeth, "They're weak. We're strong. Their time is up. Ours is just beginning."

"What did you do that got you sent here?" Ralph asked for the last time.

"Nothing," Jack said. "Nothing that you need to know about."

"You killed someone, didn't you?"

"It was nothing, believe me," Jack smiled. "And you've done some killing yourself today, haven't you?"

"I wouldn't have if—"

"You'll never know," Jack slapped Ralph on the back. "But it's okay. I understand."

Later, the man they called Commodore died.

Before morning, Jack came to where Ralph sat on a bench outside the barracks. He put his arm over Ralph's shoulders and whispered, "Now we can go home. We can go home and make them all pay."

"Are we men yet?" Ralph asked, feeling an icy hand grab him around the chest, under his skin, closing up his throat until his voice was barely a whimper.

"No," Jack said. "We're better than men. We're gods. Come on, let's play with fire. You'll feel better after that, won't you?" He stood, drawing Ralph up by the hand. "You're good at fires, Ralph. We need you. I need you."

"I don't know," Ralph said. "Yesterday it was one thing. It seemed different. Jesus was dead. They were like the Nazis."

"I need you," Jack repeated, squeezing Ralph's hand tight, warm, covering Ralph's fingers in his. "You as you are, Ralph. Not what they wanted. As you are. I want you."

Ralph felt his fingers curl slightly under the weight of Jack's. He looked down at their hands and then up at Jack's face. "I can't."

"No shame," Jack said, "We're going to live without any shame. Let's set it all on fire. Glorious fire. Let's make it burn all the way up to the sun."

"That's my dream," Ralph whispered, a shock of recognition in Jack's words, a secret between the most intimate of friends. "How did you know my dream? My first night here, I saw it in my mind, a fire going all the way to the sun."

They stood there, frozen for a moment; then, Jack slowly let go of Ralph's hand, leaving in his palm a silver lighter. "Go set fires across the land."

Before the sun rose from the sea into an empty sky, the fires got out of hand. Ralph thought that it was the most beautiful thing he had ever seen in his young life, the way fire could take away what was right in front of his eyes, just burn it away with no reason other than its own hunger. Jack told him it was the best day he'd ever had. When the burning was done, the boys went and had their showers, except for Ralph, who went in search of something new to burn.

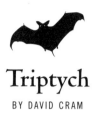

Triptych

BY DAVID CRAM

ASHES

From childhood, I hated sandy feet and grit in my food. I'd obsessively swish my clams around in broth. Everything was fine once the sand settled to the bottom. When I got home from the beach, I couldn't wait to wash my feet. Now, I love the beach and the sand. Kind of ironic, isn't it? The rhythm of the tides is soothing and the sun warms up these old bones, especially in the summer. Next time you're eating clams, look for me. See, the mortuary boys dumped me in at high tide, but I didn't travel all that far.

REAPER

They called me "pumpkin smasher." It wasn't funny. Not for those who made my acquaintance. Sometimes in the shadowy crease before waking, I see them for an instant, their faces bracketed. Their crime was being on the wrong side. Always, in that last moment, they're laughing, eating, never searching the ridgelines for danger. They had families and loved ones. I harvested them anyway. Caressing them from afar, 400-grain slugs separating them from their lives. I took them, but now they hold me, haunting my dreams, wrapping me tight in soddened sheets. They are waiting for me… on the other side.

SUMMER'S LOSS

The summer communities are quiet now. The tourists and seasonal residents have gone home to their suburban enclaves. Soon the bitter winds and storms of winter will drive the locals indoors until spring. And the next summer, like all the summers before, children will congregate, giggling, posturing, lost in their innocent play. And young couples hoping for a little peace will sit out on the breakwater dreaming of their worlds to come. And long-legged college girls will take jobs waitressing and indulge in a summer romance. And I will remember the wonder and sweet, enduring sadness of it all.

Somebody Put Me Together

BY SÈPHERA GIRÓN

SHE COULDN'T REMEMBER WHEN THEY FIRST MET.

It was one of those friend of a friend things.

It was one of those Internet connections...

* * *

There was a time when she had a life. When she would actually go for long walks by the lake, watching people, smelling the air, gazing at the undulating water, crying at the endless parade of couples holding hands... wondering if anyone would ever hold her hand again... trying to remember if anyone ever had in the past year, or two, or three. She would go to clubs, chain-smoking over rye and gingers, watching pretty androgynous men smile and flirt, while tightly wrapped women preened and primped. Sure, she went to the gym, she took classes, she even went to grocery stores on Friday nights, but there was no one there for her.

No one there...

She was beginning to wonder had there been any one there for her... ever?

Anyone that seemed to give a damn what she thought, what her opinion might be?

There was no one to ask her anything; therefore, there was no one to answer.

* * *

Once, a couple years back, there had been someone, but he was long gone. He had moved on, had a whole new way of being going on, but her... she spent a lot of time rattling around, analyzing and overanalyzing, fear of pain coating her with an inability to move on.

The ache of loneliness gnawed at her. What had once been a broken heart now was a slab of ice, slamming against her chest, chipping away at her insides, consuming her from the inside out. Whatever ran through her veins was no longer the warmth of nurturing life-giving blood. She could feel the chill pulsing through her, surging from the ice block, swooshing through her body until the cycle was complete and began again.

She was a bona fide ice queen.

The ice queen grew to hate her walks. The sight of those hands clasping, of eyes shining bright with laughter, of lips brushing against each other spontaneously brought pangs to her stomach, ache to her frozen heart. Sometimes she felt as if chips of herself fell to the ground behind her as she wandered aimlessly through the throngs of warm, rippling flesh. She felt as if she were falling apart, piece by icy little piece.

Her job as a web page designer kept her busy and people free. The more work she got, the less she had to leave her house unless it was absolutely necessary. She took comfort in that as being around living breathing people filled her with a sense of despair. L'Entranger.

One day, a friend emailed her, suggesting she check out the thread on a list somewhere. She hadn't ever ventured past email and thought it sounded like something that might amuse her. She joined the list server, and then another, and started to cruise the news groups.

And then the whole world fell away.

She wasn't sure when she started to talk to him or how they first connected. She saw his name popping up here and there on the lists, posting comments that she found amusing and thoughtful. She couldn't remember who emailed who the very first time. She couldn't remember a time that he wasn't there.

The chat rooms were next and the instant messengers. How she loved to watch her little list of people sign on and off the internet, watching when they would chat with each other, when they would need their privacy, and when the little chime would sing and a new window would pop up and they would want to talk to her.

The hum of the computer soothed her. Her pulse would quicken in the morning as she clutched her coffee, listening to the sound of the dial tone, then the connection to the server whine, that slight pause where her password may or may not be accepted, that pause where once in a while, the server was down and she would have to wait to go online and she would be so irritable when it didn't go through, then wham… she was there.

She dreamed about that sound. That pause before connection. That moment of suspension, like the edge of an orgasm. That empty space of tension.

She could crawl into that empty space, where the connection could leap. If she leaped in fast enough, she could be part of the circuitry, the intelligence that controls the computer. Could she fly along the wires, becoming at one with electricity? Could she become the buzzing throbbing pulse of energy, sizzling and soaring in that pause between connections, and in that instant, that connection, could she find her way to where she yearned to go?

She stared at the instant messenger names. Some of them weren't on yet tonight. HE wasn't on yet tonight. She puttered around, reading her mail, puffing her cigarette, designing the template for her latest assignment.

She thought about how he was taking the dog for a walk, or maybe playing baseball with his son. She thought about all the ways that he must fill his time before the siren song of the Internet called him.

She drew smoke into her lungs and wondered yet again, why all the fun guys, the intelligent guys, the guys that she really thought she might like to know, were married.

It was just like real life, only worse. There seemed to be a huge amount of married people on the lists, in the chats, wanting to talk, searching for communication, to touch another mind. She wondered if she ever married, would she still chat with her husband on line or would they have adjoining computers and still chat with strangers.

Her messenger chimed and startled her from her reverie. He was here and so impatient to talk to her today that he had barely been online for a moment before summoning her.

She felt the rock of her heart thump a little faster. She wondered what mood he would be in tonight. Would he be playful or depressed? Would they have a one sentence conversation or yak for hours? She took another draw of her cigarette and said hello.

He wanted her to go to a chat room, where they were discussing a movie they had both seen and loved. She clicked into the chat room and scanned the names. Most she recognized, and she saw his handle, Peter Pan, today.

How it suited this man she had never met. She wasn't even sure what he looked like. Couldn't be certain if what he told her was truth or a lie. She longed to believe they shared the truth. That the idiosyncrasies they shared were honest, that he wasn't just agreeing with some of her thoughts to weave a web of lies.

For he seemed to like her thoughts. He seemed to value her opinion. And that was the foundation of what was melting her heart.

When she talked to him, she could feel her heart beating, she could feel a warm flush surge through her. She heard herself laughing out loud at the jokes he told. And sometimes, they created stories.

Stories that brought out the human in her. Stories that led her to believe he really was Peter Pan, sweeping her off to Never Land, past that second star to the right and straight on 'til morning.

The places they would go, the sights they would see, the tremble she would feel when he would impulsively fling her over his shoulder and march her out of danger. How they would tease each other with suggestive words, with sly smiles and knowing winks. Sometimes her head would swim with the joy and laughter he brought to her. She treasured the light he shone into her darkness.

She ached to meet this Peter Pan.

They hung out in the chat room, watching the conversation unfold, while having their own private dialogue in another window.

He was playful tonight, making funny jokes, daring her to walk the tightrope with him. She followed, willing to go anywhere he chose to take her. She would walk on fire to be near this man who was melting her heart.

And she knew it was wrong.

It was wrong because he was married. It was wrong because she didn't really know him. Did she? If he was who he seemed to be, that was who she wanted. Then too, what if he wasn't that person at all. What if it was just a lie…

It was wrong… just because it couldn't be possible to connect so well to someone… really…

But it was all mind power. It was all brain connections. The fingers inputting the waves from the brain to pulse along until they showed up on the screen for the eyes to feed to the other brain.

Her brain throbbed with desire.

He led her across the tightrope and they faced a cave. In between punching in banal comments in the movie chat, they entered the cave, marveling at the darkness, listening to the rustling that could be bat wings, thrilling at discovering an underground stream glowing in a stream of light seeping through some unknown crack. She could see him, tall and strong, wild long hair half covering his face as his firm hands helped her pick along the rocks. She yearned to throw her arms around him, demanding that he take her in a surge of passion, right there, right now, on the rocks, in the water, on the damp cold floor of that cave…

But it was wrong…

Was it wrong? Was playing imaginary games with someone you didn't know a form of adultery? Was invading another person's brain for an hour or two a relationship? Or was it just another kind of computer game?

Tears filled her eyes as she typed.

She followed him waist deep through the stream. It was deeper than they thought, the current pushing them and now there was "something" wrapping around their legs, spurring them to hurry.

Her heart beat wildly, she could feel it. Warm, thumping against her chest, her blood boiling in her veins. Hot, so hot, she swore she could see her flesh pulsing and rippling as she typed.

He lifted her, soaking and shivering over his shoulder and she felt the heat of his body pressing against her. She wrapped her hands in his hair, binding them so that they wouldn't stray along his back, his shoulders, his neck, as he carried her through the narrow passage, the current threatening to sweep them away, the creatures slithering and slapping around them in circles.

Her thighs trembled and she squeezed them together, willing herself not to type what she wanted to type, to keep the scene a playful scene, yet her breath was coming in short bursts, her glasses fogging, a moan escaping from her mouth.

He waded through to the other side and set her gently down on a rock. She could see his face was bleeding, a scrape from something as he had carried her through that narrow tunnel. She brushed away his hair, searching his eyes in the half-light. Her face was so close to his she could feel his breath and she licked her lips.

She clutched the mouse in her fingers, willing herself not to type the words she was compelled to type. It would be wrong. It would be wrong. Her flesh bubbled, she could see a shimmer rising from her arms. Her bra was too tight and she slipped it off. Her nipples ached at the release and she fondled the burning buttons, shifting in her seat as her groin throbbed.

She patted his wound with a torn strip from her shirt, but the blood continued to flow through her fingers. He sat, catching his breath, watching her with wide, soulful eyes. She dabbed at him, pressing her hands against his head, her breast brushing against him as she leaned over him. All they could hear was the running of the stream and the sound of their panting.

She slipped up her skirt and slid the mouse against her groin, the heat of her crotch melting the plastic. She burrowed the mouse beneath her panties, into swollen lips that ached to consume.

She pulled off her shirt and wrapped it around his head, the pressure stopping the bleeding for now. She licked her fingers thoughtfully, reveling in his salty taste, as they decided which fork in the cave to take. His eyes glittered as he tried not to stare at her standing before him in only her bra and jeans.

The mouse filled her but it wasn't enough. The wires sizzled and crackled and she could feel them melding and blending inside of her. The keyboard lay across her thighs, and she pressed it against her crotch as she typed and erased and typed again.

She was chilled from the water, from the damp drafty cave so he slipped his arm around her as they started to walk again. She lay her head against his chest, listening to his heart beat. His firm hands guided her as they wandered the labyrinth. She drank in his strength.

Smoke wafted from the wires, sizzling sparks popped and crackled as she consumed the computer, tried to crawl into that space, that exquisite suspension... that gap just on the edge of connection.

They were in an enormous chamber. A chamber of gold with spiral pillars and a stone ceremonial altar. Incense was heavy in the air, there were statues and jewels and plates of food. They each grabbed an apple and sat on the altar.

She soared through the connections with ease, as if she had done this a thousand times before. With lightning speed, she was in his screen, seeing his face for the very first time.

They laughed as juice dribbled down their chins. They gazed at the statues with awe, wondering why they were all male with such amazing erections.

She surged through his keyboard, watching him type and erase and type again. Watching his lips curl up with a half smile, pressing delete with a sigh then punching in something about taking a bite from an apple. She watched him raise his eyebrow as he waited for a response. He had the face of an angel. She surged through the keyboard and into his fingers, the strong firm fingers she had dreamed about and beetled through his blood and into his brain.

It was as she had always dreamed. She shivered and quivered thrashing around in the electrical impulses, wrapping herself in his thought. She saw his thoughts were her thoughts; they merged and met, each inseparable from the other. Flashes of flying and caves and nipples and mouses. Flashes of him inside of her as she was inside of him.

Flashes of that wondrous moment of free falling, of barreling towards the earth, of riding undulating waves towards the rocks, of the suspended moment before the connection.

The heady rush of pleasure surged forth and consumed her. The colors, the sound, sensation surged and fired and buzzed as she became electric ecstasy.

Flashes of melting together.

She woke to a sensation of pulsing. A deep throbbing that stirred her essence. She was still in his head. She could hear him speaking and it thrilled her to hear the deep male voice she had never heard before. She heard him complain of a headache and heard a woman's voice offering solace.

She was with him now. She was with him when he went to his computer that night, searching for her name to pop up to show she was online. She could feel his worry as day after day, he couldn't find his playmate. She wanted to scream that she was right here, together with him always. Perhaps she did, for when she grew agitated, willing him to think of her, he would rub his temples with a heavy sigh.

It wasn't long before he found another lonely soul to play games with. To whisk off to Never Land. And as his thoughts of her began to fade, she felt like she was melting away. She didn't know how to get back and she couldn't keep her memory alive in his mind, for he could not imagine her, could not see her or taste her or feel her like she could him.

And then one day, she was disconnected.

The Girl With No Name

BY ELIZABETH HAND

I KNEW I WANTED TO BE A WRITER WHEN I WAS FIVE YEARS OLD AND SAW LAURENCE Harvey play Wilhelm Grimm in the movie *The Wonderful World Of The Brothers Grimm*. Wilhelm could create living beings out of his head—giants and singing bones, a Puppetoon dragon; elves and witches and a man with an invisibility cloak. Magic! This was the career track for me! I couldn't yet read, however, and it would be several more years before I got a better idea of how the magic worked. I was eight years old by then, the oldest of five children, on the first of many family vacations to Maine and the Maritimes.

My youngest sister was just over a year and still in diapers. Every day we would get up very early, pile into our blue Rambler station wagon, and drive to another place surrounded by pine trees where my father would set up the big green tent we all slept in. When it rained, we'd squash our faces against the window and watch as he struggled with poles and flapping canvas. Still, I don't think it rained very often. I remember gray stones, blue water, endless evergreens; a field where our tent was surrounded by grazing cows, a barn with a hayloft filled with hundreds, maybe thousands, of old comic books that I read for hours on end. And I remember the girl with no name. We were at a campground near the coast of Maine. I had a weird, exhilarated and somewhat unsettling jolt when I first saw her wandering through the pine grove: a girl my own age, vaguely attached to another station wagon with New York license plates. She looked exactly like me: tall and skinny, with crooked teeth, cat's-eye glasses, long mosquito-pocked legs sticking out of Bermuda shorts, skinny arms poking from a sleeveless madras blouse, her brown hair boy-short in what was known as a pixie cut. We looked nothing like pixies. We looked exactly like what we were—two scrawny, homely little girls. We started talking, and after a while wandered down to the lake where we spent a few hours in futile pursuit of minnows, before being called back to our campsites for lunch. After lunch we met again in the pine grove. It was a brilliant, sunny summer afternoon: green trees, indigo sky, indigo water flashing in the distance. We walked, then sat; and she started to tell me a story.

"There was this man named Frank who was driving his car down a long, dark road. All of a sudden it began to rain." The story went on for hours. A number of things happened to Frank, all of them bad. His car broke down; there was a huge dark scary house whose sole inhabitant was a skinny old man, words that the girl repeated in a soft, gleeful, ghoulish whisper. There were rooms in the house where Frank was supposed to sleep, although he didn't get to sleep in any of them. There was a four-poster bed with a suffocating canopy, another bed that flew around the room; floors that disappeared, man-eating rats, straitjackets, hypodermic needles as long as an arm; and always that skinny old man, cackling. Things ended badly for poor old Frank. The story was over. I blinked—the sun was still shining, the trees were still there. I felt a sense of astonishment, of the entire world being peeled away beneath me, just as the floors in Frank's room had moved under his feet. I looked at the girl who looked just like me, and realized—she had done exactly what Wilhelm Grimm had done. She had made living things come out of her head—all by herself, and without Puppetoons! And if she could do it... Our mothers began calling us. The station wagons were packed: it was time to go. The girl and I said good-bye, waving as we ran back towards our cars.

I never saw her again. But that was how I learned how magic worked. A few weeks later, I put it to good use for the first time back at home in Yonkers, riding on the yellow school bus with the other children at St. Eugene's CYO Day Camp (CYO stood for Catholic Youth Organization). At the front of the bus teenage counselors stood in the aisles, holding up transistor radios as they tried to tune in Murray the K and his Good Guys, Cousin Brucie and all the other dj's playing the British Invasion from sunup to sundown. Every day we went somewhere different—Playland, the Museum of National History, Rockaway Beach, Jones Beach, the Bronx Zoo, Palisades Amusement Park, Yankee Stadium; barreling past the Stella Doro factory, which smelled fabulous (they made Italian baked goods), or over the Tappan Zee Bridge to Bear Mountain, or through Harlem, where we watched enviously as other children danced around fire hydrants spewing water. When I was eighteen, I looked back on these trips and realized I'd been living inside a Ramones song. But at the time, the bus rides always took forever. The most coveted seats were in the very back, where you could play cards and gamble for money or baseball cards or Drake's Ring Dings. The older boys always staked these seats out. I had nothing in common with most girls my own age; I loved the same things the boys did—baseball, Soupy Sales, Superman, the Three Stooges, monster movies. But the boys wanted nothing to do with me—until I began to tell them ghost stories. I started with Frank and the skinny old man, imitating the same creepy voice the girl with no name had used. The boys were enthralled. They let me sit with them. They traded baseball cards with me. They let me play poker and War.

Tell us another story, one said as we headed back to Yonkers. Agh! Frank's story was the only ghost story I knew! So I did what storytellers have always done. I stole ruthlessly from another source, which was an article in *Famous Monsters Of Filmland* magazine I'd read a few days earlier. No one noticed that the plot was lifted from *Curse Of The Demon*; no one cared. For the rest of the summer, I cheerfully pillaged *Famous Monsters* and *Chiller Theater*, cribbing plots and characters from *The Incredible Shrinking Man*, *Gorgo*, *Ghidrah The Three-headed Monster*, *Plan Nine From Outer Space*, *The Monster Of Piedras Blancas*. I owed much of this early career to Roger Corman—my versions of *The Attack Of The Crab Monsters* and *Not Of This Earth* were particular favorites. Two years later we moved from Yonkers to a small town further north. I was writing my own stories by then, still mostly drawn from things I'd read or seen. The summer bus rides stopped, but I continued to parlay my skills at our village day camp.

Every morning after reveille I would hide in the woods and for the next four hours entertain a half-dozen other girls who hated the regime of games, folk songs, and feeble attempts at arts-and-crafts. I'd tell them stories until one o'clock, when the village mothers would gather in the parking lot to collect their offspring. By then my repertoire was much improved: I'd found *Great Tales Of Terror And The Supernatural* in the library, where I read "The Monkey's Paw," "August Heat," "The Wendigo," among others. "The Screaming Skull" was my favorite, and over the next few years I perfected a shriek that could shatter glass. I was very popular at slumber parties. Then adolescence intervened, as it does. I tried writing plays, a science fiction novel, Tolkien-ish fantasties. The stories I wrote had more longing in them, more sex; the plots and characters were not much better than Ed Wood's, but I didn't know that yet. I read more books, and tried to write something serious, plays in a Noel Coward vein, a story "about a mutant prostitute," as my boyfriend derisively described it: faint stirrings of what would become *Winterlong*.

More years passed. All of a sudden I was almost thirty. I had never been published, though I was always writing; I had nothing to show for my serious work except a freezer full of rejection slips. I had a dead-end job and no prospects for a better one. And then one day, I heard a voice inside my head, talking about a puppet; and I sat down and began to write a ghost story called "Prince of Flowers." It would be the first thing I ever sold. That was seventeen years ago. Not a week goes by but I don't think of that girl I met, once upon a time, the girl with no name. Was she real? She must have been: but did she really look exactly like me? My parents never let me go off anywhere by myself: how could I have disappeared for hours without them noticing? And even if it hadn't been hours—even if the time had simply flown, magically, as it does—how is it that I still remember every word she said to me? But most of all, how is it that I still hear her? Not always, but sometimes, when voices come into my head from nowhere, voices that eventually give way to those characters I love most— Sweeney and Tony and Daniel, Ivy and Jackie Finnegan and Miss Scarlet Pan. I don't see her, but I know she's here, now, sitting beside me with the Maine woods all around us on another endless summer afternoon: the girl who knows all the stories; the girl with no name.

Little Brother

BY RICK HAUTALA

A MICMAC INDIAN TALE TOLD AROUND THE CAMPFIRE

—I—

How the earth and water came to be, no one but Old One knows. How trees and rocks and animals came to be, no one but Old One knows.

Old One made the earth and the sky. He sang a sacred song as he molded them in his hands. He carved the earth with swift, gleaming rivers and filled its depths with surging oceans. He sang another sacred song as he stamped his foot on the ground to make deep valleys and push up mountains that reached to the sky. Singing another sacred song, he smoked his pipe and blew out smoke to make the clouds. He placed the sun and the stars and the moon in the sky and set them on their courses. Taking soil into his hand, he spit on it and sang many sacred songs as he fashioned all the creatures that live on the earth, fly in the air, and swim in the waters.

But after all this work was done, Old One was lonely.

When the sun fled from the sky and the moon shined her cold light over the land, Old One would sit huddled by the campfire in front of his wigwam, and he was filled with sadness.

"What's the matter, Old One?" Brother Wolf asked one night, seeing how sad Old One was.

Old One puffed on his pipe and didn't answer as he looked up at the stars, his creations, and thought long. He saw the stars' beauty, but he felt their loneliness, too. Looking across the land, he saw the valleys and mountains he had made, and the gleaming rivers and oceans he had filled; but they, too, filled him with a deep longing. He knew in his heart that none of his creation mattered unless there was someone to look at it, someone who could appreciate its beauty.

"I'm lonely, Brother Wolf," Old One said after a long while. "I look around me and see what I have made, and it saddens me."

"The world you have made is very beautiful, Old One," Brother Wolf said. "The woods and plains are filled with animals and birds. The waters are alive with fish. The hunting is good, and all that is strong grows and prospers."

"Yes, but that is not enough," Old One said sadly. "I feel the loneliness of the world, and I need someone... someone I can talk to. Someone who can share with me and enjoy the beauty of all that I have made."

"Every day after the hunt I come to your camp and we talk long into the evening. Am I not company enough for you, Old One?" Brother Wolf asked. He lowered his head and pointed his sleek black tail to the ground as he waited for Old One's reply.

Again, Old One smoked and thought long before speaking.

"No, Brother Wolf," he said finally. "Your company is not enough. The world needs Human Beings, creatures created in my image who can truly enjoy what I have made."

"But Old One," Brother Wolf said, scowling deeply, "would not creatures made in your own image also share your powers? I mean no disrespect, but would it be wise to give Human Beings such dominion over your work? Perhaps they will make things and do things to your creation that are not part of your plan."

Old One laughed loud and long, and smoke as thick as storm clouds billowed from his nostrils.

"Brother Wolf," he said sagely, "I have no plan other than to do what I have said. In the morning, I will take more soil and spit, and I will sing a sacred song as I fashion Human Beings for my world."

Brother Wolf bowed so low his snout nearly touched the ground as he shook his head from side to side.

"Meaning no disrespect, Old One, but I think that would not be wise."

Saying that, he bid Old One good night and skulked away; but in his cold, animal heart, he held resentment for Old One for not telling him that his company was enough to give him pleasure. That very night, he resolved to wait for the dawn and, before the sun could light the land in the morning, he would steal it and hide it in his den.

—2—

Old One slept, and the night was long, seemingly without end. He was not aware that while he slept Brother Wolf had stolen the sun. When Old One awoke, refreshed, he sat and smoked, waiting for the sun to rise. After a long time when it didn't come, he grew impatient and called Brother Bear to him.

"Brother Bear," he said, "I feel in my heart that many hours, perhaps many years have passed in darkness, yet the sun has not brought his light and warmth to the land. Do you know anything about this?"

Brother Bear shook his head sadly. "I do not, Old One," he said. "Like you, I have slept long and have awakened to find the world still dark. You created the day and the night, the sun and the moon, so you must know if this night will last forever."

"We shall see," Old One said, stirring the coals of his campfire. There was little wood, and the fire was no more than a feeble orange glow in the darkness. "If the night lasts too long, I will either find the sun or else sing a sacred song and make a new one."

After that, Old One called to him Brother Deer, Brother Fox, Brother Rat, Brother Raccoon, and many others. They all said to him what Brother Bear had said to him, and Old One answered them as he had answered Brother Bear. Before he could call Brother Wolf to him, however, Old One found that he was growing tired. Remembering his resolve to create the Human Beings today, he set about his work in spite of the darkness. By this time, his campfire had burned out, and he could no longer see in the darkness to gather more wood. Digging blindly into the earth, his creation, he took a handful of soil, spit into it. Singing a sacred song, he began to fashion a Human Being. But working in the dark, he was unable to see his handiwork. It was only by touch that he fashioned a Human Being like himself who walked on two legs like Brother Bear but was naked.

"To you, Little Brother, I give the gift of life," Old One said. With that, he blew gently onto the molded soil until he felt it stir with life. Carefully, he held his new creation close to his face and addressed it thus:

"Also to you, Little Brother, I give command of the earth. All of the animals I have created are for you to—"

He intended to say "for you to enjoy," but before he could continue, Brother Wolf came sniffing to Old One's campsite. Old One heard him prowling in the darkness and called out to him, "Brother Wolf, why do you come to me, skulking in the darkness?"

"I have heard from my brother animals that you are displeased, Old One," Brother Wolf said softly. "You have been asking my brothers if they know where the sun is."

"And you know," Old One said, seeing clearly into Brother Wolf's heart.

"I do," Brother Wolf replied, "for I have taken the sun from the sky and hidden it inside my den."

Old One's heart flashed like lightning with anger, yet he said nothing.

"I was saddened by what you said to me last night," Brother Wolf went on, "that my company was not good enough for you. I stole the sun to prevent you from making Human Beings."

"Go! Now!" Old One commanded, his voice rumbling like distant thunder in the darkness. "Return the sun to the sky, or else you and all of your children will perish."

Without another word, Brother Wolf departed back to his cave where he retrieved the sun and placed it back in the sky. As soon as the warm yellow light touched the land, Old One looked into his hand and saw what he had created from soil and spit and by singing a sacred song in the darkness.

The Human Being was short and stunted. His body was covered with thick scales like those of Brother Lizard. The back of his head was pointed, and his face projected forward like Brother Rat's. His eyes were round and bulged from his face like twin full moons. His shoulders were broad, like Brother Buffalo's, but his body was narrow and had long, dangling arms that ended in wide flat hands upon which were long, curved claws like Brother Mole's. He stood shakily on thin, gnarly legs that bowed outward at the knees like no creature Old One had ever created.

"You are a disappointment to me, Little Brother," Old One said, looking earnestly at his creation as he placed it carefully on the ground. "I thought, working in the dark, my hands and my sacred song would guide me, but now that Brother Wolf has returned the sun to the sky, I see that I was wrong. You are not what I had in mind at all. You are not a Human Being."

Little Brother looked up at Old One but, because Old One had not given him the gift of speech, he said nothing. The sudden blast of sunlight hurt his round, bulging eyes, and he shielded his face from the day's warmth as best he could with his wide, flat hands.

"No, Little Brother, I am sorry, but you are not a creature of the daylight," Old One said solemnly. "You were created in the night, and you are a creature of the dark, so to the darkness below the earth I will send you. But to show that I am kind, I will allow you and all of your children to come back to the upper world once every five years, there to see my creation and all the animals which I have created for you to—"

Again, Old One intended to say "for you to enjoy" but at that moment, Brother Wolf returned, approaching Old One with his head bowed and his snout scraping against the ground.

"See what you have done!" Old One said, clenching his fists and shaking them over his head until the wind rose high in the sky. "Because I was not able to see, I have created this, not the Human Being I intended. And it is all your fault, Brother Wolf. Because I have to banish this pitiful creature to the dark caverns below the ground, I also will have to punish you. You, Brother Wolf, will become a child of the night as well, and every night, you and all of your children will howl at the full moon, the pale reflection of that which you tried to steal from me!"

I Am An Exit

BY BRIAN KEENE

I FOUND HIM LYING ALONG THE INTERSTATE, BLEEDING IN THE MOONLIGHT under the sign for Exit Five. It was bad—real bad. Blood covered everything, from the guard rail and median strip to his frayed blue jeans and crooked birth-control glasses with the cracked lens. They called them birth control glasses because wearing them insured that you'd never get laid. You only got glasses like that in the military and in prison. He didn't look like a soldier to me.

Far away, barely visible through the woods, an orange fire glowed. A hint of smoke drifted towards us on the breeze.

I knelt down beside him, and he struggled to sit up. His insides glistened, slipping from the wound in his side. Gently, I urged him back to the ground and then placed my hand over the gash, feeling the slick, wet heat beneath my palm. The wind buffeted the Exit Five sign above our heads, and then died.

"Don't try to sit up," I told him. "You're injured."

He tried to speak. His cracked lips were covered with froth. The words would not come. He closed his eyes.

With my free hand, I reached into the pocket of my coat, and he opened his eyes again, focusing on me. I pulled my hand back out, keeping the other one on the gash in his side.

"Robin."

"Sorry friend. Just me."

"I was—trying to get home to Robin."

He coughed, spraying blood and spittle, and I felt his innards move beneath my palm. "She's waiting for me."

I nodded, not understanding but understanding all the same.

He focused on me again. "What happened?"

"You've been in an accident."

"I—I don't—last thing I remember was the fire."

"Sshhhhh."

He coughed again.

"My legs feel like they're asleep."

"Probably because you've been lying down," I lied. "They're okay."

They weren't. One was squashed flat in several places and bent at an impossible angle. A shard of bone protruded from the other.

"D-do you have a cell phone? I want to call Robin."

"Sorry friend. Wish I did, so we could call 911. But I'm sure someone will come along. Meanwhile, tell me about her."

"She's beautiful." His grimace turned into a smile, and the pain and confusion vanished from his eyes. "She's waiting for me. Haven't seen her in five years."

"Why is that?"

"Been in prison," he swallowed. "Upstate. Cresson. Just got out this morning. Robbery. I stole a pack of cigarettes. Can you believe that shit? Five years for one lousy pack of smokes."

I shook my head. I'd been right about the glasses. And the sentence indicated he wasn't a first time offender. Pennsylvania had a three strikes law, and it sounded as if he qualified.

A mosquito buzzed in my ear, but I ignored it. In the distance, the fire grew brighter.

"We'd been dating before it happened. She was pregnant with my son. I—I've never held him."

"They didn't come visit you?"

"Not enough money. Cresson is a long way from Hanover—almost on the New York border. We didn't have no car."

He paused, and struggled to sit up again.

"My legs are cold."

"That's okay. The important thing is to keep talking. Tell me more."

"I—I got out this morning. Couldn't wait to get home and see her and the kid. Kurt. We named him Kurt, like the singer, you know? The guy from Nirvana? She wrote me letters every single day. I used to call her collect, but Robin still lives with her folks, and it got too expensive. I've s-seen pictures of Kurt. Watched him grow up through the mail. I want to hug him. My stomach is cold."

"It's a cold night," I replied, trying to take his mind off of it. He was losing a lot of blood. The smoke was stronger now, heavier. It blanketed the treetops and drifted over the road like fog.

"The State got me a Greyhound ticket from Cresson to Hanover. Rode on that damn bus all day, and I was tired, but I couldn't sleep. Too excited. There was a McDonalds at one of the stops, and that's the first time I've had a Quarter-Pounder in five years! Couldn't wait to tell Robin about it."

His eyes grew dark.

"There was this one fucker on the bus though. Guy from Cresson, just like me. Never saw him before. He was in a different block. He was on his way to Harrisburg. He started the fight, but the bus driver didn't believe me and threw me off."

"Really?"

"Yeah!" He broke into a violent fit of coughing, and I thought that would be it, that he would expire. But then it subsided. "Fucker threw me right off the bus. Right here on the road. I had my thumb out to hitch a ride when I saw—I saw the fire!"

He sat upright, eyes startled.

"Shit, I r-remember now! There's a house on fire!"

"Yes," I soothed him, forcing him back down. "Yes, there is. But there's nothing you can do about that now. Somebody should be along shortly. What else do you remember?"

His eyes clouded.

"T-the fire—and then—a horn? A loud horn, like on a tractor-trailer; and bright lights."

"Hmmmm."

"Mister? I don't feel too good. I don't think I'm gonna make it. Will you d-do me a f-favor?"

I nodded. His skin felt icy, the warmth leaving his body.

"Give my love to Robin and K-kurt? Their address is in m-my wallet, along w-with t-t-their phone number."

"I'd be happy too."

He smiled.

"I—I s-sure-a-a-appreciate t-that, Mister." He smiled, safe in the knowledge that I would give his wife and child his love. Then he turned his head to the fire. His brow furrowed.

"I s-sure h-hope the p-people in that h-house are a-alright …"

"They are fine now," I told him. "There were four of them: Daddy, Mommy, and the kids, a boy and a girl. The Wilts, I believe their name was. Exit Four. I killed them long before I started the fire. So don't worry yourself. They'll never feel the flames."

"W-what?" He tried to sit up again, but I shoved him back down, hard.

"They were Exit Four. You are Exit Five. Hold still."

I pulled the knife from my jacket and cut his throat. There wasn't as much blood as I'd expected, most of it already having leaked out while I kept him talking. I wiped the knife in the grass and placed it back in my coat. Then I fished out his wallet and found Robin and Kurt's address and phone number. I smiled. They lived just off the Interstate, at Exit Twenty-One.

Twenty-One. And this was Five. Sixteen more, and I would keep my promise to him.

I walked on into the night, the distant wail of fire sirens following in my wake.

I am an exit.

Virtually Perfect

BY JAMES A. MOORE

CULLIE STARED AT SHEILA, TAKING IN HER EVERY CURVE AND FEATURE AND TRYING to burn them into his memory. As always, he was afraid she'd leave him some day. Not that she ever really would, but the fear was still there. Too many bad relationships in the past had made his life an endless stream of fearful thoughts and doubts about his ability to please a woman.

But Sheila wouldn't leave him. How could she? He'd made her.

The workmanship was incredible and, even observing her closely, he had trouble believing that she was anything but completely natural. He reached into the closet where he kept her and pulled her gently from her resting-place. The exercise was something of a strain: she weighed one hundred and thirty-two pounds, and he barely weighed one-sixty.

Cullie half dragged, half carried his masterpiece over to the bed, laying her down on the silk sheets he'd purchased specially for this occasion. His first time in bed with Sheila. He fiddled with her hair, making certain the long blond tresses fell just so. He toyed with her cupless leather corset and the garter belt that held her fishnet stockings in place. He readjusted the thigh-high leather boots on her long, supple legs, making certain that the slight bulge where her batteries were inserted could not be seen. He made her his, completely and irrevocably his, before he really allowed himself to look at her again.

Her eyes were just the right shade of blue, not too dark, not too pale. Her hair was as fine as corn silk, and almost as pale. Cullie smiled to himself, stunned by the level of detail he'd achieved. She really was his perfect woman. She damned well ought to be too, considering the amount of time that had gone into making her. The armature alone had taken weeks; fine tuning the ways her joints could move, making certain that the ball-bearings slid smoothly in their places, but did not exceed the norms for a real woman. Not, mind you, that she wasn't real for Cullie, because she was. As real as he would ever need.

Seventeen years in Hollywood had taught Cullie Sinclair the truth about reality, namely that it was all in the eyes of the beholder. Cullie'd spent those seventeen years training himself, mastering the art of cinematic illusion. That was why he made the big bucks: no one could pull off movie magic as well as he could, no one. Cullie had practically created "Animatronics," the art of making lifeless machines appear to move as if they were really alive. He'd made werewolves change before the cameras, and the faces he created were as "real" as the faces of the people he'd cast them from, accurate down to the last detail.

There had even been an investigation once, when one of the tabloids had seen the uncut footage from *Massacre 14*. The damn fool had actually believed the unfortunate whose face was sliced open had been mutilated in real life. The cops had a fit when they learned that the actor was unharmed, was in fact preparing for his next movie in Mexico. They'd have had an even bigger fit if they'd known that the reporter who called them had received the film from one of Cullie's assistants as a lark.

Cullie looked at Sheila's heart shaped face and sighed softly. God, she was just too beautiful. She almost deserved to be worshipped. Flawless skin, a full, sensuous mouth, almond eyes and a perfect nose, with just the right amount of curve to make her look natural. That was the real trick, making the features too stunning to notice any potential flaws. But Sheila did not have any flaws, Cullie had made absolutely certain of that. Every seam on her body was carefully concealed, hidden by the clothing that accentuated her charms instead of hiding them.

Cullie ran one finger from her collarbone down to the soft swell of her breast, marveling in the perfect resistance her flesh offered. That had been a true bitch, finding the right materials to go over the armature. He'd tried about a hundred different foams during his preliminary tests, but every one of them failed his tests; some of them crumbled if too much pressure was used, some of them lost their shape. That was the problem with foams, they never stood the test of time. In Hollywood most props were used only once or twice, and then discarded. Here, in his private home, the materials needed a longer life. Too much effort had gone into Sheila, he wouldn't risk her falling apart the first time he got a little rough. Instead he'd had to layer several different foams in Sheila's body, along with a soft rubber that always returned to its original shape. He'd even tried using just the rubber in one experiment, but that hadn't worked too well either. The stuff was too dense and, by his reckoning, Sheila would weigh just under 600 pounds if he'd gone that particular route.

Still, she was worth all of the extra time and money. Her skin was just supple enough, her muscles gave just the right yield. Her breasts were perfect, not too firm, not too soft. Cullie ran his fingers slowly down her form, feeling her body start to warm as the internal fluid systems warmed the rubber under her skin to ninety-eight point six degrees. Thank God her batteries were easily replaced. More than two nights of running Sheila at full capacity would likely drain the industrial charges completely. He had no intention of running her without all of the special equipment in working order.

Cullie's fingers slipped into Sheila's pubic hair, just coarse enough to suit his personal tastes, and plunged into the moist warmth of her vagina. The oils she excreted were the perfect temperature. He leaned over Sheila's body and felt her heartbeat; again the pulsing noise was as real as anyone could ever hope to achieve.

Cullie stepped away from her, feeling his arousal begin and deciding to hold off a while first. He turned from the bedroom and walked into the hallway, heading towards his work room on the opposite side of the house.

The room was filled with memorabilia from a dozen or more movies. Curtis Walker's head rested on a pedestal, still stuck halfway through his transformation into the Moon Demon. Behind the bestial head was a promotional poster for the same movie that failed to do Cullie's work justice but looked good just the same. Half a dozen other body parts lay around the room, mixed with alien skulls and other odds and ends. Most of the wall space was covered with shelves of materials, paints and Epoxy resins, alginates for casting heads, wax for sculpting oddities in a smaller scale.

Mixed liberally in the piles of work were photographs of Sheila Winston Sinclair, Cullie's ex-wife and the model for his love doll. Sheila Sinclair had tolerated Cullie's moodiness as long as she could, he realized that, but she'd left him in the long run, heading for Northern California with one of his assistants. Sheila was almost fifteen years Cullie's junior, and he'd fairly much known she would abandon him sooner or later. She was always more of a free spirit than he could ever hope to be: she liked to dance and to look for adventure. Cullie just liked to be with her, to experience life vicariously through her. Staying at home was safer, less chance of injury or misfortune that way. Deep down he'd always known she'd leave him. That was why he'd spent so much of his time working on her replacement.

The real Sheila, the one whose picture he idly touched and studied as he walked through the room, was a lovely girl, but he'd married her before she was ready to settle down. His Sheila, the one who waited for him in the next room, had more patience and would never complain when he was in a kinky mood. Sheila Sinclair had preferred straightforward sex, and despite a body and face designed strictly for pleasure, had never been all that fond of sexual intercourse. She'd been willing to make love, but only because she considered sex one of her "wifely duties." Towards the end she'd been less willing, and Cullie'd known about six months before she asked for the divorce that she was planning to leave him. They parted as friends, but Cullie needed more from her than just conversation and a shoulder to cry on.

So, after three years of careful planning and experimentation, Cullie had finally decided to build his own Sheila, one that would never say no to him, one that would even agree to bondage and sodomy when the mood struck him. The Sheila in the bedroom was all the woman he'd ever need and, in all honesty, he had to admit that she was all the Sheila he'd ever really wanted. True, he'd married his ex-wife too young, but in hindsight he had to admit he'd also married her for all the wrong reasons. This way was much better for everyone involved.

Cullie went at last to the cabinet where he kept the special recordings he'd created. He studied them each carefully, looking over the scripts on each Compact Disc case, and the words that would start the voice activated responses. He'd searched long and hard for the right woman to record the comments, the one that sounded the most like Sheila, and one that had been willing to imitate passion in all of the right places. Several thousand dollars later, he had every possible comment that could come up in a given sexual situation recorded and ready to go.

Working in special effects, Cullie had long ago decided, required a solid knowledge of anatomy, chemistry and even robotics. These days, it also required a great deal of knowledge in the use of computers. Hell, these days computer literacy was almost essential in every other job, why should special effects be any different? Cullie finally decided on which scenario to start with, and slid the compact disc from its jewel case. Voice commands would make certain that she responded properly to his every comment. She would never say that he was inadequate, or that she hadn't been satisfied. That was just the way he liked it.

Cullie sat down again, looking over the piles of leftovers in his work room, feeling simultaneously proud of all that he had accomplished, and saddened that he could not manage to do even more. Sheila was fully articulated, but he'd never get her to walk, and she would certainly never make breakfast for him the way the real Sheila had. These days he was far more likely to have cold cereal for breakfast than anything else. When the real Sheila had been around, breakfast was normally eggs made to order and a rasher of bacon. Oh well, at least the cereal had less cholesterol.

Cullie finally acknowledged that he was just wasting time, afraid to find that any flaws had slipped past his inspections, flaws that would ruin his greatest illusion, the one he'd created strictly for himself. He wanted the night to be perfect, no fuck-ups to mar his first time with the new, improved girl of his dreams. Time was wasting away, and he decided to take the plunge.

He walked to the small refrigerator in his workshop and pulled a chilled vodka bottle from behind a dried-out, leftover pizza. His new creation deserved a proper christening, and a little booze would help him ignore any possible errors in her programming. After swallowing a couple of mouthfuls of the chilled fire water, Cullie went back to his bedroom and the perfect woman that waited for him.

And there she lay, perfectly positioned, waiting for him with that special look in her eyes, the one that said she was ready to please him in every way imaginable. He grew hard just staring at her. Still, there were a few more final preparations before the night's session could begin.

Cullie set down the vodka, checked the CD to make certain that no dirt or scratches could be found, and set it carefully on the silk-covered pillow beside Sheila. He rolled Sheila onto her side, admiring the shape of her back, and the full swell of her buttocks. He undid the straps on her corset, exposing the ugly zipper that marred her perfect flesh. Even with his attempts to conceal the necessary wound, he could still see it. But when the corset was in place, she was once again without fault. With the skin peeled gently back, held apart by only his fingers, he slipped the CD into its caddy, and then slid the caddy into the slot where it could be read by the small computer in Sheila's torso. The small indicator light let him know that the computer was doing its job, reading the binary commands that would allow his Sheila to speak and moan for him.

Still, a test couldn't hurt. Cullie opened his mouth and spoke to Sheila close by her left ear. "Did you like that?"

Sheila responded: "Oh…. Baby. You're all the man I'll ever need. I love you." Her husky voice was perfect, just the right inflections, exactly the voice he needed to make himself believe she was real. Her mouth formed the words as she spoke, and he could feel the gentle breath that came from behind her exquisite lips. Trying not to think of the ugly opening, he gently closed and sealed the wound in Sheila's back, then tied the corset's strings back together, hiding the flaw and pushing its obscene memory away from his conscious mind.

Sheila was beautiful, and he wanted her in a bad way, but he held off a little while longer while he made the final checks. He ran a finger gently across her lips, and watched in delight as her mouth curled into a secretive smile and then opened slightly more, inviting him inside. His finger slid past her lips and the even white teeth beyond, touching the soft moistness of her tongue. Her tongue drew his finger deeper into her mouth, and her lips closed softly on his second knuckle as she began to suck the length of his finger. She moaned faintly for him. Sheila Winston Sinclair would have never considered giving him a blow job, but his Sheila was more than willing. The pressure sensitive pads under her skin were working perfectly, at least as far as her mouth was concerned.

Cullie checked her vagina with his fingers, probing deeply, and was rewarded with a lifting of her hips that perfectly matched the pace he set as he played with her and teased her. She moaned again, deeper, with more feeling. He moved his fingers to her backside and probed again, and was again rewarded with sighs of satisfaction, this time mingled with a certain amount of pain. The same sighs he had imagined countless times coming from his ex-wife. The miracles of modern science never failed to amaze him and, in truth, he had to admit that he was fairly surprised that he'd been able to carry off the level of sensation he'd achieved. He realized that his own breathing had increased, and that the only sound he could hear clearly was the sound of his own pulse in his ears. Jesus, he wanted her. And now, he'd be able to have her, whenever he decided the time was right.

Still the irrational fear was there. What if he couldn't satisfy her? What if she fell apart the first time he decided to play rough? There were just too many questions. Cullie swigged down another three gulps of vodka, trying not to cough it all back up and over Sheila. Not that she'd complain if he did, but better safe than sorry.

Cullie leaned down and kissed Sheila hard on the mouth. She responded instantly, urging him on with little sounds of eagerness. He loved the sweet slickness of her mouth, and he prided himself on his choice of flavors for the Erotic Love Oils that her tongue secreted. She was ready, waiting for him. He was almost too excited to speak. "How do you want it baby?"

Sheila sighed in response and answered, "You tell me, stallion. I'll do anything for you." Cullie practically tore the clothes from his back, eager to shove his cock into her mouth. She was better than he'd ever imagined. When he came he was screaming, and through it all she sighed and encouraged him with her tongue.

The night had only begun, and he planned on having her in every possible way before he was finished. But his body needed a few minutes to recover, and he spent the spare moments running his hands up and down her sweet form. Her breasts were perfect, her pleasure sounds were a symphony played only for him. He shoved his crotch against her pelvis and felt her respond. Not quite yet, but he was almost ready again.

He reveled in the familiar feel of her skin, the texture of her hardened nipples and the light scent of clove and cinnamon from her pores. He ran his fingers across her front, moving slowly down to her legs as he moved her onto her back. She stared up at him, that same smile once again on her angelic face. He positioned himself above her and, with minor difficulties, slid deep inside her body. Sheila rose up to meet him, and he lowered himself on top of her, eager to kiss her mouth again.

He kissed her, staring into her eyes, and reveling in her breath against his face, in his taste still in her mouth. He took in her face in close detail, studying her long eyelashes, and her thin eyebrows. He noticed with satisfaction the small scar on her forehead from where she'd fallen at the age of ten. Sheila had always hated that blemish, but Cullie had always felt it simply emphasized the stunning beauty of her face. That tiny little mark was what made his Sheila so special; that tiny little detail that he made certain would always be there.

That had been the hardest part of making his Sheila perfect; preserving his ex-wife's skin. He hated that he couldn't just slip her flesh off intact, but the scant clothes hid all of her faults. Being a special effects man meant having a working knowledge of taxidermy as well, but he'd been a little worried about how well her skin would hold up, even with the preservatives he'd administered and the oils he had used to cure her hide. He was pleased with the results, doubly so because Latex and rubber couldn't hope to imitate the feeling of flesh.

The rest of Sheila Winston Sinclair lay buried in the floor of his workroom, surrounded by a thick layer of lye to ensure that she would never decompose. But the most important part of her was with him, right where it was meant to be. He orgasmed again, and the programming worked as it was meant to, Sheila orgasmed with him, bucking wildly and screaming his name.

When he finally slipped free of her, Cullie kissed her lips again. As always, she responded eagerly, ready for him to take her in any way he desired. She was his perfect woman. He was her perfect man. "I love you, Sheila."

"Mmm, I love you too, my Cullie."

"I'm glad you came home. I missed you when you were gone."

"I missed you too, Cullie. I missed you so much it hurt."

"Promise you'll never leave me again."

"I promise. Never again. I'll be yours forever." She paused for a moment, the subtle motors in her face changing her expression from one of happiness to one of mild desperation. "Please say you'll never leave me, Cullie. I don't think I could live without you."

"I promise, Sheila. I'll be yours forever."

NECON CAMPER

Gahan Wilson

PART IV
NECON:
VISITORS FROM
ACROSS THE POND

The Burning

BY RAMSEY CAMPBELL

THOUGH CROWDS WERE MAKING THEIR WAY TO THE PARK, THERE WERE still bonfires in the streets. Patches of waste ground were heaped with flames; shadows jerked in gaping windows, made derelict houses flinch back from the creeping fire. When firemen arrived to put out the blaze, children began to stone them. Some of the crowds booed the firemen, some cheered a man who went for the children, brandishing a piece of wood and roaring. People haven't changed, Blake thought as he followed the crowds into the park.

What exactly did he mean? In the park he had no chance to think. At night, even in the open, he could hardly see his way; tonight the sky was a cave's roof of dark clouds overgrown by trees, the uneven ground was treacherous, disguised by fallen leaves. The park felt like rush hour in a blackout. He could only let the crowds bear him along.

Once he strayed onto what felt like a path—his eyes were still dazzled by the flames—where he almost stumbled into a small unlit bonfire. Around it several dim figures seemed to be awaiting a signal. He hurried to rejoin the crowds.

They weren't entirely reassuring. Apart from shuffling their feet, they made very little noise. Were they so eager for the yearly ritual that they had no time for speech? There were so many of them, crowding three deep for hundreds of yards along the fence which held them back from the display. Now they had begun to murmur, an impatient almost ominous sound, as undefined as the constant brooding of the city. He was beginning to wish he hadn't come.

Why had he come? Because it was Guy Fawkes Night, because he'd lost his job, because he had wanted to get out of the house—but those weren't answers to the question. He was here for the same reason as the rest of them; to watch a man burned to ashes.

Of course he wasn't a real man, only a guy—but there had been a real Guy, centuries ago, who had been bound to a hot stone until his flesh was seared. Perhaps Blake was just depressed, yet it seemed to him that while Hallowe'en was supposed to be the feast of the macabre, tonight was altogether grimmer. How else could one describe a night when an executioner's victim was resurrected to be burned a thousandfold?

The display was beginning. Rockets flung out streamers of fire which glared red and blue and green on the clouds. Fireworks spat showers of crackling silver, juggled whirling balls of fire. The dance of light revealed the crowd, which was even larger than Blake had thought. The bonfire writhed with shadows. Above them the guy seemed to struggle.

The glare turned the faces of the crowd into bright cardboard masks. Perhaps it was the light that made the watchers seem restless, though they had reason to be, for smoke was flooding over them from the display. There was no need to suppose they were impatient for the burning.

Blake thought they were. People hadn't changed. The crowd that had waited to watch Guy Fawkes hung, drawn and quartered must have looked as mindlessly eager—but why was this crowd so eager now, as men bearing flames converged on the bonfire? Bonfires had been for burning heretics, and also for public rejoicing; how had the two become combined? It was as though tonight's ceremony was so ancient that nobody could recall what it involved.

People were milling about now, trying to avoid the smoke. Blake's eyes were a jumble of after-images; when someone peered round his shoulder to scrutinize him he couldn't see the face. Were several people searching? Were their faces lopsided as masks that had slipped away?

He started, and came to himself. For a moment he'd known how it must feel to be trapped in a crowd through which searchers were closing in. Now they had moved away, if indeed they had been there at all.

It was no wonder that he was thinking oddly, perhaps hallucinating, when he'd had so little sleep. Every time he managed to doze, the realization that he had no job jarred him awake. There was no appeal against redundancy, nobody to blame, only the economic climate which also virtually ensured that nobody else would employ him now.

"Remember, remember, the fifth of November," a man with a megaphone was saying, "gunpowder, treason and plot. I see no reason why gunpowder treason should ever be forgot." All at once, as flames scrambled up the bonfire and the crowd cheered more loudly, Blake saw no reason either. The man up there was evil, and deserved to burn. The men who had put Blake out of a job, whoever and wherever they were, deserved it even more. His roar of approval was the loudest of any.

When he heard himself he stopped, dismayed. That was part of himself he didn't want to know. Had the searchers returned, or was everyone nearby peering at him? Ashamed to look, he stared at the bonfire. The face above it was burning now, the arms were writhing; one fell from the shoulder, into the roaring blaze. He could hardly bear to look.

It was quickly over, at least for the watchers. As far as a live victim was concerned it must have taken longer. A last flourish of fireworks spelt out GOOD NIGHT. He was glad when they faded, for their glare made the faces around him seem even more like masks.

In the dark the crowd seemed to have grown. As people began to disperse, the park sounded like an enormous playground. Of course he's known that there were many children, but now the thought dismayed him. Had children sounded so excited on the way home from public execution?

He must avoid these thoughts out here in the dark. He was thinking too vividly of

Guy Fawkes, tortured and executed centuries ago, only to be revived each year for entertainment. Blake had been thinking about death recently, since it seemed he was no use to anyone. Perhaps death was a kind of sleep—but what if you were jarred awake each year for further torments? The intervals between would seem less and less like sleep.

Suddenly he wanted to be home. At least his house was familiar, empty of surprises. He stumbled along in the midst of the crowd which filled the park. When he glimpsed people their movements looked jerky, tangled among after-images. Here and there flashlights lapped the ground, revealing fallen leaves sketched by frost. The pools of light wavered away from him. At least they were taking the children with them.

Trees closed overhead. They looked like after-images too, branded on the looming sky. He had little time to notice, for he needed to watch his feet, if he could see them. At least the crowd was thinning, though the people around him stank of smoke. The rustling of the leaves underfoot was harsh, almost deafening.

Here at last was a path; his feet had sensed it, even if he couldn't make it out. He hurried recklessly, anxious to come in sight of the main road, the streetlamps. His insomnia was oppressing him; the rustling around him sounded higher, the figures appeared to be moving stiffly as cripples.

He was in too much of a hurry. For the second time that night he almost walked into the unlit bonfire. That was the fault of the people who were crowding him and who had given him no chance to dodge. There were only a few of them; the rest of the crowd, he realized suddenly, had gone. They'd better let him through, or he would make them; he didn't care how rude he had to be.

He was turning away from the bonfire when they seized him.

They were moving as stiffly as he'd thought they were. They were rustling, though there were no leaves underfoot. Their gloved hands felt soft and lumpy, too clumsy to hold him—but before he had thought to struggle they'd twisted wire around him and stuffed a wad smelling of petrol into his mouth.

When they toppled him backward onto the bonfire he tried to lash out, but his hands and feet were bound tightly. His shoulder caught one of his captors in the face. That paralyzed Blake more severely than his bonds had done. Not only did the figure's head feel softer than jelly, but the face slipped awry, revealing a pale blur.

As Blake lay helpless on the bonfire, shuddering as though that would break his bonds, he heard a sound of scrabbling around him in the dark. They were trying to light matches. He threw himself back and forth, but that only sank him further into the bonfire; twigs scratched his face and hands. When he tried to spit out the gag, he began to choke.

A match flared, and another. He saw hands, or stuffed gloves, touching flames to the bonfire on both sides of him. Twigs and leaves blazed up. He could feel the heat through his clothes. He shrank, digging his arms into his sides until he ached.

The flames sputtered and died. The scrabbling began again, sounding vicious now. The depths of the bonfire gave way, engulfing Blake further. The snapping of twigs deafened him, so that at first he wasn't sure that he was hearing a voice: "Good God, what's this?"

All at once lights were darting about the open space, glancing at the masked figures that stood immobile around the bonfire. The flashlights converged on Blake. "God Almighty," said one of the men, the one who'd held the megaphone. "Who did this to you?"

As soon as they'd pulled out the gag and untwisted the wires, Blake fled. Even if the figures propped against the trees were still now, he couldn't bear to stay near them. As he fled, he saw the men lighting the bonfire and throwing the figures into the flames. Was it only the leaves he heard squealing?

When he reached the main road at last, he looked back. Then he ran faster, dodging traffic. The streetlamps had dazzled him; he couldn't have been sure of what he was seeing—yet he thought he'd glimpsed flaming objects across the park, hobbling toward him as best they could as they burned.

He ran down his street, past crawling piles of ash. Against a pink glow deep in one of them, he glimpsed a feeble stirring of charred sticks. He slammed his front door behind him, but couldn't keep out the stench of smoke. He stood in the empty house, wondering if anything was left in the street fires that might move.

Clearly Dead

BY SIMON CLARK

THEY RAN. THEY HID. THEY *thought* THEY WERE SAFE.
After all, there was no visible sign of danger.

I live. I die. I live again. Well... sort of. Is this the shortest zombie story ever?

I'd already told her that one before, so I opted for: "Most people don't believe in magic, but I once saw a wizard turn his car into a side street."

"What?" Her brown eyes were so wide they were in danger of rolling from their sockets.

"Okay, it's not a great joke, but—"

"No, I heard something!"

Her clothes were torn after the crazy race to reach this house on the island. Through rips in her dress I could see naked gooseflesh. Fear shivered through her.

"Oh, God," she whispered "They're here."

Okay. Picture this: There's the two of us in an attic room. It overlooks the lake. It's dusk. She's twenty years old. Slender as willow. Shoulder-length dark hair. I haven't asked her name, perhaps because a voice in my head yatters: *There's no feckin' point, stupid.*

Room's almost bare. An armchair. A table room centre. On that, a water bowl with a sponge. A wind-up gramophone. A copy of *Film Review* from November 1966. On its cover Robert Vaughn and Elke Summer with a dog. Sweet. I'd read articles aloud to distract her from a brutal reality. Some hope.

"They're following. I know they are." This became her mantra. "They're following. We'll be next." Then she'd go shivery again. "What do you think caused it? I mean, it happened so quickly. I... I just went to my brother's house and found him lying in the kitchen. Straight away, it started changing him." Then she looked at me with those big brown eyes. "I'm scared... please... will you hold me?"

And that's how we were. Me, with my arms around her when she made that stark announcement: "*Oh, my God. They're here.*"

We went to the window. The dusk made the lake look like grey iron. A sombre expanse of dead water.

"I can hear them," she breathed.

Faintly, in the distance, I heard the scrunch of feet—hundreds, *thousands!*—of feet on the island's shore.

I asked, "Do you see anything?"

She shot me a surprised glance. "See anything? As if we would."

For the first time I noticed she was wearing fake eyelashes. Despite everything... the shit hitting the global fan, cities burning, the dead walking—everything!—she'd kept the false eyelashes. Maybe a keepsake from a world we once knew... before God Almighty, or Satan, or some freaking cosmic anomaly, pulled this stunt.

Sure enough, here were signs of their presence. "Look," I told her. "You can see the water's disturbed. The grass is flattening. They're approaching the house."

She gasped. "What are we going to do?"

"I don't know..."

"There's got to be something! We got away last time!"

"Wait. Let me think."

I closed my eyes. Thought hard.

No answer came. Instead, I remembered what happened last week.

When the plague struck it was fast. People died where they stood. But that wasn't all. I watched Jo die in bed. The moment her breathing ceased her color faded. Kept on fading. Kept fading until her entire body vanished. Soon all I saw was a mound of bedclothes.

Dead.

Invisible.

Then movement.

The worse part is you cannot see them when they come for you. Now the invisible dead roam. They hunt the living.

My eyes snapped open as she cried, "Listen! They're in the house!"

I turned as the door opened. Although I saw nothing, coldness penetrated the room. Some *thing* turned the gramophone handle. Mournful funeral music droned. The copy of *Film Review* fluttered open as fingers unseen turned its pages. The sponge rose from the bowl. An invisible hand squeezed it; just for a moment cascading water formed the glistening shape of a wrist and forearm.

They reached the woman first, killing her without me even noticing.

When I turned to her, ready to grab her hand—and make that dash for safety—I saw nothing. Nothing, that is, but a pair of false eyelashes floating just in front of my face.

Then, as cold, invisible hands gripped my throat, I heard her whisper.

"Join us, my love. *Join us...*"

And so I did.

After all, who do you think is reading this over your shoulder right now?

Days of the Wheel

BY PETER CROWTHER

THE DAYS OF A FERRIS WHEEL ARE LONG, LONG IN TWENTY-FOUR HOUR TERMS and long in the life of the world... to which a wheel is not dissimilar, neither in purpose—of which it has none—nor in the way it moves, turning slowly on its fixed axis, day in and day out, ever the same, never changing, never tiring, never feeling.

Most of all, never feeling.

The woods that come together in its construction are traditionally as varied and various as those that may be found anywhere on the world, soft and hard, dark and light, their sap spent and only the bile of old-age left, the aftertaste of life, like the wrinkled old folks now watching as a parade struts down the Main Street of Forest Plains, folks like Miriam Greenhoff and Miranda Matthews, Joseph Montgomery and Duane Patterson, watching through bifocals from the windows of the Forest Plains Home For The Elderly, across lawns with grass cut so short you'd think someone had crouched there all night with scissors, whispering to the moon and the stars as the world moved on oblivious.

The eyes of these septuagenarian, octogenarian and even nonagenarian bundles of stick-bones and parchment-skin travel without moving, across picket fences white-painted by a hundred Tom Sawyer look-alikes, watching all that life and energy pass them by on the horizon of their vision, clasping mottled hands—shaped and misshaped like birds' feet covered in mottled flesh—placed on scrawny laps, their fingers wrestling silently with each other, embittered siblings never able to agree as their owners listen to the now dulled thud of their hearts, each thud sounding more faltered and more unsure, a syncopated and discordant tune that is not a tune at all, at least not any more than all the sounds that are the world are tunes, wondering whether this beat... or this one or one coming along any time now, already stacked up and waiting, will be the last.

At times like this, Miriam and Miranda, Joseph and Duane... and all the old folks in all the small towns, towns scattered across the country like duck-down from a pillow burst in a midnight fight, huddle together in the collective sentience of their souls wondering how death will feel when it comes to sit with them, how kind it will be, how understanding and gentle, and how cold or painful its touch, and they think back, while they wait, to their youth, those dim and distant days of seemingly endless sunshine, when skies were an unbroken blue and the summer stretched like taffy between the tall-tree days of spring and fall.

And they try to remember what it used to feel like riding the carnie rides.

They half-imagine, these old timers, these "senior" citizens referred to by many as Pop or Ma, old man, old woman—and by sycophantic talk show hosts and phone-in radio deejays as being 83 or 77 or 91 years young—they half-imagine that they can once more smell the fun of the fair over and above the cloying scent of sickness that surrounds them, the drifting aroma of peppermint and clocks winding down, remembering, in that faraway cobwebby place at the back of their minds, the amalgam of motor fumes, axel-grease, hot dogs and cotton candy mixed in with their own cheap drugstore cologne or perfume, cigarette smoke and well-chewed Juicy Fruit gum... half-imagining they can hear the barkers' calls

step right up!

just one thin dime!

one tenth of a dollah!

to brave the Ghost Train and the Ferris Wheel and all the other clanking rides, to see the tattooed lady and the two-headed boy, to throw wooden balls at coconuts glued onto tall pedestals, to stand in line for a fortune read by an old crone wearing too much face powder and lipstick and who talks in an incessant rehearsed whine that speaks of Des Moines or Brooklyn or Austin or Duluth and never of exotic places with exotic names, places that Miriam and Miranda and Joseph and Duane and all their kind in the myriad small towns that make up the time-embroidered quilt of America, places they only ever saw or read about in old many-owened textbooks or well-thumbed dog-eared copies of *National Geographic* back when they were all at school here in Forest Plains and able to move quickly through life and able to see so much of it waiting ahead of them, curled up like an old dog lazing in the summer sun just waiting to be called upon.

And at night, when the lights are turned down in their rooms and the time comes that, occasionally, when the conditions are just right, they're visited by friends and relations long since forgotten who sit on the edges of their beds without leaving an imprint and who cast no shadows on the wall in the light patch thrown by the moon through their windows... at night they sense the carnival again and feel the wind in their hair, hair long since grown grey and wiry, sparse and thin, like the grasses in the park outside the Library, only it's not the Library any more because the Library has gone, they suddenly remember... now it's a fast food restaurant and a savings and loan outlet and something else they forget, even though they maybe only saw it yesterday or maybe the day before when they were out in town, walking along the sidewalk feeling out of breath, cringing at the sounds of the motorcar horns and the strange rhythms blaring out of the music store onto the street.

They sit back, Miriam and Miranda, the two Emms who have buried three husbands and four children between them, and old Joe and deaf Duane, who thinks that every woman—even the steely-eyed and square-jawed Mizz Russell, the aptly-named, straight-backed matron, whose rustling, sibilant underclothes are the only quiet thing they ever seem to be able to hear... because, in some strange way

here we come... here we come for you!

it speaks to them of fear—is the wife he lost to cervical cancer long before it became fashionable and that every man is one of the two sons he lost in Korea and who visit him, from time to time, to tell him about what it feels like when a bullet enters the stomach or when a grinning madman slices off the eyelids so that the many interesting experiments he plans need not be missed by an involuntary muscle spasm brought on by exquisite and unimaginable pain... they sit back from the window, and Miriam gives a crooked half-smile to nobody in particular, seeing her reflection mimic the smile in the glass before her and wondering where the girl went that used to live behind those lips, wondering if she still lives here somewhere, wondering if maybe images never truly die the way she's heard that no sound ever truly dies but only keeps on getting fainter and fainter until only a half-crazed dog can hear it on the night winds.

　　And for a minute or a second or some other infinitesimal measurement of time gone by, time stored by old folks which, in the wealth of their experience, carries no true value because it represents such a tiny, tiny portion of all they have known, Joseph Montgomery—who, despite being called "Old Joe" is no older than any of the others and is even younger than many who refer to him thus—feels a once-familiar but now almost completely forgotten stirring, a thin and crusty unfurling of old skin stretching and old muscles hardening... an old friend come to visit, come to ask difficult questions

　　what happened to us?
　　to me?
　　where did I go?
　　where have I been?

and Miriam feels a sudden quickening and a moist warmth amidst the wizened parchment of her most private area, a crawling anxiety... a secret anticipation, a race-memory hoarded by the body to tantalize and depress.

　　And in that fragile moment, the four of them... the untold millions of them, all pulled back from windows as though hearing the sound of approaching footsteps behind them, footsteps that do not always seem to have owners when they creak arthritically around to look, they see a group of strangely attired men and women, some big, some small, a flurry of long tail-coats and stovepipe hats, ruffled neckties and flowing dresses, carrying amongst their unsmiling number a model Ferris wheel, which, large though it may be in terms of its portability to a man or woman bent by age and aches, is but a fraction of the size of the real thing, a sample-sized version of the monolithic structure pictured on the side of their horse-drawn wagon

　　a horse-drawn wagon in this day and age: I ask you!

depicting a structure of wooden beams and spokes seemingly carved to look like bones... old bones brittle with age and feisty with longing for life, and crazy-headed nuts and bolts that look for all the world like yellowed teeth and eyes laced with veins and the milky blue of cataracts, and tear-repaired mock-leather upholstery that resembles bruised skin mottled with brown whorls; it is a structure—the poster proclaims—that will soon grace the field behind the park on the edge of town, over beyond the turnpike and the old pond, a field that was once stronger and younger than it is now

than any of us are now!

a tired expanse of corn stubble... like an old man's beard, hard and abrasive and unforgiving.

Behind them—and behind the unending number of like-minded like-bodied aged folks in all the nursing homes, and in all the tenement rooms whose windows are open to the uncaring streets below, and huddled in all the night time department store doorways nursing a brown-bagged dose of memory-erasing liquid oblivion, and even in all the small one-room homes given over in plush houses owned by progeny who wear their familial allegiance on their pocketbook covers—life goes on, creaking and swishing in a familiar potpourri of disinfectant and urine and cooking food, a familiar static of radio phone-ins and TV reruns and the muted chatter of voices scarred and dimmed by age... it goes on oblivious to the spectacle outside the window or up the street or around the block, ignorant of the parade.

But not so the old people.

They see all too clearly the incarcerating struts and beams, the cold metal supports and tensile girders, the restrictive ground pinions and trammelled swing mechanisms, the formaldehyde upholstery of the seats glistening in the sunlight... they see the huge balls of Regret, finely spooled into boulder-sized twine-weaves; they see the steaming paste-pots of Dissatisfaction, and smell its pungent odor of sun-baked carcass and dried semen wafting invisibly and unstoppably through window-jams and door-sealings; they see the filigreed masking tapes of Hope and Envy, their cumulative binding power a heady brew of sunlight and shadow, of possibilities light and dark.

The parade pauses across the street, halts in its progress as all eyes turn to the window and meet the eyes of Miriam Greenhoff and Miranda Matthews, Joseph Montgomery and Duane Patterson—and, in a million other towns and cities at different times and in different settings, the eyes of countless scores of other people all nearing the end of one ride and reaching for the next... reaching with unsteady hands and nervous hearts—and for a second, all of them catch the breath in their throats as the entourage waves to them, waves its hands like a many-armed single entity, like corn blowing in the fields, moving in meticulous unison... the skeleton man and the angel, the harlequin and the harpy, the vampire and the ticket collector, the lamia and the ringmaster, the tattooed lady and the two-headed boy, a clutch of Siamese triplets joined at the head in a huge bulbous dome, their bodies bent outwards, warped by time into a gnarled normalcy, the sideshow barker waving his cane and tapping it against his straw hat, the exotic dancer switching her hips in a flurry of crinoline, eyes flashing menacingly

(*and enticingly*, Duane Patterson thinks to himself, feeling that movement again beneath his old work pants)

and all the others, and the ringmaster throws something into the air, a brief flutter of paper caught on the breeze and carried, wafting like a winged seed, across the pavement and the sidewalk and the closely-cut grass of the nursing home lawns—flying as it has flown over and around all the doorway litter and strewn washing-lines tethered across alleyways, and across the silent memory-festooned night-time rooms borrowed from sons and daughters, and over narrow hospital walkways between drips and blinking machines, and over church pews whose straight-backed seat-shelves contain leathery volumes of hymn and prayer whose covers are worn and stained by a million million hopeful and expectant fingers, and across highways littered with cars and buses, and over oceans topped by salt-spray foam, and along train tracks humming with the possibility of places to come and the memory of places gone behind— and in the Forest Plains Home For The Elderly it finds a way in, an entrance, finding a heel in this nursing-home-Achilles as it has done so many times before in all the myriad "safe" places... finding the slightest gap betwixt wood and frame, glass and holding cement, brick and mortar.

  It spirals down and up and across, catching currents and riding the air-draughts, unseen to all but those for whom the carnival waits, those for whom the Ferris wheel turns, its smooth and cold metal arm-handle wound and pulled by hands old when even the world was young, young in both world terms and the terms of the cosmos that contains it... until, at last, it falls, this breeze- and breath-carried epistle, falls onto the scrawny arms and into the claw like hands of

  Miranda Matthews!

  one of the ancient spectators.

  And then the cries ring out

  a parade!

  a carnival!

  my, will you just look at those folks!

and Miriam and Miranda, who now holds the airborne object to her eyes but who has not yet read the swirling writing and curlicued script it bears, and Old Joe and Deaf Duane look around in surprise, wondering how it is that the others can see and thinking that maybe this is not their time, that this is nothing more than a simple parade, a circus perhaps, a fair come to their town to spread cheer and merriment and laughter, but then, as Miriam frowns and curls up her nose, they hear another cry, a muted call unsure of what it says:

  gas!, the call echoes, *can you smell gas?*—a question voiced to any who might respond and in that same flickering instant, that same pause between now and soon, when anything and everything is possible, Miriam Greenhoff glances up the room towards Wilbur Portain, scrunched down in his wing-backed armchair, deaf to the world and uncaring of it, oblivious to the parade in the street outside, busy tamping down the tobacco in his curved Meerschaum with a blackened thumb, a worn silver lighter in his other hand, placing the pipe into his wizened mouth between teeth worn down and yellowed by time and nicotine, lifting the lighter to the bowl, flicking it... once, when it doesn't catch—and Miriam wants to cry out

  no! leave the pipe, don't strike the light!

and then she glances to her side, sees Miranda reading the simple card in her hand, sees Old

Joe leaning across blinking through his reading glasses, sees Deaf Duane staring out of the window, a slight smile on his face as he lifts his hand to return the waves from the street… and she turns back—and he tries a second time… Wilbur Portain, whose son and daughter-in-law put him into this place so long ago and never so much as a birthday card let alone a visit, and this time Miriam does not want to cry out but instead is suddenly concerned that the increasingly louder cries of something smelling around the silent room of old people might halt Wilbur Portain in his efforts, and then, still unsuccessful, he tamps the tobacco some more and shakes the lighter as Miriam looks around and Miranda looks up from the swirling letters, a frown and a smile fighting for control of her face, and Old Joe reaches over to take the card as Deaf Duane calls out his wife's name, watching the word spiral across the manicured glass at the other side of the window… spiral across the street to the waiting fair folk, one of whose number he has suddenly recognized, her face peering over the shoulders of the sideshow barker, and…

The click of the lighter is drowned beneath a tidal wave of fire, buried beneath an avalanche of flying masonry and wood-splinters, swept up in a tornado of spinning reading glasses, photo frames, favorite books, letters from dutiful sons and daughters and brothers and sisters, each filled with awkward words and phrases… the air outside the Forest Plains Home For The Elderly is black with debris and smoke, the carefully-manicured lawn covered with smoldering remnants of furniture, building materials and people, and the wind carries the smell of toasted meat out over the rooftops of the houses across the street, out over the turnpike and the old pond, out across the fields to the stubbled corn.

Listen:

Far away beneath the sound of the first sirens speeding along Sycamore, and a dog barking and someone crying, you can hear a calliope droning its sombre-sweet melody into the October wind, hear the step-right-up banter of the sideshow barker, hear the click and groan of the gears of the Ferris wheel…

ride!

Fifteen Painted Cards from a Vampire Tarot

BY NEIL GAIMAN

0. THE FOOL

"What do you want?"

The young man had come to the graveyard every night for a month now. He had watched the moon paint the cold granite and the fresh marble and the old moss-covered stones and statues in its cold light. He had started at shadows and at owls. He had watched courting couples, and drunks, and teenagers taking nervous shortcuts: all the people who come through the graveyard at night.

He slept in the day. Nobody cared. He stood alone in the night and shivered, in the cold. It came to him then that he was standing on the edge of a precipice.

The voice came from the night all around him, in his head and out of it. "What do you want?" it repeated.

He wondered if he dared to turn and look, realised he did not.

"Well? You come here every night, in a place where the living are not welcome. I have seen you. Why?"

"I wanted to meet you," he said, without looking around. "I want to live for ever." His voice cracked as he said it.

He had stepped over the precipice. There was no going back. In his imagination, he could already feel the prick of needle-sharp fangs in his neck, a sharp prelude to eternal life.

The sound began. It was low and sad, like the rushing of an underground river. It took him several long seconds to recognise it as laughter.

"This is not life," said the voice.

It said nothing more, and after a while the young man knew he was alone in the graveyard.

I. THE MAGICIAN

They asked St. Germain's manservant if his master was truly a thousand years old, as it was rumoured he had claimed.

"How would I know?" the man replied. "I have only been in the master's employ for three hundred years."

2. THE PRIESTESS

Her skin was pale, and her eyes were dark, and her hair was dyed black. She went on a daytime talk show and proclaimed herself a vampire queen. She showed the cameras her dentally crafted fangs, and brought on ex-lovers who, in various stages of embarrassment, admitted that she had drawn their blood, and that she drank it.

"You can be seen in a mirror, though?" asked the talk show hostess. She was the richest woman in America, and had got that way by bringing the freaks and the hurt and the lost out in front of her cameras, and showing their pain to the world.

The studio audience laughed.

The woman seemed slightly affronted. "Yes. Contrary to what people may think, vampires can be seen in mirrors and on television cameras."

"Well, that's one thing you finally got right, honey," said the hostess of the daytime talk show. But she put her hand over her microphone as she said it, and it was never broadcast.

5. THE POPE

This is my body, he said, two thousand years ago. *This is my blood.*

It was the only religion that delivered exactly what it promised: life eternal, for its adherents.

There are some of us alive today who remember him. And some of us claim that he was a messiah, and some think that he was just a man with very special powers. But that misses the point. Whatever he was, he changed the world.

6. THE LOVERS

After she was dead, she began to come to him, in the night. He grew pale, and there were deep circles under his eyes. At first, they thought he was mourning her. And then, one night, he was gone.

It was hard for them to get permission to disinter her, but they got it. They hauled up the coffin and they unscrewed it. Then they prized what they found out of the box. There was six inches of water in the bottom of the box: the iron had coloured it a deep, orangish red. There were two bodies in the coffin: hers, of course, and his. He was more decayed than she was.

Later, someone wondered aloud how both of them had fitted in a coffin built for one. Especially given her condition, he said; for she was very obviously very pregnant.

This caused some confusion, for she had not been noticeably pregnant when she was buried.

Still later they dug her up for one last time, at the request of the church authorities, who had heard rumours of what had been found in the grave. Her stomach was flat. The local doctor told them all that it had just been gas and bloating as the stomach swelled. The townsfolk nodded, almost as if they believed him.

7. THE CHARIOT

It was genetic engineering at its finest: they created a breed of human to sail the stars: they needed to be possessed of impossibly long life-spans, for the distances between the stars were vast; space was limited, and their food supplies needed to be compact; they needed to be able to process local sustenance, and to colonise the worlds they found with their own kind.

The home world wished the colonists well, and sent them on their way. They removed all traces of their location from the ships' computers first, however. To be on the safe side.

10. THE WHEEL OF FORTUNE

What did you do with the doctor? she asked, and laughed. I thought the Doctor came in here ten minutes ago.

I'm sorry, I said. I was hungry. And we both laughed.

I'll go find her for you, she said.

I sat in the doctor's office, picking my teeth. After a while the assistant came back.

I'm sorry, she said. The doctor must have stepped out for a while. Can I make an appointment for you for next week?

I shook my head. I'll call, I said. But, for the first time that day, I was lying.

11. JUSTICE

"It is not human," said the magistrate, "and it does not deserve the trial of a human thing."

"Ah," said the advocate. "But we cannot execute without a trial: there are the precedents. A pig, that had eaten a child who had fallen into its sty. It was found guilty and hanged. A swarm of bees, found guilty of stinging an old man to death, was burned by the public hangman. We owe the hellish creature no less."

The evidence against the baby was incontestable. It amounted to this: a woman had brought the baby from the country. She said it was hers, and that her husband was dead. She lodged at the house of a coach maker and his wife. The old coach maker complained of melancholia and lassitude, and was, with his wife and their lodger, found dead by their servant. The baby was alive in its cradle, pale and wide-eyed, and there was blood on its face and lips.

The jury found the little thing guilty, beyond all doubt, and condemned it to death.

The executioner was the town butcher. In the sight of all the town he cut the babe in two, and flung the pieces onto the fire.

His own baby had died earlier that same week. Infant mortality in those days was a hard thing but common. The butcher's wife had been brokenhearted.

She had already left the town, to see her sister in the city, and, within the week, the butcher joined her. The three of them—butcher, wife and babe—made the prettiest family you ever did see.

14. TEMPERANCE

She said she was a vampire. One thing I knew already, the woman was a liar.

You could see it in her eyes. Black as coals they were, but she never quite looked at you, staring at invisibles over your shoulder, behind you, above you, two inches in front of your face.

"What does it taste like?" I asked her. This was in the parking lot, behind the bar. She worked the graveyard shift in the bar, mixed the finest drinks, but never drank anything herself.

"V8 juice," she said. "Not the low-sodium kind, but the original. Or a salty gazpacho."

"What's gazpacho?"

"A sort of vegetable soup."

"You're shitting me."

"No."

"So you drink blood? Just like I drink V8?"

"Not exactly," she said. "If you get sick of drinking V8 you can drink something else."

"Yeah," I said. "Actually, I don't like V8 much."

"See?" she said. "In China it's not blood, they drink, it's spinal fluid."

"What's that taste like?"

"Nothing much. Clear broth."

"You've tried it?"

"I know people."

I tried to figure out if I could see her reflection in the wing mirror of the truck we were leaning against, but it was dark, and I couldn't tell.

15. THE DEVIL

This is his portrait. Look at his flat, yellow teeth, his ruddy face. He has horns, and he carries a foot-long wooden stake in one hand, and his wooden mallet in the other.

Of course, there is no such thing as the devil.

16. THE TOWER

The tower's built of spit and spite,
Without a sound, without a sight.
The biter bit, the bitter bite.
(It's better to be out at night.)

17. THE STAR

The older, richer, ones follow the winter, taking the long nights where they find them. Still, they prefer the northern hemisphere to the south.

"You see that star?" they say, pointing to one of the stars in the constellation of Draco, the Dragon. "We came from there. One day we shall return."

The younger ones sneer and jeer and laugh at this. Still, as the years become centuries, they find themselves becoming homesick for a place they have never been; and they find the northern climes reassuring, as long as Draco twines about the greater and lesser Bears, up near chill Polaris.

19. THE SUN

"Imagine," she said, "that there was something in the sky that was going to hurt you, perhaps even kill you. A huge eagle or something. Imagine that if you went out in daylight the eagle would get you.

"Well," she said. "That's how it is for us. Only it's not a bird. It's bright, beautiful, dangerous daylight, and I haven't seen it now in a hundred years."

20. JUDGMENT

It's a way of talking about lust without talking about lust, he told them.

It is a way of talking about sex, and fear of sex, and death, and fear of death, and what else is there to talk about?

22. THE WORLD

"You know the saddest thing," she said. "The saddest thing is that we're you."

I said nothing.

"In your fantasies," she said, "my people are just like you. Only better. We don't die, or age, or suffer from pain or cold or thirst. We're snappier dressers. We possess the wisdom of the ages. And if we crave blood, well, it is no more than the way you people crave food, or affection, or sunlight—and besides, it gets us out of the house. Crypt. Coffin. Whatever."

"And the truth is?" I asked her.

"We're you," she said. "We're you, with all your fuckups and all the things that make you human—all your fears and lonelinesses and confusions... none of that gets better.

"But we're colder than you are. Deader. I miss daylight and food and knowing how it feels to touch someone and care. I remember life, and meeting people as people and not just as things to feed on or control, and I remember what it was to feel something, anything, happy or sad or anything..." And then she stopped.

"Are you crying?" I asked.

"We don't cry," she told me. Like I said, the woman was a liar.

Partial Eclipse

BY GRAHAM JOYCE

I KNOW THAT MYRA GOES TO BED EVERY NIGHT AND WHISPERS, "DEAR GOD please let the aliens come back."

It's morning, and a diffuse winter sunlight bleeds through the curtains. I roll over in bed and stroke the warm, tanned swelling of Myra's belly, feeling the quickening under the callused pads of my fingers. It's just a tiny vibration, not unlike the attack note on the E-string. Myra opens her eyes sleepily and smiles at me. It's all beautiful. I want it to be beautiful. But now every expectant mother and father wants their infant to be born with an alien inside them.

"Anything?" I say.

She gives a tiny shake of her head, *no*. Just as she has done for nearly seven years now. Just as I do when she asks me.

"You?"

But she doesn't really have to ask. She knows that if the answer was yes then I would have woken her to tell her. Instead, so we don't have to think about it, I stroke her belly, because I know that by running the heel of my hand along the rim of her thrilling pink pot I can make the baby kick. And it does. *She* does.

"I saw her foot!" I shout. I can still see it. Or maybe it's an elbow, but anyway it tracks along the curve of Myra's belly, rippling flesh as it goes, and then withdraws.

"You're convinced it's a girl," she says. "You're wrong."

Myra's awake now. She'll have to get out of bed. She's about a week away from her time, and I know the baby is pressing on her bladder. But as she swings her legs out of bed she pauses, strokes her huge stomach, and says, "There was a moment. In the middle of the night…"

"Yes?" I hardly dare breathe.

"No, it wasn't anything really. It was just…"

"Tell me."

"I can't say for sure. I had to go to the bathroom, and it was in that moment when I was waking up, half-asleep, I thought I heard my baby calling to me. Would that count?"

I lie back, thinking, *Would that count?* Would it count? I don't know.

"I mean," says Myra, "I know *he can't* call to me, so it might have been a dream. Or

I might have simply imagined it because I so badly wanted to dream?"

I nod, but it sounds to me like no, it doesn't count. You see, there have been these rumors about pregnant women dreaming. "New wives' tales," you might call them. We've been yearning for it to happen since Myra's pregnancy was first confirmed.

Nothing.

I get up and ready myself for work. I can hear our daughter Mandy stirring in her room. Myra sees me select the Blucher. I love the unusual workmanship. The belly is spruce and the back, waist, and neck are polished maple. The hole is slightly elliptical, shaping a delicious ooze and throb in the resonance.

She raises her eyebrows as I lay the guitar in my battered carrying case and gently lock the clasps. "We're re-recording Teppi's early piece." God, it's hard to sound enthusiastic.

"Not that old thing! Didn't you do that a couple of years ago?"

"Six years ago," I point out. "And we're doing this much slower. Slow. Very slow."

"Surely there's more you could do than that!" And she looks at me, because she knows it makes me sad. She kisses me, and off I go to work.

* * *

Floyd picks me up. He has his cello in the boot, so I lay the Blucher gently in the backseat. "I've got one for you," he says brightly.

My heart sinks, and I stare at the stalled traffic ahead. "Go on."

"He's six years old. Last week he drew hundreds of people in Manchester. Hundreds. The week before that, Leeds, and you couldn't get a seat."

I've heard all this routine before. "What does he play?"

"That's it. He's not a musician. He's a storyteller."

"Give us a break, Floyd! Six years old?"

"He's in town tomorrow night. You and Myra, me and Zelda."

Like I say, I've been down this road before with Floyd. Mostly with kiddie musos, admittedly, but with the occasional storyteller too. It is a road of stony disappointment every time, but Floyd is a sucker. He wants to believe. He needs to. Maybe I'm mean, but you wouldn't get me to part with the price of the tickets any more, and Floyd knows that. There are too many spivs fleecing decent, hopeful people like Floyd and Zelda.

Floyd reads my thoughts. "My treat," he says. "Now then, do you know what we're doing today?"

"Sure." It's getting even harder to sound bright. "Early Teppi."

"Aw, fuck!" says Floyd. "Not Teppi again. That really has spoiled my day." And he leans hard on his horn just to prove it, scaring a hapless cyclist.

And even though I try hard to fake it, I have to admit that down in the recording studio it's a fucking bore, all day long. It's not Teppi's fault. Teppi is wonderful, complex and varied. But it's not enough. Even if I had never heard Teppi before, even if I hadn't recorded him faster, slower, *con brio*, who cares, we just can't make ourselves bleed for him. He, like all the others, takes the awful blame for not being new.

Floyd tries. We all try. Mid-morning I see Floyd's shiny black skin, like an aubergine, perspiring from the point on his receding hairline as he works his cello for the complicated fifth. A crackling voice from the control box cuts in and we're told to take a break. Moments later I walk into the washroom and I hear Floyd weeping. He's bent over a basin so he doesn't know I'm there. I leave before he sees me.

While waiting for Floyd to emerge from the washroom I talk with Vanessa. Always bright, always jolly, Vanessa is a brick. Superb pianist. Before the aliens left, Vanessa had a dazzling career ahead of her, with three recordings of her own steely jazz-rock compositions under her belt. Of course, that was nearly seven years ago, but she doesn't seem to let it get her down.

Floyd swings out of the bathroom, chipper, all smiles now that he sees Vanessa, so he pours himself a cup of Darjeeling and treats us to one of his jokes. Old jokes, of course. He knows Vanessa will laugh. He knows I will, too. Gosh, it's a very old one. So old I see the punch line laboring up the hill like a cart horse ready for the knackers, and unfortunately I laugh a moment too soon.

The following evening we put on best bib and tucker and turn up at the De Montfort Hall, where this six-year-old is expected to perform. Myra is somewhat uncomfortable, being so big, but she doesn't want to disappoint Floyd and Zelda. Anyway, she knows we won't get out so much after the baby arrives.

"Oh, let me!" Zelda admires Myra's bump, placing the flat of her palm on the underbelly. Zelda has beautiful long manicured fingers. She and Floyd have kids of their own, but they're almost grown-up. "It's a boy," she says. "You're carrying at the front."

That's what they said about Mandy. Nobody really knows.

Then Zelda stoops and puts her cheek against Myra's bump, as if she's trying to listen through the distended skin and into the womb. "Oh please let him dream!" she says softly.

We're caught. Trapped. Left dangling by Zelda's overt remark, and we all look away. A disembodied voice on the PA tells us that the performance will commence in three minutes.

"Come on," Floyd says.

I think he looks slightly angry.

We take our seats, and I'm amazed that the hall is full to capacity. I mean, we've all been hoaxed and duped and gypped and bilked so many times over the last few years you'd think it impossible to fill a hall this size ever again. But no. As I swing round checking for faces I might recognize, I see there's not a single vacant seat. The house lights go down, there's some nervous coughing, the curtains open.

First a warm-up act, a seven-piece jazz ensemble. Floyd looks at me as if to say, not bad but not good either, though we're both pretty stern critics. I recognize the opening piece but I can't put a name to it: Floyd will know. The fact is my mind is on the kid, and I don't like it.

Six years old. That's the ticket, isn't it? Six. I just don't like the idea of this six-year-old having to carry the weight of expectation—and the inevitable disappointment—of the 1500 people in the audience. I think of my own six-year-old Mandy, at home with her babysitter, and how I would never allow her to be put through this.

But there's big money in it, and even when it goes wrong the promoters and, presumably, the kid's parents get to pocket the admissions charges. Because nothing can ever be proved conclusively, can it?

Polite applause dispatches the ensemble and the stage is rearranged for the kid. Big chair in the middle, overhead microphone, one chair either side for what I see in the program are the kid's "guardians" rather than his parents. I point this out to Myra.

"Cynical," she says. I think she means the manipulation of the kid but she adds, "You're so cynical." She strokes her bulge. I know the chair isn't comfortable for her.

The kid comes on and he's a funny-looking thing. He's wearing a starched collar too big for his neck. He's pale under the limelight, his hair is plastered to his head and his ears stick out like wing nuts. Poor little runt. But he looks precociously unflustered by the size of the audience. His "guardians" take their seats either side of him as the kid is introduced by the emcee. Polite applause dies down and the kid waits, creating a tension in the hall, and I know, I just know, he's been coached to do this.

He leans forward slightly and says, "Once upon a time."

And the audience goes wild. Rapturous applause. This is irony, you see. Laid on with a teaspoon. From a six-year-old. It's a little message for critical observers like myself, for the skeptics and the doubters and disbelievers. It's post-post-postmodern. Or something. From a six-year-old sprog. And the audience laps it up.

It takes a while for this little riot to die down before he launches into the story proper. And I have to admit it, he's not bad for a six-year-old. He delivers well, his story is pacy, he's got good kiddie timing, and he speaks clearly. What more could anyone want?

The one thing we all want. The one thing we would willingly sacrifice all the above qualities to have.

I identify the story after just a few minutes. Most people in the audience don't yet, but they will, because the narrative pattern will occur to them. It happens to be an old Romanian folktale, about a bear who walks through an anonymous landscape meeting other animals, challenging all of them to guess what he has under his hat. How do I know it? Because two years ago we re-recorded almost the complete collection of Moldovan's work—faster or slower, I can't recall—and there was a libretto borrowing from the tale. Floyd has clocked it too, because he turns to me with an expression of apology on his face. I smile back thinly.

I mean, what are we supposed to do? Interrupt the proceedings and denounce the six-year-old in front of 1500 people? Jump to my feet and shout, "This isn't original! I spy a Romanian folk tale!"

Nah. In any event, there is already a sense of slumping attention in the audience.

Many have worked it out for themselves. The familiar narrative pattern, linked with inauthenticities in the manner the kid has been trained to deliver, will give it away. But an audience in denial is an astonishing thing, and the kid holds it for twelve minutes before ending the tale.

The audience applauds loudly, but—and it's a significant but—not so loudly as they greeted his opening line. The emcee proposes a break, and promises us another performance by the ensemble before the prodigy will offer us a second tale.

Not for us. We're out of there, as are a reasonable percentage of the audience judging by the bustling cloakroom activity. "Well," says Zelda, helping Myra on with her coat. "I hadn't heard it before."

"Me neither," says Myra huffily.

Floyd's levitated eyebrows exhort me to say nothing. We adjourn to The Long Memory for a drink before home.

* * *

And a drink turns into seven or eight, as it must. There has been a lot more drunkenness these last few years, a lot more alcoholism. Drink and drugs: they give a semblance of dreaming, don't they? Helping us to remember. An approach to dreaming. A dullard's kick against the thick, thick ice.

"A man walks into a bar," says Floyd.

We're trying to invent a joke again. It's a dead loss, because there hasn't been a new joke in almost seven years, but we're pissed as newts in a pickle jar so we try anyway. Floyd says, start with the old structures, it makes things easier.

"A man walks into a bar…"

"Says, 'ouch!'" Zelda chips in.

"Old. Very, very old," Myra says. She's not drinking because of the baby. Her tolerance for our "hilarious" drunkenness is wearing thin. She's already reached for her coat.

"Really?" Zelda protests. "I thought I'd just made it up. I really did." She's slurring.

"A man bars into a walk." Floyd says.

"Give us a break!" Myra almost screams. "Come on, Jonathan, take me home."

I think it's the interpreting I miss most. Though an interpreted dream is a punctured dream, at least in those days you could be certain of a steady supply, and the fun was in the mystery, the guessing, the deconstructing, the reassembling. We can all out-argue Freud when we own the theater.

We say goodnight to Floyd and Zelda; lush, slobbering kisses all round. They stay for another drink as I shamble out of the swinging doors of The Long Memory, supported by my heavily pregnant wife. I complain bitterly about being made to leave early.

"It was time," Myra says. "You know what will happen after the next drink. Floyd will get weepy. Then Zelda will get weepy because Floyd is weepy. Then we'll all have a stupid argument the subject of which no one will remember. Come on, stand up."

"It's only the booze," I say as we reach the car.

Myra gets into the driver's seat. She can barely fit her bump under the steering wheel. "The thing is," she says, tickling the ignition into life, "in knowing when it's time to go."

* * *

Time to go. The aliens presumably knew it was time to go. Everyone can remember the moment when they quit the planet. When they quit *us*. And just as with the Kennedy assassination, everyone knows what they were doing at the time it happened: they were sleeping.

The aliens appeared to everyone in a dream. Not the same dream exactly, but almost. You see, the aliens had to take some form in which to say farewell. For some it was a grandmother, for others a long-lost friend; for others still, a pet dog they'd had as a kid: for me my beloved collie, Nelly, long dead. But the message was the same. *Thank you for hosting us,* they said. *We're very grateful,* they said. *But we've had enough,* they said.

They were apologetic that their stay was so brief. Five hundred thousand years residing inside our heads was, for them, a regrettably short stay. The twinkle of an eye. It was short but interesting, they said. But they dearly hoped that we had enjoyed the fruits of their presence as much as they had enjoyed an exhilarating ride.

Everyone remembers being addressed in the same way, whether by grandmother or dog. Polite, somewhat formal, slightly abashed. Then the dream image had transformed into a cube of black light on a black background, before infolding into complete absence. The world awoke to a stunned comprehension of what had happened.

Since which time no one has dreamed.

Not a flicker. Lacunæ on a global scale. A collective lobotomy.

* * *

Back home, Myra climbs into bed as I gargle with mouthwash and brush my teeth and try to sober up a bit. I know if I flop into bed the world will spin and I'll feel the nausea, so instead I go into my daughter's room and watch her sleeping.

I perch on the edge of Mandy's bed, just watching her. In the moment of observing her sleep her room becomes a peaceful chapel or a quiet temple. Wind chimes tinkle softly at the window open a little to the night air. I sense her sleeping spirit at large, roaming, restless, looking for something, a Neverland, a Narnia. She's flying, but she can't find anywhere to land. I love her so much I could cry. She's six years old, and she has never dreamed.

I have this confession to make: in the dark, at night, while she's sleeping, I whisper things in the delicate conch of my sleeping child's ear. Any things. Remembered fables. Old tales. Strange stories. Religious parables. Fragments. Anything that occurs to me. Heaven knows why, but the other day I heard myself saying *Allah is great, there is no God but Allah and Mohammed is his prophet.* Then I sang her a song in French about dancing on the bridge of Avignon.

Trying to create dreams for her. Trying to pierce the shell, hole the ice.

It took us a while to work out that the aliens hadn't stolen our dreams. The aliens were the dreams. It was difficult to understand initially, generations of us brought up on notions of aliens as basically humanoid with latex rubber heads, or with eggshell-blue skin, or as disembodied human brains encased in a pink gas.

The aliens residing in the consciousness of humanity for half a million years were a benevolent virus. They needed symbiosis, a host to achieve sentience, and that is what we gave them. What did they give us in return? Stories, music, religion. Tools, scientific ideas. Jokes, connections. The synaptic fire.

After their departure they became known to us as Prometheans.

Since then our stories have dried up. Our music has frozen. Our science is arrested. No one has had an original notion in seven years. We are lodged in the mud of time, fossilized. We are consigned to limbo, and the cold wind of uncreation howls in our ears like a demon. Our species, all of humanity, has become the preterite, the passed over. Our psychic teeth, pulled.

And at nights I whisper in my child's tender ear, trying and failing to incubate the glory of dreaming.

* * *

Myra wakes in the morning and, with a struggle, sits up in bed. I blink my eyes open, and she shakes her head, no, again. She hauls herself to her feet and walks naked to the bathroom, magnificent and comical, the morning light shining on the stretched skin of her huge pot. She mutters something about swollen feet, and I wonder if our baby is going to arrive on the seventh anniversary of the departure of the aliens.

We are post-dreaming now, of course. Almost a new way of dating human history, ante- and post-dreaming. For academics, at any rate. The huge joke (I use the word loosely) is that in the entire field of intellectual endeavor only certain academics—critical theorists, social commentators, and cultural analysts—proceed as if nothing has happened, busily producing unfathomable papers on post-dreaming society.

Of course, not everyone buys the idea that we've lost it. Creativity, I mean. Originality. Innovation. Breakthrough. Those slavering puppies up at the University, for example, publishing their breathtakingly incomprehensible theses and self-serving tracts. But they're about the only ones. Hence the spectacle of six-year-old prodigies conning huge audiences desperate for the succor of the new.

Myra is thinking about something. She returns from the bathroom stroking her belly, two deep vertical creases between her eyebrows. "Out with it," I say.

She sits on the bed again, but with her back to me. "What if," she begins; "what if there were not innumerable aliens?"

I think I know what's coming. It has occurred to me already.

"I mean," she continues, "it would be odd, wouldn't it, if there were exactly the same number of aliens as there were people, and they just happened to match up, one apiece as it were. Are you with me?"

"Yes. Go on."

"So what if really there was only one alien. Inhabiting all of us. And that single alien decided to leave us. That would make more sense, wouldn't it?"

"It's a thought," I say, trying to sound light.

"Then that single alien who left us. Might that be what we've always called God?"

This is too complicated. I don't want to think about this, so I just kiss Myra and go downstairs to make some coffee.

* * *

Is this the end? Have we arrived at some feeble conclusion to human history, terrible in its banality? Not the nightmare end. Not the four horsemen. Not the holocaust, nor the nuclear winter, nor the global warming, nor the asteroid storm. Just this exhaustion. Just this absence. Like a watch spring run down.

I think this might be worse than the apocalyptic ending. The absence of poetry, of music, of narrative; this muted fanfare; the end of the never-ending movie. Not by fire or ice, but by indifference. An indifference that leaves us at the mercy of eternity.

Mandy is up and awake. Warm spring sunlight streams through the windows. She has the door open and is running for the swing I erected for her under the big old lilac tree. I leave the coffee to bubble and follow her out. The lilac flower is rampant, intoxicating.

Mandy sees me. She giggles. "Push me, Daddy! Come on!"

And I push her back and forth, and she moves from shadow into light with each swing. She wants to go dangerously high. "Faster, Daddy, Faster!"

Then I see the expression change on her face, and I step back to allow the swing to slow. "What is it?"

She spits something into her hand, and it's with relief I see it's only a milk tooth, slightly bloody at the root. It's her last one. She hands me the milk tooth as if she's trusting me with a precious stone or a talisman. I'm not sure what to do with it.

"Push me again! Higher! Higher!"

* * *

First contact was something we speculated about for a hundred years. Of course *they* would be carbon-based, even roughly humanoid; of course *they* would somehow vocalize; of course *they* would occupy the same plane of time and space. Not intersecting like this. Not like a finger of smoke inserted into the brain. How could we have guessed that *first contact* was already made perhaps half a million years ago?

Mandy swings from shadow into the dappled morning sunlight, giggling, calling for me to push her higher and higher, and I clutch Mandy's milk tooth, a droplet of dew in my fist, and I think: *Is it one alien? Or is it one for each of us?* And I wonder what I'm going to tell Mandy come the day she asks me.

Myra comes out to us in her silk kimono, sleepily pushing a stray curl behind her ear. Mandy jumps off the swing to let her mother sit, a sincere gesture but one copied from adults around her these last couple of months. But she wants to push Myra on the swing.

"Gently," Myra says. "Just gently. I don't want to go high."

I go back in and bring out the coffee on a tray. Mandy pushes Myra gently back and forth on the swing, babbling happily, and I notice Myra is frowning. She mouths something at me and points to her ear, indicating I should listen.

"… And she said they were sorry. It was a long time. They wouldn't normally have gone such a long time and they didn't like to leave for longer periods than they had stayed, but they couldn't help it and anyway a long time ago is the same as the near future for them and tomorrow is half the length of only a part of yesterday and—"

I stop Mandy from talking and I stall the swing. "Who? Who said this?"

"Nelly," says Mandy still intent on pushing Myra back and forth; and the overpowering scent of the lilac makes me feel giddy and I say, "Who is Nelly?"

"Don't be silly Daddy, you know Nelly. She's a dog. She was your dog when you were a little boy. Have you still got my tooth?"

"Yes, yes, I've still got it here," and I'm holding this tray of coffee and I don't know what to do with it. "When did Nelly tell you this?"

"In the night while I was asleep, Nelly came and told me she was sorry to be away so long but she was back and all her friends would come back—

"Jonathan!" says Myra, but I'm too interested in what Mandy is saying to look up.

I sweep Mandy up in my arms and hurry back inside, where I switch on the television. Mandy is still speaking. "—And I had a little talk with Selina in Mummy's tummy because I know she's a girl though you don't know and—"

"Jonathan!" Myra calls from the garden, but it's all over the television. Reports flooding in from Auckland and Fiji, from Vladivostok and Brisbane, from Osaka and Jakarta! And from Islamabad and Nairobi, from Israel and Cairo, Eastern Europe, anyplace where people go to sleep and wake up before we do, and nearer to home, too, people waking from dreaming, rushing out into the streets in tears and madness just to try to recount what has happened to them in the night, not everyone, to be sure, but millions, yes, millions of people, maybe half the global population, dreaming dreams, gut-spilling their experiences as the report sweeps across the globe like the shadow of an eclipse, or a tsunami of unparalleled joy, or a single unbearably beautiful musical note resonating around the planet and I don't know if it was all a warning, or a punishment or an aberration but whatever it was we are going to be allowed to dream again, dream and create, and I know that this time we need to be more careful but my heart is bursting as I understand implicitly that we are to be given back our wings.

"*Jonathan!*"

I rush back out into the garden and Myra is gazing at me with a strange expression, half desperation, half appeal, and her kimono has fallen open and the sunlight flares on a mercurial rivulet along her thigh and it has started and I want to put down the coffee and to listen more to Mandy and to watch the sensational news reports on TV and to get my wife to hospital and I want to hand back the tooth and I'm staring, staring at the heraldic trickle, the catch-light of the silver manifesto, unable to do anything, paralyzed by the torrent of words my daughter is speaking while I am drunk on lilac and imminence.

"Jonathan," Myra says firmly, hauling herself out of the swing, "just put the coffee down."

So I put the tray of coffee down on the grass and I go and get the pre-packed bags and when I've got the car ready Myra and Mandy get in.

"Selina will be my sister, won't she?" says Mandy.

"Yes. Fasten your seat belt."

"Selina will have lots of dreams, won't she?"

"Yes," I say, sparking the car into life.

Mandy thinks for a bit. "Is Selina coming now?"

"Yes," Myra says. "You're very sure it's a girl, aren't you?"

"Yes," Mandy replies, "because in the night they told me that another half a million years is starting. Have you still got my tooth?"

I say yes, I still have her tooth. It is still squeezed in my fist like a token of some miraculous covenant as I drive us to the hospital, because the baby is coming.

Recipe For Disaster

BY TIM LEBBON

You will need:

A group of people randomly linked through fate; interactions of personalities coming together to make a whole; a mix of neuroses and manias chewing at each other to make a stew of struggle and counter-struggle.

Proportions do not matter. Life is not an exact science.

Take one woman:

Like this one. A giver of keys; the key to one's soul, so that locked routes to life may be opened. A preacher to the converted, maintaining a rate of recovery for those who, so little time ago, wallowed in pits of despair. Her keys are precious, lined with a belief in the power of hope.

Her eyes are wide, because she does not want to miss anything. Mostly, she loves it all. Usually, her mind is bright and free, alight with the possibilities inherent in her vocation. To bring hope. To banish hate, and fear, and depression.

But sometimes, she is sucked into the monster she seeks to destroy. It eats her up, this monster, chewing on her flesh until it tingles with acidic twitches, gnawing at the reptilian stem of her brain and pumping in suggestion after suggestion. Fear, fear, fear. Hate, hate, hate.

That's why she does what she does. She knows what hopelessness can do to someone. She was once hopeless herself.

She leaves her flat and sings softly as she walks down the darkened staircase. She has no need of the light, because today she does not fear the dark. Today, everything is light. It is cloudy outside but her outlook is bright, and she waves gaily to the postman as he scissors over dividing walls.

"Brian," she says.

"Hope."

She sometimes thinks that her parents' choice of name could have dictated her mentality, her career, her life and, ultimately, the course and cause of her death.

Other times, it's just a sick joke.

"Nice day," she says, rattling her keys against the scabbed paint of her Mini.

"Cloudy," Brian replies from across the street.

"The sun's still there, above the clouds. Any post for me, Mr. Postman?"

Brian smiles. "Oooh yes, wait a minute." He rummages in his bag, brings out letters and bills and secret words all fused together by an elastic band. Hope often wonders what all-encompassing secret she would find, were she to receive all the mail in the world for just one day. How much despair would be there, and what proportion would it amount to? It is a depressing fact that most people communicate better when they have something to get them down.

"Thanks," says Hope as she takes the wad of letters. Bill, credit card application, bill...

Letter. With *his* scrawl across the front, words twisted together like the dregs of the nightmares he suffers, each curve cutting, each barb sharp.

She feels the kiss of despair at the nape of her neck. It nestles there for a while, massaging her skin, seeking entry to her nerve cortex. She can almost feel its teeth sink into her, and she knows that if that happens, she is finished. But knowing is no defence. Only hope is a defence, and Hope sometimes loses this whenever she hears from him. He is her dark past. He is her living skeleton in the closet of her life, tucked away conveniently and sealed in with superficial imprints of happier times to come.

"Something wrong?" Brian says.

Hope shakes her head. "Nothing I can't handle." And she gets in her Mini and drives away.

Already, it is beginning to crumble.

Strange girl, Brian thinks. Lots of history behind those bright eyes. Lovely. Caring. But a strange girl, nonetheless.

Add one man:

This man. Nathan. Constantly struggling, always striving to keep the soulbiter at bay. But the soulbiter comes all too often, in his sleep when defences are down and perceived barriers are ineffective. It is sharp, barbed, all teeth and claws and bad intent. It rips his sanity to smithereens and opens up new routes through which the bad dreams can enter. Then it locks them in.

He no longer wants to sleep.

But this is just what the soulbiter wishes, because tiredness makes Nathan all too susceptible to other suggestions. Pain. Hunger. Not a human hunger, but a primeval one, a yearning for what is not his, a quest to subsume that which eludes him. For now, it is happiness. Wherever he finds happiness, he must seek to destroy it. Because he knows he can never have it for himself.

The desires manifest themselves in lethargy. He wears clothes, but they are old and unwashed, and they provide a warning signal for those in the neighbourhood who know him. They know to get out of his way. They know that if they are smiling when he passes them by, he will bite out, strike out, claw at them as if possessed of a desire to wear their insides as a scarf.

If only they knew. It's not their slippery bits he wants. He has no use for insides hanging out. He wants their smiles.

Like a figure from ancient Greece, he pursues his nemesis. Out of his home. Through the streets.

The black gash of the post-box looms ever closer. He sees the black gash, not the bright blood-red surrounding it. He sees the nothing, the darkness, and identifies with it. He tries to squeeze up a smile from inside, but it hurts. He posts the letter, knowing it can never help, she can never be there for him because the soulbiter will always eat her, rip her from him and, when there's nothing else left, lick her essential juices from his skin. But it is the only hope he has to hang onto. He needs hope. He has always needed Hope. Even when he once had her.

A man watches him from a shop window. Poor bloke. Well and truly screwed by life. Miserable as sin. And that twitch! Like he's constantly trying to run away from something but just can't pick up the speed.

Mix in an ex-husband:

Like this one. His knuckles still congealed into broken knots from the beatings he has dished out to his wife. His face a mask of indifference, a wasted mask because it resembles him exactly. Useless as blusher applied to the cheeks of a coy virgin.

He cuddles a drink, supping frequently, replenishing his glass before it is even half empty. He never wanted to be a glass half empty kind of person, he had told his wife. He always wanted there to be something positive. Even while he was beating her, he was thinking positive. Perhaps, he thinks, that's why she hung around for so long. Maybe she actually believed him.

The pub is old, grim and grey. The bar is scarred and scored with decades of abuse, like his skin. Harsh words are cut into table tops. The air is dingy and hazed with smoke, hiding the room's main features, just as his long, unhindered hair obscures his face. He can see out, no one can see in. That's just what he wants.

The clientele do not talk to him. But then, neither do they speak to one another. Some would say that this is a pub for losers, but he knows better. His glass is always half full. This is a pub for winners who simply have not yet been acknowledged. He ignores the whimpering shadows nursing empty, stained glasses in forgotten corners.

He goes to the bar. Double whiskey. He glares at the barman, and smiles; the old man looks like a fly caught in the web of his overhanging hair.

The barman serves, but does not engage the man in conversation. He does not speak to any of his customers. The only person he talks to while he's working is himself. Even then, he waits until he is alone behind the bar once more, and his customers are back on their rickety seats.

"Beat his wife, you know. Drove her mad. Then she got better. So they say."

Marinate in a far-reaching failure:

She had tried. She really had. But the golden key of her hope had failed to even dent the solid wall of despair built up around Nathan's mind. She had never thought she'd encounter a failure, and maybe that's why it bit in so hard. Clung onto her memory with tenacious cruelty. Always there.

As if she even needed to remember. He remembered for her. Sent her letters, hopeless, terrible letters begging one more chance, one more try. But she had given him a dozen "one more tries," and they inevitably ended up turning around and fucking her up instead. Dredged up memories. Opened portions of her mind which, she secretly wished, would remain forever locked.

She had seen in him the potential realised in her husband. Her husband had never begged redemption, and she knew that it would never come to him anyway. He was not evil and hopeless; he liked what he did. Whereas Nathan ... Nathan, she kept trying to save. But however hard she tried to turn the key, the barrel of his hope had rusted shut long ago.

She tried, they would say at the hospital. She gave her all. But sometimes there's just no hope.

Maybe, they would say, she should have given up sooner.

Throw in an Extinction Level Event:

Careful on the pity, here. Not too much. Because an Extinction Level Event implies humanity moving on (at the very least), and in this unknown place pity may be as misplaced as an objective youth. Things change. Hope mutates. It is different for different people. Often, optimism hangs around after the very worst calamity. Occasionally, it does not.

Hope has no hope. In a landscape awash with blood, the teeth are well and truly ground into her spine. Her nerves have been hijacked by her constant fear of regression, and all she can see when she closes her eyes are the fists, raising, falling, and his mad eyes staring through his long, sweat-clogged hair.

Not the scenes of devastation as the disease ravages the world.

Not the crying children, their tears blood-red as they nudge the bled-out bodies of their parents.

Not the mouths, hanging open but uttering nothing because screams are drowned in the blood dripping from pores.

Only the fists. The hatred driving them so pure and basic that they pummel down even when the fingers flop brokenly, like loose scarves in the breeze.

Two failures, she realises. One her fault, the other not. One she had forced herself to turn away from, the other drawn to her by her weakness, grabbing on limpet-like and only letting go after it had seemingly bled her dry.

Both of them impossible to forget. All she had was a false face to hide behind, and now even that was wearing away.

Bring to the boil:

Hope is not eternal. She wanders, trying to avoid the plague. Somehow, it misses her.

Nathan goes to find the post-box, but it is overflowing. There is no longer a dark gash in its face. It is as if a dying population had tried one last time to heal differences, swap a kind word or settle old accounts.

The bad man remains in the bar; he will be there forever. His glass is half full of the black blood that gushed from his nose and eyes in the final minutes of his miserable life.

She walks the streets. There are bodies, but most of them must have remained at home, preferring to die somewhere familiar. A final act of humanity as their insides bled out.

Nathan opens some of the letters. Vitriol spills forth. In none of them does he find salvation. In his muddled mind, he already understands that this end has been inevitable from the beginning.

Hope's ex-husband's hair is stuck to the table, elbows rooted in the pool of hardened blood covering the vandalised surface. Scratched names hidden forever.

Drain off excess:

He feels bad. The soulbiter is on his trail. It has buried its teeth in all and sundry, it seems, but his panic is just as great. Inside—somewhere deep down, where reality may no longer reach—there is a whiff of contentment. Happiness has been wiped away with the wind, swept up into a little pile of smiles against a mythical hillside.

Now, he must find Hope. It is different merely writing to her: impersonal; mysterious. Now, he has to actually find her. He has so much to say that words can never express.

Simmer gently, forever:

Hope is living in an old shop. The window was smashed weeks ago, tins snatched from shelves, water bottles fought over and killed for. Shards of glass still catch sunlight, but they reflect red. Some bodies lay on the pavement, drilled with bullets into blank death. At least they died quickly.

She is eating gone-off cheese and stale bread. She fears the outside, because that is where the disease still stalks the streets. Sometimes she sees a victim, dragging themselves along the gutter, blood spewing from their body to merge underground with the blood of a city. It is ironic that as the veins of the populace purge through pores, so the arteries of the city flow red. A vampiric liaison. Another sick joke.

She has been eaten by the monster, and now she knows only fear. Her spine is crushed between its teeth. Her eyes are still wide, but only because she cannot believe what she sees inside herself. The self-deception she has been a party to.

Nathan steps in. He sees Hope in the corner, covered with old newspapers, and he shouts out in dismay.

In her sleep, the fists keep raining down. Only now they spray blood as they go, their pores yawning, nails split and dripping.

Nathan kneels down and reaches out, aghast that a face previously so happy could now be moulded with such pain. This is one sad face he never hoped to see. His hunger should never have reached this far.

She pushes his hands away, though her eyes remain shut. Her face is bruised, blood leaking slowly from tiny splits in the skin.

He realises as he touches her that the soulbiter is here.

Hope opens her eyes. Her failure is there before her (a downfall borne of falling fists, two failures in one), reaching out, crying clear tears. But suddenly she sees long hair again, mad eyes, flapping fingers spraying red mist across her vision, and she lashes out.

Nathan staggers back and trips onto the shattered plate glass window. He feels the cool kiss of air as the skin of his neck parts. He panics, feeling the soulbiter drawing near. But then, as things become hazy and indistinct, he realises that he may not even be awake when the soulbiter takes its fill.

One prepared earlier:

They may be brother and sister. Part of a happy family, perhaps. Big house, friendly dog, parents both in useful jobs. Good prospects ahead of them, an interest in all things right. Full of hope for a rosy future. Young, viewing the world through filter lenses which hold back all the bad stuff until the teenage years, when it all comes flooding through. When they realise what the noises in the night may mean. When they see the tensions and stresses, where before there was only their own happiness to discern. When their perception spreads.

But even then, hope seems eternal, invincible. It is the horizon, shining through the dark with a promise of life everlasting. It manifests in the shape of a first love, a composite of a smile and a laugh and a long-remembered fumble in a forest. It is always there. Unchanging. A constant throughout their life.

If only they knew.

Memories Of Lydia, Leaving

BY PHILIP NUTMAN

CARPENTER DRAINS THE TENTH GLASS OF THE EVENING DRY, GRIMACING AS the generous shot of George Dickel scorches his throat.

—Three years—

Three long, lonely years. Years consumed by memories, the recollections as clear yet intangible as the faintest whiff of sour mash. 36 months of sadness. Years when days would suddenly cloud with the thunderheads of feelings past meeting the empty horizon of the present, the persistent pain in his heart temporarily alleviated by a torrent of tears.

Once, not long after she had died, he'd broken down in the street.

A mailman had stopped to ask what was wrong, but the display of concern had only made his condition worse, even if it proved not everyone in New York was a soulless bastard.

—Three years—

Occasional glimpses in the bathroom mirror

—She used to sit in there when she wanted to be alone—

show the lines on his face growing clearer, accelerated by the drinking and smoking, especially on the annual seven-day binges, the third of which he is halfway through, getting steadily shit-faced.

Three years carrying his love of a dead woman around like a ketchup stain on a shirt, not having the strength to do the laundry and try a fresh start.

—Three fuckin' years—

Lydia had been, for a short time, his everything. Confidante, soul-mate, critic, ardent supporter, lover, nymph, Muse. The Little Woman with the Big Heart. His Heloise, his Isolde, his Guinevere.

—Romantic fool—

His Lydia. His dead Lydia. Dark-haired beauty with an olive complexion, 5'2" of passion, energy, almost frightening intellect and a sense of humor Arsenio or Letterman would envy.

—My love killed her, not the razor blade she ran across her wrists—

He pours another shot of Dickel and stubs out a cigarette, immediately lighting another one. The sulfurous bulb of the match gutters in the gloom as he inhales, its acrid aroma temporarily cutting out the smell of the burning scented candles illuminating the room.

—Just the way she liked it—

The first time they'd met she'd beat him to the punch, flicking a Bic as he tugged the matches from his pocket. There was no wind that night. the flame thrusting up towards the tip of the Marlboro, the move as cool as Bogart lighting Bacall's in *To Have or Have Not*, as he and Lydia stood outside the bookstore on East 19th Street. He asked her to join him for a cappuccino. She agreed, and they sat outside Dojo on St. Mark's Place watching the street life drift by like human tumbleweed as he got wired on caffeine and she listened to his thoughts on the Escher exhibition at The Psychedelic Solution. She thought the artist's woodcut entitled *Relativity* unexciting; he politely argued its merits, lit her cigarette—she smoked Winston Lights—before she could flick the Bic, ordered more cappuccino. She had a Perrier and lime. They smoked and drank until 1:30 a.m., neither seemingly wishing to return to their respective apartments. he finally breaking the conversation with a courteous excuse so she didn't feel he was trying to pick her up. Phone numbers were exchanged; a further meeting suggested. He saw her to a taxi, then walked to his studio apartment on East 7th Street.

The memory is as clear, as fresh as the wind that suddenly descended that Fall night.

She steps gracefully into the taxi, her long black hair spraying out like the demure gesture of a Japanese maiden opening a paper fan. A delicate smile spreads across her lips, the dark brown eyes catching the fallout from the overhead lamps, refracting the yellow-white in a warm, sensual glow. A fog of taxi exhaust slides around her legs like a loyal dog as she climbs in, closes the door and, with a small wave, is gone.

His life has been running down like an old clock since the day she died. He knows it but doesn't care. There is no point anymore.

—Tonight it ends—

The glass is dry, the bottle of Dickel almost empty.

He pads barefoot to the refrigerator, plucking a Heineken from the six-pack he'd bought a couple of hours ago. It wasn't Dickel, but beer is booze. He slouches back to the desk, gazing with the eyes of a love-sick school boy at his favorite photo of Lydia.

He'd taken the picture on their short visit to Niagara Falls in the Spring after that fateful Fall. Along with his painting, his photography gave him pleasure nothing else came close to. Except Lydia. She had freed his soul from the labyrinth of loneliness. Their intimacy was more than sex; they were soul mates.

After making love to her the first time, every relationship he'd had seemed indistinct, like a watercolor left exposed to the elements, its pigments running into each other.

Before Lydia, art had been his only passion. Painting led him to another place; the truth behind the lie. But part of him—the nagging voice of self-doubt—questioned his talent. If he had the soul of an artist, why was he a bank teller? Why didn't he throw in his job?

—Because I'm afraid; I've always been afraid—

His soul screams out for expression but the Nine-to-Five Man inside laughs at the pile of unfinished oil paintings stacked in the corner of the room.

—Call yourself an artist? You'll never be a Monet or a Van Gogh. Let alone a Keith Haring.—

But tonight he would bring his work to its logical conclusion. No more continuing to labor at the EuroAmerican Bank on Park Avenue South, a junior teller processing other people's paychecks by day, trying to paint in the evenings, attempting to capture the essence of the world around him, drinking himself into oblivion to numb the pain because all he can see is emptiness and death.

If all life leads to is death, then let it end now. The photograph:

Lydia is dressed in a blue souwester with hood, her hair, that luxurious cascade of black, neatly tucked away. Behind her the water thunders down in a heavy drape, precipitation filling the air like the gossamer clouds of a dream. A head and shoulders shot, her pert breasts jut against the plastic, a promise of the flesh beneath the synthetic cover; temptation at the bottom of the frame.

Tears sting his eyes and the image drifts out of focus. Most people carry their memories as photos in their wallets; his is tattooed on his heart, each indentation a razor cut. His chest tightens, constricted by emotional cement as deep sobs rise in his throat.

—*I killed her with my love*—

The green of the Heineken bottle mirrors the lime of the umbrella she carries in the photo, the umbrella that stands in the corner beside the door. He smiles bitterly through the tears at the thought: there are more memories of her leaving than arriving, as if their relationship was nothing more than a dress rehearsal for her final departure.

Lydia dons the coat, picking up the umbrella as she moves to the door.

"I'll probably have to work late," she says as she reaches for the bolt. "Don't wait up."

Weary from the day's office politics and the crowds of people cashing checks, he drifts off into a deep sleep before she returns, dreaming of vampiric women floating down Broadway, waking with a shout as she slips into bed.

"Shhh," she coos, holding him in her arms. "It's okay, I'm here."

All their daily rhymes balanced apart from their sleeping habits, he an early bird, she preferring to rise as late as possible before running off to work.

Their love blossomed like an orchid in the hours of darkness. The first month they were together he spent an increasing amount of time in her apartment as they wrapped themselves in a cocoon of tenderness, talking, holding each other until the early hours, she telling him of her past in Chicago and he about his childhood in Pennsylvania, two kindred spirits creating a mutual space, a fortress against the abrasive assault of Manhattan's manic rhythms. Those nights played havoc with his sleep patterns, but he was punch-drunk from the unexpected intimacy and excited by the way Lydia welcomed him with open arms into her world, her sacred place.

"This is strange for me," she says one night as they luxuriate in the tranquility of post-coitus, limbs entwined, two semi-colons curled together on the couch. "I didn't want one… a relationship… those I've had… they went sour…" She pauses in some private reverie. "After the last one, I went off men. But you're not like the rest."

And so it seemed.

He rediscovered aspects of himself he'd buried since early adolescence. Lydia brought out a playfulness in him, and in return, he made her laugh, filled her with joy, ignited a fire in her eyes. She was the one who said, "I love you," first—his Lydia, his older woman who looked like a little girl, her perfectly proportioned, petite form that of a girl-child just reaching womanhood. He responded in kind, his feelings unhampered by the caution he'd felt in previous relationships. For the first time in his life, he felt loved and loved truly in return.

The wave of tears subsides. Empty, he pushes the beer bottle to one side and goes to the kitchenette to fetch another. He catches sight of his reflection in the cracked mirror over the sink. He looks like shit.

—*It's what you deserve*—

Sipping the beer, he returns to the lounge. It is almost exactly as it was when she lived there. The wallpaper is the same dark red, the black carpet still stained with spilled candle wax knocked over in the throes of passion, the book shelves dusty. He's kept most of her belongings: her books, records and tapes, knickknacks, even some of her clothes. It is morbid, he knows; probably unhealthy—or so a shrink might say. But they keep her memory vibrantly alive, He looks at the portrait of her above the TV set he never watches. She was happy the day he painted it; yet there is, he notices now, a sadness lurking behind her Mona Lisa smile. She'd said no one had been able to capture her looks or her heart the way he did, that he was the only one who could see and understand the pain she'd experienced as a child, abused by her stepfather from the age of eight until he was killed in a bar fight when she was fourteen, repeatedly raped and beaten by the boyfriend she had when she left home at seventeen. Was it any wonder she mistrusted men, that she'd been unable to maintain relationships?

—*Even ours*—

Although they spent most of the first three months they were together indulging in mutual pleasures—watching movies, going to galleries, cooking for each other, taking long walks in Central Park—there were times when she would leave for several days, often at short notice, to visit friends in Boston. He never went with her, partially because she never invited him, but mainly because he respected her freedom, and besides, it gave him the chance to see his parents in Pennsylvania.

She appears from the kitchenette as he returns from work. She is smartly dressed in a long flowing skirt, silk blouse and red shoes. He knows she is leaving and tries to hide his disappointment.

"I've got to see Jeanette. Her boyfriend dumped her, she's in a bad way. There's a train to Boston at 7:35."

"We're going to the Met to see *La Bohème* tomorrow night, remember?"

She looks embarrassed. She has forgotten he'd promised to take her after she told him it was her favorite opera.

Lydia turns away under the pretense of picking up her pocketbook, not able to look him in the eye. She's hurt his feelings but cannot find the right words to reassure him.

"Lydia?"

She looks up quickly, a distant expression on her face.

"I'll be back, I guess. Look, I've got to go or I'll miss my train."

"Okay. Let me walk you to the subway."

'There's no need, really."

But he goes with her anyway. The conversation consists of small talk. She says she'll meet him outside the Met at 7 p.m. They kiss farewell, and she seems to drift down the steps into the subway at Lexington and 86th as if the world around her does not exist.

Returning to their apartment on East 83rd Street—he gave up the lease on his so they could be together—doubt nags at the back of his mind. Look at the picture; it appears normal. Look at it again and it has changed.

Lydia is gone.

Night falls. Despite bone-weary tiredness, he cannot sleep so goes out to buy beer from the Deli across the street. He drinks until unconsciousness claims him.

He should have seen the signs but was dazzled by love. Any man in his right mind should have realized the relationship had changed, yet his heart was in his head. She loved him. It was selfish of him to expect her to be there all the time; they were settling into a new rhythm of life, and during the period of balancing, he had to modify his expectations. But it was self-deception; he didn't want to face the fact her manner was changing, that the moment of true intimacy had passed. She was withdrawing into herself, slowly pulling away, and the more he reached out, the more she pulled back. Oh, sure, on the surface everything appeared the same, but· after you lived with someone for a while, you began to subconsciously pick up on details in the other person's behavior, to see the gap between what was said and what was done. Instead of dealing with the signs, he'd ignored them, and clung to his idealism like a shipwrecked sailor clinging to a life raft. In doing so, he failed to see that she, too, was shipwrecked, adrift on the sea of her own instability, that his desire for intimacy pushed her towards the rocks of desperation.

He sits at the desk, shaking. Why is he doing this to himself? She was unstable, there was no way he could be held responsible for her death. After all, she'd made three suicide attempts before meeting him and had never told him. He only found out when he met her mother and brother at the funeral, only then learned she'd once spent six months in an institution undergoing psychiatric evaluation following the third attempt. But he did feel responsible, and still does. He'd failed to see the signs, failed to respond to her needs by clinging to his own, and in doing so, he'd pushed her over the edge.

He picks up the bottle of Dickel and takes a big pull, leaving only a drop. Barely a mouthful. It doesn't matter. The beer and sour mash are working their dark, obliviating magic. The room spins suddenly, a nauseous tilt-a-whirl, and he can hardly sit up straight, self-pity and self-disgust sloshing around inside him like oil and water; self-pity because he is alone—as he has always been—and self-disgust because he lacks the strength to overcome his weaknesses, his neediness.

It is the sixth month of their relationship. The passion has cooled, the lovemaking no longer as exciting, as all-consuming as it once was. Long periods of silence replace conversation, and Lydia is spending an increasing amount of time at the gallery she works at on Green Street. He senses she is avoiding him, trying to ignore the promise of what they've shared. She doesn't have to work the hours she puts in, so now they are living a lie: the apartment they share is not a home, it has become a prison.

They are in bed asleep. He dreams they are there asleep, waking as she gets up. She's going to the bathroom he thinks. But she does not return. He gets up to search the dream apartment.

She's not there.

The door to the hall is open. He goes outside, vulnerable, naked, The hall is not that of the apartment building, it looks like a hotel. Disoriented, he turns to go back, but the door has shut. He has no choice but to find her.

He walks the hallway, his hands covering his genitals. All the doors are locked. Then he hears voices coming from the room at the end.

Greg Vale, an old high school friend, appears with a girl on each arm. Their laughter stops as they see him. One of the girls stifles a giggle.

"Have you seen Lydia?" he asks.

"Yeah, she's left you." Greg looks sad as he speaks.

Then he and the girls wander away, absorbed in their intimacy. Carpenter walks back down the hall. Now he cannot find the door to the apartment.

He wakes with a start, his heart beating triple-time. Lydia lies beside him on her back, the serenity of sleep casting her face as a mask of innocence.

But he knows.

She has left him. Her spirit is gone.

The following night, she slashes her wrists.

The memory of that Wednesday is so clear it seems like only last week.

The day started out filled with promise, a sudden Spring after a barren Winter, and for the first time in months he felt unrestrained enthusiasm. The mail had arrived early. There was the usual pile of junk mail, a letter for Lydia from Boston. And a card from the Pictures of Lilly Gallery down on Spring Street. Another show, he thought as he turned it over. Sandreen, the manageress, was an old friend, a punky lesbian with purple hair whom he'd met while doing a night course in Modern Art at S.V.A., and she was always sending him invites to openings even though he'd stopped going, depressed by other people's successes and the mediocrity of their work.

He had to read the card three times before the truth hit home:

Hey, Jim, it read, don't be a stranger... Bobbi wants to talk business... Jim Carpenter, come on down! It's show time!—YES, YOUR SHOW!!! We want to give you a spot!

Luv, Sandy.

Three kisses and a purple lipstick smear.

It was too much to hope for... and yet. Bobbi, Sandy's lover, had always expressed an interest in his work, Were they serious? He'd give them a call once he got to work. No, he'd call them now, even if it was 7:30 a.m. They often stayed up all night partying; maybe they were awake.

Lydia was still asleep as he crept back into the apartment. He took the phone into the bathroom and dialed. On the third ring, Sandy answered, and it was true!

They wanted him and his work.

Okay, so it was to be part of a show called "Upper East Side: Visions Above 60th," and he was going to be one of five artists exhibiting, but so what? A dream was about to become reality.

Unable to resist, he woke Lydia to tell her the good news. Once she came to full consciousness, she smiled a deep, loving smile, the kind which he hadn't seen in several weeks. She hugged him, said they should celebrate. He suggested dinner at Franco's. It was agreed. He kissed her again, wishing he could go back to bed to make love, the nightmare forgotten, but he was going to be late for work so he reluctantly departed, leaving her letter on the table.

The day dragged, the bank's interior a jailhouse of lifeless angles, soulless lighting, antiseptic steel and glass. Still, nothing could contain the joy pulsing through his veins, the sense of achievement.

During his lunch break, he took a walk up 3rd Avenue to gaze at the jutting spire of the Chrysler Building, his favorite monument on the city skyline. Its Art Deco architecture always instilled in him a sense of wonder, its gargoyles sleek and otherworldly, even if they were made from hubcaps. He stopped at a pay phone and called Lydia.

She didn't sound too happy, and there was an air of hostility in her voice he couldn't fathom. Asking if everything was okay, she replied she couldn't talk with people in the office. Bad news? No, just something I've got to talk to you about. Concerned, he pressed for information.

"Look, I'll tell you tonight." She hung up on him.

He walked back to work in a state of confusion, but she called him five minutes after he returned to apologize, said her boss was bugging her and she'd started her period early. Said she loved him, said it was nothing serious, that she'd see him at the restaurant at 7 p.m. He felt better and thought no more about it.

7:15 p.m. and he sat at the bar nursing a Manhattan. Yeah, it was a cliché, but tonight it felt like it was his town. Lydia was usually half-an-hour late so her not being there was no big deal. She'd probably gone home to change, deciding to dress up for the occasion. But by 7:55 p.m., worry and hunger began gnawing at his insides. The Maitre d' said he couldn't hold the table longer than another fifteen minutes so he phoned the apartment. All he got was the answering machine.

At 8:10 p.m.. he told the Maitre d', a short, officious man with slicked black hair, to cancel the reservation. He called again. Just the machine.

His back muscles were tense with apprehension as he ran out onto 5th Avenue to hail a cab, anxiety digging sharp nails into his abdomen as the car crawled up 3rd through heavy traffic. All thoughts of the show, of the new pictures he'd been thinking of doing were erased by Lydia's absence.

He looks at the unfinished paintings gathering dust in the corner of the room. His show? Hah. Visions Above 60th—all he saw that night was a vision of Hell.

As he reaches for the door, he knows something is terribly wrong. The thought is not conscious; it comes from some dark, instinctual level below reason, and as he touches the frame, static pricks his fingertips as if in warning. As he enters the apartment the emotionally charged air rolls over him like a tsunami, sweeping away control.

"Lydia?" His voice trembles as he speaks.

There is no answer.

He goes to the kitchenette. Signs of violence: broken glass coats the floor, crunching underfoot, the sounds grating on his flayed nerves; in the sink are a pile of burnt photographs, the ashes wet leaves of nitrate paper. He picks one up, the only one not fully burnt.

It is of Lydia and someone else, but the other figure is unidentifiable, the image charred to a soggy black.

An empty Smirnoff bottle lies beside the garbage can, its neck smashed off.

He races to the bedroom.

Empty. The sheets are ripped apart. Purple pieces of cotton litter the floor like confetti. Lydia's favorite dress, a midnight-blue cocktail number in crushed velvet, is twisted in a heap on the chair.

The bathroom.

He tries the door. It's locked.

"Lydia!"

The door will not budge, He slams his shoulder against it in a futile effort to snap the lock. They make it look so easy on TV. On the fourth attempt, the frame gives a little, but his muscles agonize against the wood.

He returns to the kitchenette, panic scrabbling inside his chest, as he searches under the sink for a screwdriver. Finding it, he runs back to the door.

It takes tremendous strength to pry it into the frame, his bruised shoulder complaining as he tries to lever the lock.

"Lydia! Lydia!"

She doesn't respond and his urgent panic fuels the strength he needs.

The frame gives with a short crack, the door swinging wide, propelling him into Lydia's private hell.

She is almost completely submerged under the red water, a horror movie heroine in a scene recalling Rossetti's *Lady of the Lake* as written by Poe, a bloody razor blade lying quietly on the tub's rim.

He screams as he rushes to her, plunging his arms into the warm red not caring about his best suit, or Brooks Brothers' shirt.

He is soaked as he hauls her limp body from the tub. She's unconscious, barely breathing, and as he pulls her clear of the dark water her arms flop revealing the deep gashes in her wrists, faint lines of blood still trickling from the self-inflicted wounds.

He pulls her clear, her legs dragging over the porcelain, trying to reach for a towel in which to wrap her. A heavy rag doll, her weight is too much to bear and he slips. Lydia, his dying Lydia falling on top of him, a final breath escaping from her lips. He doesn't notice in his panic and pulls the large pink towel around her, reaching for two hand towels which he ties around her wrists before racing to the phone. He dials 911 and sobs for paramedics.

But before they arrive, he realizes she is dead.

They find him in the bathroom cradling her lifeless body against him, hysterical sobs echoing off the tiled walls.

He picks up the photo of her standing on the bow of The Maid of the Mist and begins to sob again. It was this night three years ago he last held her in his arms, the lifeless shell of the person he'd loved more than any other, and now the black weight of remorse pulls him down into the pit of total depression.

It is time to end the pain.

He pulls the desk drawer open and removes the .38 Special he'd taken from his father's gun collection last week. Three years of carrying around memories of the woman he'd loved, retreating steadily into a haze of alcohol are too much to bear. That and the terrible realization his art is meaningless.

He puts the gun to his head, His finger squeezes against the trigger. And...

Nothing.

He can't do it.

He is weak, and the thought tears him apart.

Too weak to deal with life, too weak to end it.

"You fucking coward," he whispers, placing the gun's barrel in his mouth, cocking the hammer with his right thumb.

His finger caresses the trigger.

—*squeeze*—

He tastes death—cold, hard, metallic.

Just one little squeeze and that's it. Over. Done. His hand shakes.

—*do it!*—

He yanks the gun from his mouth .

"I can't!" he cries. "I'm too fucking weak." Deep sobs of utter despair rip through him as he puts the gun down on the desk, sliding from the chair to crumple in a heap on the floor. Within seconds he passes out.

He wakes on the couch sensing someone in the room.

The candles have burned themselves out with the exception of the fat red one on the bookshelf. Confused, his eyes try to penetrate the gloom.

The kitchenette—someone is in the kitchenette.

He stumbles off the couch, his head throbbing, heart triphammering in his chest. "Who's there?"

He freezes as he reaches the doorway.

Lydia stands in front of the sink. She wears her favorite blue dress as she sorts through a pile of photographs, a Bic lighter on the counter.

"Lydia?"

She ignores him as she continues to look through the photos, pausing on one particular shot.

"Darling?"

He moves closer.

I'm dreaming. This isn't happening.

He halts at the threshold of the door as if he is staring through a window.

Lydia starts to shake, her small shoulders slumping as she begins to cry. Screwing up the photo in her left hand.

"You bastard," she hisses, reaching for a glass beside a vodka bottle. She gulps down the liquor, then hurls the glass against the wall. The smash echoes loudly in his ears.

"I hate you!" she spits at the photo, holding it up as she picks up the lighter.

He moves closer to see what she sees.

There is a man he doesn't recognize in the picture. A large, older man with his arm around Lydia, both of them smiling at the camera.

She flicks the Bic, directing the flame to the photograph. The paper catches immediately, a tongue of fire licking its way up the image. She holds the photo until the flame sears her fingers. She picks up another picture and repeats the ritual.

He watches as she holds up each photo, her face set in bitter determination as she feeds them to the flames. The stranger is in every one: holding Lydia, kissing Lydia, laughing with Lydia.

She burns out the stranger from the last picture, and turns in Carpenter's direction, gazes right through him, and walks into the lounge. She sits on the couch, the letter with the Boston postmark in her hand, shaking again, seemingly more from anger than sadness. She reads the letter then crushes it in her delicate fist, throwing it into the waste basket beside the TV.

He stands helpless, confused. He moves to touch her, reaches out to tell her it's okay—he's here; he feels her pain, can taste her sorrow. If he holds her, shares the pain, it will be okay. Together, they can drive the darkness away, fill the room with light. Isn't that what Love is? The power to change, the ability to transform?

He bends forward.

"Lydia," he says softly as he extends his left hand.

As he touches her shoulder, she fades for an instant, flickering like an image on a damaged videotape.

She suddenly stands and moves towards the waste basket. She leans down, plucking the offending ball of paper from the trash, uncrumpling the screwed up pages. She flattens them out as best she can, then folds them in half. She pauses, struggling with her tears, and goes to the book case in the furthest corner of the room. She selects a volume, and slips the letter inside. Tom Robbins' *Even Cowgirls Get The Blues*—one of her favorites—then sits back on the couch, stifling her sobs.

The room darkens.

He wakes on the couch, aware he needs to use the bathroom. He sways drunkenly as he unzips his fly as he fumbles for the light switch. Light explodes in his face.

Lydia lies in the bathtub. Tears rolls down her cheeks, a razor blade poised over her left wrist.

"Goodbye, Roger," she says softly.

The blade cuts deep.

He wakes on the couch, roused from sleep by the light touch of lips on his.

Lydia, naked, wet, pale, oh so pale, stands over him.

"I'm sorry."

He reaches out for her but she fades into the darkness.

"Release me," she whispers.

He wakes face down on the carpet, his brain throbbing with a jackhammer hangover.

"What the—," he slurs before belching, a bolus of vomit cresting his throat. He pukes on the carpet and groans.

—*dreams*—

Strange dreams.

But he never dreams when he's drunk; at least he never remembers if he does. That's the beauty of booze; it brings oblivion.

—*Lydia*—

She was here. And something else…

—*the letter*—

Stubbing the toes on his right foot, he swings himself in the direction of the bookcase. His vision rolls as he tries to find the Robbins book, gagging as he fights against hurling a second time. There. Tugging it free from the embrace of a Ludlum and a Jong, he weaves back to the couch.

He opens the book.

And the letter flutters free.

It takes him a while to focus on the neat, ornate handwriting. "My Dear, Dear Lydia,

"I don't know how to begin this, filled as I am with both sadness and joy..."

The following three lines are crossed out. "Perhaps Truth is the only way.

"After all these months, Carol and I have decided to resume living together. And in time, we hope that we will be able to work things out..."

He skim-reads the next couple of paragraphs.

"But please do not feel what you and I have shared this past year has been in vain, or the frivolous desire of a middle-aged man. Our love has meant more than words can express..."

He doesn't need to read the rest. Jeanette. Boston. It was all shit.

He staggers up off the couch towards the desk, his mind silently screaming at the terrible truth—that Lydia had lied to him, that he's lied to himself.

It is time to end the Big Lie.

He picks up the gun. Opens his mouth.

If truth is knowledge, and knowledge is power, then let that power give him strength.

He squeezes the trigger.

***

For Stan, with thanks.

"Memories of Lydia, Leaving" originally appeared in a different form in the anthology *After The Darkness* [Stanley Wiater, ed; Maclay, 1993]

CAMP NECON SKELETON

Gahan Wilson

Appendix: The First Thirty Years

1980
Chairman: Bob Booth
Location: Roger Williams University
Writer Guest: Charles L. Grant
Artist Guest: Don Maitz
Toastmaster: Les Daniels
Roastee: Donald M. Grant

1981
Chairman: Bob Booth
Location: Roger Williams University
Writer Guest: Les Daniels
Writer Guest: Peter Straub
Artist Guest: Rowena Morrill
Toastmaster: Pete Pautz
Roastee: Charles L. Grant

1982
Chairman: Bob Booth
Location: Roger Williams University
Writer Guest: T.E.D. Klein
Writer Guest: Michael McDowell
Artist Guest: Jill Bauman
Toastmaster: Alan Ryan
Roastee: Stephen King

1983
Chairman: Bob Booth
Location: Roger Williams University
Writer Guest: John Coyne
Writer Guest: David Morrell
Artist Guest: Ned Dameron
Artist Guest: Barclay Shaw
Toastmaster: Douglas E. Winter
Roastee: Alan Ryan

1984
Chairman: Bob Booth
Location: Roger Williams University
Writer Guest: Alan Ryan
Writer Guest: Whitley Streiber
Artist Guest: Steve Gervais
Artist Guest: Bob Lavoie
Toastmaster: Craig Shaw Gardner
Roastee: Douglas E. Winter

1985
Chairman: Bob Plante
Location: Roger Williams University
Guest Publisher: Donald M. Grant
Toastmaster: Douglas E. Winter
Roastee: Bob Booth
Legend: Joseph Payne Brennan

1986—No Convention
The committee ran the World Fantasy
Convention instead

1987
Chairman: Bob Plante
Location: Roger Williams University
Writer Guest: Kathryn Ptacek
Writer Guest: Robert R. McCammon
Artist Guest: Thomas Canty
Toastmaster: Craig Shaw Gardner
Roastee: Les Daniels

1988
Chairman: Bob Plante
Location: Roger Williams University
Writer Guest: John Farris
Writer Guest: F. Paul Wilson
Artist Guest: Charles Lang
Artist Guest: Wendy Snow Lang
Toastmaster: Phil Nutman
Roastee: Craig Shaw Gardner

1989
Chairman: Bob Plante
Location: Roger Williams University
Writer Guest: Lucius Shepard
Writer Guest: Chet Williamson
Artist Guest: Jeff Jones
Toastmaster: Stanley A. Wiater
Roastee: Bob Plante

1990
Chairman: Bob Plante
Location: Roger Williams University
10th Anniversary Celebration
Toastmaster: Bob Booth
Roastee: Robert R. McCammon

1991
Chairman: Steve Schleifer
Location: Bryant College
Writer Guest: Ramsey Campbell
Writer Guest: Nancy Collins
Artist Guest: Bob Eggleton
Toastmaster: Bob Lavoie
Roastee: Thomas F. Monteleone

1992
Chairman: Steve Schleifer
Location: Bryant College
Writer Guest: Craig Shaw Gardner
Writer Guest: Thomas F. Monteleone
Artist Guest: Alan Clark
Toastmaster: Rick Hautala
Roastee: Stan Wiater

1993
Chairman: Steve Schleifer
College: Bryant College
Editor Guest: Ellen Datlow
Writer Guest: Gahan Wilson
Writer Guest: Kathe Koja
Artist Guest: Rick Leider
Toastmaster: Thomas F. Monteleone
Roastee: Ginjer Buchanan

1994
Chairman: Jim Anderson
Location: Bryant College
Writer Guest: Rick Hautala
Writer Guest: Brian Lumley
Artist Guest: Rick Berry
Toastmaster: Ginjer Buchanan
Roastee: Rick Hautala
Legend: Charles L. Grant

1995
Chairman: Jim Anderson
Location: Roger Williams University
Writer Guest: Jonathan Carroll
Writer Guest: Matthew Costello
Artist Guest: Stephen Bissette
Toastmaster: Gahan Wilson
Roastee: Matt Costello
Roastee: F. Paul Wilson
Legend: Alan Ryan

1996
Co-Chairman: Patty Anderson
Co-Chairman: Dan Booth
Location: Roger Williams University
Writer Guest: Nancy Holder
Writer Guest: Joe R. Lansdale
Artist Guest: Doug Beekman
Toastmaster: Elizabeth Massie
Roastee: Jill Bauman
Legend: Les Daniels

1997
Co-Chairman: Patty Anderson
Co-Chairman: Dan Booth
Location: Roger Williams University
Writer Guest: Yvonne Navarro
Writer Guest: Chelsea Quinn Yarbro
Artist Guest: Pat Morrisey
Toastmaster: Elizabeth Massie
Roastee: Steven Spruill
Legend: Ginjer Buchanan

1998
Chairman: Dan Booth
Location: Roger Williams University
Writer Guest: Neil Gaiman
Writer Guest: Jack Ketchum
Artist Guest: Cortney Skinner
Toastmaster: Christopher Golden
Roastee: Stephen Bissette
Legend: Darrell Schweitzer

1999
Chairman: Dan Booth
Location: Roger Williams University
Writer Guest: Kim Newman
Writer Guest: Thomas Tessier
Artist Guest: Mike Mignola
Toastmaster: Rick Hautala
Roastee: Chet Williamson
Legend: Paul Dobish

2000
Chairman: Dan Booth
Location: Roger Williams University
Twentieth Anniversary Celebration
Toastmaster: Bob Booth
Roastee: Dan Booth

2001
Chairman: Dan Booth
Location: Roger Williams University
Writer Guest: Elizabeth Massie
Writer Guest: Tim Powers
Artist Guest: Nicholas Jainschigg
Toastmaster: Roman Ranieri
Roastee: Peter Straub
Legend: Craig Shaw Gardner

2002
Chairman: Dan Booth
Location: Roger Williams University
Writer Guest: Douglas Clegg
Writer Guest: Christopher Golden
Writer Guest: Graham Joyce
Artist Guest: Richard Sardinha
Toastmaster: P.D. Cacek
Roastee: Jack Ketchum
Legend: Jill Bauman

2003
Chairman: Dan Booth
Location: Roger Williams University
Writer Guest: Elizabeth Hand
Writer Guest: T.M. Wright
Editor Guest: Richard Chizmar
Artist Guest: Omar Rayyan
Toastmaster: James A. Moore
Roastee: Elizabeth Monteleone
Legend: Gahan Wilson

2004
Chairman: Dan Booth
Location: Salve Regina University
Writer Guest: Simon Clark
Writer Guest: Tom Piccirilli
Writer Guest: Tamara Thorne
Editor Guest: Don D'Auria
Artist Guest: Glenn Chadbourne
Toastmaster: Gordon Linzner
Roastee: Christopher Golden
Legend: Douglas E. Winter

2005
Chairman: Dan Booth
Location: Roger Williams University
Twenty-Fifth Anniversary Celebration
Toastmaster: Linda Addison
Toastmaster: Gerard Houarner
Roastee: Philip Nutman

2006
Chairman: Dan Booth
Location: Roger Williams University
Writer Guest: Gary Braunbeck
Writer Guest: Edward Lee
Editor Guest: Peter Crowther
Artist Guest: Gahan Wilson
Toastmaster: Steven Spruill
Roastee: Gahan Wilson
Legend: Rick Hautala

2007

Chairman: Dan Booth
Location: Roger Williams University
Writer Guest: Sephera Giron
Writer Guest: Brian Keene
Writer Guest: Tim Lebbon
Artist Guest: Tom Kidd
Toastmaster: Matt Schwartz
Roastee: James A. Moore
Legend: Bob Booth
Legend: Mary Booth
Hall Of Fame Inductee: Jill Bauman
Hall Of Fame Inductee: Bob Booth
Hall Of Fame Inductee: Ginjer Buchanan
Hall Of Fame Inductee: Les Daniels
Hall Of Fame Inductee: Craig Shaw Gardner
Hall Of Fame Inductee: Charles L. Grant
Hall Of Fame Inductee: Rick Hautala
Hall Of Fame Inductee: Alan Ryan
Hall Of Fame Inductee: Gahan Wilson
Hall Of Fame Inductee: Douglas E. Winter
Memoir Published: Bob Booth
Memoir Published: Craig Shaw Gardner
Memoir Published: Charles L. Grant

2008

Chairman: Dan Booth
Location: Roger Williams University
Guest Writer: Charlaine Harris
Guest Writer: James A. Moore
Guest Writer: Michael Marshall Smith
Guest Artist: Eric Powell
Toastmaster: Jose Nieto
Roastee: John McIlveen
Legend: F. Paul Wilson
Hall Of Fame Inductee: Donald M. Grant
Hall Of Fame Inductee: F. Paul Wilson

2009

Chairman: Dan Booth
Location: Roger Williams University
Writer Guest: Sarah Pinborough
Writer Guest: John Skipp
Writer Guest: Thomas E. Sniegoski
Artist Guest: Lars Grant-West
Toastmaster: Mary SanGiovanni
Roastee: To Be Determined
Legend: Thomas F. Monteleone
Hall Of Fame Inductee: Thomas F. Monteleone
Memoir Published: Jill Bauman
Memoir Published: Thomas F. Monteleone
Memoir Published: Alan Ryan

2010

Chairman: Dan Booth
Location: Roger Williams University
Thirtieth Anniversary Celebration
Toastmaster: Bob Booth
Roastee: To Be Determined